THE LEOPARD'S PREY

THE LEOPARD'S PREY

A JADE DEL CAMERON MYSTERY

SUZANNE ARRUDA

AN OBSIDIAN MYSTERY

OBSIDIAN

Published by New American Library, a division of
Penguin Group (USA) Inc., 375 Hudson Street,
New York, New York 10014, USA
Penguin Group (Canada), 90 Eglinton Avenue East, Suite 700, Toronto,
Ontario M4P 2Y3, Canada (a division of Pearson Penguin Canada Inc.)
Penguin Books Ltd., 80 Strand, London WC2R 0RL, England
Penguin Ireland, 25 St. Stephen's Green, Dublin 2,
Ireland (a division of Penguin Books Ltd.)
Penguin Group (Australia), 250 Camberwell Road, Camberwell, Victoria 3124,
Australia (a division of Pearson Australia Group Pty. Ltd.)
Penguin Books India Pvt. Ltd., 11 Community Centre, Panchsheel Park,
New Delhi - 110 017, India
Penguin Group (NZ), 67 Apollo Drive, Rosedale, North Shore 0632,
New Zealand (a division of Pearson New Zealand Ltd.)
Penguin Books (South Africa) (Pty.) Ltd., 24 Sturdee Avenue,
Rosebank, Johannesburg 2196, South Africa

Penguin Books Ltd., Registered Offices:
80 Strand, London WC2R 0RL, England

First published by Obsidian, an imprint of New American Library,
a division of Penguin Group (USA) Inc.

First Printing, January 2009
10   9   8   7   6   5   4   3   2   1

LIBRARY OF CONGRESS CATALOGING-IN-PUBLICATION DATA:
Arruda, Suzanne Middendorf, 1954–
The leopard's prey: a Jade del Cameron mystery/Suzanne Arruda.
p. cm.
ISBN 978-0-451-22586-3
1. Del Cameron, Jade (Fictitious character)—Fiction. 2. Women private investigators—
Kenya—Fiction. 3. Americans—Kenya—Fiction. 4. Murder—Fiction. I. Title.
PS3601.R74L46 2009
813'.6—dc22   2008021285
Set in Granjon
Designed by Alissa Amell

Printed in the United States of America

This book is dedicated with love to my brothers and sisters: Dave, Michael, Nancy, and Cynthia

ACKNOWLEDGMENTS

MY THANKS TO: the Pittsburg State University Axe Library Interlibrary Loan staff, for their tireless efforts to help me run down all the research books, especially the rogue *Red Book*; the National Wild Turkey Federation's Women in the Outdoors program, for roping lessons; Terry (Tessa) McDermid, for her help as my writing buddy; James Arruda, for help explaining ailerons; Michael Arruda, for explaining dead-stick landing; Dr. Vic Sullivan, for his hints on how to sabotage a biplane; Mr. Ken Hyde of the Wright Experience, for sharing his vast knowledge and love of maintaining and flying Jennies; Barbara Brooks of Elefence International, for her input on raising leopard cubs; Mike and Nancy Brewer, for original and inspired musical accompaniment to my Web and publicity CDs; my NAL publicists, Catherine Milne and Tom Haushalter, for all their hard work; my agent, Susan Gleason, and my editor, Ellen Edwards, for their continued belief and efforts in the series; all my family: the Dad, James, Michael, Dave, Nancy, and Cynthia, for helping me shamelessly promote the books. I especially wish to thank Joe, the greatest husband and webmaster a writer could ever want, for all his help and support; and Wooly Bear for keeping her hair balls off the keyboard.

Any mistakes are my own, despite the best efforts of my excellent instructors.

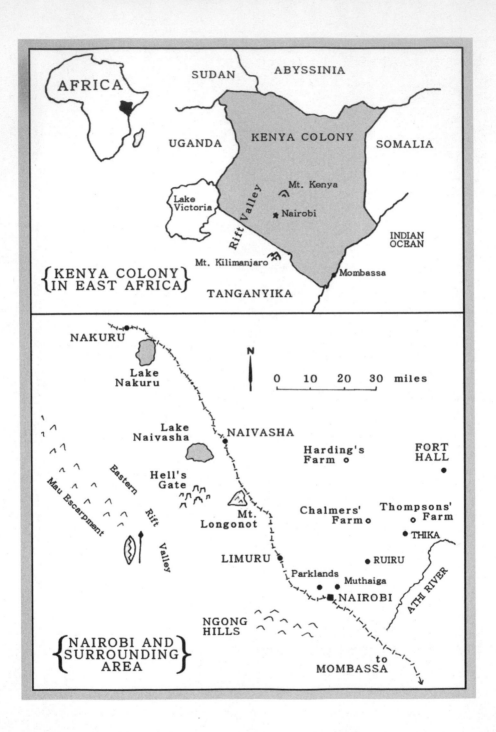

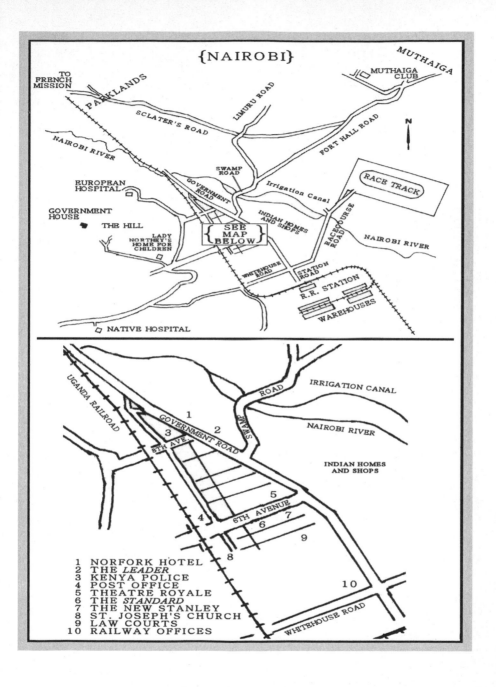

{NAIROBI}

CHAPTER 1

KENYA COLONY, *July 1920*

*There is an African proverb that runs through many tribes.
"The foolish antelope cuts firewood for the leopard." Basically, don't give
your enemies any more help in establishing your demise
than they already possess.*

—The Traveler

I'LL BE FINE.

Jade del Cameron wondered if those famous last words would soon end up gracing her headstone. The plan had seemed like a good one at the time, but it had been daylight then, the sun warm and benevolent. She'd watched the two Americans, Wayne Anderson and Franklin Cutter, enter the blind twenty yards away, and heard the three Kikuyu assistants settle into the tree that grew beside her. Soon after, darkness had swooped down upon the African landscape, a mythical black bird, immense, terrible, and predatory, devouring Jade's previous cockiness. Her quivering limbs told her this had been one of her less intelligent ideas.

I'm safer in here than during the War in that Model T ambulance with shells pounding around me. But her heart didn't believe her. It raced until the dull roaring filled her inner ears with a sound akin to a raging river. She took a deep breath and tried to relax by shifting her legs. The right calf immediately cramped, and she flexed her foot to relieve it. The cramp quit, but the left leg started twitching, the muscles fatigued from maintaining one position for over six hours in a two-foot-wide-by-three-foot-long-and-four-foot-high enclosure, built for something much smaller than a five-foot, seven-inch woman.

Get a grip on yourself. You've sat in blinds for longer than this before. That was from her head. Her stomach responded with, *Yeah, but never as leopard bait.* She shivered, her sweat-soaked shirt sucking heat from her body. When she had first entered the cage of lashed limbs, its stifling warmth had stolen every breath. Then, as Africa released its captured heat like a nightly sacrifice to Ngai, the Maker, she longed for some of that warmth. And all just to save a bit of Africa from itself.

The leopard in question was one of a pair that had menaced the pastoral tribes for several months. Both were slated for death for their crimes, the male first. It wasn't his fault. Easy game had diminished as the colonists expanded their farms. The pair of young cats, hungry and desperate, had first taken to the goats, conveniently clustered into low pens. On his last raid, the male was driven off by a brave villager, but not before the cat had slashed the man's leg and bitten him in the thigh. Worse yet, at least as far as the residents of Parklands north of Nairobi were concerned, the cat had been seen stalking someone's dog. The terrified boxer had raced onto the veranda and into his master's house through a partially open window, his tail between his legs, leaving a puddle of urine on the new rug imported all the way from Turkey.

The arrival of the Perkins and Daley Zoological Company soon after this incident had seemed like a godsend to all. They wanted specimens for American zoos, the villagers and settlers wanted the leopards gone, and the goats and dogs wanted not to be eaten. It looked as if everyone, except the goats that would still be consumed eventually, would get his wish. The company suited Jade's purposes, as well. She wanted to save these cats from extermination, and she needed the money.

Writing articles for the *Traveler* paid well enough, but traveling anywhere to write about a new location had grown more expensive, especially with the current petrol shortage. Even her photographic film seemed to cost more every time she picked up an order. It also gnawed at Jade's conscience to take advantage of her friends, the Dunburys, by staying at their home. She longed for more independence. So after asking about the company and finding that they had a reputation for honesty, she hired on as a wrangler and photographer. Somehow, she hadn't counted on ending up as leopard bait.

From lashed-together tree limbs, the company had built a double cage, one half for a goat, the other half for the cat. The leopard would try to get the goat from outside, but wouldn't be able to drive its claws through the tight network of vegetation. It would finally notice that it could more easily see the prey if it looked through the open doorway into the empty half.

The illusion of accessibility was maintained by a double layer of bars, each constructed of branches lashed at right angles to one another, and each layer separated by a foot of space. In theory, the cat would enter, tripping the mechanism that would drop the door behind it. The men in the nearby tree would jump down and secure the door before the cat could get out. In theory.

This male had proved wary, and after two nights of sniffing and snarling around the outside of the cage, he'd slipped away and stalked the village instead. The Kikuyu said they'd heard his asthmatic "chuff" outside of the injured man's hut.

Jade hadn't been with the men those first two nights. So when they and two of the closest settlers, Alwyn Chalmers and Charles Harding, said the cat would now turn man killer and needed to be shot, Jade intervened with this solution, which now had her questioning her sanity. If the cat wanted a human, she argued, let it smell and see a human in the cage. For obvious reasons, no one else had volunteered to be the literal "scapegoat."

Perhaps Jade had never really believed that the leopard would turn man-eater just because it had tasted human blood. It sounded like an old wives' tale. In fact, she doubted the cat would even approach a cage with a human in it. But the settlers wanted the animal eradicated, and the expedition didn't want to waste any more time trying to capture this pair. She was their last chance. Wild Africa, Jade noted, was disappearing, one animal at a time. She intended to save these two leopards even if it meant shipping them to a new home in Cincinnati or New York.

So why are my palms sweating? Jade knew why. She felt vulnerable. What if the leopard threw itself on top of the cage? Would the lashings hold against one hundred to one hundred forty pounds of snarling muscle? Did she trust the men to immediately release her once the animal was caged next to her? *Why the hell didn't I bring my rifle?*

Of course, there wasn't room to aim and fire, and anyway, the purpose was to save the cat, not kill it. With her right hand she reached down to the sheath on her boot, her fingers grazing the smooth antler-bone knife hilt. If she had to, she could cut the lashings and escape.

Just relax. Cutter and Anderson are out there. The two

Americans seemed competent enough. Or maybe it was just their thick Chicago accents that gave the illusion of toughness. Both of them were solidly built, but could they handle a furious leopard?

Take a nap. It's going to be dawn soon. Hard to nap when her heart was pounding one hundred times a minute. She felt her lungs constrict, as though the walls were closing in on her. She tugged at her shirt collar and gasped. *It's the cage!* That was it. Suddenly she needed to get out, to feel air on her face and space around her body. Unfortunately, the release pin was on the outside.

She shoved her slender fingers up through the narrow gap and felt for the toggle. Nothing! *Where's the blasted pin?* Jade forced her hand up farther, her knuckles scraping the rough wood, drawing blood. Her fingertips grazed the toggle, and for the first time, she wished she'd cultivated long fingernails. *Just a little farther.* There! Her index finger had the pin. She started to push it when she heard a tubercular cough.

Leopard! Jade jerked her fingers back inside the cage as something powerful brushed up against it. The soft glow from the gibbous moon, which had previously penetrated her compartment, disappeared as the leopard's body blocked it. The animal sniffed, short whuffing snorts, as he analyzed her scent. When he exhaled, the hot scent of stale carrion flooded the enclosure. Jade instinctively pressed her back against the opposite side as the leopard snarled, the sound deep and rasping like a heavy saw through hard timber.

The cat pushed his shoulder against the cage, testing it. The lashings creaked under the pressure, and Jade felt subtle movement in the wood along her spine. Her sanctuary shifted a fraction but held. She slid her knife from its sheath and waited for the next jolt.

It came from on top when the leopard jumped up to try to gain entry from above. The limbs groaned, but the green wood didn't crack. Jade heard the cat's claws scrape against the cage as he tried to find a point of entry. In the moonlight, she could see his form more clearly than before. She thought she detected a thinness about his middle. The animal was more than hungry. He was ravenous. His raspy snarls grew in volume. So did his repeated scratching and probing.

A thin piece of leather snapped, two limbs separated and a paw appeared above her. His claws swiped at empty air as he tried to reach her. Time to get him off the roof. She reached up with her knife and pricked the soft padding. The leopard withdrew the paw with an angry scream and jumped off the cage and away from her.

He landed near the open door, and for the first time, the two stared at each other. The leopard's eyes glowed with the night shine of a nocturnal animal, reflecting every fragment of moonlight back at her. Jade knew the men were getting worried out there, and if it was anything like what she felt, they would soon finish off this cat. No doubt the only reason they hadn't tried to shoot it yet was fear of accidentally shooting her. She needed to draw the animal in. Jade pricked her finger on her knife-edge, and let the scent of her own blood fill the cage.

The cat stalked her with an unnerving slowness, his broad head low between his shoulders, pausing after each step. His pale amber eyes never left hers, hypnotizing his prey into immobility. Beads of cold sweat formed on Jade's brow. She could literally feel them ooze out of her pores, a creeping sensation. She didn't move. There was no place to run.

Another step and the cat hit the release catch. The door dropped, but the animal had hesitated again and it only hit him across the top of his rump and tail. The capture crew didn't know that. They only heard the door swing downward followed by a high-pitched snarl.

Jade heard the men jump from the trees. *He's going to back out of the cage and kill them!* She needed to bring him in all the way. She forced her hand, the one she'd pricked, through the narrow openings and swiped at the cat, taunting him. A splinter made a fresh gash and a few drops of blood landed on his nose.

"Come on, *chui*," she yelled, goading the leopard with his Swahili name. "Dinner's waiting." The scent of blood drove the starving and infuriated animal to a fever pitch. He charged forward, slamming into the partition just as Jade jerked her hand back into her compartment.

She knew the men were now sliding the wooden beams across the door to secure it, but she couldn't hear them. Her senses only noted the hideous, enraged screams and those eyes—those furious, smoldering yellow eyes, glowing with hatred.

Jade didn't wait for the men to pull the pin and let her out. She sliced the lashings from her side of the prison and tumbled out into the African night, gasping for air.

One cat, one bit of Africa was saved from a death sentence, but somehow, Jade doubted that he'd ever be grateful to her. She heard a truck door slam and looked up to see one of her bosses approach. Brooklyn-born Hank Daley was built like a wrestler whose muscles had gone to flab over the years. His five foot six inches were capped by a sun-reddened face and receding hairline. A seven-inch scar on his right arm and a missing pinky finger on his right hand testified to his having survived some difficult captures in the past.

"That was one hell of a job, Jade," he said, hitching up his pants. "I thought for a moment we were going to lose one of my men. You're quite a daredevil." The forty-three-year-old second-in-command pulled a cigarette from his shirt pocket, struck a match on a boot nail, and puffed away. Together they watched as the other men loaded the cage and the furious cat into the truck.

Jade hugged herself to keep from shivering, not from cold, but as an aftereffect of the rush of danger. She tried to divert herself by asking, "What's next?"

"Well, there's that other leopard a little farther north, the one by Harding's spread," Daley said, his cigarette bobbing as he spoke. "And I still need a young rhino, some zebra, a baboon or two. Got a line on some ostrich. I also want a cheetah. I understand you have a male. Care to sell him?"

Jade shook her head. "Biscuit's not for sale, Mr. Daley. He saved my life and the life of a good friend this past January."

"Biscuit, hunh." He rubbed his chin stubble. "Well, if you should change your mind . . ."

"All loaded up, boss." The speaker, Wayne Anderson, was a bulky, five-foot, ten-inch man with a shock of carrot red hair. He flashed a big smile at Jade. Next to him stood Franklin Cutter, a well-muscled, wiry man with straw blond hair.

"Thanks, Wayne," said Daley. "You and Frank go in the truck with the cat." He nodded toward the Dodge truck, now surrounded by the Kikuyu men who stood guard over the leopard, singing a song about a brave warrior. "I'll take the Africans back with me."

Jade and her boss walked toward a hill where they'd left the other vehicles, another Dodge truck and Jade's 1915 Indian Big Twin motorcycle, which she'd purchased after she sold the French Panhard she'd acquired in Morocco that spring. After unloading the leopard at the Nairobi warehouse, the men would drive on to Alwyn Chalmers' farm and catch what little sleep they could before the next night's work began.

A soft noise in front of them attracted Jade's attention. "Someone's coming." She made out two figures. One was slender and walked with the erect carriage and sure step of youth. The other clung to him, a hunched form tottering with age.

"*Jambo,*" Jade called in greeting.

"*Jambo*, Simba Jike," said the man, calling Jade by her Swahili name of "lioness." He was a Wakamba, judging by his filed teeth. Probably from the nearby village. "This woman is my mother. She says she must speak to you."

Jade turned her attention to the old woman clutching her son's arm. She wore a leather apron stained red with soil and clutched a monkey fur cloak around her back and shoulders. Her shaved head and gnarled hands showed the liver spots of great age, but what most startled Jade were her dead eyes. Milky white, they managed to lock onto Jade's own green eyes as though the crone could still see.

"Mother, what did you want?" asked Jade in Swahili. Her son translated.

Immediately the woman spoke two short sentences with a strength and volume that belied her great age and bent figure. Jade's Wakamba was rudimentary at best, since she'd spent more time recently studying Kikuyu and a smattering of Maasai, but she did catch the word for danger, which she made a point of learning in any language.

"My mother says that you will face danger and must beware. She says you must always watch for the madness in the eyes of a killer."

Jade felt a cold chill ripple down her spine. She looked into the old woman's blind eyes, but in her mind, all she saw was the leopard's hateful stare.

MADELINE THOMPSON SAT astride a sturdy little brown Somali pony called Tea and adjusted her wide-brimmed straw hat so it hid less of her face. Tea danced nervously underneath her, his hind muscles twitching and his tail whipping at the pesky flies that landed on his withers. One must have bitten him, because he bucked slightly. Maddy shifted sideways and made a grab for the saddle, her hat slipping.

"Do you know what to do, Maddy?" asked her husband, Neville. He sat on a very placid white pony that appeared to be dozing. "As soon as I send that stallion past you, you race after him and drive him the rest of the way into the pen beside the mares."

Madeline fidgeted with her hat again. "I don't think this is a good idea, Neville. You should be on Tea, and *I* should be riding Crumpet. Tea is too nervous for me."

"Crumpet's not fast enough to chase a wild zebra, Maddy. The beast would be past her before she even thought about running. Now just be certain to whoop and yell a great deal and wave your hat around. I'll be right behind you . . . er . . . as soon as I can get Crumpet moving."

Madeline yanked her hat off her head and muttered under her breath about obstinate men and silly schemes. Two hairpins fell and released a shoulder-length strand of brown hair streaked with gray. Before she could do anything about her hair, she heard galloping hoofbeats coming up behind her. Neville shouted, "Now, Maddy!" and she dug her heels into her mount's side. Tea bolted forward just as the zebra raced past her.

"I can do this," she murmured to herself. She swung her

hat in a wide circle around her head and she hung on to the reins for dear life. "Whoop! Hyah!" she shouted. Tea responded to the challenge as though this were race week and he was running for the cup.

Just as Maddy thought the zebra was about to go into the fenced area next to a few mares from his harem, a gold-and-black blur raced past her pony's legs, heading straight for the zebra. Tea reared and Maddy pitched backward onto the hard ground. The zebra spun around to defend itself against this new enemy, and Madeline appeared to be as good a target for his anger as any.

"Roll, Maddy!" yelled Neville, as he slid off Crumpet's back.

Still stunned, Maddy looked up in time to see a pair of black hooves waving above her and a large, black-spotted cheetah beside her. She screamed and rolled away as the hooves crashed down less than a foot from her midsection. The cat ignored Madeline and nipped instead at the zebra's hind legs. In the mayhem of snarling, pounding, snorting, and high-pitched whinnies, no one heard the purring roar of an approaching motorcycle.

Neville ran up beside his wife and pulled her to her feet as a lasso landed around the zebra stallion's thick neck and brushlike mane. The noose tightened, and the zebra turned his fury toward this newest indignity. He jerked his head down and bucked, but the lasso held, mainly because the other end of the rope was looped around a post.

"Cut!" shouted a man standing fifty feet away beside a tripod and a motion picture camera. Sam Featherstone, former American WWI flying ace turned would-be filmmaker, looked up from the lens and grinned at the Thompsons. "That was fantastic!"

"I could use a little help here," called Jade as she gripped the rope she'd thrown and pulled the still angry zebra toward the pen. "Biscuit," she called to her pet cheetah, "stop annoying the zebra." The slender cat, no longer interested in his prey, turned his attention to Madeline.

Sam loped toward Jade as fast as his prosthetic right leg allowed. "It's a good thing you showed up when you did, Jade," he said. He took hold of the rope and pulled the zebra the rest of the way into the pen. Then he carefully slipped the noose from the zebra's neck. "I don't know how Biscuit got out of the house. I thought we had him shut up tight."

"Biscuit can open doors," said Jade. "Maddy, are you all right?"

Madeline leaned against her husband, who held her close and massaged her backside. "I've bruised my nether regions, thanks to your silly cat." She pushed Biscuit's head away as he rubbed up against her legs.

"Biscuit didn't mean any harm," said Jade. She motioned for the cheetah to come to her, and rested her left hand on his back when he stood beside her. "He just likes to play chase, too."

"Well, it's a good thing you showed up when you did," said Neville. "Thank you."

"Don't mention it," said Jade as she pulled off her driving goggles. "Now, will someone tell me what in thunder that was all about? Sam, I thought you were filming the life of the coffee farmer, not a Hoot Gibson Western."

"I am," said Sam, handing her the rope. After casting a sidelong glance to see if the Thompsons were watching, he kissed her lightly on the cheek. "I already filmed the recent fly harvest," he said, referring to the year's second, smaller coffee crop. "But I don't want my picture to be humdrum. I want it to tell a story about the intrepid farmers who are struggling and need money to pay off their loans. It was Neville's idea actually. He was talking about some of his past plans to raise money—"

"Like herding crocodiles," chimed in Maddy, who'd joined them with her husband.

"I never did do that, Madeline," said Neville. "I only thought about it."

Sam coughed to interrupt the family squabble. "Once you told us you were working for that zoological company, Jade, Neville took a closer look at their advertisement and decided to bring in a few zebra for them. I couldn't film our actual capture, so I restaged it."

Maddy snorted. "The *real* capture was hardly worth filming. Neville and Sam baited a path to the pen with a trail of hay. The mares came in on their own, and their lord and master followed. The action we just staged was a complete fiction."

Jade laughed. "And you know about fiction, right, Maddy?"

Madeline's chin shot up an inch. "I'll have you know, Jade, that my novels about you and your daring adventures are very true to life. *Stalking Death* did very well, and *Ivory Blood* promises to be just as successful."

"At least you weren't in Morocco with me," muttered Jade. "I'd hate to think what you would make out of *that* trip."

This time both Sam and Neville coughed.

"What?" asked Jade.

"Nothing. Nothing at all," said Neville.

Jade spun toward Sam. "Sam? Did you tell Maddy about what happened in Morocco?"

Sam pretended to be interested in the zebra and unable to hear her question. "You must admit, this zebra chase and capture does make for a good piece of film. That was some roping, Jade. But where did you get the lariat?"

"It belongs to the zoological company," said Jade. "I'm borrowing it as part of my equipment."

"Speaking of captures, how did yours go, Jade?" asked Sam. "Did you get the leopard?"

"Yes," she said. She didn't offer any details and kept her focus on carefully coiling the rope and attaching it to one of the panniers on her motorcycle.

"I understood the brute wasn't going for the bait," said Neville. "How ever did you manage to lure him into that cage?"

"We used different bait." Jade switched the topic before anyone could inquire further. "How are you going to use my roping of Maddy's zebra, Sam? I hope I didn't ruin your scene."

"Not at all. I'll shoot Neville acting out your part, Jade, and cut him into the footage. It will be a dramatic scene of a husband rescuing his brave wife. In fact, Biscuit's sudden entry gave me another idea." Both Madeline and Neville raised their eyebrows, looking at him with doubtful frowns. "It would make a wonderful scene if we used your pet lion, Percy, to stage a lion attack."

Neville pulled Madeline into his arms. "Absolutely not! I forbid it. I have no idea how tame Percy is."

"Sam, Percy was Harry Hascombe's pet lion," Jade explained. Harry, who'd once kept a cattle ranch, had sold it off and taken to leading safaris. When he did, he gave his pet cats to the Thompsons to keep. Biscuit, however, had other plans. He laid claim to Jade and traveled with her now. Percy, the lion that had been raised by humans from a cub, stayed mainly in his large enclosure. Jade recalled a night on her first trip to Africa when she'd slept at Hascombe's ranch. Even then, Percy had roared loudly to proclaim his domain when a wild lion came near, and Jade didn't doubt that the cat would have fought for primacy if he'd had to. "I don't think it's safe to let Percy out. Even in play he could seriously hurt someone. He's not tame like Biscuit."

As if Biscuit decided then to show them he was still free to follow his own head, he left Jade's side and stalked over to the new coffee dryer, which had recently been unloaded out of the way under a brush arbor. He sniffed the two-hundred-gallon drum that rested on legs beside an as yet unattached motor.

"I didn't mean to actually have Percy attack anyone, even in play," Sam said. "But I could disguise part of his cage to look like wild brush and film him roaring. Then I could cut to Madeline screaming and Neville firing away at nothing in particular."

"Why don't *I* get to fire away and let Neville be the one in danger?" asked Madeline. "Maybe I could find Neville collapsed on the ground, about to be devoured, and save him."

"As long as you scream first," said Sam. "There's nothing more riveting on the screen than a woman facing horror and certain death."

"I suppose that would be all right," admitted Neville, "as long as Maddy is not in any real danger. But you'd better do it soon. Percy is getting too expensive to keep. I'm going to sell him to Perkins and Daley along with the zebras."

Sam nodded, half listening. Already he was surveying the surroundings, picking out camera angles that would hide most of the coffee farm behind Percy's large pen. "Are you good at screaming, Maddy?" he asked.

Madeline had slipped free of Neville's embrace and strolled over to the coffee dryer to see what held Biscuit's interest. The cheetah was pawing at the large drum and making raspy cries. "Of course I can scream," Maddy said. She let loose with a high-pitched *eek*.

"That's too weak, Maddy," said Sam. "It needs to be bigger."

Jade leaned against a fence post, her arms folded across her chest, and watched the proceedings with amusement. "No one will hear it in the movie anyway."

"That's why she has to act it out, too," said Sam. "Try it, Maddy. Give me your best horrified scream."

Madeline, in the meantime, had opened the door to the dryer's cylindrical drum. She dropped the door with a clanging crash, threw her hands in front of her face, and let out an ear-piercing shriek.

"Very good, Maddy," said Jade, clapping. "But perhaps a bit overdone."

Madeline turned, still screaming, and ran to Neville, burying her face against his chest. "What's going on?" he demanded as he held his wife.

Sam opened the dryer drum, and both he and Jade peered inside. They immediately looked away, gagging. "There's a body in your coffee dryer, Neville," said Jade. "Something you care to tell us about?"

CHAPTER 2

Many African proverbs are based on observing animals.
Whereas, we might say, "The apple does not fall far from the tree" or
"chip off the old block" to indicate that children often act
like their parents, an African would say that even a small leopard
is still called a leopard. Note the inherent warning.

—The Traveler

By the time Neville returned from Nairobi with Police Inspector Archibald Finch, Dr. Matthew Montgomery, and a lone constable; Madeline had regained her outward composure. She and Jade sat on folding camp chairs while Neville and Sam assisted the officials with hauling the body out of the coffee dryer. They laid the corpse on a blanket in the shade.

"Whew!" exclaimed Sam, waving a hand in front of his nose. "He's definitely not dry roasted."

"Why, that's Martin Stokes!" exclaimed Neville once he saw the face.

"Mr. Stokes?" asked Maddy. She jumped up and hurried to look.

The inspector, a short, skinny man in his fifties, stopped her before she got too close. "Not for a lady to see, Mrs. Thompson."

"Martin Stokes?" echoed Jade as she strolled over, circumventing the inspector. Biscuit followed at her heels like a dog.

Unlike Madeline, Jade didn't always respond to the dictates of authoritative men. "Is he the same Stokes as in Nairobi's Stokes and Berryhill Store? I've been there many times, but I've never really met him."

"One and the same," said Neville. "We bought that coffee dryer from him last week. He was supposed to deliver it and never did."

"I guess we know why," said Jade.

"So I went into town yesterday and brought it back myself," Neville added.

Madeline inhaled sharply. "My heavens," she said, "he must have been in there already. How horrid!" She put her hands in front of her mouth.

"His left wrist has been slashed," said Sam.

"It looks as if he did it to himself," said Neville. "He's got some sort of knife strapped to his right hand." He stared at the fingerless leather glove, complete with a two-inch blade that jutted out near the thumb.

"Stay back from the body, if you would please," said Finch. "The doctor will decide how this man died, not you."

"A most intriguing weapon," said Dr. Montgomery. "Have you ever seen anything like it before, Inspector?"

"Never. Something for slaughtering livestock perhaps."

"It's a corn knife," said Sam.

"I beg your pardon?" said Finch. "Why would anyone need a weapon like that to handle something as slender as corn?"

Sam smiled. "I forgot. You British generally equate corn with wheat, don't you? What we call corn in the States is what you call maize. This is a new American invention. I saw one for sale in my dad's agricultural catalog on my last trip home." He pointed to the dead man's right hand. "You hold on to the ear with your left hand and slice it free with the knife on your right, all the while leaving your right fingers unencumbered."

"Most ingenious," said the doctor, squatting beside the corpse. "And it does appear from the blood on the knife and the size of the wrist wound that he did slice his own wrist with it. Of course," he added as he stood up, "I shall be able to make a more certain declaration after I examine the body more closely in my office. But at this point in time, Inspector, I believe we can safely assume that Mr. Stokes committed suicide."

"Why?" asked Jade.

"That's not for me to discuss at this point," said Finch.

Jade saw Maddy signal her with a slight hand wave. Once she had Jade's attention, she mouthed, *Later.* Jade nodded and stepped back.

"I shall send out another one of my men to assist Constable Miller here in the task of taking in your coffee dryer to collect more evidence," said Finch.

Neville groaned. "Is that absolutely necessary, Inspector? Surely the constable can just crawl into it here and do whatever he needs to do."

Inspector Finch studied the oversized drum. "We must check for fingerprints, of course, and it is better to do that at headquarters. Miller," he called to his underling, "just remove the door. Take it back to the station to test for prints. But photograph the prints on the drum here on site." He turned back to the Thompsons. "Which of you opened the door and found him?"

Madeline raised her hand. "I did."

"Then I raised the door and looked in," said Sam. "Neville was next."

Mr. Finch peered at Sam. "I don't believe we've met. You're an American, aren't you?"

"I'm Sam Featherstone and, yes, I'm an American." Sam extended his right hand, but the Inspector didn't offer to shake it.

"Mr. Featherstone is our friend and guest," said Madeline. "He is an engineer, and he has been helping my husband develop a more efficient coffee washer."

The inspector walked over to Sam's motion picture camera and tripod, still where he had left them after they discovered the body. "And is this part of the equipment, too?"

"No," said Sam. "I'm also making a moving picture about coffee farmers. The Thompsons are letting me film them at work. In return, I do handyman jobs in payment for room and board."

Finch turned away from the camera and Sam as though he was uninterested in Sam's answer. His seemingly casual stroll took him toward Jade and Biscuit. "You are Miss Jade del Cameron, are you not?" Jade nodded. "Did you also touch the dryer, Miss del Cameron?"

"Nope."

Finch arched his brows. "Indeed? I'm rather surprised. The commissioner, whom you met when you first came to Nairobi and found that dismembered corpse on Lord Colridge's estate, told me about you and how . . . helpful you were." The tone of his voice suggested otherwise.

Biscuit, perhaps hearing something he didn't like in the man's voice, chose that moment to stand and wrap his lithe body around Jade's legs. She stroked the cat's broad head and decided that Inspector Finch's comment merited nothing more than a slight inclination of her own head.

"Interesting pet, miss," said Finch.

"Indeed. You should know that Biscuit actually found the body first, Inspector. Madeline only opened the door to see why he was pawing at the drum. I'm only telling you this in case your officer finds a set of prints that don't look human. Just trying to be 'helpful,' you understand. You might need to take Biscuit's set while you're collecting ours."

Mr. Finch smiled, making a soft chuckle. "Charming." He turned back to Neville. "You said you purchased this dryer from the deceased. When might that have been?"

"Early last week. I can show you the bill of sale." Neville went into the house to get it. Finch didn't follow. Instead, he took in the stockade of milling zebras and Percy's distant pen.

"We're selling the zebras and the lion to that zoological company," said Madeline. "Anything to help pay off the overdraft."

Finch nodded. He spied a more distant fenced area and pointed to it. "What is over there?"

"My airplane hangar," said Sam.

The inspector turned toward Sam and arched his eyebrows. "Ah, you have a flying machine. I should imagine it would be hard to get aviation fuel out here."

"The OX-5 engine uses gasoline," said Sam. "One of its advantages."

Neville hurried out of the house, paper in hand, and gave it to the inspector. "Purchased June twenty-fifth," he said.

"I see. And he delivered this coffee dryer soon after?"

"No. I expected delivery this week," said Neville. "When it didn't come, I assumed he had gotten busy elsewhere. I drove into Nairobi and picked it up yesterday. Not an easy matter either."

"And with him already inside," mumbled Madeline, still fixated on the horror of her husband hauling the corpse. "Oh, Neville, he must have killed himself just before."

"I'm sure the doctor will be able to estimate *when* he died," said Mr. Finch, his gaze on Sam. "Only then will we know if he came with the dryer or was added later." He turned and waved to the doctor. "I feel certain we can leave as soon as you and Miller are ready, Doctor."

Constable Miller had quickly removed the door and treated the metal surrounding the opening with a fine, pale gray powder. He set a camera on a tripod and laboriously took photographs of any smudge he found. Jade watched with a keen interest and longed to ask him about his equipment. She restrained her curiosity, however, and contented herself with observing from a distance.

The doctor, too, waited for Miller to finish. No sooner had the constable taken his last image than Dr. Montgomery stuck his head in the dryer, using a flashlight to survey the interior. "Most curious."

"Why is that?" asked Jade.

"There's not very much blood pooled down here." He pulled out his head and turned to the body, now covered with half of the blanket. "Perhaps most of it soaked into his clothes."

"I must ask all of you to come into Nairobi to be finger-printed," said Finch. "Merely a formality, you understand. Tomorrow or the day after will be fine." He helped the constable load the body into the back of his truck and drove off, leaving four relatively stunned faces behind him.

Neville broke the silence first. "You two probably have more experience with this than I do. How long does it take before you aren't shocked anymore by the sight of a dead body?"

"The shock is always there," said Jade. "You just learn to hide it better."

"It helps a little," said Sam, "if you don't know the person."

Jade decided Maddy would do better to remove herself from the scene of tragedy. To facilitate the change, she walked toward the ponies that still waited with their saddles on. Jade unbuckled Tea's saddle and slid it off his back. As she had hoped, Madeline and the others followed her lead. "So why would this Mr. Stokes kill himself?" Jade asked.

"I think it might be because his wife ran away," Maddy said.

"He told you about that?" asked Sam.

Maddy shook her head. "We never really knew him socially, but there was that very curious insert in the personal ads of the *Standard*," said Maddy. "Let me find it." She ran into the house and emerged shortly with the thick weekly edition to which so many of the settlers subscribed. She flipped pages while Jade watered the pony. "I know I saw it here somewhere. Aha! Here it is, under the 'wanted' section." She handed the paper to Jade.

Jade read aloud, Sam following silently over her shoulder: " 'Wanted: information regarding the whereabouts of Alice Stokes, 24-year-old woman, 5 foot, 3 inches, blond hair. Reply to box 342.' " She lowered the paper. "That *is* odd. Do you know if her husband placed this ad?"

Neville and Madeline both shook their heads. "One just assumes. We could look in the *Red Book*," Maddy said, referring to the colony's official directory, "and see who owns that box number."

Sam took the paper from Jade and reread the notice. "How long has she been missing?"

"I don't remember seeing the notice before last week," said Maddy. "Do you, Neville?"

"No. And I never heard anyone speak of it either. But then, we don't go into town very often. Mr. Stokes made regular visits to the farms to see what was needed," added Neville as he started on Crumpet. "He was very attentive to all the farmers, but he never talked about anything with us except farming equipment."

"He was very accommodating," agreed Maddy. "Always very polite and so neatly dressed, even when delivering supplies. Such a cheerful man."

"Maybe he was away from home too much," said Jade. "All that attention to customers and none left for the missus? I wonder where Alice went."

"Possibly home to England like this lady," said Sam. He pointed to another notice and read it aloud. " 'Woman with two young children seeks someone to watch children while she returns to England for four months.' " He slapped at the paper. "Sounds as if someone needed a vacation from the kiddies. Maybe Mrs. Stokes also needed one away from Mr. Stokes. Chances are she'll be back on a return boat in a few months. He probably knew about it, too."

"An interesting theory, Sam," said Jade. "But if Mr. Stokes knew his wife had taken a vacation, then who placed the ad?"

Sam shrugged his shoulders and continued reading. Jade finished rubbing down Tea and turned him loose in a pen just as Neville finished with Crumpet.

"This part of the paper is very interesting," said Sam. "At least from a would-be filmmaker's point of view. So many possible stories here."

Madeline came up beside him and tried to see the paper

over his arm. "What do you mean? I read this every week, and except for the wanted notice for Mrs. Stokes, I can't say I've seen very much of interest."

Sam shifted his shoulder so Madeline could see the paper better. "Well, take this one for example: 'Lost, one brown parcel. Please return to box 16. No questions asked.' Doesn't that make you wonder what's inside? And here's another: 'Lost, one white Somali pony disappeared from Alwyn Chalmers' farm.' "

"He lost that pony two weeks ago," said Neville. "I saw the notice in last week's paper."

"That's where we just caught that last leopard," said Jade. "Probably killed the pony."

"Here's my favorite," said Sam. " 'Young woman desires situation on a farm keeping house for a bachelor farmer.' Now that's a young woman looking to get hitched."

Jade tried to stifle a yawn. "Maybe she'd like to be in your moving picture, Sam." She yawned again, only this time her mouth gaped wide.

"Mercy," said Maddy. "You're certainly a sleepyhead. Did you have to wait a long time last night for the leopard to show up?"

Jade nodded. "Till almost dawn." She rubbed her hands across the back of her neck and rolled her shoulders, working out the kinks. "After I stop at home I'm going to Chalmers' farm and try to get a few hours of sleep before we try for the other leopard tonight."

Sam's head drooped, and he frowned. "I'd hoped to give you another flying lesson today. Have you practice your take-offs and landings one last time before I give you more altitude."

Jade hesitated, tempted by the delights of flying. Then

another yawn forced her jaws apart. "I'd love to, Sam, but as tired as I am, I'd probably wreck your plane."

"You wouldn't dare," he teased. As he came closer, he noticed a few scratches on her hand and a short rip in her shirtsleeve near the shoulder. "That must have been some prickly blind you sat in last night." His dark, coffee-colored eyes searched hers, trying to read anything she might be hiding from him. Jade, able to stare down everyone but Sam, winced and looked away. The action was so unlike her that it told Sam all he needed to know. He pounced. "You said you switched baits. Don't tell me that *you* were the bait last night."

Jade remained silent.

"Jade?" asked Madeline. "Were you?"

"Sam just told me not to tell him that. So I'm not answering."

Madeline put her hands to her mouth in shock. "Oh, Jade," she murmured, "you could have been mauled to death."

"I could have been trampled by a runaway rhino, too, or had any number of things happen to me, but I wasn't. And we saved one leopard from a death sentence."

"Look me in the eyes and tell me you're not the bait again tonight, Jade," said Sam, his voice low and cool. "Otherwise I'm hog-tying you in Maddy's parlor."

Jade shook her head, pleased by his concern and irritated at his demand. "We're using a goat tonight, Sam," she said. "On my honor."

Sam nodded, accepting her sworn promise. "Good. I own you, you know," he added, referring to how he'd saved her from being sold in a Marrakech slave market that past spring by "buying" her. "Paid out perfectly good gold, too, Madeline, and what did I get? A scrappy cat. Still, I'd hate to lose my investment."

"You never finished telling me that story," whispered Madeline so Jade wouldn't hear.

She heard anyway. "Did he also tell you that my mother gave him the gold? So if anyone owns me, it's Mother and not you, Sam." Jade poked his chest for emphasis. "She and I have come to terms with that. Now if you'll excuse me, I'm going to get some sleep."

Jade climbed onto the motorcycle. Her Winchester was strapped in a leather side pocket and her personal belongings rested snugly inside red leather panniers slung over the rear seat. She readjusted the aviator's leather helmet, worn over her short black curls, and pulled a pair of goggles down over her eyes.

"Wait," called Sam. "Where *exactly* are you and the rest of the crew going to be tonight?"

"Mr. Daley had a team of natives dig a pit trap at the northern side of Chalmers' farm, on the edge of Charles Harding's property. He thinks a different approach might prove less hazardous than the double cage, especially since these cats have been wary of the cages." Jade yawned again. "I'm going to join them just before nightfall but mostly to take photographs unless they need me to rope something."

"I'll fly over tomorrow morning and see how you fared," suggested Sam, "*if* I can find a place to put down."

Jade smiled, feeling guilty for her previous grumpiness. "That sounds nice. I'll see you tomorrow, then." She started her engine and roared off toward Nairobi to check the post and, in particular, to stop at Lord Avery and Lady Beverly Dunbury's estate on the fringes of Parklands.

The Dunburys, Jade's closest friends from the Great War, had purchased a beautiful stone house and sizable grounds after their first visit to East Africa in 1919. Since then, they'd erected stables and constructed an exercise ring for training horses. For Jade's benefit, and in an effort to keep their friend from roaming too far from them, they'd added a complete film-development laboratory and a guest cottage. The Dunburys were now in London awaiting the birth of their first child, due sometime in late August or early September, so Jade had taken up residence in the main house.

As she sped along, she couldn't help but notice the difference in the landscape that a little over a year had made. What had once been an empty stretch of road now teemed with traffic. She passed two automobiles and a truck going in her direction, and met three other autos and one motorcycle in the span of thirty minutes. *Unheard of.* And Nairobi itself seemed to grow farther out every month, as settlers built their homes in the upland, parklike districts, each with its own country club.

The first time she'd traveled this route, she'd seen herds of zebra and antelope grazing nearby. She'd watched native women work small plots of sweet potatoes. Now the women were confined to their villages and the wildlife had fled in the face of noisy vehicles. The few natives who walked along the road all wore around their necks a small metal cylinder. It held their *kipande*, a paper with a set of their fingerprints, employment contract, and travel permit. The cylinder had become synonymous with the documents, earning it the same name.

Gone was the smooth-skinned warrior striding along in a monkey-skin loincloth or nothing at all, answering to no one but himself in his native land. No doubt about it. The Africa of old was dying. But, like any wild animal, it would not go down without a struggle. Jade wondered how many others would also die in the battle. Was Mr. Stokes one of the early victims?

And what about me? Is there still room here for me?

COMPARED TO THE previous night, this night's venture was a cake walk. The entire African crew slept peacefully, wrapped in their blankets on the ground, while the small retinue of Americans lounged in hammocks or on Chalmers' veranda. They sipped coffee or dozed, as the mood struck them. On Jade's advice, they decided not to wait in blinds, lest they scare off the leopard. With them was the senior partner of Perkins and Daley, Bob Perkins. The tall, white-haired gentleman, impressed by Daley's account of the first capture, had decided to drive out from Nairobi for this one. He had insisted on bringing Jade along with him.

The sides of the deep pit trap had been cut so they tapered inward toward the top, making it impossible for the agile cat to jump out once it fell in. There was only one route of access to the kid goat, and that was across the trap, beautifully disguised with thin bamboo and grass and doused with goat urine and dung in the hopes of masking any lingering scent of humans. They had nothing to do but wait back at Chalmers' house for the inevitable.

Besides, they would know when something went into the pit. Jade had rigged up a night-flash picture to be triggered by the animal once it stepped on the trap. The magnesium flash and subsequent boom would carry the distance and report their success.

Jade sat apart from the others near the back side of Chalmers' house. She'd arrived at nightfall, slung a hammock from the veranda rafters, and slept for five hours, but now she felt restless. She wished the cat would just fall into the trap and be done with it. Didn't it know that it was doomed? That it had a price on its head?

Her thoughts went back to the first leopard, and she immediately envisioned his blazing yellow eyes. She shook her head and tried to think of something else; unfortunately what came to mind was Mr. Stokes' body. While she accepted the idea that the loss of his wife might have driven him to suicide, she didn't understand why he'd crawl into the coffee dryer to kill himself. Why not do the deed in his own home? Was he afraid no one would find him there?

She shifted position and heard the crinkle of paper in her shirt pocket. *Beverly's letter.* Another, addressed to Maddy, was in Jade's day pack. Jade had picked them up that afternoon. Wanting to think happier thoughts, she took her letter out and reread it by the campfire's glow.

June 7, 1920
Dearest Jade:

I was so happy to receive your letter telling me that you were safely "home" in Nairobi and that your mother was on her way home to America. And how positively wonderful that she got the stud horse she'd wanted in Spain. I was under the impression that the Andalusians never gave up their precious horses. It makes me all the more curious to know how you and your mother managed that. Somehow I think there's a story there that you're not telling me. You didn't shoot anyone, did you?

Impending motherhood does not become me. My feet are swelling along with my midsection. Not that anyone will see me like this except Avery, and the dear man still says I'm glowing. I think the correct spelling should be "glowering." I'm quite put out by this needless sequestration. Why do we still pretend that pregnant women of social standing must be hidden? Are we trying to fool the common folk into thinking we come by children magically?

I won't bore you with all the silly committees I still take part in (behind the scenes, of course). However, I must let you in on a secret. You know Avery has all the inside news politically. He has heard a very well-founded rumor that, when Governor Northey returns to Nairobi shortly, he will announce that the British East African Protectorate will be officially known as the Kenya Colony. But keep it under your hat, darling. It's supposed to be a surprise.

Your motorcycle sounds like a great bit of fun to ride, but I'm sorry the petrol shortage hasn't improved. They'd be better off getting that Natalite plant in full production and make the fuel alcohol they produced during the war. Oh, it makes me positively restless to get back to Africa again, and as soon as little Jade or little David is born (Avery insists we name the baby Gwenevere or Arthur), we shall be on the first boat home.

Please write again and tell me all the news. I miss you all and Africa so dreadfully. I feel positively smothered here, and my sister is driving me to Bedlam.

Your dearest friend and "comrade in axles,"
Beverly Dunbury

Jade chuckled, imagining her friend chafing under society's restraints. Yes, it would be good to see Bev again, but she worried about them traveling with a new baby. She'd have to trust Avery's judgment there. She wondered how Maddy would handle this tiny addition to their group. The Thompsons, with classic British reserve, didn't discuss children much, but Jade had learned that they'd tried unsuccessfully for years to conceive. So far, with no other children close by, they'd handled their disappointments, but Beverly's baby would make it harder to bear the anguish. Maddy had become more moody ever since Beverly's announcement.

As Jade folded the letter and slipped it back into her pocket, she saw a flash of white light and heard a muffled *boom. My camera!* The men also heard it, and everyone ran to the vehicles, too impatient to wait to see their prize. Jade climbed into the front seat next to Perkins, as anxious to retrieve her camera as to see the leopard.

They sped past the stables and the horses' paddock, leaving the farm and the cornfields behind them. In the distance was one lone, scrubby acacia, pruned of its larger branches so that the leopard couldn't find anything strong enough to perch on. Jade's camera and the flash pan sat up in the remaining limbs, aimed and focused on what had been the top of the pit trap. With any luck, the cat had taken its own picture just before plunging into the hole.

But the sounds that greeted them when they shut off the engines were not the angry snarls of a leopard. Several high-pitched *whoops* followed by a cackling laugh erupted from the pit. A cold chill chased down Jade's spine and she shivered involuntarily. *Blast. I'll never get used to that sound.* With it came the image of bandaged, broken bodies, the front lines, and the horror of the shell-shocked wounded, giggling insanely. She took a deep breath and forced herself to think about the present. Best to shinny up the acacia and retrieve the big Graflex before someone knocked it out in the excitement.

"It's a hyena," said Cutter. "I thought we were supposed to get a leopard."

"Looks like someone forgot to tell the leopard," said Daley. "Do we need a hyena, Bob?"

Perkins peered at his list. "Yep!"

"Bring the cage, boys," yelled Daley to his crew. "It's a keeper."

By the time Cutter and Anderson explained the proceedings to the hired natives and hauled the wooden cage to the edge of the pit, the sun poked over the horizon, spilling liquid gold on the scene. Jade set her camera on the truck seat and retrieved a lariat and a pair of gloves.

The capture crew, expecting an agile leopard, had designed the original extraction scheme with that in mind. The idea was to first rope the animal through the mouth and pull back so it couldn't bite without biting its own gums. While the cat was preoccupied with its restraint, a bottomless cage would be dropped over him, followed by a half dozen native African men on top to weigh it down. Once they had the animal inside, the rope around the mouth would be relaxed, allowing the leopard to pull free.

It was Jade's job to wrangle the lariat around the animal's mouth. She held most of the coiled length in her left hand and held the loop, or *honda*, in her right.

"We won't need that, Miss del Cameron," said Perkins. "We can just lower the box right on top of *this* critter."

Jade shrugged and peeled off her gloves. "Suit yourself, Mr. Perkins. That leaves me clear to photograph the capture." Jade set aside the lariat, grabbed her more portable Kodak from her day pack, and positioned herself to record the proceedings.

One of the men tossed a chunk of meat into the pit. The

hyena, a young male judging by his size, fell on it with a hungry purpose. Jade wondered why he was separated from his pack. Hyenas rarely hunted alone. Perhaps there hadn't been enough game in the vicinity to support all of the animals and the young males had been driven out. Whatever the reason, he didn't flinch from his meal even as the box dropped on top of him.

Immediately, four African men jumped onto the box to hold it down while Cutter and Anderson slid into the pit, carrying a large wooden panel. The Americans inserted the panel into grooves, and slid the floor into place as the hyena lifted one foot after the other. Last, they slipped ropes under the box and tied them at the top so the box could be hoisted up.

"Done!" called Anderson.

Several Africans hurried to and from the trucks, bringing wooden beams from which they set up an oversized sawhorse with a block and tackle suspended on the central beam. The remaining men in the pit pulled hard on the rope and the hyena, now nervously whooping, was slowly raised up to the surface. Finally, a ladder was lowered for the men to climb out of the pit.

Jade took her last shot of the men carrying the cage to one of the trucks.

"Sorry we didn't get the leopard, Mr. Daley," said Jade, putting her camera in her pack.

"Call me Hank and leave that formal stuff to old Perkins," he said. "And it's all right. We needed a hyena anyway, so we haven't lost any time. We can cover up the pit and try again tonight." He clapped his hands together and rubbed them as if to signify a job well done. "I'm ready for some breakfast, or at least some coffee. Let's go back to Chalmers' and see if he's made a fresh pot."

When Jade had met Alwyn Chalmers last night, she'd been struck by how homely one man could be. A lean man to begin with, his face looked as though it had been pressed between two boards until the chin poked out sharply at the bottom from the force. At five foot, six inches, he was an inch shorter than Jade, but he made up for it with a tuft of golden brown hair that stuck up like the tassels on his own maize crop. The term "ugly as homemade sin" came to mind.

"Did you get the leopard?" he asked as Jade climbed from the truck and headed toward the veranda. She shook her head and stepped aside.

"A hyena fell in instead," said Perkins. "But we can try again tonight."

Chalmers scowled, sucking in his thin cheeks and pulling his long face down even lower. "That cat is a menace!" he said, his voice reedy. "It needs to be taken before it kills White Fire, if it hasn't already." His face reddened as his anger grew. "If you can't get it, then I'll put out some poison bait and kill it."

"Is White Fire the pony you've run the notice for?" asked Jade. "The one missing for two weeks?"

"Three weeks," snapped Chalmers. He blushed. "Sorry to be so short, Miss del Cameron, but that was my prize polo pony and best stud. Race week and the big match are coming up in another week and a half. I heard that leopard screaming nearby one night when I was working one of White Fire's colts, and he took fright. He kicked and his stall door flew open. Before I could stop him, he ran out into the night. I haven't seen him since. And he probably won't come back as long as that beast roams this area."

"I'm sorry," said Jade. "But it's possible he's already dead."

"In that case, I have a score to settle with that leopard. I was willing to let those American friends of yours try to trap it, but I can't afford to let it take another of my horses."

"Mr. Perkins and Mr. Daley are my present employers," said Jade. "I wish you'd give them another chance." She put her camera equipment in the truck.

Perkins had quietly backed down the veranda steps in the face of Chalmers' anger. Now he stepped forward at this newest request to plead his own case. "It can't hurt to let us try again, Mr. Chalmers. The pit's already dug."

Chalmers grunted; then his face blanched as a new horror popped into his mind. "White Fire could fall into it. He'd break his leg."

"I'll leave some of the native men in one of the blinds to watch for him," said Perkins. "Let's all just have some coffee and talk about this like civilized men."

Jade suspected Perkins wanted coffee as badly as she did, and all pretense of discussion was for the sake of having a cup. Chalmers mumbled that he did have coffee, and Jade offered to fetch it along with cups. Chalmers pointed out the way through the house to the back pantry while he went to the separate kitchen to get the enameled coffeepot. Jade took two steps into the abominably messy front parlor, sidestepping empty wooden crates and a mound of rags, when her attention was caught by a long Maasai spear and a leather shield hanging on the far wall. She instantly forgot all about the coffee.

The spear, as long as a man was tall, was made in three sections. The end pieces were steel joined by a central shaft of dark wood over a foot long. Two black ostrich feathers were attached to the sharp tip with a string of red and black beads. The shield, made of buffalo hide, was about three feet long and two feet wide, coming to points at each of the long ends. The hide was stretched and stitched over a wooden framework and painted a rust red, white, and black. A series of six white diamonds ran down the length in the center, bordered by a strip of red on one side and black on the other. Concentric black arcs graced the side with the red stripe and matching red arcs adorned the other half.

Below the weapons was a small table with a few framed photographs and a decade of dust. One showed five men posing beside and partly in front of a zebra with a very short-cropped mane. A younger-looking Chalmers held the animal's head with a halter. The other men weren't identifiable through the accumulated dirt. Beside this photo was a picture of Chalmers posing with a rifle. Behind these two photos was a third picture of a lovely young woman with pale, delicate features and blond hair. Unlike the other photos, this one had been wiped clean. Before Jade could study the image more closely, Chalmers came into the room looking for her.

"Did you get lost, miss?" he asked. He didn't sound angry, but Jade could tell that the question was a polite way of asking her what the hell she was doing.

"I'm sorry, Mr. Chalmers," she said. "I saw this spear and shield and couldn't take my eyes off them. They're Maasai, aren't they?" Jade followed him into the back pantry.

"Yes. I picked them up during the war when I joined some of the other chaps around here as mounted volunteer rifles." He handed two tin cups to Jade and kept four.

Jade noticed he didn't mention how he had acquired them. "Volunteer rifles?"

"A bit of a home guard, miss. Never saw much action, though."

"Do you know what the feathers on the spear mean?"

"Peace. That's why they're on the tip."

He escorted her outside and handed a mug each to Perkins, Cutter, and Anderson. Jade passed her extra cup to Daley while Chalmers poured a thick black brew into Cutter's mug. Cutter took a sip and winced. He tried another and coughed.

"Too strong for you, Mr. Cutter?" asked Chalmers.

"No," Cutter squeaked.

Jade could tell by the pungent aroma that the coffee had bubbled past the point of no return, and she knew it would be bitter. She also knew this was a test of some sort, and she was going to have to represent the Americans. She smiled and hoisted her mug in a toast.

"Here's mud in your eye," she said and, after testing the coffee with her lips for temperature, drained the cup in three gulps. "That might keep me awake." She set the cup on the veranda railing. "Thanks, Mr. Chalmers. Now, are you going to give us another chance at that leopard tonight?"

Chalmers waggled his head as though he was still thinking about it and walked over to confer with Cutter.

"We really need to give that leopard another chance," Jade said to her bosses.

Daley nodded and fished in his pocket for a cigarette. "Especially as it's reported to be a female," he said. "A mated pair sells for three times what a lone male fetches." He watched as Cutter grabbed a gunny sack and a pole from the truck and ran off to an outbuilding. "Now where do you suppose Frank's going?"

Jade shrugged. "Outhouse?" But why would he take a sack and pole? To the side, she caught sight of Chalmers chuckling as he walked into the house. *Uh-oh.* "Hey, Wayne, what's Frank up to?"

Anderson hurried over to her. "Chalmers told him there was a small animal hiding under the woodshed we could have if he wanted it. Something called a zorilla."

"Zorilla, huh?" said Daley. "Sounds like gorilla. Some kind of monkey, Jade?"

She shoved her empty coffee mug into her boss' hands. "Hold this," she said, and raced after Cutter. When she caught up with him, he was squatting next to a burrow, poking the stick into it. "No, Frank!" she yelled.

Cutter turned, pulling out the pole as he stood. "What? I can hear him in there."

"You're going to get more than that if you don't get out of the way." She grabbed his sleeve and jerked him back just as a small, bushy-tailed creature emerged, its fur bristling.

"Holy cow, it's a danged skunk!" shouted Cutter.

The black-and-white polecat sprang forward and backward on its stiff, stumpy legs, growling and screaming.

"Back away, slowly," said Jade as she took her own advice. "If he starts to turn around, beat it fast." She got to the edge of the shed and ducked behind it.

The zorilla wasn't mollified by their retreat. He pivoted and let spray, covering a wide arc, part of which caught Cutter's shoes. He let loose a furious stream of cuss words.

Chalmers was sitting on his porch stoop chuckling to himself until he saw Jade's stern look. "Very funny," she said. "What the hell were you thinking?"

Chalmers never had a chance to answer. They were interrupted by the puttering chug of a well-worn engine. Everyone turned to see who was driving up the road, and Jade heard Chalmers mutter under his breath. The newcomer was his northern neighbor, Charles Harding.

Charles Harding was a medium-built man with a protruding stomach, long, skinny legs and next to no backside, making his suspenders indispensable for keeping up his dungarees. His solar topee hat sat atop dingy yellow hair gone to white at the temples. The effect was echoed by his equally dingy linen shirt and slightly jaundiced eyes.

Harding reached into the seat next to him and extracted a large wooden crate with the words ALL-PURE CANNED MEATS painted on the side. His hands and arms bore many scratches, as though he'd been in a blackberry patch. He handed the crate to Daley, who lifted the lid.

"I'd be careful if I were you. They're small, but full of mean," said Harding. "Shot their mother last night on my land."

Jade peered over Daley's shoulder at two snarling and spitting leopard cubs, about seven weeks old.

CHAPTER 3

Leopards, due to their stealth, are feared and figure in many sayings.
"The leopard has a beautiful coat, but an evil heart"
smacks of our own "Beauty is only skin-deep." Yet "Even the
fierce leopard will not devour her cubs."

—The Traveler

BOTH MR. DALEY and Mr. Perkins stared at the box's scrappy contents as though their minds couldn't reconcile what they saw with what they heard.

"You shot the mother?" Jade asked. "The one we've been trying to capture?"

The question was rhetorical at best. Jade had even anticipated such a result, but it didn't make the reality any easier to accept. The fact that this second leopard was nursing and providing for kittens went a long way toward explaining why she'd remained in this area and hunted the domestic animals. It also made the outcome more predictable and tragic.

The first leopard had put up enough of a struggle. A mother would have fought desperately against the ropes and the box, to the point of doing serious injury to herself or the handlers. And once they'd captured her, there would have been no way to find her young. Old Africa was at war with the new. At least these cubs had survived this latest skirmish between the farms and cities versus the ancient ways of the plains and hills. The fact that they were young made them more tractable. They would adjust, but either way, another part of wild Africa was lost.

Bob Perkins' thoughts had probably followed similar lines because his protest seemed little more than token words. "You should have told us she was on your land, Mr. Harding. We might have taken her alive."

"Not without serious risk," said Harding. "And I couldn't afford to lose more livestock to her. I tracked her and shot her near her lair." He spared a glance for Chalmers and gave one short nod. "Alwyn," he said.

"Charles," responded Chalmers.

Jade noticed that the men used each other's first names, which suggested friendship, but the greetings were curt and the voices cool. Had they had a falling-out?

"It was good of you to save the kittens," said Jade.

"I expect they're worth one hundred pounds apiece," answered Harding. "Assumed you chaps would just as soon have something young rather than that hellcat anyway." He reached into the back of his truck and pulled out a swollen goatskin bag. "Here, this is full of goat's milk. I rubbed the bag against the mother so it would smell like her. Ought to take one of the corners like a teat. I wouldn't have let them starve to death. That's too cruel even for a leopard."

"We'll pay you one hundred and twenty-five pounds for the pair," said Perkins.

"One fifty and we'll call it square," countered Harding.

Perkins looked at Daley, who was still holding the box. Daley nodded. "One fifty it is then, Mr. Harding," said Perkins. The two men shook hands on it. "I've heard you're a square dealer."

Jade reached into the box and received a fierce spit and a swipe with a paw.

"They're mean as hell, miss," said Harding. "That one on the left especially. Look at her eyes—you can tell. There's a certain madness in them. I saw it with the mother, too."

Jade recalled the calculating stare of the captured male and wondered if Harding wasn't right. Then she decided that was ridiculous. "They're just scared and hungry," she said. "Mr. Chalmers, would you happen to have an old piece of flannel or a worn shirt that we could keep?"

Chalmers nodded and went into the house with a backward glance at Harding. He emerged a minute later with a towel and handed it to Jade. She ripped it in half and dropped one part over one of the cubs, the female, and quickly bundled it up so only her head stuck out.

"Now she can't scratch anyone." She nodded to the goatskin bag. "Can you poke a hole in one of the corners?" she asked Harding.

He fumbled in both his pockets, then slapped them on the outside, looking perplexed. "Seem to have a hole in my own pocket," he mumbled.

"Never mind," said Jade. "Probably make too large a hole anyway." She toted the cub over to a nearby acacia tree, and broke off a thick thorn. With it, Jade stabbed one corner of the bag and offered it to the cub. She refused at first. Then hunger took over and she sucked greedily at the makeshift udder. When the cub was finished, Jade handed her and the bag to Cutter while she dampened the other rag at the well pump. Then she undid the back end of the towel, exposing the kitten's rump, and wiped the wet rag over its backside. The cub responded by relieving her bowels and bladder all over the ground.

Cutter held the cub at arm's length and inspected his shoes. "Warn a guy next time, will you?"

"What are you worried about?" laughed Anderson. "Your shoes already stink like polecat."

Jade ignored the exchange and answered the unspoken question in her bosses' eyes. "New animals, at least cats, usually have to be stimulated by their mothers. I've seen it with our barn cats." She took the cub from Cutter, put the little leopard back in the crate, unrolled her, and bundled her brother. This time she handed the growling packet to Anderson. "Now you know how to do it. Everyone should try so the kittens don't have to rely on just one caretaker."

Anderson took the wriggling lump with all the temerity one would expect when handling dynamite. "How long do you have to do that . . . that business with the backside?"

"Oh, for most cats until they're ten months old," Jade said, keeping her best poker face during her fib. "I'd suspect another month longer for a leopard."

"But . . . but . . . by then . . . ," stammered Anderson as he mentally calculated the size of the leopard's teeth and claws.

Jade decided that the poor man had suffered enough and grinned. "Actually, they'll probably be old enough to start doing their business on their own in a week or so. But we need to keep watch in case."

Anderson let loose an audible sigh of relief and offered the dripping bag of milk to the second cub, a male. After a little coaxing, the little wildcat attacked it with vigor and the bottom of the bundle wriggled as he tried to knead his paws inside the towel. "Cute little cuss," he said.

"And you make a dandy wet nurse," said Cutter. "It looks to me as if Miss del Cameron should be the one to take care of the babies, her being a woman and all."

Daley put the box with the first cub, now asleep, on the floor of the truck cab. "But Miss del Cameron isn't going back to the States, Frank. So we all need to play Mommy here."

Cutter shoved his hands in his pockets and lowered his head. "Ahh, I didn't mean anything by it, boss."

"Think nothing of it, Frank," Daley said. "We'll train some of the natives, too. They can start taking over once we get these critters to the compound."

From a distance to the southwest came a droning purr. Everyone but Jade looked around for the sound, searching the horizon for a truck or automobile. Jade looked up. *Sam and his Jenny.* But the haze of the African sky made it impossible to see him until he came closer. Had he flown this way looking for her? Did the shiver of pleasure she felt come from the thought of seeing him, or his plane? *Both,* she decided. By then, the second leopard cub had finished his meal and had done his duty. Anderson set him next to his sister, dropped the dry towel over them, and hung the wet one over the box edge.

"We need to get back," said Daley. "I'll leave a crew here to fill in that pit, Mr. Chalmers." He directed the five Kikuyu to the task, setting the skunked Cutter as foreman to oversee the operation and return the men later. "Just don't bring me any danged zorillas."

They thanked Chalmers for the use of his veranda and the coffee, which no one but Jade had risked, told Harding where to go to collect his money, and drove back toward town. Jade noticed, sadly, the absence of any aerial noises and decided Sam had just been scouting for something to film rather than looking for her. She tried to rationalize the hazards of putting down on an uneven surface, the risk of hitting the brush, a rock, or an unwary warthog. *There isn't any safe place to land.*

She was wrong. The truck skidded to a stop on a straight stretch of the Kyambu Road.

"What the hell?" exclaimed Perkins.

"That would be my ride," said Jade. She leaped out of the truck and ran to the man standing in front of the propeller of the Curtiss JN-4, or "Jenny," that blocked the road.

Sam Featherstone was the picture of defiance and daring, his booted feet apart and his arms folded across his chest. A leather aviator's helmet covered his head and a pair of goggles masked everything above his hawklike nose and pencil-thin mustache. Once he spotted Jade, his mouth spread into a wide, pearly grin and his arms opened to receive her. Jade obliged, and he swept her up into the air.

"Told you I'd take you flying," he said.

"Sam, how long have you been here?" she asked as he set her down.

He kissed her quickly on the cheek. "Not long. This is my first vehicle blockade. I saw all the trucks at Chalmers' farm and didn't see any other camp, so I took a chance you were all heading back to town."

Bob Perkins stepped out of the truck. For a moment Jade couldn't tell which emotion would win out: his annoyance at having the road blocked by this monstrous machine or curiosity. Curiosity won, helped in part by Sam's friendly demeanor.

"Have you ever seen an airplane up close, sir?" Sam asked after Jade introduced him. Perkins shook his head no. Anderson and Daley joined them, and Jade made more introductions.

"Did this one see any dogfights?" Perkins asked. "I don't see any gun mount."

"No, Mr. Perkins," said Sam. "This was a trainer plane. It

never saw any action. We got into the war too late to use most of them. In fact, this one only got uncrated after I bought it."

"What about you?" asked Anderson.

"I got uncrated," said Sam with a chuckle, then added more soberly, "Yes, I saw action."

Anderson kept looking at Sam's left arm, wrapped around Jade's waist. "It appears you already know our Jade." His voice was flat and his face tense, devoid of any genial expression.

Sam pulled his arm away, folded them back across his chest, and stiffened. Jade noticed all the signs of male posturing. A similar situation had occurred on Mount Marsabit when her former safari leader, Harry Hascombe, and Sam had first squared off for her attention. She decided she was tired of feeling like the lone cow for all the bulls to butt heads over.

Determined to stop the sparring before it began in earnest, she elbowed Sam in the ribs. "Sam, you look like someone just starched your shorts." He let out a whoosh of air as Jade's jab struck home. Before he could regain his breath, Jade continued. "I met Sam in January up north. He's helped me out of some predicaments since then."

Anderson scowled, and Jade recognized the look. She'd seen it before during the war from "doughboys" and "tommies" whenever a pilot came into a room.

"I spent my duty on the ground with the Third U.S. Division at Château Thierry," Anderson said. He puffed out his barrel chest and raised his chin.

Sam's posture softened, his arms falling to his side. "You saw hard fighting."

"Damn right we did. But who at home ever knows about it?" said Anderson.

Jade had been right. The doughboys resented the glamorous pilots for taking so much of the glory while they paid a heavy price in blood on the ground. What the ground troops never cared to hear was the sad fact that the pilots also paid dearly. When a soldier was hurt, he hit the dirt. But that very dirt was hell and away from an airplane, and parachutes didn't always open or have a chance to. Sam, one of the lucky ones, had only paid with his right leg. All Anderson saw was that he'd just lost one more battle to a pilot.

Sam must have sensed this, too, and made an overture of friendship. "*I* know what you did. I lost some good buddies during the war to ground fighting. One was a gunner. If you'd like, I'd be happy to take you up sometime. Show you what Africa looks like from the air."

Anderson stepped back a pace and shook his head. "Couldn't get me in one of those contraptions. Just thinking about it gives me the heebie-jeebies."

Daley, who seemed oblivious to the discussion, had walked up to the plane and was peering intently at the myriad thin wires that braced the upper and lower wings. "Sure looks like she'd crumble easily. You'd have to be mighty brave or awful loco to trust your life in this."

Sam laughed. "A little of both, I guess. But I'm blocking your way, so if you fellows could give the propeller a yank, we can be off." He turned to Jade. "But *you're* doing the flying."

Jade hugged Sam hard enough to make him gasp for air. Then she stepped into the recessed stirrup and swung her long legs into the rear cockpit's wicker seat, where she donned a leather aviator's helmet and pair of goggles. "I'll pick up my Graflex later, Mr. Perkins."

"Wait a minute," said Anderson, pointing to Jade. "*She's* flying?"

"I had a few lessons during the war," Jade called back over the side, "and Sam's been teaching me when we can afford the fuel. Mostly I take off and land again back at the Thompsons' farm. Never get much more than ten feet off the ground."

"Flying's easy," said Sam. "Landing is the tricky part. But Jade's ready."

Anderson shook his head. "Whole dang world's gone stir-crazy."

Jade focused on what she needed to do to get off the ground. With Sam in the front cockpit, she knew he could take over if he had to, but he wouldn't unless it was absolutely necessary. By then, it could be too late.

They were already facing the wind, so Sam asked the men to either back their trucks up to give them a runway, or drive around them. No one wanted to take a chance that this bird wouldn't take off and plow into them, so they pulled the truck off the murram road and drove around behind them. Daley volunteered to pull the propeller, a one-man job on a Jenny, and Sam explained what to do before he climbed into the front cockpit by way of the wing-walk pads.

Jade switched off the magneto and primed the engine, pulling gas through with the choke. Then she turned on the switch and cracked the throttle. "Contact," she shouted over the side, and watched as Daley swung the propeller. It caught the first time and the engine purred to life as Daley scurried to the rear. She opened the throttle for full power and felt the Jenny pull ahead like a horse ready to race. Jade used the stick to raise the tail and keep the plane on the ground until she had attained fourteen hundred rpms. Then she pulled back on the stick and let the plane rise smoothly into the air just before the road curved.

The thrill of being aloft swept through Jade. Her pulse raced and her right hand trembled slightly on the stick. She banked into a turn, climbing in a slow spiral reminiscent of an eagle riding a thermal. Below them, Anderson, Daley, and Perkins peered up. Perkins waved once, and Jade waggled the wing in reply. In the front cockpit, Sam pointed to the northwest and Jade turned the nose in that direction.

Fifteen minutes later, at fifteen hundred feet, they left the main farms and crossed the fringe of wild Africa. She dropped to eight hundred feet and passed over a mixed herd of hartebeeste and reedbuck. Jade spotted the spread-out spiral horns of a few greater kudu along the edge. The entire herd took off as one mass at their approach, twisting and flowing like a living river. Jade tapped Sam on the shoulder and pointed. The plane had startled a rhino that stood his ground, pivoting in an attempt to spot this noisy intruder. Jade laughed at his confusion and flew on, climbing to leave him in peace. Conversation wasn't possible over the noise, so she could only hope Sam saw him, too.

She checked the fuel gauge and the water-temperature gauge, saw both read fine, but decided it was probably time to head back to the Thompsons' farm. As much as she wanted to stay aloft, listening to the OX-5 engine's throaty purr, she knew that fuel was tight and Sam's funds were limited. It would be selfish to deplete either of them, especially when he had plans to film aloft. Jade turned the Jenny's nose southeast.

They passed over Harding's farm and the acres of sisal, grown for its rope-producing fibers. The outbuildings lay in an orderly arrangement around several animal pens. Jade saw a large number of sheep in a pasture, two horses, and the usual exotic "pets," what looked like a Thomson's gazelle and a zebra. Two large dogs lolled near the house. She crossed over to what was probably Alwyn Chalmers' farm, observing the regular rows of his maize fields. More notable was the expansive stable that dwarfed his house, and the large exercise track. A few goats milled around a trough next to several horses.

From Chalmers' farm, she headed east, following the dirt road to the Thompsons' coffee farm. She buzzed the house to let Maddy know they were back before going on to Sam's makeshift airfield. Jade spiraled round to drop altitude and bring the Jenny into the wind, making sure she had a long run in front of her. She shut off the engine and angled in, gliding. The sudden absence of the purring engine gave her stomach butterflies.

This is it, kid. Don't crack her up.

Jade started to level off about fifty feet from the ground, until she was only six feet off. Soon she felt the wheels pummel the ground and the tail skid rake behind her. She pulled back on the stick to keep the nose up, lest the Jenny should pitch forward. A moment later, they were earthbound and at a standstill.

Jade removed her goggles and tugged off the leather helmet, freeing her black hair, the waves damp with sweat. Sam clambered over the cockpit sides, stepped onto the wing pads, and jumped down, ready to help Jade. She didn't need it, but had already learned that it was important to Sam to play that role, at least at his plane, so she patiently waited for his assistance. Once on the ground, they embraced, laughing, their faces flushed from excitement and the wind.

"Did you see the rhino?" asked Jade. "Poor thing couldn't figure out who to attack." She started to slip from Sam's embrace, but he pulled her back, taking her by the shoulders.

"Now I can kiss you properly without anyone around to see," he said. He leaned in and caught her mouth in his, letting his lips caress hers gently, then with more vigor and urgency.

Jade, heady from the exhilaration of soaring above her beloved Africa, reeled under the pressure. Her legs went weak, and suddenly, she couldn't feel the ground at all. After a moment she realized that Sam had wrapped his arms around her midriff and lifted her into the air. She tasted a hint of machine oil on his lips, felt the tantalizing tickle of his mustache. As her toes again made contact with the earth, Jade pulled back slightly and placed her hands on his chest.

"Nice to see you, too, Sam. Do you do that to all the people you take up in your plane?"

"No," he said, his voice husky. "Only the ones I'm in love with."

Jade was immediately swamped by the nervousness she always felt when a man expressed a serious attraction to her. She stepped away from the plane and him. "Now, Sam, don't talk that way. You've known me barely six months." She took hold of the tail to help him turn the plane. Together they pulled it by the lower wing grips into his high-walled *boma*. Jade unlatched the swinging gate to close off the entrance to curious animals while Sam took out the oil can and started lubricating the engine and Jade tied down the plane. With the rainy season over, they didn't bother with tarps and left the makeshift hangar open to the sky.

Sam put down the oil can. "I know you well enough, lady, and you know it." He came up behind her and kissed her nape. "I'm just waiting for you to realize it."

Jade turned and laid a hand gently on his cheek. "Just give me some time, Sam, please. When you talk this way, I feel like someone's trying to hobble me."

He clasped his hands behind her back. "How can you say that after I just helped you defy old Newton and his gravity? I'm not going to hobble you, Jade. I'm trying to give you wings."

"Are you, Sam? Sometimes I feel as though you want to tie me down." She nodded her head at the plane's restraining cords.

"What are you talking about?" A look of genuine surprise swept over his face.

"Well, this new job for one thing. Admit it. You weren't very happy when I took it."

"It's dangerous."

"I told you, I just handle the ropes and take photographs."

He leaned in closer. "Is that what you were doing when you played the part of leopard bait? Taking pictures? Or was that handling the ropes? Besides," he added before Jade could counter, "for all I know, you might plan on roping a crocodile next."

"Sam! I hardly think—"

He put his hands up in a gesture of appeasement. "Jade, one of the traits I love the most about you is your adventurous spirit."

"Then why . . ."

"Because one of your more *maddening* traits is your tendency to rush off on some harebrained scheme without a thought for your own safety." He threw up his hands and let them fall to his sides. "It's as if you're trying to prove something to the world."

Jade stood silently, her arms folded in front of her, and watched him, her cool green eyes studying his face. Finally, she relaxed her posture and sighed. "You're going to have to learn to trust me, Sam."

He didn't reply. She kissed him lightly on the lips. "Come on. Neville and Maddy will have heard us fly over the house and wonder where we are." She secured the makeshift hangar gate behind them.

They walked the quarter mile back to the Thompsons' house in silence, communicating by a nod and an occasional gesture just as they did in the air. Jade appreciated this ability in Sam more than she had ever thought possible. He, like her, didn't feel the need to fill every gap with banter. When they came to the house, they found a note tacked onto the doorframe. Sam made a low whistle after he read it.

"Something wrong?" asked Jade. "Did somebody get hurt?"

"No," answered Sam. Then he immediately amended the statement. "Well, yes, in a manner of speaking." He handed the note to Jade, who recognized Maddy's close, neat hand.

Sam, Jade:

We have gone into Nairobi at the "request" of Inspector Finch. You are likewise requested to come at once. It would appear that the word "suicide" has been replaced by "murder."

Maddy

CHAPTER 4

Most people either learn or instinctively feel the power that some
wield over others and adopt deferential attitudes to them,
learning to curb their tongue until it's safe. It's a temporary restraint
that is even seen in the African cultures. The Maasai have a proverb
about it: "What is said over the dead lion's body could not be
said to him alive."

—The Traveler

JADE AND SAM arrived on his motorcycle at police headquarters—
an ugly, squat, galvanized-tin building on Eighth Avenue.
They found Neville and Madeline sitting in the dingy waiting area on straight-backed wooden chairs on a scuffed and
unpolished wooden floor. A bare bulb, which probably did
little to light the room on cloudy days, dangled above their
heads. The curtainless window admitted some of the sun's
rays, but it was badly in need of washing. Neville had a newspaper in hand, but didn't seem to follow any particular story
as much as he did Maddy's nervous fidgets.

"What's all this about murder?" asked Jade after they reported their arrival to the constable at the desk and took seats
next to the Thompsons.

Maddy grabbed Jade's hand and held it tightly. "Oh, Jade,
I'm so glad you and Sam are here."

"No one is telling us much of anything," said Neville.
"Constable Miller drove out to the farm early this morn-

ing looking for us and for both of you. He said the Inspector wanted to see us *now*. Oh, and we checked the *Red Book*. That postal box is not listed in this volume so we still don't know who placed the ad looking for Mrs. Stokes."

Madeline broke in, unable to contain herself. "We reminded him that we were given a day or two to come in, at our convenience, but he said all that had changed. Of course, we asked him what he meant and he gave us a rather pert little smile and said they no longer believed Mr. Stokes took his own life."

"Did he say why?" asked Jade.

"No. Only that he did *not* seem pleased to find Sam gone, especially," she added, turning to Sam, "when he found out you'd flown off."

"I suppose they went to the Dunburys' house looking for me," said Jade.

"We told him you were with the zoological crew and wouldn't be back for a day or two," said Neville. "But you are. Were you successful?"

Jade shrugged. "Yes and no. The leopard in question had been going onto Charles Harding's property, and he shot it. But he did bring us her two cubs. It looks as though they're old enough to survive."

Madeline's head drooped. "Poor thing. *She* certainly paid a high price for motherhood."

Jade noted the pain in Maddy's voice. Apparently there was still no "bun in the oven." "Speaking of Chalmers and Harding," she said, turning the subject away from the executed leopard, "what can either of you tell me about them? They barely spoke to each other beyond acknowledging the other's presence, yet they still used first names."

Neville shifted in his chair. "I believe they *were* friends, being such close neighbors. Chalmers is a bachelor, and Harding is a widower. I think the loneliness more than compatibility bonded them together. I heard they had a falling-out more than a month ago. As I understand it, Chalmers purchased some Somali ponies from a trader. They were supposedly 'salted,' if you know what I mean."

Jade nodded. "They were either inoculated against equine diseases, or had had them and gotten immunity."

"Right," continued Neville. "Harding bought a rather promising-looking pony from Chalmers, but the animal caught fever and died. Harding is known to be scrupulously honest, and he expects the same from everyone he deals with. He claimed that Chalmers owed him a pony. Now, Alwyn is as honest as the next man, but he lost one, too, so he said that, as far as he was concerned, he sold the animal honestly and they'd both been taken."

"I feel sorry for them," said Madeline. "Two lonely men made even lonelier by silly pride."

The door to an interior office opened. Inspector Finch stepped halfway into the waiting room, once again wearing the tired-looking brown suit with frayed cuffs he'd worn to the Thompsons' farm. If he was surprised to see Sam and Jade there, he didn't show it. "I will see you one at a time now. Mrs. Thompson, would you be so kind as to come first? I should think you'd like to get this interview out of the way." He ushered her into the office with a pleasant smile and, with a nod to the others, shut the door behind him.

Neville immediately stood and began to pace. "This is monstrous," he declared. "Interrogating Maddy like some common criminal. I shall give that Finch a piece of my mind when my turn comes."

Sam went to him and patted him on the shoulder. "You'll

do no such thing, man. It's what he wants us to do. He separates us so that we'll each stew with worry about the others in the hopes that one of us will blurt out something useful."

"How do you know this?" asked Jade. "Have you made a habit of being arrested?"

"No, but it's a common interrogation practice for prisoners of war."

"But that must mean he suspects one of us," exclaimed Neville.

"The body *was* found in your coffee dryer," said Jade. "Probably the logical assumption. And I suspect the constable sitting quietly behind that desk is listening, too."

Neville plunked himself back into the chair and ran a hand through his graying hair. "Poor Maddy. She's been rather distraught these past months. She doesn't need this."

Sam and Jade both sat up straighter, matching looks of eagerness in their partly open mouths. "Are you and Maddy anticipating a baby?" asked Jade hopefully.

"No," said Neville. "We've never had any luck having a child, and I think it's telling on her, especially now that Beverly is expecting."

"I'm sorry," said Jade.

Sam responded by hunching over and fingering his hat. After an awkward silence, he looked up at Neville. "Perhaps we should distract Maddy when she comes out, especially when you go in. Otherwise . . ." He shrugged. "I know, give her the paper you have there and point out some particular story for her to read."

"Which one?"

"Does it matter? Just find one that takes a while to read."

"Aren't you two entering produce in Nairobi's agricultural show tomorrow?" asked Jade. "Is there an article about it?"

"Actually there is," said Neville as he flipped through the pages. "It's the first time Nairobi's held a fair, and I'm afraid it's been cut back at the last minute. Still, she can look at the remaining categories and tell you about her plans. That is, if you can keep her attention on it."

"Don't worry, Neville," said Jade. "We'll keep her occupied."

Sam cleared his throat. "Jade, speaking of Saturday's fair, are you attending the dance that evening? Would you allow me to escort you there? That is, if you're going."

Jade cocked her head and pursed her lips, studying Sam for a moment. "I'd love to go with you Sam, but you've certainly taken your sweet time asking. What if someone else has already asked me?"

Sam's brows furrowed. "Did someone else—"

"No."

He exhaled loudly. "That's a relief," he mumbled to himself.

Madeline emerged from the inner office at that moment, her sun-browned face looking a shade paler. Both Sam and Neville stood until she returned to her seat. She bowed her head, staring at her hands folded in her lap.

"Maddy?" asked Neville, reaching for one of her hands. Jade saw that her fingertips were stained with blue-black ink.

Madeline looked up and forced a weak smile. "I'm fine, Neville. I'm not supposed to talk about any of this with you." Neville scowled and his wife immediately added, "They just fingerprinted me and asked me a few questions. The inspector was a perfect gentleman. It's only that I find this whole subject of a murder all too distressing."

That seemed to mollify Neville, who relaxed his tense posture. He didn't get a chance to reply, though.

"Mr. Thompson, if you please," said Finch. Neville went through the door Finch indicated. Once again, Finch shut the door behind himself.

Madeline sat staring at or beyond Jade and Sam.

Jade pointed to the newspaper listings and asked Maddy about the upcoming agricultural fair. "Are you entering your flowers," she asked, "or just your garden vegetables and coffee?"

Madeline made a show of studying the listings. Jade could tell by the tense lines around her lips that her friend was distraught, but how much was due to Stokes and how much due to another failed attempt at conceiving, she couldn't tell.

"I have some nice roses I could enter, and some rather large onions and sweet potatoes," Maddy said. "I'd planned on showing my laying hens, but it seems they've cut out the animal exhibits." She dropped the paper on her lap, sighed deeply, and lapsed back into silence.

Jade looked to Sam for help, but he just shrugged. Then she remembered the mail. Jade had stuck Bev's letter to Maddy in her shirt pocket. She reached for it now and held it out. "I almost forgot. There were letters for each of us from Beverly." Jade noted that Maddy didn't immediately open the envelope. Usually, she was thrilled to get "news from the outside," as she termed it, and her uninterest only confirmed Jade's suspicions about her deeper distress.

Silence hung in the air until Jade tried another tactic. "I could use some coffee." She went to the desk and asked the constable if there was any coffee to be had or at least a cup of water. "Or is this part of the interrogation tactic?" she asked, using Sam's term.

"It is not," the young man replied, "but we only have tea." He produced four tin cups, and pointed to a pot on top of a cast-iron stove. Jade made a face. She hated tea, but she wanted something hot. She poured a cup for herself, added six spoonfuls of sugar, tested the tea, and decided it was one step above loathsome. "Maddy? Sam? Anyone else care for a cup?"

Maddy declined, but Sam came over and poured one. Jade filled a cup from a covered water jar and handed it to Madeline. "Drink this," she ordered. Madeline sipped obediently.

Before Madeline had finished, Neville emerged from the inspector's office and Sam was called in. With Neville busily directing his wife's attention to either the fair listings or to Beverly's letter, Jade was not needed. She went to a window, took out her pocket handkerchief, and swiped at the smudges and dried bugs on the glass. When that didn't clear a spot, she applied some of the tea, revealing the steeples of All Saints and St. Joseph's churches, two and three streets south. *Tea is good for something at least.* She craned her head to see Government Road.

Europeans, Indians, and native Africans went along the street intent on their business. What was absent from this view was any sense of congeniality. Everyone seemed intent on his task at hand, and Jade saw very few people greet one another beyond a quick nod. Any social intercourse in the city took place a few blocks away, on the more friendly Sixth Avenue with its many stores, or perhaps deep in the Indian bazaars. Across the street, an *askari* escorted an African wearing wrist cuffs into the Department of Native Affairs building set aside to rule over native *shauris*, as squabbles or serious discussions of any kind were termed.

What's keeping Sam? She pulled out her pocket watch and verified that he'd been in with the inspector twice as long as the others. A minute later Sam stepped out of the office, his face set in a grim scowl, his lips nearly invisible in a tense, taut line. He spared one glance for Jade and sat down with his arms folded across his chest.

"Miss del Cameron, I believe you are next," said Inspector Finch.

Jade set the mug on the constable's desk with a "Thanks" and went into Finch's office.

"Please be seated, Miss del Cameron," said Finch.

Jade sat down on another hard-backed chair. She crossed her legs, revealing the grime on her duck trousers and her ambulance corps boots. Jade hoped Finch wouldn't take her attire as a sign of disrespect. If anything, it showed the promptness with which she'd answered his summons. Then, with a patiently neutral expression on her face, she waited for him to begin.

"How well did you know Mr. Stokes?" he asked.

"Not at all," said Jade. "It was always Mr. or Mrs. Berryhill who waited on me."

"So you never met Mr. Stokes?"

Jade paused to think. "I *saw* him once this past December. I was purchasing film-developing chemicals in preparation for my safari to Marsabit. Mrs. Berryhill was filling the order when a man came in from the back. I heard Mr. Berryhill say something like 'Ah, there you are, Stokes.' " Jade leaned forward. "May I ask, sir, why you now suspect he was murdered?"

"In point of fact, our tests indicate that his wound was inflicted postmortem," said Finch. "And he had bruises on his jaw and on the side of his head." Finch looked up sharply from his leather notebook and awaited Jade's reaction to this news.

She uncrossed her legs and leaned forward, her eyes wide and mouth partly open, a picture of incredulity and surprise. "Someone beat him to death, then cut him?"

"Possibly." Finch paused to make more notations in the booklet, and Jade stifled her desire to know what he wrote. Probably nothing of importance, but an act designed to make her nervous. She certainly had a feeling of being called before the headmaster. She sat back and mentally told herself to relax. The inspector was only trying to do his job, to solve a crime, and if she was able to help, then fine. She just couldn't figure out what she knew that would shed any light on the situation. And what in the world had he asked Sam to make him so angry?

"How well do you know Mr. Featherstone?"

She hadn't expected that question. "Enough to trust him with my life, sir."

"Please elaborate. Where and how did you meet? What do you know of his previous life?"

Previous life? "I met Sam in January on Mount Marsabit."

"Then he was your safari guide?"

"No, he wasn't part of my safari at all. He—"

"He was poaching then?" The question came rapidly, designed to throw her off.

Jade had decided she would cooperate in the name of justice, but she'd rather be bucked from a bronco than let someone manipulate her. She took a deep breath, smiled a pleasant albeit insincere smile, and answered, "No."

Finch looked up, waiting for her to continue. "No?"

"He was making a motion picture about the elephant

herds. Our paths crossed." What she didn't add was that he'd come all the way to the remote volcanic mountain at the urging of the Dunburys just so he could meet her.

"I see," said Finch. "How is it then that you would trust him with your life, as you put it?"

"Because there *were* poachers on the mountain, Abyssinians by and large, led by a white man. These men tried to kill us, and kidnapped a young friend of mine. Sam went with me into the northern desert to get him back."

"And then he killed these men." It was a statement, not a question.

Jade didn't like the direction this interview was taking. "No, he didn't. He stopped me from killing them."

Finch jerked his head up and stared at Jade. She decided then to destroy any notion the inspector had of Sam being a murderer. "He also saved my life and my mother's in Morocco this past April. And again, he didn't kill anyone to do it."

"Did he stop *you* again?"

Jade realized that she'd just made herself a suspect. She recalled a similar interrogation a few months ago in Tangier. She didn't like the feeling any better the second time around. "Actually, I never tried that time. Sam taught me on Marsabit that I'm not a killer. I drove an ambulance in the War, Inspector. I *save* lives. I don't take them."

"But you did shoot that man in Tsavo when you first came here."

"I shot a hyena."

"And the man happened to be inside it?" Finch didn't wait for a reply. "So you and Mr. Featherstone are lovers."

Jade felt her cheeks grow hot and knew she was blushing, something she rarely ever did. "No, we're not. I thought you wanted to know about Sam's *past* life."

"And you are privy to that?"

"I know he attended Purdue University in the United States, where he studied mechanical engineering. He was a pilot in the American Expeditionary Forces during the war, and he lost his lower right leg as a result of shrapnel in the ankle."

"And you know this how?"

"He told me." As she said it, Jade knew her reply sounded flimsy. If Finch believed Sam had some mysterious past, he certainly wouldn't take her word for the truth. But maybe he'd believe a higher source. "You might cable Lord Avery Dunbury in London. Sam and he are friends. He'll verify all this." As an afterthought she added, "The Dunburys can vouch for me as well."

"I already have," said Finch. "Yesterday afternoon, in fact, but I have not received any such reply, which makes me question that alleged friendship. I must instruct you not to speak of any of this to either of the Thompsons or to Mr. Featherstone." He stood and motioned for her to follow him to a corner table. "I shall need a set of your fingerprints, if you please."

There on the table was a shallow copper tray, thinly inked and smudged. He took a roller and carefully ran it back and forth over the tray, smoothing out the ink film to a uniform layer. "Spread your fingers, if you will." Without asking for her permission, he took her right hand firmly but gently pressed each digit on the tray, then repeated the action, one finger at a time, across a clean page in a notebook. "And now with your left hand," he said. Jade complied. "If you would please sign your name and the date in the corner, then you are excused."

Jade signed the notebook and wiped her fingers on a

proffered towel. Why, she wondered, hadn't Avery replied immediately to Finch's inquiry? Normally she would suspect he and Beverly had gone on holiday and weren't reachable, but Beverly was over seven months pregnant; they weren't going anywhere. Had something happened? Jade stepped out of the office. Her gaze immediately sought out and found Sam's. The intensity of his expression told her that they were in more trouble than she cared to admit. *What did Finch get him to reveal? Is he worried that he incriminated me or himself?* She knew they hadn't committed any crime, but that might not matter if Finch believed they did.

Madeline, on the other hand, seemed much more cheerful than when Jade had entered Finch's office. She stood and hurried to Jade, waving the newspaper in front of her.

"Jade, wonderful news. Neville and I are going to adopt a little baby boy."

CHAPTER 5

*Ask anyone living in Kenya Colony to name the tribe that exemplifies Africa
to them, and most will say the Maasai. This is a tribe of warriors, strong in
their belief that Engai, God, made them. And then, almost as an afterthought,
He made everyone else.*

—The Traveler

IT TOOK A minute for Jade's brain to switch from being a
murder suspect to Madeline's revelation. "What? Adopt a
baby boy?" She looked at Neville, who stood by his wife,
a wide smile on his weather-beaten face. "How can you be
so certain?"

Madeline held up the newspaper. Jade recognized it as a
copy of the *Leader of British East Africa* by its unmistakable
header showing herds of zebra. Maddy turned the page and
pointed to a particular notice in the classifieds. "Here," she
said. "Read this."

Jade read aloud. "Would someone please adopt a four-
month-old baby boy of Dutch origin? Reply voucher 975, the
Leader."

"And that's it?" asked Sam. "You just claim the child and
it's yours?" His tone was skeptical.

"Why not?" asked Maddy. She seemed genuinely confused by Sam's question.

Jade, more familiar with life under rustic conditions back home in New Mexico, hastened to explain to Sam. "It might be different in your Indiana, Sam, but this is still the frontier to some extent. The governing bodies have little time or resources to devote to orphans. Anyone willing to take one is welcome to the child."

Sam scratched his head. "Back home the orphanages all tend to be run by some religious order, like as not. And if you don't have any here—"

Madeline hastened to reassure Sam that the citizens of Nairobi did care about children. "Lady Northey established a splendid home for the children left without care because of the war, but now it is primarily a place for settlers to board their children while they attend school. But this little boy in the paper needs someone. It's heaven-sent, don't you see?"

Jade looked at Maddy's beaming face and smiled. "That's wonderful, Maddy, Neville. You'll be marvelous parents." Jade handed the paper to Neville. "Makes one wonder what happened."

"I suspect his parents both succumbed to some illness," said Neville. "We're heading to the *Leader* office right now to answer the ad."

"If the authorities want any references, be sure to have them apply to the Dunburys. That should secure you," suggested Sam.

"Good idea," said Jade, hoping that Beverly would answer this query at least. "You also have a letter from Beverly with you to prove your friendship." *Only don't tell them you know us.*

Maddy's smile grew, and her eyes sparkled. "Only just think, Neville, how neatly everything has come together. If we hadn't had to come in this very morning, we might never have seen this advertisement in time, and now Jade has delivered our reference to us."

Yes, thought Jade, *if Martin Stokes hadn't been murdered and we hadn't been suspects, we might have missed this issue.* She kept such macabre thoughts to herself. "Well, then you two had better get a move on."

"Meet us at the New Stanley Hotel at one and we'll have a celebration lunch together," said Maddy. Then she and Neville hurried out the door.

Jade and Sam stepped out of police headquarters and crossed the street. Jade didn't have any particular destination in mind and doubted that Sam did either. She simply wanted to distance herself from Inspector Finch. One glance at her blue-black fingertips told her that would not be easy. She pulled out her handkerchief and wiped them again.

They walked to bustling Sixth Avenue with its Theatre Royale, post office, and the *Standard*'s office with its stationery store. Nairobi had changed so much since the war. The population had increased to an unheard-of three thousand Europeans and another eight thousand Indians. The British tended to live in the fringes in Parklands and Muthaiga districts, leaving the inner city by Swamp Road to the Indian population, which first came to build the railroad. Consequently, the colonists were more concerned with ensuring they had better streetlights and traffic signs so that they could drive unimpeded from work to their clubs for their evening scotch-and-soda sundowners, rather than with the overall health of the city. If cases of plague were a problem in the Indian slum, then the general consensus was to *keep* the Indians in the slum so the plague didn't spread. The colonists cared even less about the few native slums on the southern fringes.

Jade saw the bustling city as a veneer of civilization laid

over the old Africa. At times the veneer was so convincing that the citizens forgot that the old Africa still struggled to survive. She wondered what some of the pioneers, like Lord Colridge or Harry Hascombe, thought of Nairobi now. Hascombe with his charming smile and less than scrupulous nature now had to take his safari customers farther afield to find game.

"I should see if the new rolls of film I ordered have arrived," Jade said.

Sam raised his eyebrows. "That wouldn't happen to be at Stokes and Berryhill, now would it?" he asked. Jade nodded. "I'll go with you."

Stokes and Berryhill Ltd., purveyors of farm equipment, kitchen needs, and chemical supplies, occupied a two-story stone building on Sixth Avenue, across the avenue and three shops down from the New Stanley Hotel. The first floor looked to Jade like a general store gone berserker, carrying everything farmers could want, as long as they didn't desire fine silk dresses and the latest fripperies. The second floor was home to Winston and Pauline Berryhill and their son, Harley, aged sixteen. The store's truck, a battered black Ford with the words STOKES AND BERRYHILL LTD. painted in red on the sides, was parked in front. Jade wondered who would drive out to all the farms and settlements now that Stokes was dead.

Once inside, Sam and Jade wended past racks of canned goods, bolts of fabric, and cans of boot black. To their left, rakes, hoes, and pitchforks hung against the wall next to bins of nails and racks of saws and hammers. On the right were shelves of men's shirts and work trousers. Behind the shirts, glass-fronted cases displayed ladies' shirtwaists and handkerchiefs, combs, mirrors, and shelves of toiletries. Jade spied

boxes of Eucryl tooth powder, Yardley's hair tonic, and Palm
Olive soap. Against the far wall were home remedies and assorted chemicals, everything needed to cure croup, kill rats,
treat livestock, or bolster one's overall vigor. The scents of
leather harnesses and sacks of meal collided midway with a
recent test spritzing of lavender toilet water.

Jade's and Sam's boots echoed hollowly on the plank
floors over the hum of subdued conversation. Pauline Berryhill, a sturdy-looking woman of five foot, five inches, was
quietly proclaiming the virtues of Aertex cellular underwear
to a female customer, while her husband, Winston, pointed
out the finer qualities of the newest pruning shears to a male
shopper. Jade kept an ear to the conversations while she and
Sam stood waiting their turn.

"I'm very sorry to hear about Mr. Stokes," said the woman
customer to Mrs. Berryhill. "Such a shock! You must be devastated."

Mrs. Berryhill nodded once. "Yes, we're saddened beyond
words." She tallied up the purchase and took her customer's
money. "Do come again whenever you need anything."

"Which one do you want?" Jade whispered to Sam.

"I'll take Mr. Berryhill, if you don't mind."

"What? You aren't going to try to work your daredevil
charm on the missus?"

Sam nodded discreetly at the wife. "I'm not sure she
likes me."

Before Jade could ask for clarification, Mrs. Berryhill finished reshelving the unsold undergarments, and spying Jade,
she smiled and nodded. "Miss del Cameron, how nice to see
you. How may I be of assistance? Oh, and Mr. Featherstone,"
she added when she saw Sam. "How nice to see you again,
too." Her tone, while not hostile, didn't sound warm.

"Hello, Mrs. Berryhill," replied Jade. "I ordered a shipment of roll film a month ago. I've come to see if it has arrived yet."

"Yes, I believe it came in earlier this week. If you have a moment, I'll check and see."

Mrs. Berryhill pulled a ledger from the shelf and leafed through the pages. In the meantime, Sam strolled closer to Mr. Berryhill and examined one of the pith solar topees for sale next to a rack of suspenders. Jade had no doubt that Sam intended to pry as much information out of Mr. Berryhill as possible and left him to it.

"Yes, it's right here. Roll film for your Kodak and a box of sheets for a Graflex." She picked up a medium-sized wooden box from the bottom shelf and set it on the counter. Then her fingers ran across the adding machine buttons, pausing only to pull the tally lever. Mrs. Berryhill jotted down the numbers on a receipt book and handed the top copy to Jade, keeping the carbon for herself. "The total is forty-seven rupees," she said.

"Did the price go up again?" asked Jade. "That's much higher than what Mr. Berryhill quoted to me."

"No, but it's the import duties, you see. *They* have increased," explained Mrs. Berryhill.

Jade opened her pocket purse and counted out the money. "I'm very sorry to hear about your partner, Mr. Stokes. I'm sure this sounds rather heartless, but I imagine it puts a bigger burden on you and Mr. Berryhill, doesn't it? Will you take on a new partner or just hire another assistant?"

Mrs. Berrryhill looked up, her hazel eyes wide with surprise at this turn of questions. "You're quite right. It has put a strain on us. You're the first to make the observation. Everyone else expects us to miss his companionship." She snorted.

"I don't know how we're supposed to handle the store *and* the deliveries *or* manage a booth at the agricultural fair. Harley will help during the weekends and holidays, but he must finish his schooling."

"Mr. Stokes must have been a very important part of your store, then. Someone you and your husband thought you could rely on." Jade emphasized the word "thought," hinting that it might not be true.

Mrs. Berryhill rolled her eyes and glanced to see if her husband was listening. Then she leaned closer to Jade. "He was certainly handy at reaching out to the farmers by making personal trips to them, and I suppose that has brought us a lot of business that might have gone elsewhere, but *I* won't miss him here. We will do our best to find a strong man to do the deliveries for us. Someone who can do what he's told and mind his business. But I doubt there's a man anywhere who could manage that!"

Jade decided that Sam was only partly right in his assessment of Mrs. Berryhill. It wasn't him personally that she disliked; she just didn't have a very high opinion of men. "Did I understand correctly that he was married? I never met his wife."

Mrs. Berryhill's lips tightened. "That poor thing. I've no doubt she's left for good. Alice deserved better than him. She was such a lovely little creature. I knew her when she was a girl."

"When did she leave? Where did she go?" asked Jade, leaning on the counter.

Mrs. Berryhill shrugged. "I wish I knew."

Jade took a different tack. "Still, he must have loved her to have been so heartbroken over her leaving him that he'd kill himself. And such a dreadful way to do it, too." She deliberately left the method unspoken, hoping Mrs. Berryhill would fill in the gap.

She didn't. "I'm sorry he saw fit to do it in Mr. Thompson's dryer," Mrs. Berryhill said. "*He* seems to be a decent sort of man, at least."

"Did Mr. Stokes beat his wife?"

"Not physically. But there are marks a man's words can leave on a woman's soul. She could do nothing to please him," said Mrs. Berryhill. "He rarely let her leave home. I'm one of the few people who ever saw her. Oh, he was all slap-you-on-the-back friendly with the settlers, and I'm sure they considered him a fine fellow, but I never trusted him. I could see it in his eyes."

There it was again, Jade thought. The idea that an inner evil was revealed in a look. She could actually believe it with people. Nuances of expression were hard to hide, even for the best poker player. Everyone had his telltale look or twitch when he had something to hide, and it was possible that Mrs. Berryhill had caught on to Martin Stokes.

"If Mr. Stokes was so horrid to his wife, it makes me wonder whatever possessed her to marry him in the first place."

"Ah, well, that's it, isn't it?" said Mrs. Berryhill. "Alice was such a beautiful creature, so fair, rather like a wax doll. Who couldn't fall in love with her? Her parents doted on her, but they both died of typhus near the start of the war. Alice was only nineteen and completely orphaned. No other family. I would have taken her in, but Martin declared for her immediately, before some of the other men in the area had a chance."

"She sounds lovely," said Jade. "Have you a picture of her?"

Mrs. Stokes hesitated and shot a sideways glance to her husband, who was still busy with Sam. "In my desk."

She hurried over to it, unlocked a lower drawer, and returned with a small photograph of a dark-haired woman in her late twenties and a beautiful young girl. Jade recognized the younger face as the same one in Chalmers' picture. The other woman was plainly Mrs. Berryhill six or seven years ago. Jade thanked her and handed the photo back.

Mrs. Berryhill slipped the photograph into her skirt pocket and returned to her desk. Jade turned to see Sam, who had resorted to purchasing a new pair of work gloves and a leather-bound ledger, waiting near the front for her to join him. Once they were outside, she asked what he had learned.

"You don't suppose we'll get in trouble with Finch for this, do you?" asked Sam.

Jade shrugged. "He told me not to discuss my police interrogation with you or the Thompsons. I didn't. And currently I'm discussing my shopping experience with you."

Sam grinned. "You are a devious woman, Jade."

"Not at all. I simply took him at his literal meaning. And if I should talk to Biscuit about the terrors of police headquarters and any of you just happen to eavesdrop, I cannot help it."

"I plan to write everything down in a journal." He waggled the newly purchased ledger. Of course, if I left it lying around and someone chanced on it, I can't stop them from reading it."

"Exactly. Madeline will probably insist on writing her experience up as part of another one of her novels. Since they're usually about me, I think I should read any early drafts."

"Maybe Maddy can convince Neville to start talking in his sleep," said Sam.

"By the way," said Jade, "I don't think Mrs. Berryhill likes men at all, although she made allowances for Neville. But Stokes must have browbeat his wife. I should have asked if she thought he killed her. She was very unhelpful as far as knowing when or where Alice went." Jade related what she learned.

"I wonder, did Stokes run an ad looking for her to throw everyone off the scent? Make it look as though she ran away?" asked Sam.

"We're assuming, Sam, that Stokes placed the ad. That box number was too new to make the directory. I'd like to stop at the *Standard* office after we meet the Thompsons and see if I can find out. Did you learn anything?"

"I spent some time looking at the farm implements first and saw that he had a few of those corn knives. I said I'd seen them back in the United States and they seemed to be a handy device. Berryhill said Stokes had been going around to all the farmers that grow maize, trying to sell them on it. Then Berryhill made the cold remark that at least this suicide will serve to let people know how sharp the blade is."

"Sounds like neither of the Berryhills liked Stokes. Could they have killed him?"

"Maybe," said Sam. "Although they're hardly going to admit it. I'm not much of a detective, but I thought Berryhill looked awfully agitated. He kept his hands in his pocket, jiggling keys. And," Sam added, "he has a motive."

Jade stopped and turned to Sam. "A motive? What are you keeping from me?"

They'd paused by the Theatre Royale, its billings announcing the Leonard Rayne players in *Naughty Wives*, and a movie called *A Daughter of the Gods*, the story of a white woman sold at auction that had caused a sensation in the States. Jade frowned, recalling her own experience in Morocco's slave market.

"That scene look familiar?" asked Sam as he took her arm and escorted her across the split street. They wended their way among the parked cars in the median and across toward the New Stanley Hotel. "Recently, Berryhill discovered a discrepancy in the invoices," he said, continuing his news. "It looks like Stokes may have been embezzling from the store."

Jade whistled. "That's an interesting tidbit, but it could have been just as much a reason for Stokes to kill himself, knowing he'd be caught." She felt a desperate need to ask Sam why Finch would suspect him, or herself, for that matter.

It would have to wait. Too many people bustled around the New Stanley with its tearoom. They found the Thompsons seated in the entry lounge, oblivious to everything around them. Maddy gripped a white cotton handkerchief, which she used to dab her eyes, while Neville held her other hand firmly between both of his own, his gaze never leaving her face.

"Maddy, Neville," said Jade, "what happened? They didn't turn you down, did they?"

"Oh, Jade," said Madeline with a choked sob, "we were too late. The baby's been taken."

"What?" exclaimed Sam, loudly enough that several hotel guests turned and stared. He lowered his voice. "The notice just came out in the paper. How can the child be spoken for so quickly?"

"How indeed," echoed Neville. "The girl at the desk could only say that the ad had been closed early this morning."

"Did she say who took the baby? Or who bought the ad to begin with?" asked Jade.

Neville shook his head. "It's the second day for the notice. We don't take a daily, so we hadn't seen it. I'd assumed the baby was left at a mission, but perhaps a neighbor took in the child and decided to keep him." Madeline sobbed again, and Neville turned his attention back to his distraught wife. "There, there, Maddy. Don't cry. At least the little tyke has a home."

"But not with us," said Madeline. "Oh, Neville, please take me home."

"That's right," said Sam. "You two go on and think about the fair tomorrow."

"The fair?" exclaimed Madeline. "Oh, how can anyone think about the fair?"

"Sam is quite right, Maddy," said Neville. "You mustn't dwell on this disappointment. There will be another chance for us someday. Perhaps we might compose our own notice for the paper and advertise that we wish to adopt."

Madeline sat up straighter and clasped her husband's hand. "Oh, Neville, do you mean it?"

He smiled, his own eyes glistening with barely restrained tears. "Yes, my love. I wasn't sure of the idea when you first mentioned it—adopting, I mean. Always hoped for our own. But as we went to the newspaper office, I found that I was actually looking forward to bringing this baby home. And now I feel as if I just lost someone, too."

Madeline kissed Neville's rough hands. "Thank you, darling." She wiped her eyes with the handkerchief and made an effort to smile. "I'm sorry," she said to Jade and Sam. "I'm being selfish. We've *all* had a very trying morning."

"Oh, Maddy, stop with the stiff-upper-lip nonsense," said Jade. "You have every right to be disappointed, and I don't feel the least bit slighted because you aren't fussing over me. But I agree with Sam. You need to focus on something else."

"Right! Think about the fair tomorrow," said Neville.

"Not just the fair," said Jade. "You should go home and write this entire morning's scene at the police station for your next book."

"But I didn't think you liked when I wrote about your adventures, Jade."

"Besides," said Neville, "aren't you writing about Jade's Morocco adventure right now, Maddy?" He winced as his wife poked him in the ribs with her elbow.

Jade laughed. "It's all right. I figured as much already, and who am I to stifle your creativity? But I have an ulterior motive in mind." She explained her plan to circumvent Finch's restrictions.

"Oh, hang that," said Neville. "Everyone else is talking about Stokes. Why can't we?"

"I know *I'm* splitting hairs," said Jade, "but if we are called onto a witness stand later, we need to be able to look anyone in the face and say truthfully that we did not *discuss* our interrogations with one another, as Finch ordered." She looked to each one in turn. "So if everyone goes home and writes their experiences down, and we all just happen to read one another's notes tonight or tomorrow . . ." She made an open-arm gesture expressing her attitude that it was all accidental and innocent.

"I shall do just that," said Madeline. "*After* Neville and I write our adoption notice."

To Jade's eye, Madeline seemed more relaxed, more cheerful now that she and Neville had made plans and were taking steps. The relatively quick alteration in Maddy's mood didn't surprise Jade. After all, Madeline had not actually met this child or held it. Her attachment, and consequently much of her disappointment, had come from a quickly formed, romantic vision of a cooing baby. Not that Jade dismissed

Madeline's longing for a child. She knew it to be genuine. But with Neville's support and a working plan, Jade felt sure their dreams of parenthood would be fulfilled soon enough. Orphans, while not as common as during the war, were not rare. Many of the settlers in the protectorate's outer fringes often fell to accident or disease in their hard lives.

"Of course, write your advertisement first. Do it here while you're in town," said Jade. "I can take it to both the *Standard* and the *Leader* if you like. It will give me an excuse to ask at the first about who placed the notice concerning Mrs. Stokes."

"You don't think it was placed by her husband?" asked Sam.

"I have no idea," replied Jade. "That's what I want to find out." She repeated the information she'd picked up from Mrs. Berryhill. "Wait till you hear what Sam learned."

Sam held up his hand, signaling for a pause. "Can we eat first? I'm starved." He looked at Madeline. "That is, if you think you can. If you . . ."

"Yes," she said. "By all means. I'm all right now."

The four went to the dining room and ordered a lunch of barley soup and roasted chicken served with an assortment of fruits, sliced and drizzled with honeyed oil and vinegar. Sam attacked the bread basket while they waited and buttered a sesame seed roll. Jade settled for a cup of black coffee. The soup came quickly, and once Sam had staved his hunger, he explained Mr. Berryhill's discovery of embezzlement.

"That's all very interesting," said Neville, "but I'm not sure why it concerns us. It's not as if we are suspects." As soon as he said the words, both Sam's and Jade's mouths tightened. "Oh!" Neville said.

"I think we'll understand one another better once we've . . .

er . . . accidentally read one another's journals," said Jade. "Besides, the sooner Inspector Finch solves this murder, the sooner you'll get your coffee dryer door back, Neville."

"Constable Miller returned very early this morning with an Indian constable," Neville said. "They . . ." He stopped as the gloved African waiter removed the soup bowls and served the main course, then resumed as soon as the young man left. "They collected samples of dried blood from inside the drum."

"I wonder what that will tell them," said Madeline. She dug into her chicken, spearing a succulent piece of white meat.

"Dr. Montgomery thought there was too little blood in the drum, as I recall," said Neville. "Perhaps they plan to estimate the amount lost?"

"They can do wonders with bloodstains," said Sam. "One of my friends from Purdue is a chemist. They can tell not only if blood is human or not, but also what animal it came from, by using some serum produced from caged rabbits. More than that, human blood falls into four categories and they can use that information to identify where the blood came from."

"They can match it to a particular person?" asked Madeline.

"No," said Sam. "But let's say that Mr. Stokes had type I blood. If the blood in the dryer is a different type, then the police know it isn't his."

"But what if it *is* type I?" asked Neville. "What do they know then?"

"Only that it *could* be his, or it could belong to someone else with type I blood." Sam stabbed a chunk of meat and an orange with his fork. "As I understand it, the idea in modern police work is to not assume anything until the facts are in."

"But they did make an assumption," said Jade. "Finch and Miller assumed that Stokes committed suicide. Between the time we discovered the body and they discovered their mistake, a lot of those facts could have been lost."

"Which is probably what the killer intended," said Madeline.

"Well, it's all speculation until we are up-to-date with one another," said Neville. "So I declare an end to this morbid conversation until tomorrow. We need to get home and prepare our entries. We can all meet at the fair and discuss it then, along with all our blue ribbons."

They finished their lunch talking about Madeline's produce and Neville's coffee bean entries and agreed to gather at the roses tomorrow at noon. Before they parted, Maddy and Neville wrote out their advertisement twice, on two pages ripped from Sam's new ledger.

"One for the *Leader* and one for the *Standard*. We'll have the replies sent care of our post office box rather than to the newspapers," said Madeline.

Jade read over the notice. " 'Farming couple wishes to adopt and provide a loving home. Respond to Nairobi post 54.' " She looked up at Madeline. "I see you did not stipulate an infant."

Maddy shook her head. "Neville and I decided we would be happy with any child."

"That's very good of you," said Jade, touched by her friends' generous hearts. "I'll pay for the ads. Consider it a present."

The Thompsons drove home, leaving Sam standing outside the hotel with Jade. She held up the Thompsons' ads. "Shall we investigate alone or together?"

"Together," said Sam. "I want to hear what you find out."

They went to the *Leader* office first, ignoring the book and stationery store to one side and heading directly for the newspaper's business counter, where a freckled young girl in her late teens stood. Jade saw how the girl's eyes brightened as Sam approached, so she slipped one of the notices into his hands and stepped aside but not out of earshot.

Sam put on his most engaging grin and leaned his left elbow on the counter. "Good afternoon, miss," he said. "I'd like to run this notice for a week in the daily and once in the next weekly." He handed it across with a hundred-rupee note.

The girl took one look at the request for a child and her face became crestfallen. "You and your *wife* want a child?"

"Oh, it's not *my* ad," he said. "It's my employer's ad. I'm not married," he added.

The girl brightened again, her smile renewed. She batted her eyelashes. "That is very sweet of them."

"Isn't it, though?" said Sam. "They saw that someone had a Dutch baby boy for adoption, but it seems someone snatched the little tyke up right away. I just can't see how anyone else could have gotten here so fast, though." He let the statement dangle.

"I don't know much about that," the girl said as she handed change for him.

Sam put the money in his pocket and straightened. "Too bad. Well, nice talking to you."

He turned to leave and the girl made a grab for his shirtsleeve. "I could look something up for you," she suggested. "See what's on the sales receipt at least."

Sam smiled, his teeth flashing under the brown mustache. "That's very nice of you. I must own to being curious."

The girl sashayed off to the vertical filing cabinet, adding a few extra wiggles on the way. Jade caught Sam's eye and rolled her own.

The young lady returned. "I found the bill of sale for the ad," she said. "It was sent through the mail with the money, but there was no name on it."

"But the ad said to reply to voucher nine-seven-five. Someone must have come in to pick up replies."

The girl shrugged. "Now that you mention it, that is rather odd. I've been here most of the day except to go to lunch and this is the first I pulled the file. Wait a minute and I'll ask Viola."

Jade watched as the girl went to the desk of an older lady, presumably Viola, and wondered if this new search for more information was merely another pretense to walk for Sam. *Strap a pint of cream on that backside and you'll have butter by the time she returns.* A tiny voice in her head asked her if she wasn't thinking like a jealous woman.

This time, Viola returned with the girl, handed her the file, and sent her back to the cabinets to put it away.

"I understand you're interested in that adoption. You're the second person to ask today. There was a nice couple in earlier."

"Yes," said Sam, "that would be my current employer. I just placed an adoption ad for them." He pointed to the paper still on the counter.

Jade joined him. "They were so disappointed," she said. "We thought if we could assure them that the child had been well placed, it would ease their sorrow."

Viola nodded. "That's very kind of you, I'm sure, but even if I knew, I'm not certain that I could relinquish that information. However, I can tell you this. I did a bit of looking myself after that nice couple left because I didn't recall anyone else coming in about the notice. It seemed odd in a way."

"And did you discover anything?" asked Sam.

"In a manner of speaking, yes. The notice saying that the child was already taken was mailed here just as the original ad was. So whoever adopted the child must have learned about it from another source because they didn't apply through us." She picked up the Thompsons' notice. "I certainly hope that this brings them the child they want."

Jade and Sam said goodbye, and Sam waved to the girl who'd first helped him. She didn't return the gesture or the smile.

"You broke that poor child's heart, flirting and leaving," said Jade as they left.

"You handed me the notice," said Sam. "I was just being friendly."

Jade elbowed him. "See if *I* fall for that devilish grin of yours next time you try it on me."

"Oh, that was just my being friendly grin. I've got a completely different smile for you."

He flashed one at her, and she threw her hands in front of her eyes, pretending to be blinded by the dazzle. "Come on, Sam," she said. "We've got another stop to make."

They hurried to the office of Nairobi's other newspaper, the *East African Standard*, and this time, Jade decided to try her luck, leaving Sam to wait for her in the foyer. The middle-aged woman behind the counter looked tired. Jade hoped she might be happy for some friendly conversation, especially if it involved missing people, murder, and other tantalizingly grisly topics. She placed and paid for the Thompsons' ad, then said, "So much has happened recently. First Mrs. Stokes disappears and then Mr. Stokes commits suicide." She gave the other woman a chance to speak.

"I have a friend who works at Dr. Montgomery's office," the woman said. "He took over for Dr. Abercrombe, you know. My friend keeps me very informed. She telephoned me at lunch to say that Mr. Stokes couldn't have killed himself. There wasn't enough of his blood to have died by bleeding out."

"But I heard he was practically drowning in blood in that dryer where they found him," Jade said, embellishing her information so the woman would contradict it to set her straight.

"It wasn't all that much," she said and leaned closer. "And it wasn't his blood!"

"No?"

The woman shook her head solemnly. "No. It was from some kind of bird. They have ways of telling what type of animal it came from. But you are nearer the truth with the drowning part. He had some kind of liquid in his lungs."

Jade put her hand to her mouth to express her pretended shock. "So did he fall into a well or a pond?"

"Likely he fell into something else. The doctor is still doing *chemical* tests on it."

Jade shook her head and made *tsk* sounds. "I hope nothing horrid happened to Mrs. Stokes. I saw the notice in the wanted section looking for information regarding her whereabouts."

"I'm afraid for her," said the woman. "I knew her from church when she was a girl, though I can't say I've seen her more than once since she married." The woman dropped her voice. "She should have married that Alwyn Chalmers instead of Martin Stokes. A man's looks aren't everything. I'm sure she wasn't the happiest lady and I can imagine her running off to England maybe, but I can't see her abandoning her baby."

"She had a baby?" asked Jade. This time she didn't have to pretend to be shocked.

"I don't suppose many people knew about him, her always being at home and the Stokeses living out of town. Dr. Abercrombe delivered a sweet little boy about, hmm, four months ago, just before he left for England. My friend told me."

CHAPTER 6

The Maasai lump all other peoples together as ilmeek, *or "aliens."*
Europeans are sometimes called iloridaa enjekat, *which means*
"people who enclose their flatulence" due to our custom of wearing trousers.

—The Traveler

"Mrs. Stokes had a baby boy?" asked Sam.

"Yes! The same age as the child that Maddy and Neville tried to adopt," replied Jade.

"Did this lady know that the baby was, in fact, left behind?"

"No, but I'm not one to believe in coincidences. There aren't that many children available for adoption anymore. And both of these just happen to be the same sex and age."

They stood to the side of the *Standard*'s stone building, out of the general foot traffic. Both of them pondered the possibilities for a few moments before Sam broke the silence.

"Let's assume then, for the moment, that you're correct. That it's the same child. It doesn't prove that Alice Stokes was murdered. Maybe she abandoned both husband and child."

Jade frowned. "It's possible, and Stokes didn't want the baby, so, after he tried unsuccessfully to find his wife, he gave it up for adoption. But that doesn't fit the timing. True, he could have mailed the notice to the paper before he was killed, but who sent in the more recent notice that the baby was already taken? By then, he'd been dead for several days. No, my bet is that she handed the baby off to keep it safe, then ran away herself."

"That would mean there was someone else involved, at least with the baby," said Sam. "Maybe that person had already handed off the child to another couple or to a mission."

"That's possible," agreed Jade. "Or what about this idea? Stokes killed his wife, posted the ad seeking information to cover his tracks, but someone found out and killed him for it."

"What about the kid?"

Jade shrugged. "He probably gave it away earlier. The notices for the adoption might not have been from him."

"Maybe he was holding the child hostage to bring back his runaway wife, and *she* killed him," said Sam. "That woman at the *Standard* said he had liquid in his lungs?" Jade nodded. "Well, there you have it," he said.

"Have what?" asked Jade.

"She pushed him in a horse trough. They still have them around here despite all the automobiles." He extended his arms in a "ta-dah" motion to emphasize his point.

"But he wouldn't drown right away," said Jade. "She'd have had to hold him under for a while, and that suggests the strength of a man, not of a woman."

"Then maybe she had an accomplice who killed him for her. Women have been known to hire someone to finish off a husband."

Jade shuddered as she thought of one in particular and the murder that first brought her to Africa after the Great War. "Possibly. And she took back her child," Jade finished. "But the woman hinted that this liquid wasn't ordinary water. And why run the ad?"

"That is confusing," agreed Sam. "It would certainly help if we each knew what happened in our respective interviews with Finch."

"You're right, Sam. I may have to wait until tomorrow to read Maddy's or Neville's material, but for reasons that will become clearer when we . . . um . . . accidentally exchange notebooks later, I don't think either of them will have much to offer."

"I don't know. Madeline looked awfully upset."

"Probably just knowing Stokes was murdered would make her upset," said Jade. "And it's one thing to hear about it. It's another to actually find the body in your coffee dryer. I think it's time we each found out what the other knows. Will you please take me home to the Dunburys'? We can write in our journals there and accidentally pick up the wrong one later."

They walked back to the police station, where Sam had left his Indian motorcycle, an olive drab model used during the Great War. It had originally lacked the second seat that Jade's had, but Sam had engineered one over the rear wheel. Jade again climbed on after Sam, wrapped her arms around his waist and held on tightly.

Just as in the airplane, the cycle's noise didn't allow for much conversation. Not that there was much time to say anything during the short, three-mile run to the Dunburys' Parklands estate—besides an "oof" said everything that needed to be said concerning the street's sad condition.

Jade invited Sam into the parlor and headed to the exterior kitchen to see about some coffee. No one else was around. Avery and Beverly kept telling Jade to hire some of the native Kikuyu as cook and maids and general help, but Jade felt she was never home enough to warrant a full staff, or even one person for that matter. The only one she would have welcomed was Jelani, the Kikuyu boy who'd impressed her with his bravery and quick intelligence when she had first arrived in Africa. She'd taught him to read and write, then sent him back to his village to study with the old shaman. No, she didn't want Jelani to be *anyone's* house servant. Occasionally she hired someone to tend the grounds, and was grateful for the solitude once they were gone. Naturally this meant Bev's roses were suffering from neglect. *Maybe I'll prune back the dead canes later this evening.*

Jade returned after a short while to the parlor with two mugs of steaming coffee and set one in front of Sam. He had already found the ink bottle and a pen and was well under way writing his own account. Jade, who preferred a sharp pencil, took out her own newest leather journal and flipped past the pages concerning the animal captures.

At first she wasn't certain where or how to begin, so she started with a brief summary of observations she'd made the day before. That freed her mind up enough that she could recall almost verbatim her conversation with Finch. When she was finished, she tossed the notebook on the low ebony table next to Sam's book.

"I need to get to work, Sam, and I know you need to get back, too."

Sam shoved his hands in his pockets and let his head droop. "You want me to go?"

Jade wondered if men practiced that "lost puppy look" or if it came naturally to them. She smiled and slipped her hand around his arm. "Stop that, Sam. You'll make me feel like a heartless beast that turns strays out in the cold."

He grinned and leaned close. "So does that mean you'll take me in?"

Jade looked into his coffee brown eyes and felt her face flush. Like the African night, his gaze seemed to contain all sensual feeling, enough to make her heart race and her knees quiver. The thought that someone could have that much influence over her emotions made her uncomfortable. She never was one for letting people or situations control her life, and ever since she'd met Sam, she'd felt as though she'd lost part of that control. What scared her the most was the temptation, at times, to turn it all over to him.

Jade squeezed his arm gently and released it. "You don't need me to take you in," she said, stepping to the side. "You have a movie to make and a plane to tend to, and I have film to develop and I want to check on the leopard cubs and pick up my Graflex."

He folded his arms across his chest, a pose Jade had come to call his "serious and imperious male" posture, one that made her hackles rise. "I don't think you should go wandering back into Nairobi tonight, Jade. I'll take you to the animal compound if you want and stay until you're finished."

"It's perfectly safe, Sam. The animals are all in cages."

"I'm not worried about the animals. There's a murderer on the loose."

Jade had to admit she hadn't thought about that. "Surely you don't think *I'm* in any danger. Whoever killed Stokes most likely had a personal grudge against him. For all we know, it was his partner. You said that Berryhill looked angry about the missing funds. There's no reason for anyone to be after me." She studied his face to see if he knew something she didn't, something revealed in his journal. Well, she'd read it first to find out. "I won't stay late."

"Define 'late.'"

Jade clenched her jaw, biting back a retort. "I'll be home

just after sunset. And I'll take my rifle if it makes you feel any better."

Sam let his hands drop to his sides. "You can't fire your rifle in town anymore." He reached for her and took her by the arms. "Stay home. I'll pick you up here and take you to the fair tomorrow. I could come by early."

Something about the way he said "early" made Jade's heart beat double-time. *Better not risk temptation.* "I'm going out and I'll meet you at the fairgrounds tomorrow," she said. "You won't have room for me on your cycle with your film equipment."

Sam sighed. "You're a cruel lady, Jade del Cameron, breaking a serviceman's heart this way." He let his hands slide down her arms in a caress.

Jade's skin tingled at his touch. *Maybe he can stay for just a little while longer.*

"That Anderson fellow can handle the cubs," murmured Sam as he bent to nuzzle her ear.

Jade tilted her head, allowing him access to her neck. Sam's mustache tickled the sensitive skin just under her jaw. Her eyelids drifted down, shutting out everything but his touch as her own hands felt their way up his arms. He needed to go, but Jade was having a hard time remembering why. Something she'd once learned about nice girls.

Someone knocked on the door.

"Damn," muttered Sam in her ear.

He released her and she ran to the foyer, grateful the temptation had been removed. Jade half expected to see Inspector Finch coming to arrest them.

"Wayne," she said when she saw Anderson, "has something happened?"

Sam came up behind Jade. "Anderson," he said, a growl edging his voice.

Jade jabbed her elbow into Sam's ribs.

"Featherstone, fancy seeing you here." Anderson gave a curt nod, then ignored Sam entirely. "Brought back your big camera, and the boss needs you at the compound."

"Thanks. I was just about to head out," said Jade. "Is something wrong?"

"No. Bob is trying to train some of the hired natives to take care of the cubs, and he wants you to show 'em how it's done." He set her Graflex on a chair.

In other words, thought Jade, *everyone's afraid of getting scratched or peed on.*

"Tell Mr. Perkins that I'll be right there, please."

"I can drive you in," said Anderson.

"Thanks, but that won't be necessary. I've got my motorcycle." She smiled, trying to look polite and grateful without appearing encouraging.

Anderson spared a quick glance at Sam, frowned, and nodded at Jade. "All right then, Jade. I'll wait for you in case your motorcycle doesn't kick in right away." He walked slowly back to his truck and leaned against it.

Jade rolled her eyes and turned away from the door. "I'll see you tomorrow morning, Sam." She gave him a quick kiss on the cheek. "Don't forget the journal."

"Right. I'll be at the grand stand at half past seven."

Sam reached for her journal on the table, and Jade deliberately turned away to get her Winchester. When she returned, he'd left, allowing them both the chance to maintain their facade that he'd grabbed the wrong notebook. Jade shoved the other one into her day pack along with her camera equipment, locked the door, and headed out to her motorcycle.

The 1915 Indian Big Twin had a second seat, but Jade had installed a rack over it from which draped a set of panniers. She put her pack in one, slung her rifle over her back, pulled on a set of goggles, and kick-started the engine. It responded immediately, testimony to her careful maintenance. She waved her right hand in the air, a signal for Anderson to lead the way. While she didn't really want to eat his dust, she didn't like someone at her back either.

THE ANIMAL COMPOUND was set up in one of the large warehouses that had cropped up along the railroad tracks. The buildings were initially intended for a lumberyard, but the warehouse's owner had filed for bankruptcy in a year's time and left everything to the city managers in return for an end to his debt. Perkins and Daley had immediately seen the advantage to being so close to the railroad when it came time to ship the animals to Mombassa and a waiting freighter. The fact that the warehouse was also near a poultry and pig slaughterhouse made getting meat for the carnivores that much easier. It also meant Jade could smell the location long before she saw it. She pulled her motorcycle up on the far end of the vehicle line and cut the engine.

"Ah, Miss del Cameron. Good, you're here," said Perkins. "You did such a keen job earlier today that I wanted you to demonstrate to the crew how it's done." They walked past an open trough full of cattle dip used to treat the herbivores for mange and went inside.

"You mean they haven't been fed since this morning?" asked Jade, aghast.

"I fed them at noon," said Anderson.

"You see," said Perkins as he drew Jade aside, "a few of the men seem to be a bit superstitious about this pair. They seem to respect you, so I thought if you showed them it's all right, they'd stop balking."

Jade looked at the men, primarily Kikuyu, hoping to recognize someone from Jelani's village. She saw the young man she'd interviewed more than a year ago concerning Gil Worthy's death. "Wachiru," she said, calling him by name, "how good it is to see you."

They exchanged pleasantries in "kitchen Swahili," which all the Kikuyu spoke, but which the other Americans did poorly. Knowing the language afforded Jade a degree of privacy. After she inquired after Wachiru's family and that of the other men from the village, she pursued the matter with the leopard cubs. "Bwana Perkins says no one will feed the *chui totos*. Is this true?"

Wachiru, acting as spokesman for the group, replied again in Swahili, "We are not afraid of the *totos*, Simba Jike, but the big leopard watches us when we touch them. His eyes, they glow with his hatred, and he attacks the cage when we wrap them up."

Jade nodded. "I understand. Then we must move the *totos* so he does not see them." She wondered why no one had thought of such an obvious solution. Then it came to her. *Because they never asked the men what the trouble was. They just assumed they were afraid of the cubs.*

She explained the problem and the solution to the Americans. "It makes more sense to put the cubs over by the goats anyway," she said. "Then you don't have to carry their meal so far once you've milked the nanny." After the cubs and their pen were relocated away from the other carnivores, she once again demonstrated on the scrappy female how to feed and clean them. Wachiru followed her example with the more docile brother and everyone laughed to see how eagerly the little fellow attacked the bag of milk.

"You need some baby bottles," said Jade. "This bag is getting ripped by their teeth."

"I'll send Frank out to buy some," said Perkins. "Thanks for the help. What did you ever do to get so much respect from those men?"

"I once killed a hyena that was bothering them, that's all."

"Really? What is that they call you?"

"Simba Jike, 'lioness.' " She changed the subject by asking what their plans were for tomorrow. Both Cutter and Anderson came up to listen. Cutter had changed his trousers, but the aroma of polecat still clung to his shoes. Anderson took three steps away, waving his hands in front of his nose.

"Since that big agricultural fair starts tomorrow," said Perkins, "we thought we should take advantage of the crowd to see if anyone else has animals to sell. That's a lot easier than rounding them up on our own. Maybe locate some ostrich. We're also having trouble filling the order for a young rhino. Do you think that pilot friend of yours could go up and scout around for us? If we knew where to go, it would sure save us a lot of time."

"I'm certain Sam would do the job, but you'll have to haggle payment with him. The cost of fuel's gone up with the shortage. But he'll be at the fair, too, so you can ask him yourself. In the meantime, what do you want me to do?"

"Now that the men are feeding the cubs, we don't need you right now. But we will in a day or two to help wrangle into the trucks those zebra your friends caught. And we're taking them up on that big lion of theirs. We'll need your help with him, too."

"I'll let the Thompsons know," said Jade. "Well, if that's it, I'm going to take some pictures of the stock. Have you given any more thought about my writing up an article for you?"

"Certainly. The story of how we safely captured these animals and all the pictures will be a great asset to us. We'll have copies sent out to circuses and zoos all over the States. Should bring us a lot of business."

Jade went back to her motorcycle and retrieved her Kodak and a magnesium-powder-flash apparatus. First she photographed the leopard kittens outside; then she asked Wachiru to help her move an empty crate in position to use as a support for setting up a flash shot. She wanted a photo of the myriad animals in the warehouse, or at least one corner of it.

"How is Jelani?" Jade arranged the camera and the flash powder. "Does he still study with the *mundu-mugo*?" she asked, calling the village healer by his title. Jade directed Wachiru to turn his eyes away from the bright flare as she took her picture.

"I have not been back to the village." Wachiru waved away the residual white smoke and fingered his *kipande*. "I cannot go back yet or I will be arrested for not working and for not paying my hut tax."

Jade moved the camera and set up her next shot while she considered Wachiru's statement. When the colonists first arrived, they thought they'd found a wealth of labor in the local tribes. They quickly discovered that the natives weren't interested in the colonists' money. It held no value to them. Besides, they had their own *shambas* to cultivate. So, in order to make the natives work for them, the British decided to make the men pay a hut tax. There was, Jade admitted, some justification in that. Part of that tax paid for soldiers who patrolled and protected the agrarian tribes from the raiding tribes, but the tax quickly became a monster.

If a man had more than one wife, each with her own hut, and an aging parent unable to work, he might have to pay four hut taxes. And while the men were only required to work six months out of the year, it was often the same six months they needed for their own farm plots. Since most of the men worked on farms far from their villages, they could not go home daily to their families. The wives at home carried the full burden of village work alone, and many of the men took up with temporary wives to cook for them while they were away from home. Other men never went back home. The missionaries wrote letters in the newspaper decrying the breakdown of the tribe's social life and the decline in the birth rate, but the letters usually fell on deaf ears.

Eventually, each man had to wear his *kipande* and was heavily fined if he didn't have it. Natives were also required to have permits to walk anywhere outside of their villages. Most of this trauma fell on the agrarian tribes since they were seen as the more docile labor force. Beyond relocating the Maasai to a large reserve, the government gave up trying to mold them into anything other than what they were: a proud people with no use for anything but their cattle.

Jade wondered what would happen to Jelani. By her reckoning, he was nearly thirteen years old. Would he be allowed to stay on as the *mundu-mugo*'s student? Or would the officials decide the village didn't need another healer? Perhaps she should pay a visit to the village sometime, after this job with the collecting crew was over.

"Do you like this job?" Jade asked.

Wachiru nodded. "It is good, but it will not last long. Then I will have to find another. My brothers work for Bwana Harding. Perhaps I will go there, but I hear he keeps strange creatures."

Wachiru went back to distributing hay and water to the large number of penned antelope. Jade finished her picture, picked up her equipment and wandered up and down the rows of pens and cages until she found the male leopard.

He'd been moved into a wood-and-wire cage three feet wide by six feet long and four feet high. A metal pail half full of water sat in one corner, and Jade saw a box close by on which a man could stand to pour the water through the top slats to refill the bucket. The stained floor showed where buckets of water were hurled into the cage from the sides to wash out some of the wastes. She wondered how they fed the leopard. Then her gaze rested on several long, stout poles. The cat was probably forced to the back of the cage and held there with the poles while someone would quickly opened the cage and tossed in some meat.

As Jade approached, the cat crouched low and followed her every move with his hypnotic yellow eyes. The animal had definitely fed better in his captivity. Gone was the gaunt look about his ribs and middle. In its place were rippling muscles, tensing under the gorgeous spotted fur.

"Jambo, chui," Jade said in greeting. "You look well."

The cat launched himself against the front wires, slamming into them with enough force to bow the wooden braces. Jade jumped back, nearly dropping her camera. The animal hadn't lost any of its hatred. Did he respond that way to all humans or did he remember her role in his capture? The leopard screamed, enraged by his inability to reach her, the shrieks echoing back from the warehouse walls till it sounded as though several cats were loose. Wachiru, hearing the noise, ran to see what was amiss. He held a pitchfork in front of him as a weapon.

"I thought he broke free," said Wachiru in a hushed voice.

"Does he attack when you feed and water him?"

Wachiru shook his head. "He tried the first time, but now he knows that we bring him things he wants. We still use the long sticks, but he goes back willingly. He did not like when we put the cloth around the cubs, though."

"He's probably the father, but that is still very odd," said Jade. "The male leopard doesn't have anything to do with his young."

Wachiru studied the leopard, which never took his eyes off Jade or ceased growling. "Simba Jike, you handled the cubs and the towel. I think this animal smelled *you*. It is *you* he hates. It is not safe for you to be around him."

Jade couldn't agree more, and together, they quietly backed away from the area. Jade mounted her motorcycle and returned to Parklands. But while her eyes and ears tried to keep alert for road hazards, all she saw was the hot, burning glare of yellow fire in the leopard's face, and all she heard was the blind woman's warning.

CHAPTER 7

*The Maasai may have descended, at least in part, from the
Hamites of North Africa, where Roman legions held dominion in
ancient times. Certainly, they show a strong Roman influence
in their togas, their short swords, but most distinctly in their hairstyles,
which resemble Roman helmets.*

—The Traveler

SAM DIDN'T WAIT to get back to the Thompsons' before reading Jade's journal. He found a quiet spot close to the genera-
tor flumes and pulled off the road. Once he shut down the
engine, he raised his goggles and took out her notebook. For
a moment, he glanced through some of her notes and pencil
sketches, admiring her ability to capture the form and feel
of the animals in so few lines. He found the section on the
leopard-trapping expedition and hissed with a sudden in-
take of breath as he read of her ordeal in the pen.

Reckless little nincompoop. Ought to turn her over my knee.

Sam scowled in a way that would have put Jade on the
defensive. Then, suddenly feeling sheepish about reading
more than he was supposed to, he flipped past the remainder
of the notes and found her interrogation account. Heat radiated from his neck as his anger grew.

How dare that damned Finch suggest Jade is a murderess!

His fist clenched as he longed to connect with Finch's jaw. Then he realized what he was doing.

That's what got you in trouble to begin with, buster. You're his chief suspect.

Sam started at the beginning and reread everything, trying to absorb all the details, the fact that Stokes had drowned after someone slugged him in the jaw. The bruise on the side of the head was suggestive. It sounded as if Stokes had spun around, hit his head, and landed unconscious in some water, and the killer had left him there. The second time through he noted that Jade had defended him, a thought that made Sam smile.

What's she going to think after she reads my account? Will she still believe I'm innocent? Or will she think I hit Stokes hard enough to make him fall and drown?

He needed to think, and the best place to do that was fifteen hundred feet in the air. Fuel was hard to come by, but he had two barrels at the hangar. And when that ran out? Well, he'd worry about that later. This needn't be a long flight. He'd head west over those farms Jade's crew had visited. He stopped long enough at the Thompsons' house to borrow one of their men to help him take the plane out of the hangar and pull the propeller.

ONE OF THE first things Jade did each morning was to light the Dunburys' new oil-burning range and start her breakfast of coffee, bacon, one egg scrambled, and pan-fried potatoes. This morning that ritual took a backseat to reading Sam's journal. She'd read it twice last evening, but she still felt the need to review it one more time, one section in particular.

Finch knew how to get under my skin. First all those questions about Jade, insinuating that she was capable of killing someone, then twisting my words until it looked like I was defending her because she's my lover (his words). I told him that he was no gentleman if he spread any more of his bullshine against Jade. Then his next question made it seem as though he was changing the subject completely. He asked me where I purchased my airplane fuel. I explained that the Jenny's OX-5 engine runs on regular gasoline that I order by the drum from Stokes and Berryhill. Finch made one of those meaningless "Ah" sounds and asked which man I dealt with. I told him Stokes took the last order. I assumed he also delivered it but I wasn't around when he did. I knew where Finch was going with this. The exchange went something like this: Finch: "I heard you had a bit of a row with Stokes over by the yards." Me: "The charges were all wrong on the bill. We had words." Finch: "You shook your fist at him." Me: "With the billing. I waved it in his face." Finch: "But that is not what I heard from an independent witness. This person said you hit him on the jaw." Me: "It was an accident, and I barely grazed him. I didn't kill him." Finch: "Stokes was struck. You hit him. His wrist was cut with that maize knife. You knew all about the knife, and I'd bet we'll find your prints on it, too. You're familiar with the Thompsons' equipment as well."

Jade scanned the remainder of the account, which differed little from hers. Finch went on to ask Sam how long he'd known what a corn knife was. Sam repeated his previous statement, that he'd only seen them in his father's catalog when he had gone home in February. Then Finch asked Sam if he'd handled the one on display in the store. Sam didn't record his answer.

Jade closed the journal and went out to the kitchen to cook her breakfast, starting coffee on one burner and a pan of bacon on another. *Who is this independent witness?* Did someone come forward on his own or was Finch interviewing regular customers? No wonder Sam looked so angry and upset when he had come out of Finch's office.

She turned the bacon, then sliced two small potatoes into a bowl and salted them. Once the bacon was done, she put the strips on a plate and fried the potatoes in the drippings, adding a generous amount of pepper. *Eggs or toast? Toast!* She cut a thick slab of bread and propped it close to the flame.

If Finch thinks Sam is a suspect, he's not going to look anywhere else. She thought about Finch's points as she stirred the potatoes and turned the bread. Sam was seen arguing with Stokes and supposedly taking a punch at him. Stokes had a bruised jaw. Sam knew what a corn knife was, and the body was set out to look as if Stokes had taken his own life using one. The killer had even added animal blood when he found out that slicing the wrist of a dead man didn't produce much blood. But Sam knew about those serum tests, which made it unlikely that he'd try to fool the police with animal blood. If she told that to Finch, maybe he'd look elsewhere.

Flames coming from the toast interrupted her meditations. Jade grabbed the burning bread and smacked the fire out with the palm of her hand. It was still edible, by and large, and the parts that weren't? Well, that was what preserves were for. She removed the skillet of potatoes and turned the knob to shut off the oil. Jade smeared a large dollop of Maddy's mango pawpaw preserves on her burned toast and bit in, chasing the mouthful with a gulp of coffee.

Did Sam handle that corn knife? And what if he did? Surely a lot of other people touched it. Finch can't make much of that, can he? She hoped by now the inspector had found another print and matched it to a known criminal. That would be the end of it. She finished her breakfast, pumped water into the sink, and washed her dishes, then set them in a rack to dry. After locking up, she motorcycled out to the racetrack's grounds, where the fair was being held.

The track facilities needed work, probably one of the reasons the town fathers had decided to hold a fair to begin with. If a few people were inconvenienced because the grounds were dilapidated, or because the fence work was rotten in a few spots, they would rally to improve the area. Not in time for the upcoming races, but hopefully before the New Year's race week.

At present, no one seemed to notice or mind any inconvenience. Hundreds of people from as far away as Voi, 230 miles to the south, had turned out to enter their produce, and an equally large group of Nairobiites had closed their shops and homes and come to see the exhibits. Stores catering to the needs of the farmer-settlers had set up closet-sized booths and hawked the latest tools, seeds, saddles, tack, and outdoor wear. Hastily built of spare lumber and corrugated tin with a sawdust floor, they reminded Jade of the small shops in the Moroccan *souks*.

While none of the fancy-goods stores dared risk displaying the latest French gowns or hats, some of the store owners had recognized that a large number of city dwellers would be in attendance, people with money who might want to buy the latest home or kitchen gadget or perhaps decide on a new pocketbook. Close by were purveyors of automobiles and motorcycles, most only with large pictures of the vehicles, although the newest Hupmobile was displayed next to a food stand that sold pork sausages on a hard roll.

By far, the proudest displays were those entered by the farmers. Restricting the entries to vegetable matter made the fair decidedly smaller than any held at Nakuru, but much sweeter smelling. Jade had never seen so many varieties of roses in one small space, each one competing with the others in size and color. The brilliant tea roses with their tightly held petals stood as the epitome of grace and elegance next to the older variety cabbage roses, but the latter won in fragrances from sweet to spicy.

Jade had looked for Sam that morning, but after waiting for forty-five minutes, she went off on her own, disappointed, searching for Madeline. She saw her waiting anxiously nearby as two prim-looking women in broad, flowered, and feathered hats examined each entry for mildew or rust. Madeline was very properly dressed in a pale blue cotton dress and sturdy yet feminine walking shoes. She wore gloves like most of the ladies there, and a broad straw hat with a blue ribbon. Her graying brown hair, which Jade had cut short a year ago, was now pulled back in a low roll and held in place with a shell comb.

"Maddy," said Jade as she waved to her friend, "have they judged yours yet?"

"No. They're just finishing the tea roses. I entered two dark purple cabbage roses." She pointed to the end of the table.

"They're beautiful," said Jade. "You can't lose."

Maddy chewed on a glove finger as the two judges conferred over their notes with much bobbing of heads and ribbon flowers. The sight reminded Jade of some gaudy birds' elaborate courtship ritual. Finally the judges reached an agreement and placed a broad blue ribbon in front of a velvety red tea rose. Muted applause rose from the gloved spectators, followed immediately by the buzzing hum of whispered conversations.

Maddy gripped Jade's arm as the judges began on the cabbage roses.

"Where's Neville?" asked Jade.

"Either with the potatoes, the onions, or the coffee."

"And Sam?" Jade also wanted to ask Maddy where her notes were so she could read them, but she knew that her friend's mind was centered on the judges.

"Sam's around somewhere. He brought his camera. I think he's taking footage of Neville and the coffee competition." She clutched Jade's arm. "Oh, look. They're examining mine now."

Jade allowed Madeline to squeeze her arm and concentrated on watching the crowds rather than on the painful constriction. *St. Peter's mother, but Maddy's strong!* But then, what else would she expect of a hardworking farmwife? It made Jade wonder if Stokes' killer was a woman and not a man. Maybe his wife hadn't run away after all, at least not very far. Had she come back for her child? Had there been a struggle in which Stokes hit his head and fell into a tub of water? Mrs. Stokes was a small woman and not a farmer. Still, fear or fury could lend a lot of strength.

The scenario didn't feel right to Jade, mainly because of what had happened afterward. While she admitted that a mother might resort to murder to get her child back, she couldn't conceive of a woman of Alice Stokes' small stature hoisting her husband into the coffee dryer or staging a suicide. *Maybe she had help. But then why leave the child behind?*

Whoever it was knew about the corn knife Stokes was demonstrating. *Who grows maize around here?* A name immediately flashed into her head: *Alwyn Chalmers*. But just as quickly, she rejected the idea. Anyone coming into the store could have seen the gadget. It didn't even have to be one of the farmers. The most likely candidate was his own partner, Winston Berryhill. Just how angry had he become when he found out that Stokes was cooking the books?

And how, Jade wondered, could she divert Inspector Finch's attention away from Sam and onto Mr. Berryhill? Surely the embezzlement had been reported to him. As she speculated on what information she needed to convince Finch, she felt her arm being jostled.

"They're making their decision," whispered Madeline.

Once again, the ritualized bobbing of plumed hats began. Beside Jade, Maddy jiggled ever so slightly in tightly controlled anticipation. Then one of the ladies draped a blue ribbon around Madeline's roses, and Maddy squealed with delight. Jade cheered her on with a "Hooray, Maddy!" while the audience looked on with mixed reactions and patted their gloved hands together. A few women frowned at the overt emotional display, most smiled politely and wished it had been their roses, and several nodded to one another as if to say, "What else would you expect from a country bumpkin and an American?"

"Oh, wait till I show Neville," Maddy said as she stroked the precious ribbon.

Sam walked toward them from the edge of the crowd. "Well done, Madeline," he said. His linen shirt was open at the throat and his sleeves were rolled up. He had his tripod and camera slung over one shoulder and gripped a leash with his other hand.

Jade felt something butt her legs and looked down. Biscuit had greeted her in his own cheetah fashion. "Sam! I missed you this morning. I was afraid you didn't come. And you brought Biscuit. Thank you. I've missed him at the house."

"He had a good run alongside my motorcycle." Sam pulled out a pocket handkerchief and dabbed at his forehead. "Sorry I was late this morning." He tried to stifle a grimace.

"Are you all right?" asked Jade.

Sam nodded. "I'm fine. Just a headache. I flew over those farms yesterday. The ones you'd been working at. Saw some interesting things." He lowered his tripod to the ground and leaned on it. "Well done, Madeline. That made a great sequence for the motion picture."

"What?" Maddy exclaimed. "You were filming me?" She immediately patted at the stray hairs that refused to stay back in the roll. "I must have looked a sight."

"You looked lovely," Sam said. "I hope you don't mind. I thought about asking you but I didn't want you to be self-conscious. You were certainly more fun than the group with the potatoes. Most expressionless lot I've ever seen."

"Did we win?" asked Madeline.

"Not on the potatoes," said Sam. Madeline's shoulders drooped. "But your bag of coffee beans took first." Maddy's eyes opened wide and she bounced again. Sam laughed along with her. "I got Neville's reaction on film as well. He was a bit more restrained, but he had a great grin as the men around him all clapped him on the back. I left after that and he went on to the onions."

"That's wonderful, Maddy," said Jade. "You beat the Karen Coffee Company. You can ask a higher price next time you sell."

"Yes. Assuming we get our coffee dryer cleaned and the door back before we need it in another six months for the big crop."

Jade saw this as the opening she needed to discuss their

information. She broached the topic obliquely to begin with, since there were so many people in earshot. "Neville should ask for the door back, in a firm manner. Finch should be done with it by now."

"That chicken or duck blood should not be too difficult to clean out," Sam said. Then he added more recent news in a softer voice. "Especially since Constable Miller was back yesterday with battery lamps. He went into the drum and dusted and photographed and scraped everything he could off the insides. It's probably cleaner in there now than it was when Neville bought it."

Jade wondered what sort of materials Miller found inside. Hairs? Fibers? She'd read an article in a popular magazine about the information that police could find by photographing these items under a microscope. As a photographer herself, she found the topic fascinating. As a suspect or a friend of one, her interest took another, less academic direction.

Biscuit, restless from standing too long in one spot, tugged on his leash. "I want to talk about this more, but not now. We should separate," said Jade, "and gather information."

"How?" asked Maddy.

Jade shrugged. "Eavesdrop. Or, in your case, since the body was found in your dryer, use that to initiate conversation. Maybe someone has heard something useful."

"I'll find Neville," Maddy said. "I'd rather do this with him nearby. By the way, I want to thank you, Jade, and you, too, Sam, for putting those notices in the papers. I bought a copy of the *Leader* this morning." She pulled the paper from her large handbag and gave it to Jade.

Jade flipped past the steamer arrivals to the public notices and Maddy's ad. From there, her attention turned to an article headed *Native Trouble Brewing?* It mentioned a Kikuyu named Harry Thuku who was urging villagers to stop working. Next to it was an essay on native superstitions. "Let's hope it does some good," said Jade, handing back the paper. "Now, everyone skeedaddle and get to work. We'll all meet up this afternoon at Bev and Avery's house, where we can talk in private."

Sam waited until Madeline left to find Neville before speaking his mind. "I think we should stick together, Jade. You and me."

"No, Sam. You have a perfect excuse to infiltrate and study people." She pointed to his camera. "You could even use it as part of the subject matter. Tell them you want to document the horrified reactions of the townspeople to this outrageous incident. You don't even have to load film if you don't want to. They won't know that you're cranking empty reels."

"But you could come with me." Sam found an empty bench and sat down.

Jade saw his face, flushed just a moment ago, blanch. "Are you sure you're all right, Sam?"

"I'm fine," he said. "I've probably caught a cold." He forced a grin. "It is winter here in Nairobi, you know."

Jade chuckled. "Right. As if moving a few miles south of the equator makes a difference." Then she had a thought and sobered. "Your leg isn't becoming a problem, is it?"

Sam laughed. "That's it. I've got termites or a tree fungus."

Jade laughed in spite of her concern. "I meant your real leg on top. I would think that having that wooden one underneath would rub sores or something."

Sam shook his head. "Nope, but," he said, taking her

hand and pulling her down onto the seat next to him, "I do appreciate your concern."

Biscuit butted his head before Sam could show his appreciation. "This cheetah needs to walk, Sam," Jade said as she rose.

"Wait," said Sam. "About Finch and what happened with Stokes . . ."

Jade sat back down and waited for him to continue. People milled around them, making any private conversation nearly impossible.

"I hit him," Sam said. "I didn't intend to, but I did." He studied her face.

Jade frowned, then nodded. "And that's why Stokes suspects you. But how do you unintentionally hit someone?"

"I know fuel costs are rising, but that last bill was outrageous. In light of his skimming off the books, I can now see why. I yelled at him and waved the bill and . . . well, maybe I waved it a bit too close to his jaw on purpose. But he was still standing when I left."

"But Finch probably doesn't believe you," Jade said.

When Sam shook his head, she said, "Then I need to do something about that. Can't have Finch locking up my friends." Jade stood up again.

"Where are you going?" Sam asked.

"Hunting."

SAM WISHED HE FELT BETTER. Right now his head felt like two bulls butting, and the headache wouldn't go away despite those aspirin Jade always recommended. He was running a bit warm, so he'd loosened his collar and rolled up his shirtsleeves. It was possible that he *had* caught a chill while flying yesterday. *Should have worn your leather jacket, you dolt.* But even with his self-chiding, Sam didn't believe it was a cold. No, it was worry. Was Finch focusing only on him? Men had been convicted on less evidence before. True, Jade was on his side, but her reason stung.

What was it she said? Can't let Finch arrest my friends? Friends! He wanted more, much more. *One thing at a time, partner. Can't ask a woman to marry you when you're going to jail.*

He'd just have to clear his name. Find out something to remove him from suspicion. That was when Sam saw four men standing in front of the Stokes and Berryhill booth, and decided that if there was ever an opportune spot to gather information, this was it. A teenage boy who Sam presumed was Berryhill's son, Harley, stood behind a plank desk, looking as bored as only a young man impatient to mingle with his friends could. Sam stood the tripod on the ground in front of him and introduced himself to the group.

"Gentlemen, I'm Sam Featherstone, and as you can tell by my accent, I'm an American. You can probably guess by this camera, I'm also a motion picture maker, and I sure would like to include some of this fine fair."

The men, curious about the camera, stepped closer.

"I say. Are we in your way or something, young fellow?" asked the oldest. Unlike the others, he hung back.

"No. As a matter of fact, I want you *in* the picture." Sam nodded to the Berryhill boy. "You, too, if you don't mind."

Suddenly, everyone stood a little straighter, and several of the men took off their hats and ran their fingers through their hair to set it in order. As if on cue, they formed a line and struck a pose together.

"Oh, no. You misunderstand me, gentlemen," said Sam.

"This is a *motion* picture camera. I want you to move and talk to one another, just as you were doing before."

"I say," repeated the old man. He blew out his bushy mustache. "Just what sort of motion picture is this that we would want to participate?" His companions nodded in agreement.

"I am actually filming the life of the coffee farmers Mr. and Mrs. Neville Thompson to be exact. That includes this fair and the people at it."

"Indeed! Well. Hmm, that is an altogether different matter, then," said the elderly man. He pushed up the brim of his solar topee, exposing a crop of hair as snowy as his mustache. "I know the Thompsons. First-rate people. Good workers. Smart fellow, that Thompson. Took my advice last year on an engine. Naturally we shall help then. You'll be documenting that, I presume. Of course you will. Might have expected it." He waved his companions forward. "Snap to, gentlemen. Look lively, now. Help this young fellow out. Er, what did you say your name was?"

"Featherstone. Sam Featherstone. I'm an engineer, so I'm also working for Thompson."

"Naturally," decreed the old man. "Only decent thing to do. Interesting people, you Americans. Good of you to help out in the war. A bit late, though."

The men, having the approval of the old man, outdid one another in their dramatic endeavors. First they kept finding pretexts to face the camera until they appeared to speak to young Harley over their shoulders. Next they fumbled about picking up a gadget or two and struck excited or incredulous poses complete with forehead slapping and wild gesticulations, all except the elderly man. He watched his companions with what appeared to be a great deal of amusement. Every few moments, his shoulders shook and his magnificent, bushy white mustache fluttered as he blew out a puff of air.

By this time, a small crowd, including two small boys and a Great Dane, had gathered to watch the antics. Sam waited patiently for the gawkers to get bored and leave, and bribed the two boys into going with four rupees each. Only the dog, which had settled itself in a shady spot and appeared to be staying for the duration, refused to go.

"Gentlemen, I want to film you doing just what you were doing when I arrived."

"But we were merely discussing the fair," said one man. "That and the latest *shauris*."

"Exactly," said Sam. "It is a perfect scene of gentlemen farmers at the fair." He stepped forward from behind the camera and examined the items in the booth. His gaze quickly found what he wanted, the display of new maize knives. "I have an idea." He motioned for the elderly man to stand just to the right of the display.

"You're Lord Colridge, aren't you, sir?"

Colridge nodded. "Who else would I be?"

"Then I know that I can count on you to lead the way." Sam picked up a trowel and placed it in Colridge's hands. "You, sir, will be examining this trowel."

"Pish tosh! I'm not interested in a trowel," protested Colridge. His mustache fluttered with an exasperated snort.

"If you would only *pretend* to be interested, sir."

"You can act interested in a trowel, can't you, Colridge?" asked one of his companions. "After all, you do an excellent job of *acting* interested whenever the commissioners try to talk you into something. That trowel is probably more animated than any of them."

The other men chuckled at this joke, including Colridge. "All right, all right. I shall play the part and I daresay you won't find a better actor anywhere short of the Theatre Royale."

With the apparent ringleader settled, the rest of the men fell into Sam's plan easily enough. "When I say, 'Action,' you gentlemen," he said, indicating the other three men, "will come walking by and see your friend here examining this trowel. You will stop and shake hands and begin talking about the fair. I need you to look lively, but not exaggerated. That's the hard part. It should look like a very interesting discussion without appearing staged."

Sam snapped his fingers as though a great idea had just occurred to him. "I've got it. I heard where one of these gloves with the knife attached was found recently on a dead man. One of you will look up at the display and point to these knives and comment on how it figured into the recent tragedy. Then just continue talking about what you've heard."

"Wait just a moment, lad," said Colridge. "I daresay that will make for a lively discussion but I don't know that I want it on record. Will anyone know what we are saying?"

"Oh, no," said Sam. "Sound doesn't record and I doubt anyone will be able to read lips."

"Especially with that broom covering yours, Colridge," said one of the other men.

"I do believe you are safe there, sir," said Sam. "I will make up some words to appear on the screen. Probably something about a marauding lion in with your stock or something of that nature. The audience will love it."

While the men got into position, Sam noticed the lad behind the counter kept clenching and unclenching his fist as though he burned to say something. "You're important in this scene, too, young man," said Sam, noticing the youth start-ing to sputter in irritation. "You're the proprietor. Feel free to add whatever you like to their discussion."

Then he went behind the camera, removed the lens cap, called, "Action!" and rolled film.

WITH NO PARTICULAR plan in mind, Jade decided to stroll and let fate or Biscuit make the decisions. She was an American, an outsider, and as such, her questions about Stokes might make some people defensive. The Nairobiites would feel the need to defend one of their own rather than open up about him. *How did that proverb go? Something about "even the fierce leopard does not devour its cubs."*

Instead, she intended to rely on her two best allies for bringing people to her: Biscuit and her Kodak. Having a tame cheetah made her more like one of the more eccentric locals, and taking pictures for an international magazine like the *Traveler* often brought even the most reticent and stuffy person around. Everyone, it seemed, wanted to be famous.

She wended her way past several Dutch-speaking Boers in heavy shirts, thick trousers, and broad hats. She took a pho-tograph of them with the produce display in the background and walked on. Next Jade strolled by a cluster of young ladies busily eyeing the nearby gentlemen, then past the bachelor herd itself decked out in pale linen suits and boater hats, fe-verishly discussing the latest cricket matches.

She heard snippets of conversations from gloved ladies in airy flowered dresses discussing the upcoming return of Lady Northey and when they would host the next benefit for the children's home. A Pomeranian on a leash, too fool-ish to realize it was edible, yapped at Biscuit, who ignored it with the disdain of one with better taste than for small dogs. Petite Cherie's mistress pulled back on the leash, glaring at Jade. Jade smiled back, assuring the ladies that Biscuit was no threat. The women eyed Jade's jodhpurs and boots and gave her a cutting look.

Ahead lay the store booths. Jade heard a strong male voice proclaiming the merits of a new coffee pulper.

"There's no dead body in it, is there?" quipped one of the male onlookers. "I won't pay extra for coffee equipment just because it holds a dead body."

The others laughed at this macabre joke, and Jade moved closer to listen.

"That's only a problem at the Berryhill store," said the proprietor. "We don't carry those maize knives, and you can't get the corpse without first having one of those."

Jade shuddered at the callous remarks. Then she recognized one of the chuckling onlookers as Mr. Holly, a banker that she'd once met at the Muthaiga Club. If memory served, he'd been roaring drunk at a party in her honor and made a pass while they danced. She hoped he didn't remember the punch to the eye she had given him.

"One would get the impression that Mr. Stokes was not well liked," she said.

Holly turned and, recognizing her, smiled broadly and tipped his hat. "Miss del Cameron, how pleasant to see you." He ogled her figure. "Still as lovely as ever, if I may say so." Biscuit brushed against his legs, and he started momentarily. "Oh, and you have a cat."

"His name is Biscuit," she said.

"Hascombe's cheetah?" Holly asked.

"Not any longer," Jade said. "He handed him off to me

when he took up safari work for good. But, Mr. Holly, you were saying something about Mr. Stokes." She knew he wasn't, but it didn't hurt to prompt him.

"Call me Stuart. I actually always found Stokes a very likable chap. A good man on the football field, too. But there are others who weren't so keen on him."

"Oh?"

He stepped closer and leaned over to pass his confidences to her alone. Jade suspected from his greeting that he had other reasons for getting nearer. *Good thing Sam's not here.*

"Mind you, I'm not certain of any facts," Holly said, "but I heard that he was positively monstrous to his wife. Never letting her go out without him, never letting her join any of the ladies' clubs."

"I heard she disappeared," said Jade. "Do you think she'll return now that he's gone?"

"Yes, presuming that she will have a way of knowing he's dead—a friend perhaps, or the paper. More to the point, presuming *she's* still alive."

"Still alive? You think he killed her?"

He shrugged. "I heard gossip that there was a child."

"A child?" asked Jade. "How old? Where is it now?"

Holly raised one eyebrow. "Where indeed? I got the story from a friend who heard it from a doctor's assistant. Delivered at home three, maybe four months ago. Boy, I believe. I have no idea where it is. Just so long as I don't have it."

Clearly, Holly wanted to impress her with his inside knowledge. Since Jade already knew all this, she decided to fish for more. "Well, he must have felt terrible remorse to commit suicide in that manner."

"You think he killed himself?" He chuckled and nudged

her with his elbow. "My dear young lady, you have it all wrong. I have it on good authority that he was murdered."

Jade put her hand to her open mouth and opened her eyes as wide as she could. "Murdered? So he *didn't* slit his own wrist with one of those horrid glove knives?"

Holly took her by the elbow and escorted her to a shady spot closer to the back side of the booth. "I heard from a *very* reliable source, a 'hello girl' to be precise, that Martin Stokes was already dead when his wrist was cut. Apparently there would be a lot more blood, and it wouldn't have come from a bird at any rate because that was what was in the dryer drum."

Jade didn't reply, hoping Holly would "up the ante" and add the next layer of information. He did.

"What was most intriguing was the report that he had *arsenic* in his lungs."

Jade gasped. "He was poisoned?"

"No. He drowned in it. Cattle or sheep dip, or something like that."

Jade thought about all the arsenic-based dip in use in the colony, employed to kill a variety of skin parasites. Stokes could have been killed at any number of locations.

"Drowned in cattle dip! Are you sure?"

Holly put his right hand over his heart. "I swear on my dear old grandmother's grave. And I certainly hope the police nab the culprit," he added with a solemn bow. "The team's out a perfectly good midfielder."

Jade felt a wave of disgust at the man's shallow acknowledgment of Stokes' worth. Since Holly didn't appear to have any more information, she decided she'd had as much of his company as she could stomach for another year. She tugged on Biscuit's lead. The cheetah chirped and wound around her legs.

"It looks as if Biscuit wants to keep moving," Jade said. "It was very interesting talking with you, but I must be going."

"You are attending the ball at the New Stanley tonight, aren't you?" Holly asked. "I don't believe we ever got to finish our last dance at the Muthaiga last year." He took off his hat and scratched his head. "I can't recall why, either."

"I think you weren't feeling well that evening," Jade said. "Some of your friends took you outside for fresh air." In reality, they'd laughingly tossed him into one of the cars to sleep it off after Jade punched him. But, she thought, what he didn't know wouldn't hurt him. Sam might, though, if this man tried anything again this time. "I am attending, but I already have an escort."

Holly didn't appear to take the hint. "But you'll save some dances for me, won't you?"

It would have been a waste of breath to reply. Instead Jade gave Biscuit his head and walked off with a "Goodbye, Mr. Holly" tossed over her shoulder. As she left, she wondered what she'd really learned that might be of any use. Drowning in a tank of mange dip narrowed the scene of death from just plain drowning, but it was still too broad an area. There were so many containers of dip that the health department had recently raised concern about arsenic spilling into the soil and into streams and causing human liver damage.

And just because Stokes was found in the coffee dryer didn't mean he was killed near it. That was when Jade realized that she didn't actually know where the dryer had been placed. She'd assumed that since Neville had bought it from Stokes and Berryhill, it had been somewhere near the store. But it was a big piece of equipment, and not something anyone wanted to haul around. Perhaps it had been in a rail yard. She'd have to ask Neville.

Did Finch ask him that? Jade remembered that she still hadn't read Maddy's or Neville's accounts of their interrogations. She also needed to find out what Perkins and Daley had planned for Monday's work. She decided to find them next.

CHAPTER 8

Celebrations among the Maasai are marked with feasting, singing,
and dancing, much like in any other culture. But more impressive are
the male competition dances where warriors leap into the air,
each going higher than the other, shoulders trembling at the peak.

—The Traveler

SAM CRANKED THE camera, actually rolling film. Not that he could use any of it as proof, but it did make for good action. His ears were tuned to the conversation, which had started out stilted but soon took on a more genuine note.

"So Stokes was killed with one of these knives?" asked one man.

"That's what I heard. Cut his own wrist."

"We'll miss him on the cricket field."

"And the football field."

"I won't miss him," shouted Harley Berryhill. "Good riddance to him." All heads turned to stare at the youth. "I know at least one person better off now that the leech is dead. A man's affairs are his own."

"See here, young man," said Colridge. "What do you mean by that?" He turned to Sam and held up his hand. "I believe you should desist cranking that machine you have there."

Sam stopped and listened. Harley's face reddened as the men turned to him.

"Well, out with it, boy!" commanded Colridge.

Harley hesitated for a moment, his youthful bravado diminished. "Mr. Stokes was taking money in return for silence," he said.

"Blackmail!" said Sam. Here at last was a motive he could get his hands on. "Who?"

"I can't say anything specific," the boy blurted. "That would defeat the purpose."

"On my honor!" exclaimed Colridge. "You're defaming a dead man, son. With accusations of extortion, no less. This is unheard-of!"

One of the other men cleared his throat. "Don't be too hasty, Colridge."

The old lord snapped around. "What's that you say, Griswell? Don't tell me you agree?"

"There's some truth to what young Harley said. I . . . I've heard . . . uh . . . of another account of extortion by Stokes."

Sam tried to read Griswell's face. A few beads of sweat, the man's general hesitation, and the way he fidgeted with his coat buttons hinted that *he* was the one who had been blackmailed. "You should report this to the police," said Sam. "It may have some bearing on the case."

"I don't see how it would help," protested Griswell. "Stokes killed himself, and reporting this incident would only put my . . . er . . . friend in trouble of public exposure, the very thing he wished to avoid." Behind him, Harley nodded his head vigorously.

"Hmm," murmured Colridge with another puff and mustache flutter. "Quite right. Best to let sleeping dogs lie."

The men dispersed, leaving Sam alone with the boy. Before he could question Harley further, a customer approached, and Sam left to find his friends. His pulse quickened with the keen excitement of discovery. *Ha! Wait till Jade hears that Stokes was a blackmailer.*

A man's affairs are his own. Was Stokes blackmailing married men to keep their infidelities a secret? Was he blackmailing the kid's own father, Winston Berryhill? Maybe he was blackmailing the boy? *Nah. What could he be doing that was worth blackmailing? Strike that. Probably plenty he wouldn't want his parents to know.* But somehow, thought Sam, blackmailing a sixteen-year-old hardly seemed lucrative. It was a shame that Griswell wouldn't reveal anything. How many more victims were there?

Whoever the victim, extortion certainly gave someone a motive for killing. Sam wondered how much credence Inspector Finch would place in any of this information coming from one of the prime suspects, namely himself. Especially since no one else was willing to come forward. But it might at least put Finch on a different track.

Suddenly, Sam didn't want to wait until they met up at the Dunburys' house. He wanted to find Jade now, look in her incredible eyes of moss and light, and tell her his bit of news. But where to find her? Had Perkins and Daley set up a booth to talk to farmers about selling the unusual pets the settlers seemed to keep? She might be there, checking in with her employers.

Sam picked up the pace, at least as fast as his tired body, artificial leg, and heavy equipment let him, and scouted each of the booths he passed. That was another thing that worried him: this damned job she had as rope wrangler for some half-baked outfit out of Chicago. Sitting inside a cage as bait for a leopard? The thought still gave him chills. *When we get married, there's not going to be any more of that bull!*

He had to laugh at his own arrogance. *When we get married? Hell's bells, man. You haven't even proposed yet.* And he couldn't until he cleared his name. He didn't know about life in New Mexico, but in northern Indiana, decent girls didn't marry murder suspects, innocent or not. Then he needed to convince Jade that she needed him, which was going to be hard since Jade was a woman who didn't really need anyone. After rescuing her and her mother in Marrakech, he'd thought he had a shot. He'd planned out his entire courtship, too, wooing her in the air.

And now she calls me her friend! A sensible man ought to chuck it and go, he thought. But Sam had a Midwestern stubborn streak. It had served to keep him flying as a green pilot when his courage first faltered under fire, and it frequently helped him to see a job through when patience had long since got up and left. Now he'd be dogged if he was turning tail and going home to lick his wounds. He'd win Jade or get shot down trying.

And you know all about that. He reeled as a wave of dizziness hit. *If she accepts you, man, will you be able to control her wild streak? Will you even want to?* That gave him pause. No, not Jade. *Gotta let varmints be varmints.* The question was, could he live with that?

"Excuse me, young man!"

Sam stopped abruptly and blinked. In his mental wanderings, he'd run right into a large male. "I'm terribly sorry," said Sam. Then he recognized the man from Jade's descriptions. "Beg pardon. Aren't you Charles Harding?" Harding nodded. "I'm Jade del Cameron's friend, Sam Featherstone. Have you seen her today?"

"No, I'm afraid I cannot help you there, Mr. Featherstone."

"I'm glad I bumped into you," said Sam, then realizing how that sounded, quickly added, "I don't mean literally, of course."

"Of course," echoed Harding. He put a hand where Sam had accidentally jabbed him in the stomach and winced.

"It's just that I saw the most amazing sight the other day while I was flying and I thought you'd like to know about it."

"Oh? And what might that be?"

"I flew over your farm yesterday afternoon and I saw what looked like a zebra mating with one of your horses. It was—"

"You flew over my farm and paddock?" Harding's face reddened and his lips tensed into a tight line.

Sam stepped back a pace. "Well, yes, but I didn't swoop down or buzz the place, if that's what you're worried about."

"I don't care two straws for what you call whatever you did. You stay away from my place. I don't need a ewe throwing a lamb because she got scared of your blasted flying machine."

Alwyn Chalmers was walking by and stopped to see what the commotion was about. "Your ewes are throwing lambs, Charles?"

Harding glared at the newcomer, then composed himself by tugging down on his tweed jacket and stretching his neck. "No, but they're likely to if this here flyboy keeps flying over my property."

"I only wanted to tell you what I saw—"

"I don't care what you saw," snapped Harding. "Wildlife wanders onto the farm often enough, and as long as it's not a predator, I don't pay them much mind."

"While we're on that topic, young fellow," said Chalmers, "my farm is just south of his and I'd appreciate it if you didn't fly over it, either. I've lost my best polo pony already. I wouldn't care to have any more animals scared off by one of those machines."

Sam clenched his jaw to keep from saying something he might regret later. Instead he touched his hat brim in a polite salute, turned on his heels, and left. From the corner of his eye, he saw Inspector Finch watching him. He also spied Perkins standing next to his two hired men, Anderson and Cutter.

Might as well check if they've seen Jade. He stopped and asked.

"Not today," said Mr. Perkins. "But I've been wanting to speak with you. I want to hire you to fly over some of the western region, near the Maasai land. See if you can scout up a young rhino. We'll pay for your fuel and fifty American dollars on top of that. If you spot anything that we can get to and capture, we'll throw in a hundred-dollar bonus."

"Make it seventy-five for the search plus fuel and bonus, and you've got yourself a deal."

"Done," said Perkins. He and Sam shook on it. "We're loading up some zebra and a pet lion tomorrow afternoon, and Monday we're picking up that young buffalo the governor's kept as a pet. Apparently he butted a lady the other month, so they're looking to find him a new home. Point is, we wouldn't be ready to go after anything before Tuesday."

Sam felt his head throb again. Surely this headache would be gone by then. "I can go up at first light Monday."

JADE PULLED OUT her pocket watch and decided it was getting late. Time to take Biscuit home. The cat had already had a good run today alongside Sam's motorcycle, but the three miles to the Dunburys' wouldn't tax him. She'd probably discovered as much as she could here anyway and had bumped into Mr. Daley and discussed work as he wandered through the fair. He wanted her to help Sunday afternoon loading up Percy and the Thompsons' zebras. Jade chirped once to Biscuit and headed for the parking grounds and her motorcycle. Halfway there she saw Anderson signal to her. She stopped, thinking that there might have been a change in plans.

"I suppose you're going to the dance tonight with that Featherstone fellow," he said.

Jade sighed. This was the last thing she wanted to deal with. "Yes, I'm going with Sam and the Thompsons." Wayne seemed like a nice man, but she was never one for playing the field, and right now, Sam had her attention.

Anderson grunted. "I wanted to warn you about your flyboy," he said. "If I were you, I wouldn't want to take any chances. I have it on good authority that he struck and killed a man."

He turned and walked away, leaving Jade no opportunity, short of calling after him, to ask for more details. Did he know the supposed eyewitness that Finch had mentioned? Or was he just trying to drive a wedge between her and Sam?

THE BALL AT the New Stanley Hotel was a lavish affair. Bandmaster Harvey and His Merry Men, an orchestra well versed in all the latest songs, filled a dais at one end of the ballroom, and a sumptuous assortment of cakes, tarts, cheeses, fruit, and tiny watercress sandwiches was laid out on the other side. The punch bowl was kept full of a bubbly champagne punch, and a cash bar provided for anyone in want of something stronger.

Ladies posed and glided in straight sleeveless gowns of wispy tulle, silk, and satin. The older ladies chose darker hues of black, violet, or midnight blue. Younger women, or those pretending to be, opted for pastels in peach, green, rose, or dainty blue. Jade wore the same apricot gown that Beverly had given her last year. Its style was one year behind the times, but she didn't care. Madeline, a bit more fashion conscious, had once again remade her blue gown by loosening the waist so it hung straight, as was the current vogue.

Both Neville and Sam looked dapper, albeit uncomfortable, in their black ties, stiff collars, and black dinner jackets. Several of the younger men, Mr. Holly included, sported midnight blue jackets, reported to be the latest in men's fashion.

The Thompsons had brought their journals to the house. Jade had read them, but neither had had anything new to add. Jade had hoped to share what information they'd garnered during the day, but Madeline, giddy over her blue-ribbon roses and exuberant about the prospects of adopting a child, could talk of nothing else. Even Neville was elated enough by his blue ribbon coffee that his partially dismantled coffee dryer didn't disturb him. They had money from Maddy's books and the prospect of higher pay for their crop, and both trusted that Inspector Finch would soon return the dryer door to them.

The Thompsons had arrived at Jade's door around midday, shortly after she returned to Parklands, and by the time Sam got there, Maddy had Jade shut away in a back room helping her make last-minute alterations to her old gown. With one or another in the bath or dressing, there was no opportunity for Sam and Jade to swap news. Then Madeline insisted on sitting in the back of the car with Jade to talk about building a nursery onto their house, and Neville drove them all to the dance. And now, when Jade hoped finally to hear from Sam, they discovered that any semblance of serious conversation was impossible over the noise from the dance floor.

Not that Sam particularly wanted to dance. He found it impossible to keep up with the fast fox-trot, Peabody, or turkey trot tempos, which were primarily what the dancers clamored for, along with ragtime and jazz. The more sedate castle walk and waltz, both of which Sam managed very gracefully, were rare, and as soon as Jade and he moved back off the dance floor, some man grabbed Jade's hand and whisked her out onto the floor without even asking if she wanted to dance. This last time, it was Cutter who held Jade in a bear hug, leaning in close and pumping her right arm up and down in tune with *Loving Sam, the Sheik from Alabam*, a popular stateside song. At least he'd changed his shoes, so he didn't smell too much from polecat. Jade saw Sam scowl and move off to the corner, his arms folded across his chest. She also spied Inspector Finch, in evening attire, watching from near the punch bowl.

When the band finished, Jade thanked Cutter for the dance but declined another and hurried off the floor before anyone else could grab her. *Stand by the food and act like you're eating.* She shoved a finger sandwich in her mouth, as the band struck up "Choo Choo," grabbed another, and looked around for Sam. She didn't see him anywhere. She did spot Pauline Berryhill and hurried over to her just as Anderson turned in her direction.

"Mrs. Berryhill, how are you enjoying the dance?"

The woman might have been sucking lemons for her grimace. "It's amusing if you care for this sort of thing." She smoothed the skirt of her plain indigo dress. A single locket on a gold chain relieved the austerity of the bodice's narrow pleating. It was not a homely dress, per se. "Dignified" was the word that came to Jade's mind, and to an extent, it became Mrs. Berryhill. "I really cannot be staying long though. I have offered to make some of the deliveries myself tomorrow. Winston deplores driving."

"Deliveries on a Sunday," said Jade. "That's very dutiful of you."

"It's practical," replied Mrs. Berryhill. "The store will be closed then, so I am not needed behind the counter."

Jade set the uneaten sandwich in her hand on a nearby empty tray set aside for used punch cups and champagne flutes. "Mrs. Berryhill, I'd like to talk to you about Mrs. Stokes' child."

Mrs. Berryhill raised her chin and pulled back her head. "I'll not spread any gossip about that innocent creature."

For some reason Jade wondered if she meant the child or Mrs. Stokes. She decided it didn't matter and pressed on. She already felt that Mrs. Berryhill knew more than she was letting on. "I'm not looking for gossip. Good friends of mine, Madeline and Neville Thompson, wanted to give a baby a home. They answered an ad to adopt a four-month-old baby boy the day after it was first published. Later I learned that Mrs. Stokes had a baby boy that age. I'm not one to believe in coincidences, so I think they were the same baby. The baby was already taken, Madeline was devastated, and I think she deserves some explanation as to how that child in the ad managed to get adopted so quickly."

Jade waited a moment while all this registered in Mrs. Berryhill's mind. Then she added more gently, "You placed that ad, didn't you, Mrs. Berryhill?" Jade found that direct statements often got better results than questions. She wasn't disappointed.

The woman nodded. "Yes." She fidgeted with the locket a moment, then tugged at her dress bodice. "I'm sure you can see that the child needed a decent home."

"You seem to be the only person who knew Alice Stokes or cared about her, Mrs. Berryhill. When did she leave? Where did she go?"

Mrs. Berryhill toyed with the locket and looked everywhere but at Jade. "I don't know when *or* where she went. I just know she made plans. You see," she explained, meeting Jade's eyes, "I knew when her husband would be away on his calls. Most of those times I couldn't leave the store, but on a few occasions, I could see her, make certain she was all right. *I'm* the one who brought the doctor, or she'd have delivered that baby on her own." Mrs. Berryhill glanced away again. "Then not long ago, my husband and I found her baby in a crate in back of the store."

"Why do you suppose she left her child behind?"

"Secrecy, I suppose," said Mrs. Berryhill. "If she disguised herself, she could probably board a train and not be noticed as she would with an infant."

"So you don't believe Mrs. Stokes is coming back?" asked Jade. Mrs. Berryhill shook her head. "Who adopted the boy and how did they manage to get him so quickly?" Seeing the woman's hesitation, Jade added, "Please, it would help my friend if she knew the child went to a loving home."

Again, the woman played with her locket. "There was a . . . farmwife. From up north. She was in town getting supplies and took the child straightaway." Mrs. Berryhill raised her chin again, as if defying Jade to contradict her.

"She replied to the newspaper office right after reading the ad?" Jade couldn't keep the skepticism from her voice. According to the secretary, no one had applied to the paper.

"Well . . . no. She came to the store and *saw* the baby. She admired it. Said she wanted one herself. So I let her take him."

"You gave the baby to a total stranger?"

"Of course not! I've done business with this woman before. Not often, but enough. You may assure Mrs. Thompson that this lady is a clean-living, decent woman."

"Thank you, Mrs. Berryhill. This will certainly help my friend."

"You're welcome, I'm sure," said Mrs. Berryhill. "Now if you'll excuse me, it is getting late. I must find my husband and be going home."

Jade watched her leave just as the band struck up "Broadway Crawl," and Anderson appeared at her elbow.

"How 'bout we share this dance, Jade?" he asked.

Jade didn't see Sam or the Thompsons anywhere, but she did spy Mr. Holly weaving uncertainly in her direction. While she really wanted to find her friends, she decided it would be rude to outright reject Wayne. After all, she did need to work with him, and it *was* just a dance. *Better to dance with him than to deal with Holly again.* Besides, she wanted to ask him about his earlier statement.

"Certainly," she said. Wayne took her right hand and pulled her close for a fox-trot. He wasn't a bad dancer, but Jade didn't like to be held so close. She slid her left hand to the front of his shoulder to give herself a little more breathing room.

"I'm curious as to why you felt the need to warn me about Sam," she said. "He didn't kill anyone."

"Hasn't that inspector told you? Featherstone was spotted giving that Stokes guy a wallop to the jaw."

"Really? I'm not sure I believe that, and anyway, it doesn't prove that Sam killed him."

"Makes him dangerous in my book. I think you should steer clear of him, that's all. Guys like that can blow up pretty quickly once they get in a lather."

"Guys like what? Do you mean pilots? Is that why you dislike Sam so much?"

"Hey, I'm no apple knocker," he said, referring to an unworldly country bumpkin. "I've been in Chicago a long time. I've seen some characters."

"I'm sure you have, but you're wrong about Sam."

The song ended; Jade thanked Wayne for the dance and excused herself to find her friends. *Where the blazes is Madeline?* Jade saw her on the far side talking to a pretty young woman barely out of her teens. Neville and Sam were near the bar having a drink. Luckily, the orchestra announced it would take a brief respite, which meant no one would tug her onto the dance floor in the next fifteen minutes. As Jade made her way to Madeline, she studied the room. Jade had to hand it to the New Stanley Hotel for hiring and training efficient staff. The five white-gloved waiters, all native Africans, were busy taking glasses from people as soon as the glass was empty. The overall effect was immaculate without the usual party residue. *Shame they can't move some of these people out of my way.* After several "pardon me's" Jade arrived just as the girl left.

"There you are, Jade. I was looking for you," said Madeline. Neville and Sam joined them. "I wanted you to meet that nice girl. I had the most interesting conversation with her." All male eyes turned to the departing young woman in her very modern, low-cut dress of green taffeta with puffy tulle sashes at each hip. The entire dress was held up by two thin straps.

"She's a 'hello girl,' " said Madeline.

"I can see that," said Sam to no one in particular.

Jade tossed a sidelong look at him, but he was still staring after the girl. "What was this conversation about, Maddy?" she asked.

"She overheard me speak to Mrs. Palmer about Mrs. Stokes' disappearance. Everyone talks of it, but no one knows anything. Nobody really knew the woman at all. So, Nancy— that's her name—she approached me and said she had an idea about who placed the ad looking for her."

"How did she find that out?" asked Neville.

"She overhears a great many things in her line of work," replied Maddy.

"I can imagine," said Sam.

Jade, impatient, urged Madeline on. "What did she say?"

"Well, she's very good at recognizing voices, and she said this man had a high-pitched, reedy one. She thought it sounded like Alwyn Chalmers."

"She didn't see him?" asked Sam.

Maddy shook her head. "No. Why would she?"

Sam scratched his head and stammered a bit. "Well, it just seems . . . I mean, I would assume. . . ." He shook his head. "But I'm surprised at you, Maddy, talking to her."

Madeline opened her eyes wider and placed a hand on her chest. "Why shouldn't I? Of course there is a difference in our ages, but she seemed very polite and nice."

"But, Madeline . . . ," sputtered Sam. He turned to Neville. "Surely you don't approve of your wife chatting with her?"

Neville drained his scotch and soda and shrugged. "Spoken with her myself several times."

"Sam," said Jade, "I think you're confused. The title 'hello girl' is just a cute name for the telephone operators."

Sam blinked twice, slowly, like a startled owl. "A telephone operator?"

"Of course," said Madeline. "Because they always say 'hello' when you place a call. What did you think she was?"

"Never mind," muttered Sam, red faced.

Neville chuckled. "Very good. Very good, indeed."

Madeline, still confused, looked to Jade for an explanation. Jade leaned in closer and whispered, "He thought she was a woman of ill repute, a streetwalker."

Madeline's hand flew to her open mouth; then she giggled. "Oh! Hellooooo," she said.

Sam rolled his eyes. "Honest mistake. Sorry."

Jade smiled and turned the conversation back to the more important revelation. "That's really very intriguing, Maddy. Why would Chalmers place an ad to find information about Mrs. Stokes?" No one had an answer to that, but thinking of Chalmers made Jade recall the leopard cubs and, consequently, her job. "By the way, I think we're collecting Percy and the zebra tomorrow afternoon."

Neville nodded. "Good."

"Perkins hired me to fly over close to the Maasai reserve to scout for a young rhino," said Sam. "I'm going up early Monday morning. Will you come along, Jade?"

"Yes, as long as Perkins doesn't need me." She saw the orchestra members return to their seats and pick up their instruments. Soon talking wouldn't be possible. "Quickly, before they start up: I learned that Stokes drowned in some animal dip after being hit. They found arsenic traces in his lungs. Did anyone else discover something?"

"I just reported my news," said Maddy.

Neville shook his head.

"Stokes may have been blackmailing someone," said Sam. "That's according to the Berryhill kid and another man, a Mr. Griswell. Neither would be more explicit, though, which makes me suspect that Griswell, at least, was being blackmailed. Other than that, I overheard a lot of men rehash the same material we've all heard before: good football player, solid in cricket, but nothing much about him personally. I got the distinct impression that one old man, Lord Colridge, knew a lot about everyone else but kept his cards close."

"You met Lord Colridge?" asked Jade.

"I filmed him," said Sam. The orchestra tuned their instruments in the background. "You know him?"

"I met him when I first came to Africa," said Jade. "He took me along on that hunt for the man-eating hyena."

Sam nodded. "He seemed fond of you two," he said to Neville and Madeline. "Once he knew I was your friend, he was tickled pink to let me film him." He still held his empty scotch glass and looked around for a place to deposit it. There were no trays or waiters nearby. Sam nudged Neville and pointed to a distant tray by the back wall, then to himself.

By now the orchestra had jumped into "Oh, by Jingo" and the couples took to the floor. Further serious conversation was at an end as everyone else around them practically shouted to be heard over the music. Jade motioned to the door. "Shall we leave?"

Maddy nodded. "I agree, don't you, Neville?"

"What?" Neville asked over the noise.

"We want to leave," repeated Madeline.

"Fine," said Neville.

Jade looked around. "Where's Sam?"

"He went to put his glass down over there." Neville pointed to the back wall, but there was no Sam nearby. "Where did he go?"

"I don't see him anywhere," said Jade as she stood on tiptoe and turned a slow, complete circle, scanning the room.

They each searched the ballroom, looking for Sam, but after fifteen minutes, they still hadn't found him. Cutter stopped Jade as she was about to look outside, and asked her for the next dance.

"I'm sorry, Frank, but I was about to leave as soon as I found my friend."

"Are you looking for that pilot fellow?"

"Yes, Sam Featherstone. Have you seen him recently?"

Cutter nodded. "Saw him go out the back way with some man ten minutes ago."

Jade thanked him, grabbed Maddy and Neville, and headed for the back door. But when they went outside, all they saw was the empty alleyway.

CHAPTER 9

*Lions are the scourge of the Maasai herds. A warrior is insulted by a lion
boldly roaring by the kraal at night. But as long as a lion still eats raw meat
instead of roasted like a man, he cannot challenge a Maasai.*

—The Traveler

JADE LAY AWAKE, listening for Sam to return. After hearing
he'd left, Neville had gone up and down the dark alleyway
while Jade and Madeline searched out front. Next they waited
by the Thompsons' car for an hour. Still no Sam. Finally,
Maddy suggested that he'd missed them somehow and gotten another ride back to Parklands. They drove to the Dunburys' residence, but Sam wasn't there either. Neither was his
motorcycle. His camera and tripod, however, were still in the
back pantry, where he'd left them. He must have come back
and driven off.

Where did he go?

For that matter, *why* would he go and not tell them?
What had anyone said that drove him off? Or had he seen
something suspicious and followed it? Had something happened to him? He hadn't looked too well recently, but with
typical male reticence, he kept claiming that he was fine.

Exasperated with chasing sleep, Jade got up and slipped

her trousers and a shirt over her linen camisole and drawers. She shook out her boots and tugged them on over a clean pair of socks. She needed something to occupy her time and mind, and developing pictures was as good a plan as any. She took her flashlight and padded out to the outbuilding the Dunburys had built for her lab. After unlocking the door, Jade went in and lit a lantern fitted with a red glass chimney. Next she mixed a fresh batch of chemicals and started the process, focusing on her watch's second hand, and the careful rinsing of each roll in the developing can.

Finally, she studied the negatives by the dim lantern light, looking for the exceptional picture among the blurred or mediocre shots. Jade felt a stirring of pleasure and relief to know that the picture of the hyena in the pit showed promise. Her bosses would be glad for it in their advertising packet.

She clipped each of the developed rolls on a line to dry, cleaned up the lab, and went back to the house. It would be dawn in a few hours. Since she'd taken up residency in the Dunburys' home, she'd been attending Sunday mass at St. Joseph's in Nairobi, but today she felt the need for additional spiritual help. She decided to lie down, still dressed, for an hour before motorcycling to St. Austin's, the French mission church in the care of the Fathers of the Holy Ghost.

The mission, with its coffee farm and school, lay tucked between the confluence of a seasonal tributary and the Nairobi River in the beautiful highlands east of town. The drive would help her think, and she loved visiting the French Fathers there as she'd done when she first met them, looking for help. Maybe Sam would be back when she returned, but by this time, he'd probably gone back to his room at the Thompsons'.

*　　*　　*

SAM FOUGHT THE urge to punch his fist into a wall. First Inspector Finch had pulled him from the ballroom and then had the unmitigated gall to "suggest" that Sam spend the rest of the night at the police headquarters rather than disturb his friends by coming in so late. Finch even had one of his constables retrieve Sam's motorcycle for him so he'd "have it in the morning" when they turned him loose. And why? Because they had found his partial thumb print on the corn-husking glove.

Well, why the hell wouldn't they? He'd hauled the blasted body out of the dryer, for Pete's sake. He'd also admitted in his interview that he'd looked at one in the store and handled it. So had a lot of other people, he imagined. Sam told Finch what he'd learned about Stokes: how the Berryhill kid and Mr. Griswell both seemed to think he was blackmailing someone. Finch only seemed mildly interested and countered by asking if Stokes had blackmailed Sam as well.

"Was that why you were so angry with him?" Finch had asked. "Is that why you hit him?"

Sam repeated that he hadn't knocked Stokes down. That he'd been upset about being charged five pounds more for the barrel of fuel, waved a billing in his face, and grazed him. He wanted to know who this so-called witness was who claimed to see him punch Stokes. Finch said he couldn't divulge that, making some claim that it was to protect the witness.

"Am I under arrest?" Sam asked.

"The case against you is looking better, but no, not at this point," Finch had replied. "But we would suggest that you don't go flying off anywhere."

"I'm supposed to fly early Monday," Sam said. "I have a job for that Perkins and Daley outfit. They want me to scout a young rhino for them." When Finch didn't respond, Sam added, "Jade is planning to go with me."

"Ah, Miss del Cameron," said Finch. "A most interesting young woman."

Sam couldn't tell if Finch's comment about Jade was geared to provoke a response or intended to suggest that she might be involved in Stokes' death as well. He decided not to reply. Anything he said would be misconstrued anyway.

"What does she think about your being seen arguing with Mr. Stokes?" asked Finch.

"You told me not to tell her about my previous interrogation."

Finch smiled. "So I did. But women are generally so curious."

Sam kept his mouth shut and his eyes on Finch's.

"She told me you rescued her and her mother in Morocco," continued Finch. "I checked into that and learned that Miss del Cameron had been held by the police as a murder suspect in Tangier." He cocked his head and watched Sam. "What I found most interesting was that she slipped away from them during the night."

Sam felt his jaw tighten and forced himself to remain calm. *It's all an act. He's trying to provoke me.* He folded his arms across his chest and leaned back in his chair.

"Of course, we have applied to Lord Avery Dunbury about all this, as Miss del Cameron claims he is a character reference," said Finch. "It is curious, isn't it, that Lord Dunbury has not deigned to reply?" He leaned forward, looking to Sam for an answer to the implied question.

"Maybe he's simply not at home right now," said Sam.

Finch put his palms flat on the table. "Perhaps." He gave

the tabletop a slap and stood. "Well, I should imagine that you are very tired, Mr. Featherstone. It is rather late."

"I'm free to leave?" asked Sam.

"If you insist, of course," said Finch. "But when the constable brought your motorcycle to the station, he noticed that your lamp was out. Of course it would be out of the question for you to drive it at night. After six o'clock headlight rule and all, you know. You *would* get arrested for operating a vehicle without the proper lighting. You could walk, but we have a perfectly comfortable bunk here at the station." He smiled as though he were offering a friend a spare bedroom with a bath.

Sam took a deep breath and let it out slowly as he stood. "Thank you for your consideration," he said. "It seems I have little choice."

Which was why, sitting on the bunk in what was nothing more than a jail cell, Sam wanted to punch his fist into the wall. Instead, he flipped the mattress over in case there were lice, tossed the pillow to the floor, and rolled up his dinner jacket to use in its place. He didn't bother to dismantle his artificial leg before retiring.

I'll be damned if I let him see me as anything less than a whole man.

JADE GOT UP again at five, pulled her old ambulance corps skirt on over her trousers, left a note on Maddy's bag, and rode off to the mission on her motorcycle. The early-morning air felt cool and refreshing on her face, the speed good. Biscuit had chirped and strained at his lead, begging to run alongside her, but Jade decided the Fathers didn't need a cheetah interrupting their Sunday. Instead, she left Biscuit tethered in the backyard with a chicken carcass for breakfast.

Jade took the Kikuyu Road south and cut east at the Nairobi River. From there she followed the river, avoiding the roads and relishing the open grasslands. She crossed the dry tributary, puttered into the mission's coffee plantation, and rode past the convent and school grounds to the church. As she dismounted, she adjusted her skirt so that it hid her trousers above the boots. Then she slipped a scarf over her head and went inside.

After mass Father Jacquinet invited her to breakfast, but Jade declined, albeit with some regret as she thought about the fresh breads, jams, clotted cream, and the Father's wonderful coffee. She explained that she needed to get home and on to the Thompsons' house before the zoological crew arrived. Besides, she was anxious to find Sam and ask what had happened to him.

"Are you certain you do not have time for perhaps a petite visit?" Farther Jacquinet asked, holding his thumb and index finger a few millimeters apart.

She pulled out her pocket watch and checked the time. Seven forty-five. Madeline and Neville would possibly still be abed on a Sunday morning, and something told her she wouldn't see Sam there either. "Perhaps there is time for just one cup of coffee," she said.

"*Bon!*" exclaimed Father Jacquinet, as he led the way to the refectory.

Inside the cool dining area, Jade helped the younger Father Duflot set the table while Father Jacquinet assisted the more infirm, older Father Robidoux to a seat. Jade was sorry to see that the old priest had declined so much physically since she last saw him, but was glad to note the alert expression in his soft blue eyes. His mind, at least, had not aged.

They said grace and broke their long fast on warm bread and jam. Jade regaled them with her adventures in Marrakech, but she could have recited the merits of her motorcycle and they would have been just as happy as long as it was in French rather than in Swahili or English.

"It is good that you helped the old woman in Tangier to go back to France," said Father Robidoux. "But selling the Panhard? Bah! That was a mistake, mademoiselle. That is a fine French automobile."

"True, but I find my Indian Big Twin much more practical," she replied.

"And now? What do you do now?" asked Father Jacquinet.

Jade told them about her writing and her extra job working for Perkins and Daley. She spoke about Sam and flying, and about the most recent problems. "Did you know this Mr. Stokes?" she asked. "Did he deliver food or supplies here?"

Father Robidoux shrugged. "Sometimes, but I never spoke with him. He came, he delivered, we paid him, he left. Voilà." Then he smiled and his eyes seemed to twinkle. "And so," he said in a cracked voice, "you have yet another puzzle to solve."

"Why do you think, Father, that this is a puzzle for *me* to solve?"

"Perhaps I am a bit of a detective myself, no? You tell us of this Mr. Featherstone, who helped you and your mother in Morocco. And you tell us of rides in his flying machine. Then you say that the police think he may be a suspect." He chuckled. "You will not let them accuse this young man. Oh, no." He smeared jam on another chunk of bread and bit into it, still chuckling.

Jade blushed. "Sam and I are friends, Father. Of course I do not wish to see him accused. And yes, I'm trying to assist, but I don't know what else I can do."

"You have already said you must find out where the coffee dryer stood," said Father Duflot. "Perhaps there is a tank of this animal dip nearby? You will play like the great French detective, M. Edmond Locard, no? You will search for the hairs, and the buttons, and the faint but telling footprints. And do not forget there is planning in covering up this crime."

"Yes," said Jade, "slitting the wrist and adding animal blood to make it appear to be a suicide." She looked at the mantelpiece clock and noted the time. "Nine o'clock! Oh, dear, I must be on my way," she said. "Thank you so much for the delightful breakfast."

"Please be certain to let us meet this young man soon," Father Robidoux said as Jade excused herself. "Bring him next Sunday," he called to her back.

SAM LEFT THE police headquarters as soon as someone opened the door for him at six thirty. He felt as if bugs were crawling all over his legs. *Damn lice-ridden jail!* He rode on to the Dunburys' house, intent on explaining where he'd been and retrieving his everyday clothes, but not until he filled a tub with water and scrubbed himself raw to get the bugs off him. When he arrived, it was to an empty house.

Avery had purchased a good house to begin with, but had also invested some money adding all the best amenities. Consequently, the bathroom had hot and cold running water, as long as someone lit the pilot and turned on the gas to heat the water. No one had. Luckily, in this climate even the cold water wasn't too bad. Sam filled the tub a third of the way full and scrubbed hard with a bar of Palm Olive soap he found on the shelf. Wrapped in a towel, he found the clothes he'd left behind when he'd changed into evening wear and gotten dressed.

Now he felt human again. He wadded the dinner jacket, trousers, tie, and cummerbund into a ball, rolled them into a newspaper, and tossed the bundle in a corner on the front veranda to keep any possible lice from contaminating the house. He'd worry about them later. Right now he had other things on his mind. He felt a desperate need to see Jade.

He looked for a note, found none. Sam checked his watch and decided she had gone to mass. From his visit in town last January, he remembered that they'd gone to St. Joseph's together. He got back on his motorcycle and headed back into Nairobi.

By the time he arrived at seven thirty, the service was just beginning. Sam knelt in the back pew, his eyes scanning the crowd for Jade. From their build and general height, two young ladies could have been her, but he couldn't see their hair for the broad-brimmed hats on their heads. Somehow, neither the hats nor the dresses looked like anything Jade would wear. An hour later, he emerged discouraged at not finding her. He suddenly felt very much alone in Africa, like a man shot down in enemy territory. The pounding in his head didn't help either.

He decided to retrieve his equipment and go back to the farm. He slipped out of the church and motored back to the Dunburys'. His head spun a little as he bent to take the key from under a flowerpot. He attributed the weakness to lack of sleep, went inside, and headed for the back pantry, where he had left the camera and tripod yesterday. They were gone!

JADE RODE BACK to Parklands, thinking about Father Duflot's suggestion. If she could find something to show Finch, something that would lead him away from Sam as a suspect, it would be worth any time and effort. *I'll ask Neville where the coffee dryer stood as soon as I see him.* Finch had either not asked Neville that question, or Neville hadn't remembered it when he made his meager entries in his notes.

At the Dunburys' she found a note from Madeline in her room. It said that Neville and she had driven off to their farm at six fifteen but left Biscuit behind since he was still eating. They added that Sam had not returned, and since they expected to see him at their home, they took his camera equipment with them in the motorcar. Jade wadded up the note and tossed it in a trash can. Then she removed her skirt and hung it in her closet. In the bathroom, she saw a wet towel and wondered if either Maddy or Neville had bathed that morning or if Sam had returned. She hurried to see if he was in any of the guest bedrooms. *Empty.*

Deciding Sam had already gone back to the Thompsons' farm, Jade locked up the house and headed for her motorcycle. That was when she saw the bundle tossed into a corner of the veranda. A quick check revealed Sam's evening clothes.

Why did he leave them wadded up here? Why didn't he wait for me? She rerolled the clothes in the paper and set them back where she'd found them, searching for some reason why he'd be angry at her. She came up empty. Deciding that the answers waited for her at the Thompsons', Jade went to fetch Biscuit. She undid his tether and led him back to her motorcycle. A quick check on her watch showed it was nine forty-five. Time to get moving.

The sleek cat pranced and tugged at his lead, letting Jade know how excited he was by the prospect of another good run. Jade made sure the lead was firmly wrapped around her right hand, kick-started her engine, and let Biscuit set the pace. If anything, she had to restrain him several times. Her motorcycle was capable of 60 mph, but the road was not, and Jade didn't care to connect with one of the many ruts and bumps at that speed. Two miles from the farm, she stopped, untied the lead, and let Biscuit have his head. He could run full out for as long as he could endure it and trot the rest of the way in.

When Jade pulled into the farmyard, Biscuit was there waiting as Madeline pumped water into a large enamel pan for him. Since the cat was impatient, much of the water went directly onto the cheetah's broad head, which he stuck directly under the flow. Jade looked around and saw no sign of Sam's motorcycle.

"Hi, Maddy. Sam back yet?" she asked as she removed her leather helmet.

Madeline shook her head. "No, and I'm worried. Neville even went out to see if his plane was still in the hangar. It is."

"I'm going back to town and tell Finch something happened. This isn't right. It's not like Sam to disappear without telling any of us." Jade went to the well and, once Biscuit had finished drinking, pumped another burst of water into a bucket. She caught the tailings of the flow in her hands and splashed the water on her face, then took a dipper and drank deeply.

Madeline offered Jade a towel to dry her face, just as Biscuit raised his head and stared at a distant cloud of dust. Then he chirped. Jade knew immediately that he'd recognized the sound of Sam's motorcycle.

"Here he comes now," Jade said.

As the engine's rumble became clearer, Neville came from one of the outbuildings, where he'd been working, and joined them. Everyone, human and cat alike, stood in a row, watching the dust cloud approach. Within minutes, Sam rolled into the yard and shut down the engine. He pulled off his goggles and helmet with uncharacteristic silence. Jade could practically feel the tension roll off him. Madeline took the towel from Jade, dampened it, and handed it to Sam. Jade followed with a dipper full of water. No one spoke, letting Sam have a moment to collect himself.

Finally, Jade couldn't wait anymore. "Are you all right, Sam?"

He handed the dipper back to her and managed a thin-lipped smile. "I'm fine," he muttered through gritted teeth. "I was riding around thinking, that's all." He saw his camera and tripod on the veranda and sighed. "At least the damn camera isn't gone. Sorry. Bad language," he said with a side-wise glance at Madeline and Jade.

"Tell us about it," said Jade.

Neville had run into the house and come back out with a whiskey and soda, which he handed to Sam. "You might need this more than the water," he said.

Sam started to reach for it, then dropped his hand and shook his head. "Better not. Got a bad enough headache as it is, but thanks anyway, Neville." Neville shrugged, took one look at the glass, and drained it himself.

"Finch hauled me into police headquarters for the night," Sam said.

"Why?" exclaimed Neville and Madeline in unison.

"Said my prints were on the murder weapon, which as we all probably know by now was not *really* the murder weapon, but try to tell that to Finch."

"But of course your prints are on it," said Neville. "You pulled Stokes out of the dryer, Sam. As I recall you had him by the wrists, and I had the feet."

Sam nodded. "And I handled a corn knife in the store. If not that one, then another. But it seems that makes *me* a prime suspect."

"He didn't officially arrest you?" asked Jade.

Sam shook his head. "Implied it's only a matter of time. Told me I shouldn't go flying off anywhere."

"What about your job tomorrow morning?" Jade asked.

Sam shrugged. "Be damned if I'm losing that money. But he'll probably haul me off for sure when I get back." He looked at Jade. "Maybe you should fly and I'll just sit in the front and scout. Then when he arrests me, I can tell him that I didn't fly, just like he ordered."

Madeline clucked an "Oh, dear," and Neville looked longingly at the empty glass. "I'll be back in a moment," said Sam as he headed for the outhouse.

"Neville," said Jade as she watched Sam walk off, "I meant to ask you. Where was the coffee dryer when you originally picked it up?"

"By the freight yards. Not far from your bosses' warehouse in point of fact. It was supposed to be sent on up to Thika, but I finally just took the truck and picked it up myself."

"How in the world did you manage to lift it?" Jade asked. "Surely you must have noticed that it was particularly heavy, for a supposedly empty drum?"

"I might have, but I didn't lift it," Neville replied. "I paid six of the rail yard natives to load it and got my own men to unload it here. Remember, Jade. It wasn't a particularly large drum since we air-dry most of our coffee. Wanted it to finish the drying in wet years. I liked that model because it had one large door instead of the usual two smaller ones."

"Lucky for the murderer," muttered Jade.

Neville's stomach rumbled and he patted it. "Maddy, I'm starved. What say we go in and have an early luncheon?"

"It's barely past ten thirty," said Madeline.

"Then we have early elevenses," said Neville. "Besides, once that crew arrives, there won't be time for meals, and I'm sure Sam will want something to eat."

Madeline nodded. "You and Sam come join us, Jade. I'll cut some cake and put on hot water for tea and brew some coffee for you."

"Don't bother, Maddy," said Jade. "I had breakfast at the mission. But I'll tell Sam."

She sat on the front step and waited until Sam came around. "They went inside for a snack," Jade said. "Neville's stomach decided you were hungry."

Sam nodded and headed for the door. Jade snatched at his trouser leg and tugged him to stop. "I'm sorry about what happened, Sam," she said. "We waited at the car for you for over an hour. Then when we saw your cycle was gone, we assumed . . ." She shrugged. "Well, to be frank, we didn't know what to assume. Mainly that you'd come back here."

Sam nodded. "I tried to catch you this morning," he said. "I must have just missed you."

"I was at church."

Sam pulled back, started to say something, then clamped his mouth shut. "Church. I see," he said finally. He turned to leave.

"Where are you going?"

"I have no idea," he said. With that, he walked off toward the line of coffee trees.

Jade got up and trotted after him. "Sam, wait." He stopped, half turning to face her. "What's wrong, Sam? I don't understand."

He took a deep breath and let it out. "I went to church this morning, looking for you." His dark eyes bored into hers. "You weren't there."

Jade let her head fall back. "And you think I was lying to you just now?" She stepped closer and peered into his eyes. "I went to the French mission." Sam's shoulders drooped. "I'm sorry, Sam. I had no idea. . . . I left Maddy a note, but I guess she threw it away after she read it."

"Sorry, Jade. I'm as bad as that damned Finch, accusing you of deceiving me without more evidence."

"You've had a bad night," she said by way of excuse. "And you look like hell." She placed a hand on his shoulder. "You ought to go lie down and sleep. I can go for a doctor or—"

"I don't need a doctor and I don't want a damned nurse-maid!" Sam snapped.

Jade pulled her hand back. "Maddy's slicing cake if you're hungry. I need to see to my equipment, get ready for loading those zebra. You'll probably want to set up your camera." Her lips twitched in a weak attempt at a smile; then she walked back to her motorcycle for her lariat. All the while, she wondered if Sam was hiding something.

THE FIRST TRUCK, a large flatbed with a lidless wood-and-wire cage built around the inside of the truck bed, arrived just after eleven, with Daley at the wheel and four Africans riding in back. Cutter rolled in ten minutes later in an identical truck. Madeline invited the men to sit in the shade of the veranda while they discussed the upcoming operations. Jade and Neville joined them, and Sam filmed part of the discussion. Half an hour later, Anderson pulled into the yard.

Anderson drove a smaller truck with stout wooden planks on the outer sides rising three feet from the bed's bottom. A wooden gate, which slid into place in the back, lay loose on the floor next to an empty wooden cage. The others went out to meet him.

"We'll load the zebra into the larger trucks," said Daley. "If we pack three in each one, they won't have room to move. Won't take a spill and break any legs that way." He patted the last truck on the side wall. "Your lion will go in here. In a cage of course. We've got some poultry netting covering the gaps in the wood so he can't get a paw out and claw someone."

"Percy wouldn't claw anyone," said Madeline. "He's been a pet since he was a cub."

"He's going to be unhappy about the move, ma'am," said Daley, "and that means frightened. So there's no telling what he'll do."

"Mr. Daley is quite right, my dear," said Neville as he placed a hand on her shoulder.

Madeline nodded. "Of course. It's just that I feel sorry for Percy. He *will* be frightened."

"Don't worry too much about your lion, missus," said Daley. "I've got a zoo in Florida that wants him, so he'll have a nice, warm place to live and all the meat he can eat. We even have a young lioness to keep him company. Just bought her from a man in Nakuru."

"He's lived most of his life penned up, Maddy," added Jade. "You couldn't set him free. He's never hunted and he'd probably get shot within a week."

"Right," said Neville. "Let's get these animals in the trucks."

Anderson called for the African men to bring out the loading ramp and set it up by the paddock gate while he backed the first truck into place. The ramp had slots cut into the side, and the men slid wide planks into place as barricades to prevent an animal from jumping off the sides.

"Do you think they'll go in easily?" asked Anderson.

"They're just zebra," said Cutter. "Should be like loading horses, right?"

"Have you ever loaded wild mustang?" asked Jade. "They don't tend to be very cooperative. Keep out of the way of their hooves, especially the back ones. I've seen them kick."

"Well, that's your job, isn't it?" asked Cutter. "Aren't you the rope expert here?"

"That's what they're paying me for," said Jade. She'd pulled on leather gloves and retrieved her lariat. Like Neville, she now wore a wide-brimmed straw hat that shielded her face from the sun. She inspected the rope's coils, checking for kinks or unwanted knots.

"What about flyboy?" asked Anderson, hooking a thumb over his shoulder to point to where Sam stood with his camera. "Isn't he helping?"

"Only if he volunteers," said Daley. "I can't hire too many workers here or I won't make any money. His job'll come tomorrow. If he can find us that young rhino, it'll make this expedition." He clenched his right fist. "If we only had more time, but we're already booked for the boat home and every day we have to feed caged animals eats into our profit."

"Well, I'm betting that all we have to do is open the gate, and they'll be so glad to come out that they'll run right on into the truck," said Cutter. Without waiting for a "Go ahead," he swung the gate inward. Immediately the stallion nipped at one mare's flank and sent her and the other mares running to the opposite side, where they milled and reared in confused panic.

"Get out of there and shut the damn gate," yelled Jade. "The mares aren't going to cooperate until we get their lord and master out." She clamped her hat tighter on her head, made sure her pocket kerchief was handy, and climbed over the fence halfway between the gate and the milling herd. "Maddy," she called over her shoulder, "would you please fetch Biscuit but hold him until I'm ready? Wish I had a good border collie here."

A good dog, she knew, would single out an animal and cut it from the herd. She'd have to do that herself, and right now, it didn't look as if the stallion had any intention of moving away from his harem. She needed something to draw him out. That would be Biscuit's job.

"Get ready, Maddy," Jade yelled. She loosely held the extra rope as coils in her left hand. Her right hand held the lariat by the knot as she swung the loop over her head, smoothly rolling her wrists. "Okay, now," she called. "Biscuit, to me."

Biscuit immediately raced to Jade's side. The sleek cat slunk low on all fours, his broad head down between his hunching shoulders. He let loose a raspy *rowr* as he eyed the stallion.

The zebra recognized the same animal that had threatened him a few days ago. He reared and pounded the ground in front of him, daring the cat to risk his deadly hooves.

"Stay, Biscuit," said Jade in a soothing voice. "Stay." Biscuit remained rooted in place, out of reach but close enough to irritate the stallion and keep him in front of his mares. Jade inched to the side, still swinging her rope overhead, until she had a clear shot at his head. She let the rope fly and it fell true around the zebra's neck. A quick tug and the loop tightened.

"Biscuit, away," Jade ordered, and after a moment's hesitation about leaving the fun, the cheetah trotted back to

Maddy. Jade raced to the fence nearest the gate and passed the rope around one of the stout posts. Then, using it as a pulley, she tugged on the rope, dragging the zebra closer. Anderson jumped over the fence and lent a hand. When the animal was halfway to them, she called a halt. "Let me get another rope on him," she explained.

Jade took a second rope from Cutter and tossed another loop onto the ground just behind his hind legs. "Give him a bit of slack," she called. The zebra took the slack and stepped backward into the loop. Jade pulled and ensnared a leg. "Now he can't buck. Together, on my count. Gently." As Jade counted up, she and Cutter pulled together, with him at the head and Jade with the rear. Each step allowed the zebra to inch forward until they had him by the gate.

Jade handed her rope off to Anderson and pulled the kerchief from her back pocket. "Neville, do you want to do the honors? It ought to be your face in the scene." She handed the kerchief to him, and he took her place in front of the zebra.

"I'll be danged," said Daley. "They're dressed alike down to the same hat, too."

"That's because Neville and Madeline are the stars of this show," said Jade. "Tie the handkerchief around his eyes, Neville. He'll settle down once he can't see the danger."

True to her word, the zebra did quiet himself, and the men were able to lead the animal up the ramp and into the truck. Without the stallion pressing them back, the mares followed a few at a time until all six zebra were loaded.

"Were you able to get all that on film, Sam?" asked Jade.

He looked up from the camera and nodded. "Should be okay."

Jade thought he looked pale and noticed the lines tightening around his mouth. "Sam?"

"I'm fine!" he insisted. "I told you, I'm just tired." Biscuit trotted over and butted his head against Sam's good leg. He reached out and scratched the cheetah behind the ears, and Biscuit erupted in a deep, resonating purr.

"Fantastic job, Jade," called Daley. "Now all we have to do is load up that lion."

"You won't need me for that," said Jade. "Maddy hasn't fed him yet. Put some meat in your cage, set it door to door with his, and he'll go right on in."

"You heard the lady," Daley called to his crew. "Get the cage set up." He turned back to Jade. "We may still need you to help unload these animals into the holding pens in Nairobi. We'll put them into a freight car with built-in stalls so they'll be ready to ship out Tuesday."

"Tuesday?" asked Jade. "I thought you were staying on through the week."

"We are," said Daley, "but Bob wants to load up the hoofed animals early. He's taking them by train late Tuesday to Mombassa and supervising the loading. I'll stay on here until we get the rhino. Then I'll take it and the predators to the ship."

Jade nodded as she watched Sam relocate his tripod and camera to film Percy's transfer and loading. His answer to her query had sounded curt and snappish to her ear. *Maybe he is just tired. You're tired, too.* But as she watched him smile at Maddy and give stage directions to Neville, she knew something else was wrong. Was he jealous of her dancing with Anderson last night? It hadn't been her choice. She couldn't think of anything else.

She hoped that a good night's sleep and the prospect of flying tomorrow would put Sam in a better disposition. Until then, Jade decided to stay out of his way lest she inadvertently say something about Finch or Stokes to remind him of his humiliating night in a jail cell.

As she predicted, Percy followed his stomach and went easily enough into the cage. He started once and snarled as they put the barricade in place and again as the men hoisted him up into the truck, but once they left him to finish his meal in peace, he quieted down.

Jade went to the pump and splashed water on her face, letting it run down her shirt. The afternoon sun immediately dried her and she felt her tension evaporate along with the water. Someone touched her shoulder and she jumped.

"Sorry," said Madeline. "I didn't mean to startle you."

"I was just daydreaming, I guess."

"You must be exhausted," said Maddy. "Come inside and have some lemonade. There's still cake, too. Neville is the only one who ate any earlier."

"Is Sam going in?"

Maddy frowned. "Yes, but he said he wants to lie down and sleep. He must have had a very bad time of it last night." She peered at Jade. "Did you two have a row?"

Jade shrugged. "I wish I knew that myself. We're supposed to fly tomorrow morning, and now I'm not sure if I shouldn't just stay away."

Madeline grabbed Jade's arm. "Oh, don't do that," she said. "I'm sure he's just worn-out. Neville can be a grumpy lion when he's tired, too, but he'll never admit to it. Silly male pride."

Jade felt her fatigue returning. "I'm exhausted, too. It looks like Mr. Daley wants to get these animals squared away now, so I'm going to have to leave. Thanks anyway."

"But you'll come back for supper?"

Jade shook her head. "Thanks, but no, Maddy. I'm going

to soak in a tub and sleep. I'll see you tomorrow bright and early, in case Sam still wants me to go up."

She waved goodbye to Neville, put on her helmet and goggles, and started her motorcycle. Not wanting to eat everyone's dust, she led the way to the Nairobi warehouse, taking note that the place where Neville's coffee dryer had stood was a few hundred yards from the holding pens. *That's close to where our trough of cattle dip is, too.* If the dryer was a convenient place to shove a body, then the murder site would be close. There was no other dip trough nearby.

If she had any hope of finding some footprints or impressions, though, it was dashed by the innumerable tracks made by men filling buckets of dip to fill pump sprayers. So after the zebra were safely in their stalls, she didn't search the area around the trough, especially as the hired Africans were busy treating the new arrivals.

"Join me for a drink?" asked Anderson.

"Thanks, but no, Wayne," replied Jade. "I'm not a drinker and frankly I'm just too tired to socialize. But thanks for your help hauling in that stallion. I couldn't have managed by myself."

"Well, I'm a pretty handy guy," he said. "You know, if you change your mind about hanging around here, you could come back to the States with us."

"I don't think so," she said. She headed for her motorcycle while Anderson followed.

"Hate to see a pretty American wasting her time here in this forsaken hellhole."

Jade didn't bother to answer. She just waved and headed north to Parklands. She'd left Biscuit behind with Madeline, and as she pulled into the lane, she suddenly wished she'd brought him back with her. The house was too big to rattle around in alone.

Jade had stuck her key in the lock when she noticed it was already unlocked. Immediately, her senses went on alert. She opened the door a crack, listened, and hearing nothing, crept inside. Something clattered to the floor, the sound coming from one of the back rooms. Jade reached down to her boot and pulled her knife from its sheath.

She was definitely not alone.

CHAPTER 10

When a Maasai warrior went to war, he wore a lion's mane headdress.

—The Traveler

THE SOUND OF shuffling feet followed the clattering. Jade pressed herself to the wall, trying to determine the number of intruders. If it was just one, she could take him, but if there were several, she needed to make a dash for the nearest policeman. Unfortunately, by the time they returned, the Dunburys' house could be thoroughly looted.

Then another thought came to her. Maybe this wasn't a thief. Maybe someone wanted to find out how much she knew about Stokes' murder. In that case, she definitely needed to capture this person. She gripped her knife in her right hand, the edge of the blade resting back along the sleeve of her outer forearm. The antler hilt felt cool and familiar in her grip.

The shuffling stopped, followed by a low groan. Was someone hurt? Had there been a falling-out between two thieves? Her knee didn't hurt, so presumably the danger wasn't mortal. *No sense taking chances.* Jade looked around for something to protect her exposed left flank and immediately chose the ornate Wakamba shield hanging on the wall above the leather couch.

Nothing like the genuine article.

Armed and protected, Jade padded to the open doorway and into the narrow hallway. In front of her was the door to Avery's study. To her right lay a small sitting room and, beyond that, the master bedroom. She paused in the doorway, waiting for another noise to guide her next move. She heard a drawer open in the bedroom.

A petty thief.

From what Jade read in the papers, these were generally one of the poorer natives, often a child, looking for something they could sell to pay their hut tax. If that was the case, the thief would most likely be unarmed. But Jade didn't intend to take any chances. A nagging voice in her head suggested it could still be the murderer looking for information.

Jade decided on the element of surprise. She charged the open door with a battle cry worthy of the lustiest warrior, shield out in front of her, and her knife hand raised. A clang and a shrill scream met her outcry.

Jade stopped abruptly inside the bedroom and lowered her weapons. "Beverly? What in the name of St. Peter's bait bucket are you doing here?"

Lady Dunbury, her fair face even paler than usual from fright, plopped herself into a nearby chair. "I live here. My stars, Jade. You nearly scared me into labor."

Jade dropped the shield to the floor, slipped her knife back into its sheath, and stepped into the room. Her eyes told her this was her best friend, but her head couldn't register the fact. "But you're supposed to be in London having your baby. What are you doing here? Where's Avery? My Lord, you're . . . huge!"

Beverly planted her feet apart and gripped the chair's arms. "Oof," she said as she pushed herself up. "I feel like I'm carrying a pumpkin inside."

Jade hurried to help her. "No, don't get up. You should sit. You shouldn't be here."

"Oh, hush and give me a hug."

Jade clasped her friend in her arms, trying to avoid crushing the bulging abdomen. "Bev, I can't believe this. You're really here." By now Jade's head, aided by touch and sound, had caught up with her eyes. She felt a giddy elation, an exuberance that lifted her soul as high as flying did her body. She felt something else, too: a bump against her own middle. "Was that the baby?" Jade asked. "Did I just feel the baby kick?"

"You did. The little tyke kicks all the time now." They hugged again, rocking from side to side. Beverly started to sob.

"Bev, what's wrong?" asked Jade, worry replacing her joy. She suddenly remembered that she hadn't seen any sign of Avery and a horrible anxiety cut through her heart. "Where's Avery?'

Bev eased herself, a little ungracefully, back into the chair and waved her hand in the air. "Avery's probably still at the train station, trying to get our luggage here. I was tired, so I took a rickshaw home."

Jade knelt beside her and placed one hand on her friend's arm. "Then what's wrong? Why are you crying?"

Beverly dabbed at her eyes, which always reminded Jade of the blue one saw in watercolors. They seemed even more so now that they were moist with tears. "I cry all the time," Beverly answered. "I hear a sentimental song, I cry. I eat a scone, I cry." She turned to Jade and smiled. "And even the

remotest memory of Africa or you, and I blubber like a baby."
She reached over and hugged Jade again.

"You cannot know how much I—*we*—missed you and
our home here," Beverly continued. "I positively *hate* London
now. It's so noisy and smelly, and there aren't any zebra to
come running down the street when a lion scares them."

She sniffed, and Jade stood and fetched one of Beverly's
embroidered handkerchiefs for her. "Thank you," said Bev
after she blew her nose. "And my sister has been impossible!
She insisted on moving in to take care of me."

"That sounds very loving, actually," said Jade.

"My aunt Fannie's bustle," Beverly retorted. "She's always wanted to live in a big town house and she thought that
once she was moved in, she'd never have to leave. I think she
was planning to be the baby's governess." She dabbed her
nose again, but by now, indignation had replaced her previous emotional outburst. "When I wrote that last letter to you,
it was all I could do to stop crying. That's when Avery decided we should just chuck it all and come back where we
belonged."

Jade shook her head. "It sounds too risky to me. Surely
your doctor didn't approve."

"Oh, pshaw on him, old fuddy duddy. We—well, Avery—
ran into Dr. Burkitt that very day in London. He came to
see me and declared me as fit as a Cape Buffalo. So we threw
everything into the trunks and caught the next boat out. Dr.
Burkitt is returning to Nairobi with the governor, so he'll be
here to deliver the baby. We wanted little Jade or David to be
born in Africa."

"No. Absolutely no. You are not naming that child after me."

"Obviously not if it's a boy."

"I mean it, Bev. So help me. . . ."

"So help you, what? What could you possibly do? Refuse to stand as godmother? You know you wouldn't do that." She hoisted herself up again and straightened her dress. As usual, Beverly wore the latest style, and since the waistlines this year were very loose, only the bulge pushing out from the pretty peach organdy gown gave any clue that this was a maternity dress. As she stood, her handkerchief fell to the floor.

"Be a dear and pick that up for me, will you, Jade? I do not bend so easily."

Jade retrieved the handkerchief and then the silver glove box that Beverly had dropped when she screamed. Beverly, in the meantime, started waddling toward the door. "In point of fact," Bev said, "Avery and I have not decided on names. I just wanted to see what your reaction would be to those so we'd know whether to consider them or not."

"Not," said Jade, following her. "Where are you going now?"

"To the main parlor. I want to ooze into that soft leather chair and never get up."

"You sit in that and you probably won't. Not without a couple of porters at least."

Beverly slapped at Jade playfully and settled herself into the chair. Jade went back, picked up the shield, and hung it back on the wall.

"Good to know that you haven't changed, Jade," said Beverly. "Let me see your tattoo."

Jade undid her left cuff and exposed the crescent lion's claw she had received along with her Swahili name, Simba Jike.

"Not that one," said Beverly. "The one those Berbers gave you in Morocco."

Jade swept up the short black waves that normally graced her forehead and bent over so Bev could see better. At the hairline were five tiny blue marks, three below and two above, representing a lion's paw. "Satisfied?" asked Jade as she straightened.

Beverly made some *tsk*ing sounds. "Soon it will be impossible to take you into any fine establishment. But at least that one is easily hidden by your hair."

"I didn't ask for it, you know. I thought it was henna and would go away after a while."

Beverly grinned. "It's what Avery and I love about you, Jade. You're becoming a walking bit of Africa." She looked around at her home and sighed. "I know we haven't lived here very long, but we do love it: the animals, the flowers, the wonderful people." She suddenly stopped and listened. "Speaking of people, Jade, why don't I hear any? Didn't you hire *any* help at all?"

"There's a man, Nanji, who trims the bushes every month," said Jade. "His wife brings eggs and milk twice a week. You'll like her. Her name is Bisa. She also sells chickens to me for Biscuit. Not that they're hard to come by. Some native's always hawking chickens by the depot." As she said this, she realized that was possibly where the bird blood had come from.

"But who cooks for you, or cleans?" Beverly ran her finger along a nearby table, then inspected the dust streak. "Hmm, never mind the last question. I see the answer to that."

"Bev, you know I don't want to manage a household. You also know that you don't just hire a cook here. You also hire two or three kitchen boys, and someone to wait tables, and—"

Beverly waved her hand as a signal to stop. "Yes, I know

all about it. I'll see to it myself tomorrow. Maybe your Bisa can recommend someone."

The sound of a motorcar and a truck pulling into the drive interrupted their conversation. Slamming doors and male voices shouting in Swahili brought Jade to the window. Beverly tried unsuccessfully to hoist herself out of the chair. "Is that Avery?"

"Yes. He just stepped out of a brand-new Hupmobile. The truck seems to be hired. It's your luggage and enough men to carry it all inside." She opened the door for Avery and received a kiss on the cheek for her reward.

"Jade, damn good to see you. Ah," he said, looking to where Beverly struggled against the cushion, "and there is my darling wife and our little bun in the oven."

"That bun is the size of a full loaf now," said Jade. "When *are* you due?"

"We thought early September, but now we're not so certain," said Beverly. "Dr. Burkitt believes August is more likely." She held out a hand. "Help me up so I can direct the luggage."

"You'll do no such thing, my love. Jade, I'm counting on you to see to it that Beverly does not get up."

With that, he stood at the door and, after a quick look at each label, directed the crates and valises to their appropriate rooms. Most were personal items for the master bedroom, but a few went into Avery's study. The men worked quickly. Avery paid them handsomely and sent them on their way with the truck. Then he eased himself into the matching leather sofa.

"I bought a motorcar, my dear. A new Hupmobile. It's imperative that we have transport, so I saw no reason to beat about the bush." He clapped his hands on his knees to underscore his statement. "By thunder, it's marvelous to be home again, and to see you, too, Jade."

"Why didn't you wire that you were coming?" asked Jade, sitting on a footstool by Beverly. "I'd have met you at the train."

"Beverly and I wanted this to be a surprise." Avery looked at his wife. "Tell me, Beverly, was Jade surprised to see you?"

"Not half as surprised as I was to see her," Beverly said.

When Avery looked confused, Jade chimed in, "We sort of startled each other."

"Ah, indeed," he said. "Wish I'd have been here to see that. Well, bring us up-to-date on all the news. Tell us what Maddy and Neville are up to. Oh! And how is Sam? Is he still out at the Thompsons' making his movie? Are you two still . . . you know . . . an item?"

"You might have to ask Sam that," said Jade, the smile evaporating from her face. "He's been a bit . . . distant just recently, but then, he's also a murder suspect."

"What!" the Dunburys yelled in union.

"Can we not leave you alone for a minute, Jade, without your getting kidnapped or involved in something unseemly?" asked Beverly. She folded her arms across her chest. "Tell us everything. Start at the beginning."

So Jade began with finding the body in the coffee dryer and reported on all she'd learned since then. She explained Maddy's desire for a child and finished with Sam's snappish tone and her confusion over what she might have said or done to provoke it. "We're supposed to fly tomorrow morning to find a rhino calf for the company, but Inspector Finch told Sam not to fly off anywhere, and even if he doesn't, I don't know if Sam still wants me to go with him."

"You don't suspect him, of course, do you, Jade?" asked Avery.

"Certainly not," said Jade. "He knows I'm trying to find evidence to clear him." She frowned. "But this new job keeps getting in the way, so I'm not making much headway. Maybe that's what's bothering him. Maybe he thinks I'm dragging my feet."

"Don't you see, darling?" said Beverly. "He's had a terribly humiliating experience being hauled off to jail like that. He's probably hurt that you didn't make more of it."

"Or try to bust him out," added Avery with a chuckle. "But it looks as though I need to have a word with Inspector Finch. If he's been waiting for me to respond to a wire that I never received, he might have his suspicions about the both of you. And speaking of this other job, why on earth are you working for them?"

"Two reasons," said Jade. "I'm trying to save a few animals earmarked for extermination, and I need the money."

"But your articles," said Beverly.

"I still send in copy, but traveling to write about someplace new costs money, Bev. Plus I don't like being so beholden to you and Avery. You know how I value my independence. I should rent my own rooms somewhere," said Jade. "I feel as if I'm being kept."

Avery lit his pipe and puffed away while his wife muttered something about being too independent for her own good. "Hmm," he mumbled as he studied Jade's face.

"What?" Jade demanded.

"Nothing." He looked at his watch. "Getting late in the day now. I'll see Finch first thing tomorrow morning. I'm famished. I don't suppose we have any food, do we?"

"We do, and I'll be happy to be your cook, kitchen help, and waiter this evening," said Jade, "in return for my keep." She went out to the little stone well house, where they kept the eggs, and brought in six along with a cut from a wheel of cheese. Next she took a good-sized portion of smoked ham from the larder along with several large potatoes and an onion.

After lighting the stove and setting up the coffeepot, she melted a dollop of butter in a skillet. Jade peeled the potatoes, sliced them paper thin, and threw them into the butter along with some salt and pepper. She diced the ham and onion, adding them to the potatoes. Once the mix was sizzling, Jade beat the eggs with paprika and pepper and poured them into a second, buttered skillet. She stirred the mixtures frequently, pausing only to grate some of the cheese into the eggs. Finally, when the eggs were done, she divided everything onto three plates.

"Voilà," she said as she served them. "Home-fried potatoes with ham and scrambled eggs." She went back to the kitchen and returned with the coffeepot and a loaf of bread.

"This smells delicious, Jade," said Avery. "Doesn't it, love?"

Beverly's mouth was already full of food. She settled for nodding vigorously. "I can see why you didn't hire a cook," she said once she'd swallowed.

"Just a basic Western breakfast," Jade said, "but equally delicious for a late supper."

"Maybe we should hire you," said Avery. "Except I'd never see tea again, would I?"

Jade apologized and started to rise. Avery stopped her with a "Don't trouble yourself," and went to the pantry to rummage around for tea. He returned juggling a teapot, loose tea, a creamer, a cozy, and the sugar bowl. Jade assisted him in setting the supplies on the table.

"Sure you left anything in the pantry, Avery?" Jade asked.

"I couldn't find any lemons," he said. "And I must go back for the kettle of water."

This time Jade told him to sit and fetched the hot water herself. "So what do you make of the Stokes murder?" she asked while she poured water into the pot.

"Most curious," said Avery. "I met the man, but I can't recall much about him. What about you, my dear?" he asked Beverly. "Do you recollect anything about this person?"

Beverly shook her head. "Cannot say that I do." She put the cozy over the teapot to keep it warm while it brewed. "I think I met his wife once after church. Quiet little creature."

"Physically beaten?" asked Jade.

"Not exactly," said Beverly. "Those women seem to pull into themselves. When you do get them to speak, they're always so apologetic. Always assuming they are at fault." Bev shook her head, her corn silk blond curls jiggling just above her shoulders. "She seemed to have built barricades and was in for a long siege. I remember thinking of that old phrase about still waters and all that."

"So," Jade summarized, "to keep with this fortress metaphor, you had the impression that she had hidden capabilities, possibly even the ability to attack."

"I suppose I did, though it could be that she was merely planning her escape. But it's hard to imagine any woman leaving her baby behind," added Beverly. She placed a slender hand on her bulging tummy, an action that spoke of both possessiveness and protection. "And how perfectly awful for poor Maddy to raise her hopes about adopting, only to have the child swept away from her like that. I feel dreadful going on and on about ours in my letters. Do you really think that was Mrs. Stokes' baby?"

Jade nodded as she swallowed her coffee. "An unhappy wife making plans. But she'd need resources. A boat ticket to England costs money. Mrs. Berryhill said Alice Stokes' family all died of typhus at the start of the war. That's why she married Stokes, someone to take care of her. And she seemed to slip away without telling anyone. No one can even tell her that her husband's dead. She might want to come home or at least have her son rejoin her."

"For myself, I would be interested in knowing how many people this Stokes was blackmailing," said Avery. "Finch should interview that Berryhill lad. Harley, is it? Or that other man, Griswell." He looked at Jade. "Or perhaps you should."

Jade poured another cup of coffee for herself and buttered a slice of bread. "I *could* do that, when I get back tomorrow, but I don't know that the boy would talk to me. *You* should see him, Avery. Have a man-to-man talk with him."

"He doesn't know me at all," protested Avery.

Beverly pulled the cozy off the teapot and poured for her husband and herself. "Then order something, my dear," she suggested, "fifty pounds of flour or something else rather large, and have the boy deliver it. When he comes, I'll stuff him with cake and you interrogate him. It's all very simple."

"Not so simple, my love," said Avery as he poured milk into Beverly's tea and added a sugar cube to his own. "You forget that we have no cook, and hence, no cake."

"Then I'll open a tin of biscuits and ply him with those. Sweets are all one and the same to a growing boy, I should think."

Jade chuckled at her friend's scheming. "Then I'll leave you to that job," she said and stood. "In the meantime, I'll wash the dishes and hit the sack. I have an early date with an airplane tomorrow, assuming that Sam is still letting me go along."

"Convince him that he needs you either to fly or to work his camera," said Beverly. "But don't tell him or the Thompsons that we're back. We want to surprise them all with a party tomorrow evening. Just get them to come to the house at seven."

Jade stacked the plates on top of one another. "I doubt I'll get them to come, Bev, not without giving away your secret. You know Maddy and Neville don't leave their farm very often, and they were just here this weekend for the fair and the dance."

Beverly frowned. "I'll think of something. Perhaps I—" Her words were interrupted by a commotion outside as someone drove fast into the lane. "Whoever could that be?"

Jade put the plates back on the table and went to the window. "It's Neville," she said. "And he looks worried, too." Jade opened the door just as Neville got to the top step, her mind racing with horrid possibilities: Maddy mauled by a lion, their house burned down, Sam crashing.

"We need you, Jade," he said. "Sam's collapsed in a raging fever."

CHAPTER 11

It's hard to imagine recovering from severe injuries resulting from these
fierce exploits, but that's when the valor of a warrior shows through.
Healers will remove splintered bone, rejoin the broken ends,
and sew up the wound with sinew. If this cannot be done,
the healer will make a ligature and cut off the limb, all without
benefit of a sedative.

—The Traveler

"WHAT HAPPENED?" JADE asked as she ran to the edge of the porch. She peered over Neville's shoulder toward his truck as though she expected to see Sam lying in it. Avery hurried up behind her, while Beverly struggled to rise out of her chair.

Neville blinked several times in rapid succession. "A-Avery?" he stammered.

Avery put his hand on Neville's right shoulder and drew him into the house. "That's right, old friend. We just arrived today. Sit down." He pushed him into a nearby chair. "Have a brandy. My stars, man, you look awful."

"I'm fine," said Neville, bouncing back up immediately.

Jade, in the meantime, had grabbed a red-and-black bag woven from wool in serpentine zigzags and diamond shapes, a gift from a grateful Berber clan. She threw anything useful that she could think of into it: jerky from dried antelope meat, her flashlight, matches, and a pocket compass, among other things. If she was going to be gone for a while, she wanted to be ready for anything. "You said Sam's already in the hospital? What happened to him?"

"He went to his room not long after you left. Said his head felt like a rhino was inside slamming against his skull and that his back and legs ached. Maddy called him for afternoon tea, but we didn't think much of it when he didn't respond. After all, the man looked exhausted. But when she went to take him something to eat later, she found him soaked in sweat and raging out of his mind. It took two of my men to help me get him into the truck."

"Malaria?" asked Beverly.

Neville nodded. "That's what the doctors at the hospital think. A look at his blood under the microscope should prove it."

"What can we do to help?" asked Avery.

"Nothing." Neville nodded toward Beverly. "I should think it would be risky letting your wife go to the hospital. Never know what a person can catch there. But Sam's still thrashing and the nurses are having a terrible time getting any quinine in him. We thought maybe if Jade were with him, he might recognize her and settle a bit."

"Is Maddy there now?" asked Jade.

Neville shook his head. "There wasn't room enough for her in the truck since my men rode with me to hold Sam down."

"Delirious from fever, I imagine," said Avery, his face taut with concern.

"How horrid," said Beverly. "Oh, if only Dr. Burkitt were back."

"If Burkitt were back," said Neville, "he'd have had Sam stripped down to nothing. It's his favorite treatment for *any* fever."

Jade gave Beverly a quick hug. "Don't wait up for me." She turned to leave, stopped, and added, "For that matter, don't expect me back anytime tomorrow either."

"I'll come to the hospital tomorrow morning," Avery called to Jade's back.

Jade simply waved goodbye without turning around and headed for her motorcycle. "I'll follow you there, Neville," she said as she pulled down her goggles. Neville nodded, started his truck, and led the way to the hospital.

Most of Nairobi had been built in flat, swampy land near the Nairobi River with little thought to clean air, water, or sanitation. The European hospital, however, was constructed on a hill on the northeast side of town not far from the Government House. Unlike much of the city, it possessed a tolerable sewer system, which drained into a septic tank. Both the airy elevation and the decent sanitation increased the odds that anyone brought there sick would actually recover. It was a welcome idea in Jade's mind, which churned with concerns.

Sam figured into several troubling thoughts. She felt his attraction keenly, but always with an underlying wariness, like a prey being tempted by the all too irresistible bait. She knew that once she gave in, she would be hooked. Married.

Caged. In a way she understood the plight of those leopard cubs. They would have a good life in the zoo. They'd be pampered, fed, cared for, and never know the threat of death by some set of thrashing hooves or a bullet. But at what price? Oh certainly, Sam said he loved her adventuresome spirit, but later, would he expect her to settle into a more moderate routine? Already he'd disapproved of her newest job and demanded her promise to act more sedately.

She thought about Beverly, so happy in her impending

motherhood. Where was the Beverly she'd once known? The Beverly who threw all caution to the wind on an ambulance run had become the Beverly who also worried whenever Jade got a little too daring. Maybe, like the leopards, there wasn't any place for the free spirit anymore. *Am I a dying breed?*

Another part of Jade told her that Sam was different. He wouldn't cage her. She could trust him. But just recently he'd been gruff, and Jade worried that she'd offended him somehow. She'd been right all along. He hadn't been well, but her suggesting it had angered him, pushing her away. *How ironic. Maybe my worry about losing my independence is a moot point.*

Then there was that nasty bit of business involving Stokes. Sam, it seemed, had become Finch's key suspect, and while Jade didn't believe Sam had killed Stokes, some supposed eyewitness did. Had the real killer seen the argument and taken advantage of it to kill Stokes and then blame Sam? That last thought made Jade shudder.

Her reflections ended as Neville left his men in the truck and led Jade into the hospital. They headed for Sam's ward, where a zealous nurse in stiffly starched whites stopped them.

"Visiting hours are over," she said. "You must return tomorrow."

Jade didn't intend any such thing. "I've come to see the American Sam Featherstone." She kept her tone cool, nonadversarial, and very matter-of-fact, hoping that she spoke with an assured authority.

The nurse immediately looked her over, taking in the dusty boots and jodhpurs. "Mr. Featherstone," she repeated. "Then you must be Jenny?"

Jade felt a momentary sting, knowing that Sam had called

for his plane instead of her. She didn't show it. "Yes," she answered without hesitation.

"I'll take you there right away. The doctor thinks you might be able to calm his delirium. We haven't been able to do much with him. Can't even draw blood safely." She nodded to Neville. "You shall have to wait until tomorrow, though, sir. Hospital rules."

Jade turned to Neville. "You'd better get yourself and your men back home. Maddy will be anxious enough. Thanks for coming for me."

The nurse marched ahead of Jade down a long corridor, turning right into one of the side rooms, a ward for male patients. Rows of beds, most empty, lined both walls with a narrow walkway between them. A few men lay sleeping under white sheets. One watched Jade pass by.

Jade had no trouble telling which bed was Sam's. She heard his moans as soon as she entered the room, and they tore into her heart. For a moment she felt transported back to the battlefields, where she'd helped to load the wounded. *All those beautiful, brave young men.* As Jade drew nearer, she could see that they had strapped Sam into the bed around his chest and upper arms and again around his knees, but in his fevered delirium he still thrashed against the restraints.

"Haven't you gotten *any* quinine in him yet?" Jade asked.

"Some," said the nurse, "by pinching his nose shut and forcing his mouth open, but I'm afraid he's vomited most of it back out."

She knelt beside the bed. "Sam, I'm here. Sam. Can you hear me? It's Jade."

"Jade?" snapped the nurse. "*You* said your name was Jenny."

"It's a nickname," said Jade with a dismissive wave. She turned back to the feverish man lying drenched on the bed. His cheeks looked sunken, emphasizing the bold, straight nose that grew from his brow. His gaunt appearance made Jade shudder. Sweat trickled from his high forehead and pooled briefly on his pillow before soaking into the casing. His lips worked as he struggled to give voice to his deliriums and his left foot shifted restlessly under the sheets. Jade noticed that his right leg disappeared about midcalf.

"We removed his prosthetic leg," said the doctor who had appeared at her elbow.

Jade picked up a cloth and patted his sopping brow. "Sam," she called again, this time getting closer to his ear. For a second, his moans stopped, and his eyelids flickered. "Rest easy, Sam. No one's going to hurt you. We want to help you."

The doctor held a glass to Sam's lips. "Mr. Featherstone, you must drink this."

Sam's left forearm flew up and he swatted at the doctor's hand. "German swine! You'll get nothing from me!"

"He apparently thinks it's the war, and the Germans have him prisoner," said the doctor.

Jade felt her stomach wrench. He'd never given any hint that he'd been taken prisoner, but then like most soldiers, he didn't like to talk about the war. For that matter, neither did she. *Is it true?* She remembered Sam talking about interrogation tactics back at police headquarters.

"Give me that," said Jade. She sniffed it and smelled the lime, which made the bitter quinine in ordinary tonic water remotely palatable. But in here, the quinine dosage was higher. "He's not British. I don't think he's used to your usual sundowner," she said, referring to the nightly gin and tonic.

"I have an idea. Do you have a lemon? And I need an empty glass."

"Nurse, fetch a lemon sliced in two," ordered the doctor. He looked at Jade. "Don't Americans like limes?"

Jade shrugged. "Never had one myself before I came here." The nurse returned with the two halves of a lemon and the empty glass. Jade took the glass of tonic water from the doctor and squeezed one lemon half into it. "When I give the word, put the *empty* glass in his right hand."

She held the second lemon half under Sam's nose, her fingertips brushing his mustache. "Sam," she said softly, "it's a hot summer day. You've been working hard in the field. It's time to come to the porch and drink a cool glass of lemonade." She nodded to the doctor. "Now."

Sam's lips moved in a voiceless response. His nostrils twitched, then flared as he inhaled the clean scent of lemon. After a moment, his right hand gripped the empty glass and lifted at the elbow. At the same time, Jade held the glass of quinine water to his lips. Sam drank slowly at first; then, with the doctor supporting Sam's head, he gulped the rest just as he might have drained a glass of lemonade back on his home farm in Indiana.

"That was delicious, wasn't it, Sam?" Jade said, her voice soothing and calm. "Now you should take an afternoon snooze here on the hammock."

"Work . . . Jenny," Sam muttered.

"Don't worry about Jenny," said Jade. "She's fine. I'm taking care of her."

Sam's body relaxed as he drifted into sleep. The doctor took a syringe full of Sam's blood for observation.

"That was brilliant, miss," said the doctor. "I'm most grateful to you."

"Once his fever's down, you'll probably find him more pliable," said Jade. "But you might have to resort to this deception again. If you don't object, I'd like to stay by him until then."

"Not at all," said the doctor, ignoring the nurse's shocked glare. "Your presence appears to me most soothing to him. But I'm confused. I thought you were Jenny. You're not?"

Jade shook her head.

"Then is this someone we should send for?"

Jade's lips twitched in a brief, wry smile. "Hardly. It's his plane, Doctor. A pilot's first love."

"Oh, I see," mumbled the doctor. Then his eyes opened wide and he held Jade's gaze. "I daresay, that's a bit of a stunner for you, miss . . . er, what *is* your name?"

"Jade del Cameron. And it's probably no more than I deserve." She smiled weakly. "He's a good man and a war veteran, as you probably gathered." Jade nodded toward the stump where his lower leg should have been. "I expect you to treat him as such."

"Of course, Miss del Cameron. All our patients receive the best of care. I must own I wondered about that leg. Tough break for the chap, but I've seen worse."

Jade met his eyes. "So have I."

Something in Jade's emerald eyes made the doctor wince, as though she projected all the pain and sorrow she'd ever experienced hauling the wounded and mangled in her ambulance. He stood. "Nurse Harper will be in the ward, of course, and I will make rounds again in a few hours. If he, or you, should need anything, let us know."

Jade thanked them both, then settled into a wooden chair by Sam's head. She folded her arms across her chest and leaned her head back against the wall. *Might as well catch a bit of sleep before Sam wakes again. It's going to be a long night.*

She catnapped, slipping out of sleep every time the nurse walked by or whenever Sam shifted in his bed. Then, as soon as her brain registered that all was well, or at least not any worse, Jade drifted back into her fragmented dreams. Her body rested, but her mind worked at sorting and organizing her many questions and her scant information. As a consequence, she dreamed of Biscuit chasing raggedy, half-starved zebras into newspaper offices full of orphaned babies.

The doctor returned at four a.m., and together, they repeated the last ruse and tricked Sam into swallowing the bitter concoction. He thrashed less than before, and drank willingly if less eagerly. This time he didn't speak. He continued to perspire, but seemed less feverish than before. The nurse brought fresh sheets and a clean nightshirt.

"Wait outside, miss. It would not be proper for a"—she paused, eyed Jade's clothes, and nearly choked on the next word—"*lady* to be present while the patient was bathed and dressed."

"I was an ambulance driver during the war," Jade said. "I've been around men while they're being cared for." She pointed to the restraints. "What if he gets violent again? You know you shouldn't be doing this alone. If you don't want *me* around, then get a second nurse in here or the doctor."

"The doctor is resting at the moment," said the nurse, "and we only have one nurse per ward during night shift."

"Then you're stuck with me."

The nurse scowled. "Very well, but I do not approve."

"I'll keep that in mind," said Jade. "Now, you're in charge. What do you want me to do?"

Knowing that Jade was willing to follow her directions placated the nurse's sensibilities. "Undo the chest strap only. If he begins to thrash, apply firm but gentle pressure to his shoulders and I'll redo the restraints. We must work quickly."

Jade did as she was directed and kept her hands on Sam's shoulders, moving one only when the nurse pulled the backless shirt from first one arm, then the other, and again when she slipped the clean linen gown on him. She felt the firmness of Sam's muscles under her hands and recalled the night he'd held her close in the hammock on Mount Marsabit, protecting her against the cold with his body heat. That night, her own overpowering fatigue had dissolved in his strong but gentle embrace.

The nurse quickly washed Sam while Jade kept her gaze focused on his face and the mop of damp brown hair that clung to his brow. They undid the leg restraints next.

"Roll him toward you," said the nurse. Jade complied and the nurse slipped the wet sheet from under him and slid in a fresh one. "Now I'll turn him toward me, and you finish that side of the sheets."

Jade tugged the sheet tight, averting her eyes from Sam's exposed rear. They rolled Sam onto his back again and pulled up a fresh top sheet, leaving the restraints off. When they were done, the nurse once again looked Jade over.

"You're a cool assistant—I give you that," the woman said. "At least you're not one of those flighty women who faint."

Jade smiled at the term "flighty." For her, it had a different meaning. "Thank you, Nurse. Mr. Featherstone appears to be calmer now. I doubt you'll need any help next time."

"His fever *is* dropping. He shouldn't sweat out another set of sheets so quickly." The nurse started to leave, then turned back to Jade. "You should consider becoming a nurse yourself."

Jade shook her head. "I dealt too closely with death during the war. I doubt I could maintain my composure as well as you do."

The nurse accepted the compliment with a nod and returned to her rounds. Jade went back to her hard chair and another attempt at sleep. She managed half an hour. Then the iron grip of a hand clamped on her wrist startled her awake. She turned to see a pair of black eyes staring at her.

"Sam," she said, "you're awake." He only stared, his eyes slightly glazed as though he was trying to comprehend the situation. Jade came to his rescue with a whispered explanation. "You're in the hospital, Sam. In Nairobi," she added, lest he was still feverish and under the impression he'd been shot down.

He tried to speak and managed to croak out, "Why?"

"Malaria, from the looks of it. I'll bet you haven't been using your mosquito netting. You've had a pretty wild fever. I've seen broncs that bucked less than you were doing."

He tried to rise and fell back against the bed.

"Lie still, Sam." Jade took a cloth, dampened it in a basin, and wiped his face. "You had me pretty worried." She noticed his left foot shift, searching for the right one. Did he feel his missing leg, she wondered, or was he only trying to find out if the wooden one was attached?

"Should I call the nurse for you, Sam? Is there anything you want?"

His grip on her wrist tightened. "What day is it?" he said, his voice weak and breathy.

Jade placed her other hand on his, stroking it, hoping

he'd relax the pressure on her wrist. "It's not yet dawn on Monday."

His nearly black eyes took on a pleading note. "I need to leave. The job. The Jenny."

Jade shook her head. "You can't fly right now. They'll have to wait on their rhino."

"No!" he said more forcefully. "They can't wait. Contract."

Jade sighed. Although the plane and a spare engine had only cost him two hundred fifty dollars from the Curtiss Company, Sam had spent a lot more having it shipped overseas last year. He'd put nearly everything else he owned into the Akeley motion picture camera and film. This job was important to him. "I could talk to them if you want," she said.

"No! You fly."

CHAPTER 12

Initiation into manhood means respect, freedom, and the fellowship of other warriors. Initiation into womanhood means the end of freedom and marriage to a junior elder at least twice as old as she. Yet the women sing constantly.

—The Traveler

You FLY! THE command echoed in Jade's ears, stirring myriad conflicting emotions. Exuberance and excitement clashed with sadness and fear. She thrilled at the thought of going solo, then rebuked herself for forgetting the cause of this honor. Sam was still in a bad way. But a sense of pride surfaced, because she knew that she could help calm his mind by removing one of his concerns. Fear that she wasn't ready to fly plowed right into pride. *What if I wreck his plane? He'll never forgive me.* A sneering voice reminded her that she needn't fret there. If she wrecked his plane, she'd probably be dead anyway.

Jade leaned closer to Sam and kissed him lightly on his forehead. "Sam. I—"

She was interrupted by the renewed grip on her wrist. "Please," he pleaded.

Jade patted his hand. "All right, Sam. If it will help you to rest, then I'll take her up."

He sighed, closed his eyes, and collapsed back on his pillow. His right hand slipped from her wrist and fell to his side. Jade readjusted his cover sheet before reaching into her bag for a pencil and her notebook. She tore out a back page and wrote a note to Avery, remembering his plans to visit in the morning.

Avery: Sam had a job scouting for rhino. He's asked me to go up for him. I'll be home later this evening.

Jade

She looked over the brief note, decided it was adequate, and folded the paper. She wrote *Avery* on the outside, and set it on the chair seat.

The nurse saw her head for the door. "You are leaving now?"

"Yes," said Jade. "Thank you for taking such excellent care of him." She pointed back to the chair. "I left a note for a friend of Mr. Featherstone's, someone who'll come by later."

"What shall I tell Mr. Featherstone if he wakes and finds you're gone?"

"Tell him I'm taking care of Jenny."

When Jade arrived at the Thompsons' farm, the sun was just breaking over the horizon, and the warmth felt good on a chilly morning. The Thompsons were already giving directions to their workers for the day. The smaller fly crop had already been picked and pulped. Now it waited for the fermenter to loosen the residue left on the beans in preparation for washing.

Biscuit greeted Jade first with a chirp and a head butt. A

small black feather with white spots stuck on his chin told Jade that her pet had found a wild guineafowl for breakfast.

"Jade," called Madeline when she spied her friend, "how is Sam? We're going to drive in and see him later this afternoon if we can get away."

"He's doing better, Maddy," Jade said. "We managed to get the quinine in him and his fever finally broke. I left him sleeping, and Avery's going to spend time with him this morning. They're limiting his guests anyway." She clapped Neville on the shoulder. "Thank you, Neville, for bringing him in last evening and for coming to get me."

Neville's mouth gaped, as though taken aback by the thanks. "Of course," he said after a moment's pause. "One might deal with lesser bouts of the blasted disease at home but not one of that scale. The good news is some types of malaria don't seem to come back again, so this may be it for Sam."

"It was good of you, Jade," said Maddy, "to come out here so early to give us news."

"It's not my only reason," said Jade.

"Yes, of course," said Madeline. "You came to tell us that the Dunburys have come home. Such a surprise. I cannot imagine what you must have thought. Neville, of course, told me yesterday evening. I must own that I would never have expected Beverly to make such a long voyage in her condition, but I'm sure she's glowing."

Jade waited until her friend had stopped prattling, something Maddy did when worried. "No more surprised than I was. It appears they missed Africa and all of us too much to wait. Bev's fine. She wanted to surprise you by having you come to the house later today."

Madeline's eyes brightened and her smile relaxed the worry lines on her forehead. "Of course, we shall come. After we see Sam, we'll go straight to their home." She turned to Neville and peered up at him pleadingly, one palm resting on his shirtfront. "Won't we, Neville? We won't stay the night, of course. It would only be for the afternoon."

Neville patted his wife's hand. "Of course, darling. If the coffee washer operates, we can take one more afternoon off. Kimathi can see that the final work gets done."

"Speaking of Kimathi, I need to borrow him this morning to help me drag out the plane and then pull the prop." Jade explained the need to take Sam's plane up and scout for a young rhino. "I won't keep him long. He'll be back before it's time for your elevenses."

"Oh, Jade," said Madeline, "are you ready to solo?"

She nodded. "I can handle it. I've had the best teachers." The plain truth was, Jade herself didn't feel as confident as she sounded. She knew she'd only logged a grand total of sixteen hours of flight time in her life. But Sam trusted her and she couldn't let him down.

"Do you need my help as well?" asked Neville.

"Thanks but no. Kimathi has been through this procedure many times with Sam, so he knows what to do, and it only takes one man to turn the prop."

Neville called for Kimathi, a tall Kikuyu who had taken on the role of foreman several years ago. "Memsabu Simba Jike will fly Bwana Mti Mguu's aeroplane," he said, referring to Sam by the Africans' name for him, "tree leg." "Come back here when she goes up, but listen for her return and help her again."

"I'll buzz the house when I'm back," Jade suggested. "You won't be able to miss me."

Biscuit started to follow her as she climbed back aboard her motorcycle and invited Kimathi to ride aboard the seat over the rear wheel. "No, Biscuit, stay." She didn't want to worry about him being in the way during takeoff. "Maddy, can you get Biscuit?"

Madeline took Biscuit by the collar and held on to him. "Be careful," she called over the noise of Jade's cycle. It was an unnecessary admonition. Jade had every intention of doing just that. She adjusted the throttle, and she and Kimathi rode off north to the edge of Neville's farm and Sam's makeshift hangar.

Jade first reoiled all the engine holes. Then she began her walk around the plane, checking the tail skid, twanging all the wires to see if they were tight and unfrayed. She studied the fabric skin on the wings, looking for any rents or holes. She added a few drops of oil to the hinges on the ailerons as well as those on the rear elevators and rudder. After that, she squatted down and inspected the wheels, making sure that the bungee cords that acted as shock absorbers were tight and the bracing wires were intact. What should have taken an hour took two as she did everything twice and more slowly.

In her mind, she re-created Sam's motions, never deviating from his routine lest she overlook anything. But imagining Sam brought back her last sight of him in the hospital, haggard and worn. She tightened her lips and forced herself to focus.

This is no time to get maudlin.

The honor of his trust in her was more than counterbalanced by the burden of responsibility. Jade was a good mechanic, having maintained her old flivver, or Model T, ambulance during the war. She also felt at home with her Indian Big Twin motorcycle's motor. But all those machines had been hers *and* they stayed on the ground.

While Kimathi stood by, Jade stood on the wheels and

drained a little fluid from the bottom of the fuel tank, removing any water that might have settled. Then Kimathi pumped gasoline from Sam's barrel into a *debe*, climbed up onto a stack of crates, and filled the tank while Jade inspected the rubber hosing. She filled the radiator, checked the prop, and finally decided she was ready to take the plane up. She and Kimathi grabbed the plane's wing holds and moved it out of the little hangar and into the slight morning breeze.

Sam had purchased a trainer, a plane with controls in both cockpits, but instruments only in the rear one. In practice, a trained pilot sat in the front while the student flew from the rear. If the student "froze" or otherwise put them in danger, the real pilot could take over. Jade had sat back here before, but this time there was no one in the front. The sight of that empty front seat sent a quiver into her stomach.

Get ahold of yourself!

She put her left foot in the recessed stirrup and stepped up. Behind the pilot's head was a little space to store a canteen or some other small item. Jade shoved her Berber pouch in there next to Sam's logbook and a spare canteen. Time to mount up. She swung her right leg over the side and pulled her left leg in. The narrow cockpit gave the pilot just enough room to sit, not to fidget. This backseat felt even more constrained because Sam's friends, the "Bert Boys," had rigged his rudder bar to work from a hand control as well as with the feet. Sam had discovered that his wooden leg didn't impede controlling the rudder as much as everyone had feared, so he rarely used the new controls. But they were still there, and her knee brushed them when she tightened her restraining belt.

This is it, girl. From her elevated position, she watched Kimathi move nearer to the propeller.

As before, Jade retarded the magneto switch and primed

the engine. Then she turned on the switch and cracked the throttle. "Contact," she shouted over the side. Kimathi swung the propeller and moved out of the way. Once again, Jade was caught by the sensation that the plane, like a good horse, had a will to run and only waited for Jade to let her have her head. Jade opened up the throttle, and swept down the field, keeping the plane on the ground until the rpm gauge registered fourteen hundred rpms. She felt the plane jostle over the bumpy terrain as the grasses turned into a blurring rush of olive green. Above, to her right, she spied a black-shouldered kite, his wings outstretched as if in rapturous praise. Then, with a pull on the stick, she experienced the sensation of being suspended as she let the Jenny rise and joined the bird, soaring over the grasslands.

The cool air helped with takeoff, especially as the morning sun did its part in creating breezes. The OX-5 engine sounded soft and sweet to her ears, its low, throaty purr reminiscent of Biscuit's peaceful rumblings. Beyond that, silence. She increased her speed, climbed gently to one thousand feet, and began her turn. As she circled back over the hangar, she waved to Kimathi. He waved back and started the walk back to the house and his duties in the coffee fields. Jade was left alone, swaddled in fine Irish linen and a sapphire sky.

She peered over the side, feeling the slipstream caress her face. Keeping the sun on her right, she headed north toward Fort Hall, then due west toward the more open land. Bob Perkins had thought Sam might find a young rhino near the Maasai reserves. She'd already decided that the most interesting route would be to head to Naivasha, skirt the lake's southern side, and slip southwest into the rich plains between the Mau Escarpment and the Ngong Hills.

Maps didn't always mean much out here. Most of the existing ones were old and didn't include the newer settlements or show anything beyond the farthest reaches of the Uganda railroad. Rivers were scrawled more or less haphazardly with bends where they didn't exist.

Sam had taken the best map he could get, made notations, and even drawn in a few of the newer homesteads and dirt tracts. Jade had found it with his logbook in the same tiny compartment where she'd stowed her water. She'd looked over the map that morning, plotted a course, and written down compass bearings. If she spotted a rhino, she needed to be able to get the location back to her employers as accurately as possible. Check that. She needed to get the information to Sam to give to them. This was *his* job.

She planned to fly within sight of recognizable landmarks as much as possible. Below her stood Fort Hall, with its lone trading post and civic station. Just southwest of there they had caught the first leopard. That meant Alwyn Chalmers' maize farm was close by. She doubted his missing polo pony was still alive, but if it was, she might spot it from the air and help the man out.

Horses were social animals. If it hadn't come home, then it had probably found company with its closest African relation and was keeping to the edge of a zebra herd. Jade spied what looked like a herd of something a few degrees south of her intended path. She banked, her feet adjusting the rudder bar while her right hand on the stick moved the ailerons to keep a smooth turn. Once again, her thoughts turned to Sam and his description of flying.

Most of it isn't done with hands or feet, he'd said. *You fly with your head and by the seat of your pants.* Then he joked that since some pilots he'd known had their heads up their rears, they thought they could fly better than him since the communication from brain to butt was shorter. *It doesn't work that way,* he'd concluded.

The herd was a mix of zebra and wildebeest. Jade pushed the stick forward and dropped enough to see the animals better. Nothing that looked like a pony stood out. *Too bad.* She climbed back up and headed toward the railroad crossing at Naivasha.

Naivasha, home to cattle auctions and a gorgeous lake, boasted a hotel in addition to the railway station. Recently it had become a popular holiday spot for Nairobiites looking to get away for a day, hoping to see the wildlife they had evicted from their own lands. She turned south just past the railway station and followed the rail line. A black vehicle approached from the west, one of the district farmers perhaps. To her right, Naivasha Lake gleamed, a cobalt gem circled by pink flamingos.

Jade flew toward the lake and dropped to get a better look. Two hippos lounged in the papyrus-fringed shallows, and several pelicans sat on the shore in attendance. An African fish eagle rose beside her, riding a thermal. She took in his white head and back flanked by great black wings. Her heart beat faster as she shared his dominion. Deciding she'd better not share it too closely, she veered toward the land just as the eagle dove for a meal. Jade tore her attention from the freshwater paradise and concentrated on the grasslands. After all, she wouldn't spot any rhino in the lake.

Mount Longonot rose in a graceful blue haze to the south with more than six miles of scrubby plains between it and the lake. Jade held the stick between her knees and consulted the map. She was in the Great Rift. About twenty miles west of her position rose the Mau Escarpment, but before that, there was a spot identified as Hell's Gate, where red volcanic rock

jutted out in dramatic columnar walls and steam vents exhaled Satan's breath. Maasai land. Maybe not a good place to
fly. She'd stick to these plains.

A quick glance over the side revealed a herd of grazing buffalo, then several giraffe browsing among the acacia
trees. Nearby roamed some tiny creatures that might have
been dik-diks. No rhino. As she again turned the Jenny's nose
west, she spied a decrepit-looking farmhouse nestled against
Longonot's gentler tip. The dirt tract leading up to it looked
fresh enough to still be in use. Jade didn't see any evidence of
cattle or crops and wondered if the place had been recently
abandoned. Then she noted the even more dilapidated truck
parked under a lone acacia tree. *Perhaps not completely abandoned.*

Jade crisscrossed the plains twice before fortune blessed
her just south of the lake's lowest reach. If her eyes didn't
deceive her, a pair of black rhinos lounged under an acacia
just ahead. She passed by, but the tree blocked part of her
view. One definitely looked like a calf, but she couldn't quite
make out the mother. She circled and came back around.
Sure enough, there was a calf, but now Jade could tell that the
mother was not lounging. She was dead, and the baby had no
intention of leaving the only protection it had ever known.

"Hot biscuits!" Jade exclaimed. Many collectors, she
knew, captured calves by shooting the mother, a practice Jade
abhorred. Since a mother rhino wasn't easily run off from her
young, killing her tended to be the only way to get the calf.
Jade wondered how this mother had died. The railroad was
only a few miles east of them. Perhaps she'd had a run-in
with the locomotive.

Rhinos had been known to charge the puffing engines,
usually to the animal's demise. If this female had survived

the immediate confrontation, her injuries might have been severe enough to eventually take their toll. Most animals died on the spot when they'd been dealt a bullet to the heart or brain, but as Jade knew from her experience in Tsavo over a year ago, someone always forgot to tell the rhino. They had a tendency to run on pure momentum and anger.

Another war casualty. But, like the leopard cubs, this calf had survived its brush with civilization. She'd turn back, pass on the information, and then let her bosses pick up the calf.

Her engine shuddered. *What the hell?* Maybe she'd just hit one of those invisible booby traps where the air changed density. She was close enough to Hell's Gate that there might be steam pockets where rising gases supplanted the oxygen needed for the engine to operate.

The engine sputtered again, an old man's cough replacing the throaty purr.

Definitely time to turn back. If she could get as far as Naivasha, she could put down and get tools from someone there.

But then, the engine went dead, and only primeval silence filled the cockpit.

CHAPTER 13

Warriors value the companionship of other warriors and, at some point later in their career, will live in the manyatta, *a warrior village. We might think of it as an exclusive men's club.*

—The Traveler

SAM WOKE TO the pungent scent of disinfectant and the feeling that someone had replaced his tongue with a cotton wad. He didn't think he could form enough spit to shine an ant's shoes. He forced his eyes open and stared at the arrangement of beds, ordered like a barracks. His mind felt as foggy as his mouth, and he couldn't comprehend the sight. He thrashed and his right arm brushed the top of the chair, knocking Jade's note to the floor and under the bed.

It must have been those dreams. So real. He could hear the roar of wind race past his ears, feel the plane buck against a strong crosswind, forced into a turn in a dogfight. But the wildest part was that he was flying a Jenny against the Germans. *I flew a Spad.*

Sam closed his eyes and tried to gather his wits. There had been other sensations, other illusions or, more accurately, delusions. He'd felt the phantom pains in his missing lower leg and absentmindedly tried to ease it by rubbing the other leg against it. But he couldn't move. His legs were pinned. He shuddered and once again felt the terror of his capture and imprisonment. *Maybe I wasn't dreaming. Maybe I'm still in the camp.* He pushed the fear further back in his mind before it could take hold. Instead, he focused on one of the last thoughts he remembered. He could have sworn that he was home in Battle Ground, Indiana. He knew it was impossible, yet the feelings were so genuine, he could smell the fresh-cut hay and feel the sweat on his back. His mother brought him something to drink, lemonade, and he gulped it down before rejoining his brothers in the field. *Gotta make hay while the sun shines.*

He thought he remembered hearing Jade's voice once, but that made no sense. *Jade doesn't live in Indiana.* He drifted back into oblivion once more.

You can do this, Jade told herself. *It's just a landing.* The problem was finding the best spot. With Hell's Gate in front of her and to the south, and the lake to the north, her options were limited. The beautiful grasslands had too many obstacles in the manner of wildlife.

Even without power, the plane could glide for a while, especially if she could catch an updraft and ride it back up a little, like a vulture. It gave her a bit of time. She glided west, riding into the airstream pulled down from the distant Mau Escarpment, which created a small headwind. Huge cliffs, made from column after column of basalt, acted like a gate, beckoning her to enter the wild lands beyond. A few isolated volcanic towers dotted the landscape to the south. Here all the air became heated by the sun baking the red rocks. Too many rocks. She needed to set down now. She spied a level-looking patch without any wildlife to clutter up a decent runway.

Hard on a plane, colliding with a wildebeest.

Jade was too high to make this field, so she executed a gentle spiral to decrease her altitude. Even then she felt she was coming in too fast, so she used her rudder and turned the plane's nose a few degrees out of the wind in a sideslip, letting the breeze hit the fuselage to act as a brake. *So far so good.* She was now about six feet above ground and had a decent stretch in front of her. She straightened out and put the nose right into the wind.

Jade felt the wheels make contact and eased back on the stick to bring the tail skid down. Immediately she felt the plane jolt and buck. The grass was deceptive. It hid myriad dirt clods, dried dung chips, and volcanic rocks.

The Jenny skidded to a halt with one final buck. Jade jerked forward. Her head struck the panel and she dropped into black silence.

"SAM, ARE YOU awake? My stars, man, you had us worried."

The familiar voice completely disoriented Sam. He stared at his visitor, blinking stupidly, his mouth agape. Finally he managed to croak out one word: "Avery?"

"Well, you recognize me at least. That's something. You look like bloody hell."

Sam's mind worked feverishly to reconcile the facts with this visit. Avery was in London. Avery was talking to him. *I'm in London?*

"Am I dying?"

Avery laughed. "No, man. Just a nasty run of malaria. You'll be right as rain in no time." He patted Sam's shoulder. "Don't blow a gasket trying to make sense of it. I didn't come all the way to Nairobi just to see you. Beverly and I came back because we couldn't stand London anymore. Arrived yesterday just in time to have Neville drop in trying to find Jade. Told us you had collapsed in a raging fever."

Sam groaned. "No wonder . . . I feel like . . . something the mule passed."

"You need some water," said Avery. "Nurse, here please. Bring this man some water."

"There's water in the pitcher there, sir."

"Yes, and it's been sitting here so long it's got fish swimming in it. Now fetch something fresher. Come along, look sharp." He held out the pitcher. "That's a girl."

The nurse grabbed the pitcher and ran off, seemingly eager to put distance between herself and the imperious man in the chair.

"Jade?" asked Sam.

"She came right away. I assume she spent the night by your side. Probably off somewhere trying to take a nap." The nurse returned with the refilled pitcher. "Nurse," said Avery, "when did the young lady who was sitting here leave?"

"I wouldn't know, sir. I only came on duty an hour ago. There was no one here then."

Avery poured a glass of water for Sam and held it while he drank. When Sam was finished, he sank deeper into his pillow.

"Buck up, man. She'll be back," said Avery.

"This is Monday?" Sam asked. Avery nodded. Sam sighed. "I was supposed to be flying this morning. Scouting for a rhino. This just cost me a *lot* of money."

"It's only money. If they really want their blasted rhino, they'll wait and give you another crack at it. After all, it's even more money for them at the end of the line."

Sam shook his head. "They have to ship out soon. Costs too much to wait around." He closed his eyes. "Simple matter of economics." He wondered how long Jade had stayed. He assumed she'd reported to work for Daley and Perkins. Otherwise, Avery would have run into her at his house. In his mind, he could picture her standing by his plane, a stray black curl peeking out from under her soft leather helmet, the chin strap undone. She would be laughing at something, her joy a matter of expectation as they prepared to free themselves from gravity and all their mortal ties to earth. He felt the need to take her in his arms and kiss her. A gentle punch on the arm roused him.

"Sam, perk up. The doctor said you can leave tomorrow, assuming you look a little less like hell. I'll bring round my shaving kit before then."

"What time is it?" Sam asked.

Avery pulled out a gold pocket watch. "Pushing nine o'clock. Tried to see you earlier but you were sound asleep and the nurse wouldn't let me in." He stood to leave. "*This* nurse is all set to run me out already, but I'll be back later and see you all ready for inspection. Oh! I'm supposed to tell you that Beverly apologizes for not being here or sending a pudding or some other concoction. She's interviewing cooks today, so we'll be lucky if we get anything to eat ourselves. She said to tell you she sends her love."

Sam managed a thin smile. "Tell her thanks. I should have asked you how she's doing."

"Healthy as a horse and swelling like a hippopotamus. Now you get some sleep. Ah, here comes your nurse with some lovely gruel." He leaned close to Sam's ear. "I know it's tasteless swill, but take it like a man. I'll try to get back today if I can. Maybe round up a roast chicken?"

"Bring Jade with you."

"I shouldn't think I'll have to. I'll wager she'll be here before the afternoon's out."

JADE DRIFTED IN and out of consciousness, her thoughts meandering like an aged river. At times she felt a breeze caress her cheek and thought she was still flying. Then, at the drone of a fly buzzing about her forehead, she returned to the war and heard the Sopwith Camels pass overhead on their way to the front lines.

She fell asleep, and dreamed of a rearing stallion, pawing the air above Maddy's pregnant body. No, it wasn't Maddy. It was some little blond woman, Mrs. Stokes. The zebra looked sleek and muscular. Then someone rode up on a polo pony and swept the woman away just as the deadly hooves crashed to earth and hammered into Martin Stokes instead.

In a moment the scene changed and Jade was trapped. Through the shadows she detected a pair of pale yellow eyes, snapping cold fire and madness. A leopard? She heard the old blind woman's warning, but there was nowhere to go. The furious animal snarled inches from her face and Jade screamed.

She woke with a start and jerked upright, her own cries ringing in her ears. Momentarily disoriented, she looked around for anything familiar. The problem was, she couldn't recollect what *should* be familiar. Ambulances and trenches? Her head cleared a bit more. No, that was behind her. Nairobi? The Thompsons' house? Her right hand rested on the side of the cockpit.

Sam's plane!

Jade tried to stand, only to be jerked back by a sharp pull to the stomach. The restraints. Her hands fumbled with the buckle.

Don't let the plane be wrecked. Don't let the plane be wrecked!

The restraint came free. Jade clambered over the side and slid to the ground. Her knees buckled under her, and she plopped onto her backside. Her head throbbed and she felt a knot on her temple. *Ouch! Better not get up too fast.* She noted, while she was on the ground, that the plane's fuselage, what she could see of it at least, was intact. The underbelly looked good even if her landing approach didn't.

From her position, a line of scarred earth and flattened grasses appeared to have been plowed by a drunken farmer. *What the hell happened?* She remembered the engine's seductive purr and peering over the side, the slipstream rushing past her ear. The engine had coughed, chugging once like an old man clearing his throat. Then that empty silence such as humans rarely heard except on mountaintops with the rest of the world far away.

"I couldn't have run out of fuel. I'd only been in the air an hour at the most." She should have been able to return with fuel to spare. Jade pulled off her pilot's helmet, releasing a mop of damp black waves. She felt dehydrated, so she stepped onto the stirrup and grabbed her supplies from behind the seat. A long pull of water did a lot toward clearing her head. Jade followed it with a strip of jerky. Then, still chewing, she walked around the plane, examining it carefully.

Everything looked good, and she was just about to feel a bit better when she saw the rip in the right lower wing, where a sharp rock had cut into it.

Hell's bells and little fishes! The rent was less than five inches long, but that was more than she was willing to chance in the air again. Assuming she could get in the air again. Why had the plane acted as if it had had no fuel? She'd watched Kimathi fill the tank. Was there too much water in there? No, she'd drained it off before starting.

Well, there was only one way to check. It was now pushing four o'clock. She'd been unconscious for the better part of the day. Maybe the engine had cooled enough for water to settle. Judging by the high air temperature, she doubted it, but she had to do something. She scrambled up on the wing walk and leaned into the front cockpit to retrieve a small set of tools from under the seat. Then Jade took the cap off her canteen, went to the front, and carefully cracked open the bottom drain valve, preparing to capture a little water or fuel in the cap.

Nothing came out at first; then she saw a drop form around a thin green tip. Jade pulled out a fragment of grass. More fuel dribbled out, so Jade captured some before closing the valve. When she looked at it, she saw some fine sediment.

Someone contaminated the fuel.

But that didn't make sense. True, it may have taken a while for enough sediment to settle down the gravity-fed line to clog it, but it should have happened before she even hit Fort Hall. She dug her flashlight from her bag, stepped back up onto the lower wing walk, and climbed into the front cockpit. From there she shinnied over the windshield and stood, straddling the plane to get a look down into the gas tank. What she saw horrified her.

A thin string hung down inside the tank, stuck gingerly to the lip with the smallest dab of gum arabic. She pulled up the string and found a partially dissolved paper mesh, like a tea bag, dangling at the other end. Inside was a lump of crumbling mud and grass, leaching out a tiny rip in the bottom. It was a booby trap, set to release sediments after the plane had been aloft for a time.

Jade sat down in the shade of a wing to contemplate the ramifications. Someone had tried to kill her. *Why? Who? Wait. Slow down.* That was not the only possibility. Maybe someone wanted only to prevent her from taking off. Either way, this person had played with her life. Cracking up on takeoff could have had its own share of disasters. Was that the intent? To damage the plane so she couldn't fly? Then why not just take a knife and slice the wing's skin or snap a spar? No, the saboteur likely intended for the plane to take off and then crash.

You're not the target.

Sam was supposed to fly this morning. She wasn't even sure anyone else knew she was going along. So who wanted Sam dead and why?

Jade stood and paced, her nervous energy about to explode. She took a deep breath and forced herself to slow down. *Think! Who knew Sam was flying?*

As far as she knew, only Mr. Perkins or Mr. Daley. She had the information from Sam because she hadn't been there when one or the other of them offered him the job. There could have been any number of people within earshot.

Anderson? He might have been with his boss. He certainly didn't like Sam, but Jade couldn't imagine him hating Sam enough to want to kill him. Then again, maybe he'd only intended the plane to sputter to a stop on takeoff.

She thought back to the Sunday afternoon when they had been loading the zebra. Anderson had come on his own in a different, smaller truck. *And he was late.* Had he been back at the hangar then?

None of this helped her situation. Sam was in the hospital

with malaria and she was stuck several miles from Naivasha. Not only couldn't she bring back word on the rhino calf— she couldn't pass on this information to Sam or Inspector Finch. If someone was trying to kill Sam, he could still be in danger.

Why would anyone want to kill Sam? Her mind turned to Anderson again, the only person she knew who had displayed any animosity toward Sam. *Stokes drowned in cattle dip. There's cattle dip at our animal compound.* Jade stopped dead in her tracks. Had Anderson killed Stokes? Was he pinning the blame on Sam? *I've got to tell Finch.*

Jade climbed back up to the rear cockpit and retrieved the map and Sam's logbook. She'd seen a farmhouse near Mount Longonot. Could she reach it and get help? She located Mount Longonot and then tried to pinpoint her own location. She knew she was somewhere in the area the old-timers called Hell's Gate, an area frequented by Maasai.

The Maasai didn't worry her. Well, not much anyway. Cattle disease had taken a toll on the tribe and now they dwelt relatively peacefully in their reserve. Of course, she'd just landed on the edge of it. If her estimated position was correct, she was probably seven miles west of that farmhouse. That meant seven miles of wildlife, and she had no weapon other than the knife in her boot.

The long shadows told her that she was fast running out of daylight. She also worried that there wouldn't be much of a plane left when she eventually returned. By the time the giraffes and other herbivores got done chewing on the doped-up linen skin, some Cape buffalo would probably decide that the wooden frame looked like a dandy back scratcher.

Get ahold of yourself. Sam's safe in the hospital. You're safe in the plane, and the plane's safer with you guarding it. Besides,

Kimathi would tell Neville and Maddy that she wasn't back and they'd send someone to find her. *And how will they do that if they don't know where to look?*

That momentary panic was eased when she remembered that Sam would tell them his flying plans. So it seemed there was nothing to do but get comfortable and wait. Jade's stomach growled and she pulled out another chunk of jerky. She also found Sam's flight jacket in the front cockpit and put it on.

Maybe I should start a fire. Right. With my luck, I'll burn up the plane.

Instead, she pulled out the logbook and browsed through it. Sam had made notations on the scenery and wildlife from each of his flights, some with a little camera drawn in the margins to indicate what would make good aerial footage. He'd been over Thompson falls, noted a hippo pool along the Tana, and jotted notes on some of the more picturesque farms worth filming. Harding's sisal fields didn't show as well from the air as Chalmers' maize. In the margins by Harding's farm, Sam noted a pet zebra trying to mate with a horse. Chalmers' polo ponies and exercise area seemed promising for footage, as did the sheep pens. Following that were notes on aerial Nairobi, including the busy rail yards. Jade shut the book and put it away.

A jackal yapped somewhere to the north, and followed it with an explosive *bwaa*. Jade worried about the rhino calf. From what she had seen, it was not an infant by any means, so it might be able to defend itself should a family of jackals find it. She wondered what other predators wandered among the game and decided she'd best be prepared. In the final hours of daylight, Jade gathered up a pile of rocks and set them carefully on the footboard inside the cockpit. Then she settled in to wait out the night.

THE NURSE FIRST dosed Sam with that hideous quinine concoction, then insisted on watching him swallow every bland spoonful of the flavorless oatmeal and cold toast.

"Has anyone else been by to see me?" he asked.

The nurse nodded. "Lord Dunbury stopped again. Tried to bring some chicken. You were asleep, so I sent him and his chicken packing."

Sam sighed. Why hadn't Jade come back? The nurse fluffed his pillows, took his pulse, and gave him a drink of water. As he drifted off to sleep, he thought he saw her stoop and pick up a bit of paper from under the bed.

SOMETHING LARGE TROTTED to Jade's right an hour before sunset. She felt the vibrations first, which translated into gentle shudders in the cockpit. She opened her eyes and caught a bulky shadow gliding parallel to the plane. Buffalo. Maybe a few fires wouldn't be such a bad idea after all, especially if someone came looking for her. Besides, she needed something to do. Just sitting in Sam's grounded plane made her uncomfortable. It focused her attention on the last time she had seen him and his frightfully gaunt face.

Jade climbed back out of the plane and set to work gathering stones for a fire ring. She didn't need to look far. There were dozens of big ones less than seventy yards from the plane. She made several trips and lugged back enough volcanic debris and another armload of dried branches to make three rings about a foot in diameter each. She placed one several feet in front of each wing tip and another past the tail.

The sun's bottom just kissed the horizon. She had about ten minutes of daylight left before she was plunged into the dark African night. There was no dusk this close to the equator. Knife in hand, she slashed off every dead branch she could find and several greener ones. Her boot kicked a dried buffalo chip and she made a search for them, retrieving more than a dozen. Then, just as the sun set, she pulled a match from her bag and lit the first fire.

Above her, the stars made their appearance as she lit the last stack of wood and dried dung. The dried chips burned, but the fire didn't produce much light. Well, it would have to do. She didn't have anything else to contribute.

A few glowing eyes blinked in the dark. One stared long enough that she hurled one of her smaller rocks at it. The jackal yelped and ran off. In the distance, a hippo splashed its way onto shore for a nocturnal feed. Another pair of eyes blinked from the underbrush as the animal coughed. Jade felt the hair on her arms stand on end.

Leopard? She pulled her flashlight from the bag and played it over the grass. The little spotted genet blinked, hissed, and ran away.

Jade shut off the light and told herself to relax. There weren't supposed to be many large predators out here. But every pair of glowing eyes made Jade think of the leopard. *He's in a cage in Nairobi, for the love of Pete.* Why did she feel as if she was losing her nerve? She'd been in the bush alone before.

Yeah, but always with a tent and gear and always because it was where you planned to be. This time you're stuck because you cracked up Sam's plane. She reminded herself that it wasn't really cracked up. The rip could be easily fixed with some good linen cloth and glue. And once they drained the fuel tank and cleaned out the line, it would fly good as new. She climbed back into the plane and tried to lean back and look up at the brightening constellations, not an easy trick in a cramped cockpit. Seeing the black sky made her think of Sam. *He has eyes like that.*

She missed him and wished he was with her to share the night sky. She wanted to sit beside him by a decent fire and feel his strong arm around her shoulders. She wanted to hear his laugh and have him sing one of his funny old songs in that gravelly deep bass. Avery had once laughed at Sam's singing voice, said it sounded like a bull elephant grumbling, but Jade liked it. It had a raspy, scratchy undertone, which, while not musical, was intriguing. She had told Sam his voice reminded her of olives. You either liked them or you didn't, and if you did, you weren't sure why, but you did for the very reason that they had an indescribably distinct taste.

Sam. She'd hated to leave his side this morning; he had looked so pallid and broken. Her mind fretted, thinking of the worst possible ramifications of malaria. Some forms flared with alarming frequency. Others ended in the deadly blackwater fever. As she prayed for Sam's health, she realized how much he meant to her. She knew then that losing him would turn Africa into an empty place, one she'd never feel at home in again.

He'll be fine, she told herself. *Probably never have another attack.* But what then? Before, at the Thompsons', he'd seemed upset and at least part of that emotion was directed at her. Was it simply a result of his illness, or because she'd danced with Anderson? Either way, she'd find out what this *shauri* was about. She'd do that just as soon as she cleared Sam's name of those murder suspicions. *And how do I do that when I'm stuck out here?*

Jade closed her eyes and drifted to sleep. Maybe it was a change in the predawn air or the faint whiff of tanned leather and ocher in the air, but Jade woke to the prickly sensation that she was being watched.

She was surrounded by nine Maasai warriors.

CHAPTER 14

Mature warriors and junior elders, acting as mentors, live in the manyatta, *where these "fire-stick elders" teach the warriors about Maasai customs. Joining them are the warriors' mothers and a few girlfriends. No uninitiated boys may enter.*

—The Traveler

THE NURSE MUST have slipped him some sort of sedative, for Sam didn't wake up again until just before daybreak. Promptly at five a.m., Avery reappeared with his shaving kit, a mirror, and half a roasted chicken. The latter was tucked into a napkin in his kit.

"Had to sneak it past the ward nurse. Quick, eat while she's still at her desk."

Sam glanced at the nurse at the far end of the room. She sat hunched over some paperwork, writing. He devoured one leg quarter and a part of the breast without taking his eyes off her. As soon as Sam finished, Avery wrapped the remainder of the chicken in the napkin and shoved it back into the recesses of the leather kit. Then he whipped up some lather in a mug.

"Can you do this, or shall I act as barber?" Avery asked.

"I'll do it," said Sam. "If that doctor comes back round, I want to look fit enough to get out of here. *You* might take off half my mustache."

Avery held the mirror while Sam lathered up and then carefully swiped the thin blade over his face. He took extra care around his mustache, keeping it to a thin line. When he was through, he felt more tired, but less diseased.

"Thanks, Avery. I feel like a new man."

"And you look as helpless as a newborn."

"Surprised the nurse hasn't run you off yet. How did you get in this early? Did you bribe her?"

Avery grinned. "Better. I held up a note from your doctor saying I had permission to act as your valet before your release."

"That was pretty decent of the doctor," said Sam.

Avery laughed. "The doctor knows nothing about it. But who can read their signatures anyway, right?"

Sam smiled. "Avery, you old devil. You're a forger."

"It's a skill every lord should have. But it looks as though my luck might be running out." He nodded to the corner, where the night nurse was showing her notes to the day nurse. "Looks like a changing of the guard and the end of my early visit."

"Stick it out, man," said Sam. "If you leave, it's just me and my gloomy thoughts."

Avery squirmed in the chair as though he felt as uncomfortable listening to a man's confidences as his backside did sitting on the hard seat. "I say. None of that now. You'll be out today and soon back in the saddle." When he saw Sam's frown, he crossed his legs and settled himself for the long haul. "Let's have it. Best to spit it out."

"Jade never came back yesterday to see me."

"Is that all? Hell, Sam, she's probably out roping more wild zebras or capturing an entire pride of lions. Or she came back and you were asleep."

"Yeah, you're probably right," said Sam. "Although that's part of what worries—" He stopped as a ruckus at the door attracted everyone's attention.

JADE PEERED OUT of the cockpit and saw shapes, cutout silhouettes tacked against a black sky and backlit by dim firelight. A ring of men surrounded her, each standing storklike on one leg, the sole of the other foot resting against the inside of the knee. Gradually, she realized that only one man faced her. The others looked out onto the grassland and rocks. The man facing her stepped into the dim firelight and looked up at her.

She'd only known two Maasai before, Ruta and the old tracker and witch Memba Sasa. Ruta had been a handsome man with a proud carriage and a strength of mind and body. The man facing her reminded Jade of him. He wore his shoulder-length hair like thin ropes twisted with red ocher and animal fat. Most were pulled behind and held in some as yet unseen clasp. The top ropes, however, were directed forward as forelocks. They came together in a tight twist, making a triangle, the point falling between the eyebrows in a metal disk.

The warrior wore an ocher-stained leather apron wrapped around his loins and a red cloth as a short toga across one shoulder. When the breeze ruffled his cloak, Jade glimpsed a well-muscled chest, bare except for a thin crisscross of beads, and an armlet of colorful beads bound his upper right arm. His legs were coated with pale pink earth with rippling stripes of skin showing through. Above the knee, he wore a thigh bell made from metal strips tied with leather thongs. At the moment, a thin shank of bone locked the strips into place and kept them from jangling. Jade knew that, on the hunt, the shank would be pulled, allowing the metal to clang together. The noise would confuse a lion, driving it where the warrior wanted the beast to go.

Almost as striking in appearance as the man was his oval shield. Made of stretched hides, it was painted in bold white and red patterns, chevrons, rippling lines, and dots. To complete his regalia, he held a spear as long as himself and carried a bundle of wild sage leaves, clamped under one armpit as a deodorant. He grasped something that Jade couldn't see in his left hand.

"Maasai" meant "the speakers of Maa." She knew some Maa, thanks to her studies, but had never gotten a chance to practice it outside of a book. Ruta never spoke to her or anyone else except Harry Hascombe. But for all of Ruta's pretenses, she'd learned that he understood both Swahili and some English. She took a chance that this man might have had dealings with colonists before and could speak Swahili as well, in case her Maa failed her.

"*Jambo,*" she greeted in Swahili, then added the traditional Maasai greeting, "*Kesherian ingishu,*" literally, "How are the cattle?"

The man watching her didn't move. Jade didn't know if she should get out of the plane or not, but somehow it seemed cowardly to stay there and she knew the Maasai were not a cowardly people. They wouldn't respect caution in others. She stood and lifted a leg over the side and found the stirrup, swung the other leg out, and jumped down. Then she went around the wing toward the propeller. The warrior walked forward, holding his spear erect, and stopped three paces from her. He extended his left hand and offered her a clump of green grass, a peace offering.

"*Jambo, Simba Jike,*" he said, and proceeded in kitchen

Swahili peppered with a few English words. "We welcome the slayer of evil, the friend of my brother."

"Ruta? Yes. I was friend to Ruta," Jade said, taking the grass. The Maasai who had been Harry Hascombe's gun bearer and the caretaker of Biscuit had been a brave man. She had always wondered why he was so far from his own land. This man looked younger by several years.

"That man was my brother. He left the *kraal* the year after I became a warrior. I am Tajewo Ole Ndaskoi," said the warrior, introducing himself as a son of Ndaskoi.

How did he know that his brother was dead, or for that matter, who she was? Then it occurred to her that Harry Hascombe now led safaris. He'd probably come himself and related the brave death of a fellow warrior.

"We saw this cloth *tumaren* land on the earth yesterday," continued Tajewo, pointing to the Jenny.

"*Tumaren?*" Jade was unfamiliar with the word and wondered if it were Maasai for "bird."

Tajewo looked around until he spied a dragonfly patrolling inland for food. "*Tumaren,*" he repeated as he pointed to the darting insect. "Tales have come to us of it and the man with the leg of wood that flies in its heart. We came to see this man for ourselves."

Jade couldn't tell if he was disappointed that she was flying or not. She did find his description of the plane as a dragonfly remarkably accurate. Most people, in trying to explain the plane to a culture unfamiliar with mechanized flight, called it a bird. But with the two wings on each side and the delicate, long tail, it did more closely resemble the insect.

"Bwana Mti Mguu taught me to fly the *tumaren*, the airplane," she said, giving it the English word. "I came to find a young rhino, a *kifaru toto*. I found one whose mother was dead." She pointed in the direction of the young rhino. "I would go back and tell some men, and they would come and save the *toto*. But someone has thrown dirt inside of the airplane and made it foul. It will not fly now and I tore the skin on the wing." She pointed to the rip in the linen.

Tajewo glanced at the tear, then peered at the motor and the propeller. "The . . . ar-plane is like the . . . ah-toe-mu-beel?"

"Yes," said Jade. She pointed to the motor. "The motor makes it fly."

The warrior nodded, understanding now. He'd seen his share of land vehicles before: trucks and autos driven by Europeans on safari or government agents making certain the Maasai kept to their reserve. "We watched when the ar-plane stopped making its growl. We saw it come down. Then we saw the fires, and thought the Bwana was hurt or his ar-plane was broken. We kept guard during the night."

As he spoke, the sun rose and spilled golden light and long fingers of shadows across the dusty landscape. The grasses here grew sparsely and looked browner as the dry season stretched on. In the daylight, Jade again saw the fierce, volcanic pillars and cliffs to the south, a forbidding, harsh landscape. She knew she was lucky to have escaped with only a torn wing.

"Thank you," said Jade. "I am grateful. I need your help." All this time, the other warriors did not turn around or approach the Jenny. Their discipline amazed her. Anytime *she* saw a plane, she wanted to touch it and peer up into the motor. And she'd seen plenty of them. "I must leave the airplane and walk back to Naivasha town. If I stay here, the men will find the *kifaru toto* too late, and it will die. If I leave the airplane, an animal will chew on it or scratch its back against it."

"And the man with the wood leg will beat you?" Tajewo didn't wait for her answer to his rhetorical question. To him, it was obvious.

Tajewo called to the men. They gathered in a clump, discussing the matter. She caught the occasional surreptitious look at the linen-and-wood contraption beside them and even more open stares at her. After a few minutes, three of the men set off at a trot to the east.

"Three warriors will find the *kifaru toto* and bring it back here. If it is too young to eat grass, they will take it to the *kraal* and give it milk." Tajewo pointed to the southwest. "It is a half day's walk to the village. The rest will guard the ar-plane. In this, I can repay the one who killed my brother's killer."

"Thank you," said Jade. "Now I can find the farmhouse I saw and see if someone can help me go home."

"*I* will take you to that *kraal*," he said, using the term for the "village." "But I do not think anyone is there. It is filled with emptiness for many years. Then I will take you to Nai'posha," he said, giving the town the original pronunciation.

"That's odd," mumbled Jade more to herself. "I was sure I saw a truck there." Well, perhaps it was too old and broken down to bother with anymore when the settlers gave up and left. Perhaps someone new had taken over the farm recently and Tajewo just didn't know it yet. She gathered her few supplies from behind the cockpit seat, replaced Sam's jacket, and fell into step beside the tall Maasai.

"You can't go in now, sir," said the night nurse. "Visiting hours have not begun yet."

"I have to see Mr. Featherstone. It's most important."

"Mr. Featherstone is in need of his rest and . . . sir!" she shouted as Neville pushed past her. "Stop this instant!"

"It's all right, Nurse," said the doctor, who'd just come in to make his morning rounds. "We can give him five minutes."

The nurse turned on her heel with a huffed "Well!" and went back to her desk. Neville didn't wait for anyone to change their minds and hurried over to Sam's bedside.

"Good to see you alive and kicking," said Neville. "Hello, Avery." He fidgeted with his hat, as though nervous about something. Avery rose and nodded toward the chair, offering it to Neville.

Sam shifted his stumpy leg under the sheet. "Only kicking with one foot right now, Neville. Thanks for bringing me here. I heard you brought Jade, too," Sam said. He made the statement sound like a question, hoping for some information that would dispel his worry that she'd gone off on another wild escapade.

Neville, still standing, nodded. "I think she stayed most of the night. Yesterday morning she came by the house to tell us they finally managed to get the quinine down you with some subterfuge. As I understand it, she made you think it was a lemonade."

Sam started. So that was where the memory of home had come from. "Is she in the waiting room or at the farm with Maddy?" he asked, his voice hopeful.

Neville shook his head. "That's why I needed to see you. She's not back yet."

Something in his voice made Sam sit up straight. "Not back from where?"

"I'm not sure," said Neville. "Wherever you planned to go, I assume."

Sam's bass voice dropped to a low rumble. "Are you telling me she went up in the plane?"

"What are you talking about?" asked Avery. "What happened?"

Neville looked from one man to the other. "Jade said that Sam told her to go up without him." He looked directly at Sam as he finished. "She said you *insisted* on it, wouldn't take no for an answer."

Sam's eyes opened wide and his face blanched. "And she's not back yet? I didn't ask her to go up alone." He threw back the covers and began searching for his clothes. "Doctor!" he yelled. "Where's my damn leg!"

"Calm yourself, man," said Avery. He pushed against Sam's chest in a futile attempt to keep him in bed. "Neville, a hand here, if you please, and tell me what the deuce is going on." Then to himself: "How can a sick man be so bloody strong?"

The doctor raced over to them. "Mr. Featherstone, get back into bed this instant."

"Where's my leg?" demanded Sam, still resisting Avery's increasing pressure. "Neville, find my leg."

Neville straightened and peered around the room as if the leg would suddenly appear floating in front of him. "I don't know—"

"We'll find your leg, Sam," said Avery, "*after* you get hold of yourself and tell me what the blazes is going on."

Sam collapsed back against the pillow, beads of sweat breaking out on his forehead. His breath came in shallow pants. "My stars, I'm weak as a kitten," he mumbled.

"The hell," muttered Avery.

"That's why you aren't to be released yet," declared the doctor. "There is no reason for—"

"There is every reason in the world, Doctor," growled Sam. His ebony eyes glared at the doctor. "Miss del Cameron has crashed somewhere, and I have to find her."

"What?" shouted Avery. A stern "Shush" and an equally harsh glare came from the nurse standing two beds over taking a patient's pulse. Avery scowled, but dropped his voice. "What the hell is going on?"

Sam held up one hand, indicating that he'd speak as soon as he got his breath back. "I was supposed to fly Monday morning for that zoo company. Scout for a rhino calf. It seems our Jade flew off alone in my place."

"She said you told her to. Begged her, in fact," said Neville.

"Well, I didn't!" said Sam. "At least not consciously. I was probably raving or something."

"Has Jade soloed before?" asked Avery.

Sam shook his head. "She's handled takeoffs and landings on her own and a complete flight once, but I've always been in the front seat, ready to take over if necessary."

"And was it ever necessary?" continued Avery. He poured a glass of water and held it out to Sam.

"No. She's good." Sam stopped and took a drink. "She controls the plane smoothly, understands allowing for drift, and she knows how to scout for an emergency-landing site."

"So what's the worry?" asked Avery. "She sounds like a competent pilot."

"The worry is that she's not back yet. She should have been back two hours after takeoff. It's been an entire day. Something's happened."

"She probably stayed out too long and put down somewhere to refuel," said Avery. He looked at Neville. "When did your man tell you that she hadn't returned?"

"An hour ago. I had machinery problems most of the day yesterday, and Maddy helped me. We didn't get back to the house until dark. Kimathi kept watch from the fields all day and then all night by the hangar. When Jade didn't return during the night, he hurried back to tell us."

Avery frowned. "It *does* sound as though she's had some sort of trouble."

Sam pushed himself to a sitting position and steadied himself with both hands on the bed. "And there are places in the bush where you don't want to be stranded. Now, if you're all through mollycoddling me, I intend to go and find her."

"You really shouldn't leave," said the doctor, who had remained silent during the discussion.

Sam took hold of Avery's shoulder and hauled himself up. "I'm leaving, Doctor. Give me whatever pills I need to take, but I'm leaving. And bring me my leg!"

The doctor motioned the nurse forward and instructed her to bring Mr. Featherstone's effects. She scurried off, her steps hastened by four pairs of stern male eyes on her back, and returned with a bundle of clothes, a pair of boots, and a wooden leg. She dumped the entire assemblage on the foot of the bed and hurried away again after Sam's particularly frightful scowl.

"I want to make it clear that your leaving goes against my advisement," said the doctor.

"Understood," said Sam as he pulled on a pair of drawers followed by an undershirt. "It's not that I'm ungrateful, mind you, but there's more at stake here than my rest."

The doctor fidgeted with Sam's boot. "If this is the young lady who was here Sunday night, I can certainly understand your desire to assist her. But she seemed a capable young woman. I'm sure she's in no *real* danger. Didn't strike me as the type to just fly off, as you put it."

Sam rolled his eyes. "You mistook the statement for something metaphorical, Doctor. I'm speaking literally." He finished attaching his prosthetic and tugged on his trousers. "She did fly off. And in my airplane."

"Oh, dear," muttered the doctor.

"And you have no idea," continued Sam as he buttoned his shirt, "just how much trouble that little green-eyed varmint can get into." He steadied himself against the back of the chair before sitting down in it. "My boots, if you please."

"Let me give you a hand there," said Neville.

Sam shook his head. "Thanks, but it's actually easier to pull it over the leg than have someone push." He pointed to the sides of the wooden foot, showing where countless rubbings had polished the wood to a fine sheen.

"Do you have any idea where Jade went?" asked Avery.

"Probably. If she pulled out my map, she would have found my notes. I'd intended to head west past Naivasha and to the edge of the Maasai reserve. Supposed to be good game there."

Neville nodded. "Indeed. Planned to take Maddy there on a holiday. The lake is splendid."

"I have my vehicle at hand," said Avery, "If we can round up some chaps with cars, we can make it there quickly enough to conduct a broad search."

"She's probably at Naivasha waiting for us," suggested Neville.

"Maybe," said Sam. He didn't sound hopeful. "Who did you have in mind?"

"There was a dinner last evening," said Avery. "A reunion of Volunteer Mounted Rifles."

"Right," said Neville. "I saw the notice in the paper. They meet once a month at the Norfolk Hotel."

"Do you think they'll help?" asked Sam.

"They'd damn well better," said Avery. "After all, they are, or were, a military unit."

"Of sorts," said Neville, "but strictly volunteer and no one really saw much service. They mainly patrolled the rail lines and some of the fringes of the territory in case of enemy invasion or warring natives."

"Then it's about time they did something to earn their keep," said Sam. "And we can find someone from that Perkins and Daley company, too." He stood. "Let's go." Avery and Neville flanked Sam to the door. Once outside, Sam leaned against the outer wall.

"I'm sure Jade's all right, Sam," said Neville, trying to sound hopeful.

"I pray that's the case," said Sam, "and if she is and she smashed up my plane, I'll kill the reckless little minx."

CHAPTER 15

And just what sort of activities would one expect in such an exclusive club?
They plan and carry out cattle raids, go on lion hunts, and learn the customs
so that they can become valued elders in their turn.

—The Traveler

TAJEWO COULD HAVE loped easily across the grasslands, but Jade was too worn-out from the previous night trying to sleep in a cramped cockpit to keep up for very long. After a few hundred yards, she slowed to a brisk walk, and Tajewo did the same. They traveled in silence. A chunky rock hyrax popped its head up over a red rock and ran back into the shadows. Jade watched a giraffe stride with its languid, liquid grade to an acacia tree. Its long blue-black tongue stretched upward and wrapped itself around a leafy branch, stripping it bare as it retracted into the gaping mouth. A second one joined the first giraffe at the opposite end of the tree.

Jade took in the high shoulders and sloping back. A fascinating creature, especially when it splayed its forelimbs to drink. There was nothing remotely like this animal in the United States. It was no wonder people wanted to see them in the zoos. Such sights occupied Jade for a while, but finally after a quarter mile, curiosity about Ruta and the Maasai warriors in general won out.

"Do warriors often leave the *kraal* like Ruta did?"

Tajewo kept his eyes on the grasses for any danger, a hidden predator, a sleeping bull who would not appreciate being awakened. "No. A warrior must never eat alone, for this means that a warrior, no matter how poor, will have food."

"Then why was Ruta alone?"

"He was a great warrior. Once, he was throwing his spear to keep his arm strong. A new warrior did not see. He ran in front of him and was killed. His family said my brother did this thing to win a girl. But he did not. They would try to kill him now. It was best that he hide, so he left."

"I'm sorry," said Jade, noticing that Tajewo didn't speak Ruta's name. *Taboo?*

"Never mind. Engai is still present," Tajewo replied, invoking the Maasai's belief in God's watchfulness.

"But you are traveling alone now," Jade observed.

"I will be back before sunset," he explained. Tajewo's own curiosity apparently got the better of him, too, for he began to pepper Jade with questions as they became more comfortable conversing in their blend of Swahili and English with occasional sprinklings of Maa. "My brother's friend, Bwana Nyati, the man you call Hascombe, told us of you when he came with news of my brother. He said you could shoot a rifle well." He glanced at her shoulder to indicate that she didn't carry a rifle now. "You do not hunt anymore?"

"Only for meat when it is needed," she said.

"Then why do you want this *kifaru toto*? It is not meat."

Jade tried her best to explain the concept of zoos and people paying to see animals they had never seen before. She heard him grunt once and wondered if he had experienced something similar in his own life. After all, more safaris seemed to be intent on seeing the "wild natives" and their villages as much as the animals. Ever since the cattle sicknesses had hit the Maasai's herds, the once feared tribe had been reduced to living in their own reserve, unable to raid for the cattle promised them by Engai, the Maker. To do so would mean the loss of their spears and they'd be unable to defend from lions what herds they had left.

"There are no *kifaru* in your land?" he asked her.

"No. No *kifaru* and no *simba*. We have a smaller *simba* in the mountains." She held her hand out to indicate the general height of a mountain lion. "But it is shy and does not come down to people very often. We have no *chui* either." She told him about her experience as bait to trap the fierce male leopard and about his rage when he saw her.

"Engai did not give *chui* the strength in his jaws that he gave the lion. But he gave him fierce, raking claws and a wildness in his heart. He does not have *simba*'s roar, but he has mad yellow eyes to strike terror in his prey's heart. Some say it frightens the soul so it cannot flee. Such is often the way. Animals often possess something to make up for the strength they do not have. Even some men are like this. Those that are not strong of body may have fierceness of heart. Those that lack the arm to throw a spear may use poison or secret weapons."

He cast another, longer look at Jade. "And do you still hunt witches?"

Jade let out a breathy *huff* and her shoulders twitched. "In a way. I hunted for a man who killed the great *tembo* for their ivory tusks, a man who sold slaves and guns. And I hunted for a witch who stole my mother far to the north."

Tajewo nodded. "You are a lioness. The male lion is bigger and very dangerous, but it is the female that hunts for the pride. Who do you hunt for now?"

Jade started at his insight. It was true—she was hunting again, although less actively than before. She remembered trying to explain this to her mother when she'd finally told her about the adventure on Mount Marsabit. Jade had summarized it in the following words: "There was a great evil that ran rampant during the War. I couldn't do anything about it, but I could do something about the one on Marsabit." She still believed it, too. In a way, she felt she was doing her part to rid the world of some of its cruelty. But this time she hunted for a killer to clear an innocent man's name.

"A man was killed in Nairobi. I hunt for his killer." Perhaps it was the fact that she knew he wouldn't tell anyone else, perhaps it was the strength he radiated, but for some inexplicable reason, she felt the need to unburden herself to this strange man. "His wife is missing, too. I would like to find her."

"Why do you seek the woman? Did she kill her husband?"

"No." Jade paused and shrugged. "She left her *toto*. Why would a mother do that? Maybe she was also killed. Or maybe she hides from the killer."

"So you hunt for animals for the white men to take, you hunt for a killer, and you hunt for his wife." Tajewo shook his head. "It is not good to do too much at once. We have a saying. A man cannot walk on two different paths at the same time. It will crack his buttocks."

Jade tossed back her head and laughed. "That would explain a lot, Tajewo." The fresh coolness of the morning air joined with the exhilaration of being alive in the company of Africa to renew Jade's strength. She became impatient with her own pace and fell into an easy, loping run. Tajewo released his thigh bell and matched her step as they ran across the plains, startling an occasional ground bird or antelope. The metallic jangling of Tajewo's bells gave most animals ample warning and cleared the way of anything potentially dangerous.

They soon passed the first set of warriors, now returning with a confused young rhino trotting between two of the men and in front of the third. Jade waved at them as they went past and they saluted her with their spears held high. The new pace ate up the ground and very soon the old farmstead appeared. Window curtains hinted that the home had once again become inhabited. Tajewo was not impressed.

"I will not leave until I know you are safe. But I will hide here." He pointed to a distant stand of euphorbia trees, which looked like candelabras hoisting green tapers atop bare trunks. A clump of thick succulents clustered at the base.

Jade stepped up onto the rickety veranda and knocked at the weather-beaten front door. No one answered, but she thought she heard a noise from within. A quick glance to the window revealed a small woman trying to spy on her. Jade waved and smiled. The curtain dropped, and the door opened a foot, enough for the woman to step out but not enough to give any appearance of hospitality.

The young woman stood several inches below Jade. She had fiery red hair with a touch of orange pulled back in a tight bun. The color reminded Jade of the hennaed hair she'd seen in some of the Berber women of the Atlas Mountains. Wearing a sacklike dress of navy blue cotton and stout work boots, the woman looked haggard and frightened.

Her pale skin showed no freckling, indicating she'd seen little sun, unusual for a farmwife. If she had just recently taken up residence, Jade reasoned, she probably still saw every person or noise as a potential threat. Jade guessed her age to be somewhere in the twenties. Something about her face seemed familiar.

"Good morning. My name is Jade del Cameron. I'm an American living in Nairobi. I was flying an airplane and had to set down west of here. I was hoping you could give me a ride to Naivasha. I would pay you, of course."

"Can't help you. I have no automobile."

"Then the truck behind your house doesn't work? Perhaps I could see what's wrong with it. I'm a good mechanic." Jade could have sworn she had seen vehicle tracks leading to the house when she flew over before.

"It's out of petrol." From behind her came a faint gurgling coo. The woman started to turn to listen, then quickly snapped back and faced Jade again. "If you need water, you can help yourself to the pump out back."

"Thank you. That's very kind of you. It's been a long walk," said Jade. "When I get to Naivasha, should I tell someone that you need petrol? Do you need food, too?"

"No! I have what I need already. Now you'd better get moving on, elsewise you'll still be walking when the sun gets high." The woman started to close the door, but Jade stopped it with her hand.

"You wouldn't happen to have a tin cup or something that I can drink from, would you?"

The woman considered the question a moment, then nodded. "Wait here."

She left the door a few inches ajar and went into a back room. Jade stepped in closer and surveyed what little she could see of the house's interior. An idea had come to her when she heard what sounded like a child's voice. The front room was sparsely furnished with one chair near a fireplace and a small square table. In the near corner stood two crates labeled NESTLÉ'S MILK FOOD and WEBLEY'S TINNED BEEF. Both were stamped STOKES AND BERRYHILL. Jade stepped back outside just before the woman returned with a battered tin cup.

"Here," she said as she handed the cup to Jade. "Just leave it hanging on the pump when you're finished."

"Thank you," said Jade. "Is your husband hunting right now?"

The woman blinked twice, her blue eyes mirroring the brilliant sky. "Yes. Hunting. He's hunting now. Should be back tonight."

"That's good. I'd be worried about you alone out here otherwise. Are you sure I can't send someone out to check on you? Maybe someone from Nairobi?"

"No! Goodbye."

The woman shut the door in Jade's face, and she heard the bolt slide across the door on the other side. Without waiting, Jade went around back to the well pump and used the cup to refill her canteen. Tajewo joined her, but declined the use of the cup, preferring to dip his head and drink directly from the flowing stream of water.

He straightened and wiped his mouth with the back of a hand. "This person will take you to Nai'posha?"

Jade shook her head, all the while looking at the grasses behind the truck. "No. The woman says the truck does not work."

Tajewo leaned on his spear. "I think perhaps she lies. The grasses are bent close by."

It didn't take a great hunter to notice the recent track left by some wheels. But they ended a few feet behind the old truck. "No, I think another automobile has been here instead." Jade longed to check the fuel level, but decided it was pointless. She hung the tin cup on the well pump and walked away, following the tire tracks. Whoever drove in hadn't come straight to the house. Instead, he'd bypassed it and doubled back, reminding Jade of how a protective mountain lion mother would avoid a direct path to her den lest she lead another predator to her cubs.

"Why would this woman lie to you?" asked Tajewo, falling in step beside her.

Jade knew now why the face had looked familiar despite the severely styled red hair. She'd seen it before in two different photographs. "Because she is the woman I told you about. The one who is missing. I do not think she wants to be found."

SAM LEANED BACK in Avery's car and stared at the ceiling. How did one deal with knowing that the woman he'd come halfway around the world to meet might be lying in a broken heap in the African wild? You took action and found her—that was how. He wished he could have jumped on his motorcycle and gone off immediately, but at present he felt as limp as a soggy scarecrow and even more useless.

What the hell is keeping Avery and Neville? He glared at his watch. He'd been waiting outside of the hotel for an hour. *To hell with this.* He got up and made his way into the front parlor, where he promptly collapsed into a leather easy chair.

We should have left on our own. We'd be halfway to Naivasha by now. He wished he'd gone to the rooms to rouse the men with Avery, but Avery had warned that he'd be back in the hospital if he pushed himself too hard. So he'd let Avery and Neville organize the search while he watched precious time slip past him.

Avery reappeared in a moment, alone. "Sorry, Sam. Not much luck there. Must have put on quite a bender at the dinner last night. They're by and large in no condition to go anywhere." He snorted derisively. "A host of drunken sots. I don't know what the Volunteer Mounted Rifles amounted to in their heyday, but right now it's an excuse to get a snoot full. I was astonished by how rapidly I could galvanize these men into doing nothing."

Sam's eyes widened with the realization that they'd just wasted valuable time. "You couldn't rouse a single man out of a host of former soldiers?"

"One, a farmer named Harding, seemed cogent enough, especially when he learned it was a woman who was flying."

Avery and Sam moved to the car while Avery continued his account. "I asked him if he could recommend any other men from his group. He said Berryhill had gone home drunk last evening. Thought a Mr. Chalmers could be of use, but he didn't come to the meeting. I hope Neville has more luck, but it seems the governor returned yesterday to declare us the Kenya Colony and everyone else ran off to see him. I told Harding we'd regroup at the Naivasha Hotel," he continued. "We can see if anyone there heard an airplane fly over or fly back."

"Then we'll split up and patrol the area south of the lake where I'd planned to fly," said Sam as he got back into the car to wait for Neville. "If anyone finds her unharmed, they should fire three shots in rapid succession, then bring her back to the hotel. Four shots will mean . . ."

"Keep a good thought, Sam. We'll only need to fire three shots."

"I WILL WALK with you to Nai'posha," said Tajewo, "since this woman will not help you."

Jade heard the disgust in his voice. "Do not be too hard on her. She is afraid of someone."

"Her husband? But he is dead. You must tell her. Then she will not be afraid."

"I think she already knows," said Jade, remembering the boxes labeled STOKES AND BERRYHILL and the black truck she'd seen from the air. Mrs. Berryhill had probably made a supply run recently, and brought more than canned foods. Jade was certain she'd heard a baby, and there had been a lot of canned milk. The question was, who was Alice Stokes hiding from now? Her husband's killer? And why would someone want to kill Stokes?

Several ideas came to mind. Winston Berryhill found out Stokes was skimming money from the store. Or a blackmail victim had killed Stokes. Or Chalmers, who kept Alice Stokes' picture and had apparently placed the ad looking for her, was in love with her. Maybe he had killed Stokes to protect or free her. But none of those reasons threatened Stokes' wife. If Avery or Beverly hadn't already talked to Harley and convinced him to tell what he knew to Finch, she'd have to talk to him when she got back. In the meantime, she'd keep Mrs. Stokes' secret.

"When you return home," asked Tajewo, "you will still hunt the killer, even though the woman did not help you?"

"Yes."

Tajewo shook his head, his forelock jiggling. "You are like

the elephant. He does not tire of carrying his tusks. But you must be careful, Simba Jike. This man, he might kill you. It is not possible to dodge the spear before it has been thrown."

"No, but maybe I can stop him from throwing it."

After I check on Sam. She wondered how he'd fared after she left. Had the fever recurred? It frightened her to realize just how much she counted on Sam being a part of her life and how empty it would seem without him. And it wasn't only the malaria that endangered him. Someone had fouled the engine, attempting to severely injure or kill him. Why? *I need to get back and warn him before anyone finds out Sam wasn't in that plane and tries again.* She felt the urgency squeeze her heart, making it race.

Sweet Millard Fillmore. You're in love! And you just had to put a rip in his plane.

A herd of zebra raced off in the distance, startled by a noise. Jade held up her hand to signal a stop and listened. In the cool morning air, the sound of a puttering motor carried from the east. Perhaps it was her wishing it, but she thought she detected a puff of dust where a vehicle churned up the dry soil.

"Maybe it is Bwana Mti Mguu," said Tajewo, "come to find his ar-plane. Will he beat you for hurting it?"

Jade turned her head to look at him and detected a wry smile on his face, as though he wondered if she would fight back. After all, she had a reputation now. "No. He is a good man. He does not beat women and children. And his airplane is not hurt badly. There is only a cut in its skin. We will sew a new piece of skin over the cut." *And clean out the engine and the fuel lines.*

"Come," she said, and pointed to the distant vehicle. They broke into a long, loping stride, eating up the ground over the grasslands. She hoped it was just someone out to see the lake and not the saboteur looking to find a smashed plane and equally broken pilot. Then she brightened with the thought that Sam might have sent a search party out to find her.

After a minute, the driver must have spotted them since the truck turned to meet them and sped up. Tajewo stopped a few feet away, his hand resting on his spear. Jade recognized the driver as Alwyn Chalmers.

"Mr. Chalmers, I'm glad to see you."

"Miss del Cameron," he said in his reedy voice, "it would be an understatement to say that I'm surprised to see you alone out here. And on foot, to boot."

"Then you weren't searching for me? I just assumed . . ."

Mr. Chalmers coughed into his fist. "I *was* searching, in point of fact. For my polo pony. Still missing, you know."

"Yes. Sorry. I haven't seen him. So you aren't going back to Nairobi then?" She let the disappointment show in her voice. The thought of walking on to Naivasha and waiting for a train south suddenly seemed too tiring and too time-consuming. She needed to see Sam again, alive and well.

"Oh. Right. Of course. Wouldn't think of stranding you." He reached over and opened the passenger door to his left. "Climb aboard."

"Just a moment, please, if you don't mind. I wish to thank my friend for his protection." Jade turned back to Tajewo and held out her hand. The Maasai warrior transferred his spear to his shield hand and clasped her hand in his. "Thank you, Tajewo, brother of Ruta. Thank the other warriors for me, too."

"We will guard the ar-plane, Simba Jike, until you or Bwana Mti Mguu come for it. And we will take care of the *toto* for you."

"I promise we will come for them soon. Until then, good-bye, and may Engai watch over you and give you many cattle and children."

"Goodbye, Simba Jike. Good hunting. May Engai shield you with his wings."

With that last wish, Tajewo again gripped his spear in his right hand, turned, and loped off, his thigh bell jingling in clear metallic notes. Jade watched him run, his long shadow the advance guard. When he and his shadow blended into one, she turned back to Mr. Chalmers and climbed into the front seat. As soon as she settled herself, exhaustion took over. But as much as she wanted to drift off to sleep, she couldn't let down her guard. Not yet.

My knee doesn't hurt. That's something in Chalmers' favor. But Jade never really knew how much stock to place in her war-wounded knee. Its tendency to ache just before a rain-storm or when someone was trying to kill her never really sat well with her, no matter what the old Berber woman had said about walking with death. *Besides, it didn't hurt before I took off. Shouldn't it have given me some advance warning then?*

She pondered that idea for a moment, feeling the warm-ing air breeze past her as the truck jolted and bounced east-ward to Naivasha. She already knew the answer. No one knew she'd be in the plane. They'd expected Sam. She sat up straighter and forced herself to stay awake.

"How did you manage to strand yourself out in this area, Miss del Cameron?"

"Engine malfunction," she said without explaining that the engine belonged to an airplane.

"Oh. I say, that's too bad. Where did you break down?"

Jade jerked her thumb over her shoulder to the west. "Near Hell's Gate."

Chalmers turned to look at her. "That's a far distance, miss. You're lucky that Maasai was friendly." He studied the faint track in front of him, squinting into the sun. "Must have been *your* tire tracks I was following then." He sounded disappointed.

Jade didn't contradict him and let him assume she'd been in an automobile. "Sorry, Mr. Chalmers. You were probably hoping you were on the path of someone who might have seen your pony, I suppose."

"Hmm, yes. Indeed." He squinted some more and dodged a wallow. "Say, you didn't happen to notice any signs of habitation out that way, did you? I understand more people are moving into the lake area."

"They must be closer to the lake, then," said Jade.

"Yes, of course. Sensible thought, I guess. I suppose you would rather I took you back into Nairobi or should I leave you at Naivasha?"

Jade heard the hope in his voice when he said Naivasha. Clearly, he didn't want to go all the way into Nairobi and preferred to resume his search, but she suspected it wasn't the pony that he was looking for. He was too far from his farm to expect to find it out here. If she was going to keep Mrs. Stokes' secret, Jade needed to draw him farther away.

"I do need to get back to Nairobi," Jade said. "My friends will be very worried about me."

"Very well." Instead of circling the lake and heading north up its eastern side to reach the town of Naivasha, Chalmers kept the truck nosed due east, intending to intersect the road south to Nairobi.

Jade decided to gauge his impression of Sam, hoping that an off-the-cuff question would catch him off guard. "I believe you've met one of my friends, Sam Featherstone. What do you think of him?"

Chalmers didn't so much as blink. "I can't say as I thought anything of him." He shrugged. "I suppose he's your young man?"

"We're good friends," Jade said. "But *you* never married, Mr. Chalmers?"

"No." Chalmers kept his eyes on the path ahead and found a spot where the Uganda rails lay low to the ground. Jade held on to the door and the seat as the truck rocked and jolted over the tracks. After the silence ran on for a minute longer, he added, "There were not always as many women here in the colony as there are now."

And, thought Jade, *there was probably always someone more handsome to attract them.* A pity, really. His gaunt, pinched face could have belonged to Abe Lincoln's homely brother, but it had character. Besides, he seemed to be a stable man, quiet and hardworking. That should have gone far with a woman out here.

"Pity about Mr. Stokes, isn't it?" she asked. "Wonder what happened to his wife. What was her name? Anna?"

"Alice," he said, reciting it as one might a prayer.

"That's right, Alice. Where could she have gone? Did you know her?" Jade thought about the photo on his table, the only clean object in a filthy house.

"I knew her." The words were whispered, a treasured memory slipping away. He didn't add anything else.

They hit the Limuru Road and turned south to Nairobi. The road's pounded murram soil was rutted in spots from the last rains, and the truck springs worn to nothing. Between her fatigue and the jolting, Jade decided further conversation was not only useless but also painful. Her head ached. She settled for watching the surrounding land for any sign of wildlife. With the exception of one warthog off to the side, she didn't see any. No wonder newcomers could claim that they'd never seen a lion or a rhino. As they neared the Limuru bridge with its warped boards, Chalmers asked her where he should leave her.

Good question. The logical place would have been Neville and Maddy's farm, since she'd taken off from there. She knew Maddy would be frantic by now. But Jade's concern for Sam's well-being overrode all else. Every moment that he was unaware of the attempt on his life was a continued risk. She had to warn him first and see for herself that he was all right. Then she could ease her friends' anxieties.

"The European hospital," she said.

Chalmers gave her an openmouthed stare. "Are you hurt?"

"Nothing serious," she said and smiled to give some appearance of truth. "Merely precautionary." If he had tried to kill Sam, she didn't want him to know where he was.

Her chosen destination seemed to make Chalmers nervous, and once he'd crossed the rickety Limuru bridge, he sped up and raced down the road. He nearly collided with a rickshaw taxi where the road intersected with Sclater's Road and Forest Road.

"Slow down, please, Mr. Chalmers. I'm okay. I'd like to stay that way. You'll get a fine."

The thought of riling a constable went far toward tempering Chalmer's driving. He turned onto Government Road at a more reasonable speed. Then, just as he veered right toward the hill, Jade saw something that made her heart skip a beat. *Sam!*

"Stop!" she shouted.

Chalmers hit the brake fast enough to throw them forward. "Did I hit someone?"

"No. Sorry, Mr. Chalmers. It's just that I saw my friends in front of the Norfolk. They will be looking for me, so I'd better go to them first."

He pulled to the edge of the road, and Jade jumped out. "Thank you so much, Mr. Chalmers. You've been a godsend. I don't have any money with me at present, but I promise I'll repay you for your gasoline."

"Think nothing of it, Miss del Cameron. I wouldn't dream of taking advantage of a lady in distress that way. Er, are you quite certain you're all right? I can take you to the hospital."

"I'm fine. Just fatigued, that's all." She smiled and held out her hand. When he took it, she shook his and thanked him again, using a blessing she'd learned from the Berbers. "God reward you according to your merits, Mr. Chalmers." It was a handy blessing, especially for someone you didn't know well and might just as well curse if you did.

She raced across the broad street, dodging the few rickshaws that were about that early in the morning. Luckily, most people of Nairobi didn't rouse themselves until nine a.m. at least, and it was barely past that now.

Sam, Avery, and Neville caught sight of her running toward them and shouted to her. Broad grins spread across their faces, and Avery tossed his hat into the air with a whoop. Behind them, she spotted Mr. Harding. Was he part of a search party in the formation? Harding's expression wasn't as exuberant, but showed that he was either happy to see her alive or happy not to have to mount a search. She didn't care. Her attention was fixed on Sam. His angular face, pale from his illness, showed a palpable relief.

Sam stepped forward, his arms open and extended, ready to receive her. She ran into them, nearly bowling him over. Their words tumbled out, flowing together like water joining at a confluence of streams.

"It's so good to see you, Sam."

"Thank heavens, you're all right!"

"You're out of the hospital! I was so worried."

"Are you hurt?"

"You should still be resting."

"You don't look bruised," he said, studying her face.

"Why didn't you tell us earlier that you felt sick?"

"What were you thinking, going up alone like that?" He held her at arm's length.

"You told me to. You begged me."

"I was delirious!"

"How the hell was I supposed to know you didn't mean it?"

"A dim-witted child could have told that."

"Yeah? Well, I'm neither a dimwit nor a child, Sam Featherstone." She poked him on the chest and broke free. "And if you hadn't been sulking around like a pouty child, you might have shared some of those symptoms beforehand."

"Sulking? Pouty?" He threw up his arms before wagging his finger at her. "That really fries my fritters! I'm not the one deceiving people."

"Deceiving!" Jade's fist clenched and she gritted her teeth. "You'd better have a good explanation there, pal, or . . . Just when did I deceive you?"

"When you went off to catch that first leopard. You never said you were the bait. You made it sound like just another easy capture."

"It was a spur-of-the-moment decision, buster! I didn't know I needed to get your permission. And you could've let me know where you were going at the dance instead of leaving me waiting for you."

"I got arrested!" His voice rose in volume.

"I'm sorry, but *I* didn't arrest you, so don't take it out on me."

"And you don't need to take it out on my poor plane. You broke my plane!"

"I didn't break the plane. It's just a rip on the wing fabric."

"What'd you do? Try to land on a rhino?"

"Ooooh! You big lummox. For your information, the engine cut out, and I had to land."

"You didn't drain the water beforehand? How many preflights do you need to know you *always* drain the water out of the gas?"

"And do you usually peer down into the tank to see if anyone's planted a wad of dirt and grass, too? 'Cause I missed that one."

Sam's jaw dropped and he stared at her angry face for a few seconds. "Someone sabotaged my Jenny?"

Jade nodded. "Someone tried to kill you."

"*You* could have been killed?" he said at the same time.

He reached for her and pulled her into a tight embrace. They held on to each other as though the other would evaporate like a morning dream if they let go.

"Sam, I was so worried about you."

"I'm so sorry, Jade." He kissed her brow and her hair, and he had just parted his lips to engulf hers when someone coughed behind him. Sam released Jade and stepped back a pace.

"Glad to see you safe and sound, Jade," said Avery. "We've been in quite a stew since we found out you'd disappeared." He pulled out his pipe and filled it with tobacco.

"Sorry we didn't look for you sooner," said Neville. "I was into the machinery all day, as was Maddy, and Kimathi didn't report you missing until late last night."

"It appears you no longer need me anymore, so I'll just go on back home."

Jade peered around Sam to see the speaker. "Ah, Mr. Harding. Thank you very much for being part of the search party. I'm sorry if I inconvenienced you." In the morning light, the man looked sickly, his face more like yellowed parchment bleeding into his eyes. *Liver trouble?*

Harding touched his hat brim. "Not at all, Miss del Cameron. Just glad to see you alive and unharmed." He nodded to Sam, Neville, and Avery. "Gentlemen."

"Mr. Harding, thank you again," said Sam, extending his right hand.

Harding looked mildly embarrassed, ducking his head a bit, his lips tight. Then he shook Sam's hand. "Sorry the others weren't in any shape to help out. Not that it mattered in the end." He pulled his hands back and shoved them in his pockets. "Was that Chalmers driving you in?" He looked across the street to where Chalmers had just parked his vehicle and was getting out.

"Yes, I ran into him just west of Mount Longonot. He was looking for his missing pony."

Harding shook his head. "That's why he didn't come last night. Bloody fool." Then he glanced at Jade and reddened. "Pardon me. Strong language."

"Damn right it is," said Jade with a grin. Mr. Harding

managed a wan smile, touched his brim again and got into his truck. Jade and the others watched him drive away; then Sam slipped his arm around Jade's waist.

"So," said Avery, puffing on his pipe, "someone deliberately fouled the engine?"

"Yes. When I looked in to see if it had gone empty, I saw the remnants of a paper wrap and thread. Someone bound up dirt and grass inside and hung it in the fuel tank. It took a while for the paper to dissolve enough to release the contents. So the bastard clearly wasn't trying to prevent takeoff."

"You need to tell that to the inspector," said Neville. "And I need to get home and assure Maddy that you're safe and sound." He shook his head. "Someday, maybe there will be telephone service out to the farms."

"Thanks, Neville," said Sam, "for everything. I owe you."

"Think nothing of it. Just get back to helping me with that new washer as soon as you feel up to it." He shook hands with Avery, got into his own car, and drove off to his coffee farm.

"Neville's right, Sam. The inspector needs to know about this."

"Where did you put down, Jade?" Sam asked.

"South of Lake Naivasha, near Hell's Gate. Don't worry about the plane. There are a half dozen Maasai warriors guarding it for you."

"No fooling?"

"One is Ruta's brother. *And* I found a rhino calf. I think its mother rammed the train and suffered the worst for it. She died west of Longonot, and true to form, the calf stayed with her. The Maasai have taken the calf back to their *kraal* until Perkins and Daley come for it."

Sam lunged for Jade and grabbed her in a tight lock, hoisting her off her feet. "You saved my job. You're the bravest, most wonderful—" He leaned in to kiss her, but stopped short and glanced sideways at Avery.

"Pay no attention to me," Avery said as he turned his back. "A man's got to do what a man's got to do."

Sam grinned. Before Jade could remark that there were other people about on the streets now, Sam had already swooped in for the kiss. He tasted of bitter quinine and lime, but Jade didn't mind. His kiss still made the back of her neck tingle.

Someone driving by tooted their horn at them, and Sam released Jade. "I'll go to your compound and tell Perkins right away," he said. "Where should I direct him?"

Jade pulled out her notebook, tore out a page and drew a map showing the lake, Longonot, and Hell's Gate. "When they get to the plane, they should ask for Tajewo. He can lead them to the *kraal*. They should tell them that Bwana Mti Mguu sent them."

"Who's that?" asked Sam.

"You. You're Bwana Tree Leg." She grinned as she watched his response. "You're rather famous, actually. Word's gotten around about the man with the tree leg who flies the big dragonfly across the sky."

"Makes sense," agreed Avery. "I'm jealous. I'm just known for my pipe."

Sam folded the map and slipped it into his pocket. "Wait. I can't go see Perkins now. I need to accompany you to the police," he said just as Chalmers joined them.

"I'll take our Jade to the constabulary," said Avery. "Finch might toss you behind bars again if he thinks you tried to sabotage your own plane to hurt Jade."

Sam ran a hand through his hair, pushing the longer strands on top back from his brow. "You're right. He probably would." He noticed Chalmers for the first time. "Ah, Chalmers, thank you for rescuing Jade."

"My pleasure," he said. "But did I just hear you say your *aeroplane* was sabotaged?" He looked at Jade. "Is *that* what you meant by engine trouble?"

Jade felt her face grow warm. "That's right."

"Huh. Well, that's interesting," he said more to himself than to her. Then he touched his hat. "It seems you're in capable hands now, so I'll push off. Good day to you all."

"I'd better leave, too," said Sam, "if I want to catch Perkins or Daley at the warehouse."

"Take my car, Sam," said Avery. "Meet us at my house as soon as you're done."

"Thanks, Avery," said Sam.

"Watch your back," Jade cautioned. "When someone finds out that you weren't in that plane, they may try again." She frowned, realizing that both Chalmers and Harding already knew. How long before word spread?

"Will do." Sam reached out and touched her hand before driving off in the Hupmobile.

Jade felt more joy than she had in several days. Just knowing Sam was out of the hospital, alive and not angry at her for busting his plane, did wonders for her.

"You probably would rather not walk anymore," said Avery. "I'll call for a rickshaw."

"Don't. It's not far, and I don't feel so tired now."

Avery laughed. "Fancy that."

They followed Government Road toward the Tin Shanties that served as the police headquarters, but when they were just outside of the New Stanley Hotel, they heard a loud ruckus of shouting and police whistles.

"Sounds like quite a *shauri*," said Avery.

They hurried ahead to the Court Building to see what the commotion was about. To Jade's horror, one European constable and three African constables were dragging away a half dozen native prisoners, all of whom where vehemently protesting their arrest. Foremost in the group was Jelani.

CHAPTER 16

*The colony frowns on cattle raiding and hunting the lions that
would make sport for others, so they are taking steps to shorten the
amount of time warriors may stay in a* manyatta. *Of course,
Maasai are not proving so tractable as other tribes.*

—The Traveler

"Jelani!" Jade shouted above the din. The boy looked up at hearing his name. The native man next to him had his hands up protecting his head from a club wielded by one of the African constables. It was Jelani who surprised Jade. She knew the lad had courage, but she'd never seen such a look of defiant superiority on anyone's face before. It was as though he was willing to be martyred for a cause. She pushed through the growing crowd toward him.

"And just where do you think you are going, miss?" said a constable, blocking her path.

"I demand to know why you are arresting these natives. I know one of them personally."

"We're not arresting them," he said. "Did that yesterday. We're taking them to court today to charge and sentence them." He pointed to Jelani. "That boy there. He's the reason for this *shauri*. Trying to incite a riot, he is."

The officer didn't stay to continue the conversation. Once

the African policemen had the group firmly in hand, the white officer directed them in hauling the offenders into the building.

Jade saw the grim set of Avery's jaw and knew he was as upset as she was. "Can you do anything, Avery?" she asked.

"I'll do what I can," he said, "but it will have to be through the court. My title might not carry much weight here. I'm not sure who the magistrate is these days. I've been gone awhile."

They entered another flimsy-looking building, went into a courtroom set aside for native cases, and took seats two rows behind the prisoners. Jelani and his companions weren't the only ones awaiting judgment. An assortment of natives, mostly male, mostly Kikuyu, filled the first three benches behind the European constable. Everyone rose, willingly or not, when the magistrate entered.

The first case involved a native woman selling *tembo,* a euphemism for home-brewed alcohol. She was fined ten rupees, an unheard-of sum for a poor native woman, or had to face thirty days in the native prison. Unfortunately for her, she hadn't made that much selling the drink.

Jelani and his companions were the next case to be decided. The officer read the charges: refusing to work and, for Jelani, inciting a revolt. The magistrate's brows rose at this last charge as though he couldn't believe a boy of Jelani's young age could foment a riot. Jelani, for his part, did his best to give the impression that he was capable of that and more. He straightened to his full height, nearly five foot, five inches, and jutted out his chin.

Avery stood and addressed the magistrate. "Your honor, I would like to speak in defense of these men."

"And you are?"

"Lord Avery Dunbury."

"Are these your laborers?"

"No, sir. In point of fact, I do not know any of them except Jelani." He motioned to Jade. "This young woman knows the lad as well."

The magistrate turned to Jade, who also rose. "And your name, miss?"

"Jade del Cameron, sir."

"An American, by your voice."

"Yes, sir."

"Very well, speak your mind, but I should warn you that I take a very dim view of lazy natives. As they are not your workers, I doubt you will be able to convince me otherwise."

Jade took a deep breath and kept her eyes on Jelani, waiting for Avery to have his say.

"I have known the lad, Jelani, for over a year, as has Miss del Cameron, who has acted as his tutor, teaching the boy to read and write. We are concerned first of all about this charge of refusing to work, especially as the boy is not yet old enough to fall under the laws requiring poll and hut taxes.

"Is this true, boy?" asked the magistrate, addressing Jelani. "Are you still a child by our reckoning?"

"I do not know how many long rains I have been alive," Jelani answered. "But I study with the *mundu-mugo* in my village, and he has passed to me a symbol of authority. I have also gone through the manhood rite, so I am a man." His young voice, still cracking, resonated clearly.

Jade felt a surge of pride as she watched him. He'd grown in the past months, like new grass shooting up after a fire. From where she stood, she couldn't see his heel, but she knew that he bore the scars there proudly, a sign of his bravery in escaping slavery barely six months ago. *Yes,* she thought, *he is as much a man as any of the others standing with him.* But it was the English standards that decided who paid taxes, and by that standard, he should still be exempt.

"How old is this boy?" asked the magistrate. He looked at Avery for an answer.

"We don't know, you honor. Possibly twelve."

"And more likely thirteen by the looks of him," said the magistrate. "In which case he is required to pay the hut tax and work to earn it. When he is not working, he should be in his village, and not wandering without travel papers. But," he added before Avery could protest, "I will dismiss *this* charge on the grounds of uncertainty. We will register him as being of age starting next month." The magistrate turned to the officer in charge. "See to it that this boy is fingerprinted and registered. We will deal with this other charge in a moment."

If Jade expected Jelani to show some relief at avoiding one of his charges, she was in for a surprise. His lips tightened and his brows furrowed.

"As to these other men," said the magistrate, "they were all found away from their current employers with no papers to justify their movement." He nodded to the officer in charge. "Repeat offenders?"

"Only one, your honor," replied the officer. "A man called Ngigi."

"Very well." He held up his hand when Avery attempted to speak again. "Hold your peace, sir. I am passing sentence. I fine all the first-time offenders ten rupees each. Mr. Ngigi will face thirty days' imprisonment." He waved his hand in dismissal. "Take those men out, Officer, but leave this boy, Jelani."

The officer in charge directed the African constables

to take charge of the men while he waited behind to see to Jelani. Jade saw Jelani's gaze follow the men, and wondered if he knew them well. She thought she recognized one of the constables herself, but didn't get a second look.

"Now," said the magistrate, "about this second charge, inciting a riot." He folded his hands together and leaned forward, as though expecting a tale of some sort.

The officer in charge explained. "All of the men had been reported as missing without leave by their employer. We located them at their village and were proceeding to take them into custody when this . . . this boy came out of a hut and told the runaways that they should refuse to go back and demand the right to quit their jobs. He even told the native *askaris* making the arrest that they should stand by their brothers and refuse to arrest them."

Jade exchanged a sidelong look with Avery. *Our boy's becoming a leader earlier than I expected.*

The magistrate leaned over farther and addressed Jelani. "It sounds as if you have been listening to Harry Thuku."

At the name of the outspoken African leader, Jelani squared his shoulders.

"Well, answer me, boy."

"You did not ask me a question," said Jelani.

Jade heard Avery draw in his breath. She looked back at the magistrate to ascertain his reaction. He did not appear amused.

"These people," he said, indicating Avery and Jade with a hand wave, "are present on your behalf. They have asked to hear your side of the story. If you do not explain your actions, you will do them a great dishonor, especially as I understand that the lady has taught you to read."

"I will not dishonor Memsahib Simba Jike or Bwana

Dunbury, but I will not say anything about the man called Harry Thuku. I said these things to my tribesmen because they are true. One man returned home because his father was very ill. He said he would go back to work for his bwana. Why wouldn't the bwana wait? Should this man tell his father not to be sick now? Wait until my servitude is over? Do they need a white man's permission to walk in their own country?"

Jade's pulse raced at the words. She admired the strength of a youth who was willing to become a man and risk everything for his people. Surely the magistrate had to be equally affected, but his face was impossible to read, so well had he trained himself to school it in front of the assemblies.

Jelani continued to list the reasons the men had left their employers. One bore the marks of the *kiboko*, or hippo-hide lash, on his back. Another was frightened of what he thought was white man's sorcery. "He said the bwana changed an animal from one kind to another and back again. Another man felt ill and wanted to consult the *mundu-mugo* for medicine. The last man wanted to visit his wife."

"I see," said the magistrate. "While I am certain each of these men felt his reason was important, it still remains that they broke their promise. They agreed to work for their bwanas for a certain amount of time. In return they would be paid so that they could pay their taxes and have money left to buy things."

"There is nothing they want to buy," said Jelani. "They do not care for lanterns and metal pots. It is the white man that wants them to buy these things, so he has to work. That is why they have to pay the tax. It is so they will work."

"You don't think work is important? Men should not work?"

"Yes, but they should do their *own* work." Jelani took a step forward but the constable stopped him. With a quick glance at the officer, Jelani continued. "Who takes care of the village *shambas* or protects the goats now?"

The magistrate placed his hands palm down on his desk and took a deep breath. "You *have* been listening to Thuku. I recognize his words. But you're just a boy and do not fully understand the importance of these laws. The hut tax is not an excuse to make men work. It pays for soldiers to protect the villages. It takes care of the roads that go from village to town."

"Roads we are not allowed to walk on without travel permits," said Jelani.

The magistrate stood. "Enough! I don't intend to explain the law to a boy. In light of my earlier decision regarding your age, I declare you to be too young to pay the penalty for such activities. Instead, I release you to these people, whom you seem to respect. They will see that you return to your village after you are properly fingerprinted. You will be expected to work starting next month. Case dismissed." He waved them out of the room and waited for the next case.

Jelani walked without a word toward Jade and Avery, who escorted him out of the courtroom and into the street. Jade struggled the entire way with what to say to him. But everything she came up with sounded patronizing. What did one say to a fallen warrior?

SAM HADN'T FELT this rotten or this good since the Armistice. He remembered that day clearly; he'd been drawn, wasted, and wounded. His right leg, gone from the shin down, still taunted him with phantom pains, especially at night. But knowing the war was over, and that he'd soon be released from the German camp to go home, overrode the pain and loneliness he'd felt for those last five months.

And so it was today. His body struggled to move after suffering through fevers, deliriums, and a diet of thin oatmeal. But Jade was alive! His pulse quickened as he thought of her. No doubt about it, she was definitely top drawer. It didn't hurt that his plane wasn't too badly damaged either, and that Jade had saved his job by finding the rhino calf. Yep! Things were looking up.

I'll report to Mr. Perkins. Then I'll pick up some Irish linen and a sewing kit to fix the wing. He mentally added to the list as he reviewed what else Jade had told him. *Wrench set, clean rags, as many of those two- and three-gallon cans of fuel as I can find.*

Suddenly his good mood shifted. Somebody had deliberately fouled his engine. Not only that, but they'd done it so as to ensure he'd crash. The fact that they had nearly killed his girl by mistake only made it worse.

Low-down, stump-sucking, dung-brained, maggot-ridden son of a mule's backside. When I find out who did this, I'll kick his face in so hard he'll have to chew through his rear.

But who? And why? Someone had wanted him to take the blame for Stokes' murder. That was why Finch had hauled him in, because someone had said he'd struck Stokes hard. But he'd found out that Stokes was a blackmailer, drawing motive away from himself. Did the real killer hope that his death would end Finch's investigation? That he'd just assume the murderer had died and close the books? Or had Sam seen or overheard something incriminating and not known it?

A driver honked his horn at Sam, who hit the brakes before they collided in the intersection. *Pay attention.* It wouldn't help matters to wreck Avery's new Hupmobile. He shifted back into first and crept forward, then into second gear as he sought the side street that would take him to the old ware-houses.

Okay, he could believe someone needed him to be the fall guy here. But was there some other reason for wanting him out of the way? As soon as Sam turned the corner, he saw Perkins talking with Cutter and Anderson. *Anderson!*

Now there was a man who didn't like him. Anderson wanted Jade for himself and the former doughboy resented Sam for being a pilot. *And crashing would certainly make me look bad!* Trouble was, thought Sam as he set the hand brake, he had no proof. He kept an eye on the men's faces for any reaction to seeing him.

"Mr. Featherstone," said Perkins, "we'd just about given up on you."

"Mr. Perkins," Sam said as he shook his hand, "my apologies for being late. I had some difficulties."

He watched the other two men as he spoke but saw no sign of surprise or anger. Cutter listened with the air of a man ready to get to work. Anderson's lips twitched in a slight sneer.

"Difficulties," repeated Perkins, as Daley joined them. "Nothing serious, I hope." He frowned. "You look like hell."

"He looks like he's been crapped out of the south end of a north-facing bull," said Cutter.

Sam nodded. "Feel that way, too." Seeing that they all expected more, he elaborated. "There was a problem with the airplane's engine. Some fouling forced a landing." He didn't bother to tell them that he wasn't the one who had put down in the bush. Again, he kept his eyes on all the men, especially Anderson. "However, you do have a rhino calf waiting for you. An orphan. It's in a Maasai village right now."

All four men grinned and whooped at the news, which

surprised Sam. He expected Daley and Perkins to be happy, but he'd have bet money that both Anderson and Cutter would see retrieving the rhino as more hard work.

"This is great news, Mr. Featherstone," said Perkins. "Not only did you find us a calf, but we don't have to contend with its mother. You've earned your pay for sure. We'll all get a hefty bonus if we can bring this animal back safely."

That explained their exuberance. It also made Sam question Anderson's role in fouling the engine. If he wanted this bonus that much, he'd ally himself with the devil before he did anything to muck it up.

"How far is this village?" asked Daley.

Sam explained the location, drawing a map for them. "If you leave by noon, you can get to the village by sunset."

"Camp out in a truck with a bunch of killer natives around us?" said Cutter. "Hell, why not stay at the Naivasha Hotel tonight and get an early start tomorrow? Not *too* early, though."

Daley agreed. "I'd like Jade to join us to take pictures. Ought to be some zingers with those Maasai warriors in there. Would you tell her for us?"

Sam saw Anderson's face erupt in a big grin that Sam wanted to smear in the dirt. Instead he made a counterproposal. "I need Jade to help fix my plane. She's a top-notch mechanic, you know. How about I take her out there today? We'll camp and work on the plane at first light. You pick up Jade later on your way to the village. Then, after you've loaded up the rhino and Jade has the pictures, leave her with me on the return trip so she can help me finish up."

Mr. Daley looked at his partner and shrugged. "Suits me. I'll pay you the rest of your fee on our return trip, once we've caged the rhino."

They shook on it, and Sam watched Anderson's face fall. Perkins and Daley headed into their office, leaving Sam alone with the two Americans.

"Well, flyboy, you're a real smarty-pants, aren't you?" said Anderson. "Bet that pilot crap works on all the skirts, doesn't it?"

Sam could put up with a lot of things, including insults to pilots, but calling Jade "a skirt" wasn't one of them. He stepped closer to Anderson until they were only inches apart.

"I don't appreciate your talking about Jade that way," Sam said, his gravelly voice a low rumble.

Anderson didn't move, but Cutter put a hand between them. "Break it up. Wayne, you know the rules on fighting." He turned to Sam. "I don't think he meant any disrespect to Jade—did you, Wayne?" When his friend didn't reply, he shot him a look. "Did you, Wayne?"

"No insult meant for Jade," Anderson said, inferring there was one meant for Sam.

"Well, then," continued Cutter, "that's that. If you'll excuse us, we got work to do."

Sam nodded and let Cutter lead Anderson away. He wondered at how quickly Cutter had stepped in. Almost as if he'd been afraid for his friend. Had he been the one who saw Sam's argument with Stokes?

"You're lucky, Anderson," Sam said, calling after him.

"Oh?" asked Anderson, turning. "And how's that?"

"You're lucky *Jade* didn't hear you call her a skirt. That lady throws a mean right."

AVERY AND JADE took Jelani to be fingerprinted and documented before they brought him back to Avery's home. The three rode in a bicycle-propelled rickshaw, which Avery hired. Jelani hadn't spoken much throughout it all, but Jade placed a reassuring hand on his shoulder in case he worried that he was in trouble with them as well as with the Bureau of Native Affairs. They arrived home at the same time Sam did.

Beverly's delight at seeing Jelani turned immediately to worry when she heard of his arrest. "You poor dear," she said, "did they hurt you? Avery, please find the boy something to eat. Oh, I've got to hire some staff."

"I am well, Memsahib Dunbury." Jelani remained standing in the fancy parlor.

Jade noted that he'd switched from the more colloquial term "memsabu" to the more formal "memsahib" since their last meeting. "Jelani, please sit down. I want to talk with you, but as long as you are standing, I feel as if I'm interrogating you."

Jelani lowered himself to the polished parquet wooden floor next to a zebra-skin rug. Jade sighed. He gripped his *kipande* in his right fist, refusing to wear it.

"I will not treat you as a boy, Jelani. Not after what I saw and heard today. Tell me, as your friend, what has happened."

She saw Jelani take a deep breath and bite his lower lip as the frightened boy inside struggled to stay hidden behind the developing leader. She knew then that he longed for a comforting embrace or a sympathetic smile, but was forcing it back. A soft gasp from Beverly told Jade that her friend saw it, too, and wanted to give in to her growing maternal instincts. Jade held up her hand to stop her.

Avery returned with a tray containing a chicken quarter, a banana, and two pawpaws. He set the tray with a glass of water on the floor next to Jelani and went to stand behind his wife. Sam leaned forward in an armchair, his forearms resting on his thighs and his hands clasped. Jade wished Biscuit was there. His presence would go far toward easing the lad's troubled mind. She tried another tactic.

"You're probably angry at us for coming to court. I can't say as I blame you." Jade was gratified to see Jelani look up suddenly at those words. *At least I have his attention.*

"The magistrate treated me like a child." Jelani ignored the food but drank the water.

Jade nodded. "He would have done that even if we hadn't been there. He doesn't know or care what deeds you have done in your youth." She looked at his wounded foot, which peeked out from under his crossed legs. Instead of a rounded heel, the foot ended in a flat, callused plate. Another flat red circle appeared where the ankle bone should have been.

"He judges me by my size," he said, looking up at Jade.

"He judged you by English law," said Avery, holding up a hand when Jelani would have protested. "I think he knows now that you wield as much power over your village as if you were a man of twice your years. But if you are not thirteen years of age, then he must, by law, still treat you as a boy. But the next time he won't. He's declared that next month you will be a man."

"And made to wear the *kipande* and told where I may go and where I may not go." Jelani dropped the small metal cylinder by his feet, put his head between his hands, and sighed deeply. When he looked up, his soft brown eyes were moist. "My mother is too old now to work and pay her hut tax, and my father is dead."

"What?" the others shouted in unison. "When did this happen?" asked Avery.

"Last month," said Jelani.

Jade closed her eyes and silently reproached herself for not visiting the boy sooner. "I am sorry, Jelani."

"Do not be, Simba Jike," said Jelani. "He died at peace, knowing that I would be the *mundu-mugo*. But I must work on some bwana's farm for six months to pay the hut tax for my mother and for the *mundu-mugo,* since that is now my hut. And I must also have a hut to live in on the bwana's farm, since wherever I go, it will be too far to come home each day. Then I must pay tax on that hut as well."

"Indentured servitude," muttered Sam. "Only one step removed from slavery."

"And if I am working away from the village, how will I learn to be the *mundu-mugo* like the elephant told me? My master has already dreamed of his death. It will be after three more long rains. I have much to learn."

"I'll pay your hut tax, Jelani," said Avery, "and your mother's."

Jelani produced a thin, grim smile. "You are a kind man, Bwana Dunbury. But what of the others in my village? Many men do not come home anymore after being away so long. Their wives cannot leave the village and cook for them, so the men take new wives. The village has not so many babies now. The *mundu-mugo* has seen his future. I have seen my village's as well. It will die unless I help it." He put his head down again and rocked to and fro. "I do not know how."

No one spoke for a while as they looked from one to another and back to the sorrowing boy before them.

"I would be happy to hire you," said Beverly, "but I don't think it would solve this dilemma. And," she added, "I shouldn't like giving you orders to fetch and carry."

Avery slapped his leg and paced the floor. "Well, the entire system is completely fouled." He jabbed his finger in the air as though pointing to a culprit. "The case against it has been argued over and over again back in London, you know. There are even antislavery leagues back home protesting, but no one here seems to think it's a problem."

"Avery, love," said Beverly as she reached out her hand and took hold of his. "*This* is our home, now. You must get on the governing council and try to change things. Speak to the governor when he returns. Surely your voice will carry some weight."

Avery patted her hand and smiled. "Only with you, my love. I'm afraid I will not have nearly as much influence as the older settlers, but I will do what I can. How can I not? But it still won't solve our immediate problem."

Jade smiled as he labeled the problem "our" instead of Jelani's. "I'll hire you, Jelani."

He looked up. "I do not understand how that will help. If I must travel with you, how can I study with the *mundu-mugo*?"

"You won't travel with me. You will live at your village and be my source."

"Source? I do not understand, Simba Jike. Do you mean sorcerer? I have heard that word. I will not be something evil."

Sam sat up straighter. "I think I understand, Jelani. A source is a beginning, a place where something starts, like the spring at the head of a river."

Jelani frowned as he looked from Sam to Jade.

"You'll be the source of my information," Jade said. "I'll write about the Kikuyu and you will tell me what I should write."

"By thunder," said Avery, "that's a splendid idea."

"You should write as well, Jelani," said Beverly. "You should sell articles in your own words to the *London Times*."

"Earn his own money, rather than depend on us for wages," said Sam. "Beverly, that's inspired."

Jelani lifted his head higher and squared his shoulders. "Would it work? Would this paper pay for my stories?"

"We cannot make promises for them," said Jade, "but I think so, yes. Still, until the money comes, please accept my offer."

Sam leaned forward again. "If you're going to write about what is happening to your people, Jelani, then I think that you need a bigger view of Africa. I can give you that."

Jelani's eyes opened wider, but, Jade noted, not with that innocent sense of excitement she'd seen in the past. Instead, his eyes held the gleam of a general who had been offered a view of the enemy camp.

"In your airplane?" Jelani asked. Sam nodded. "Thank you. Yes, I will go up."

"Good," said Sam. "I'll take you aloft as soon as I get her back and running."

"Well," said Beverly and clapped her hands together, "that will be three authors among us: Jade, Maddy, and now Jelani. Perhaps I should try my hand at it next."

Avery kissed his wife on the forehead. "Give it up, my dear. You cannot bear to write so much as a letter."

"That's not true. Jade, tell him what a fine correspondent I've been."

"I've received one letter from you since the end of last January when you went back to London. One entire page in large hand, so you are definitely not ready for a novel."

Beverly stuck out her tongue at Jade.

"And what happens now?" asked Avery.

"I need to find my plane," said Sam, "and get it cleaned, repaired, and back in the air." He looked at Jade. "Your bosses are going out today as far as the Naivasha Hotel and then on tomorrow to the Maasai village. Perkins wants you to photograph them at the village. Thinks it will be great publicity or something." Sam explained how Anderson had expected Jade to be with them in the Naivasha Hotel and how he'd smashed that idea by telling them he needed Jade with him as a mechanic. "We should leave soon so we can get to the plane before nightfall."

"And how are we going to get there if we don't ride with Perkins?" asked Jade.

Sam cast a hopeful glance at Avery. "I was hoping we could use the Hupmobile?"

"And if you're flying back, Sam, and Jade is still with the crew documenting their great rhino capture, what happens to my new automobile?"

Sam scratched his head. "Dang. Guess I sort of overlooked that part in my haste to salvage my plane and," he added with a sidewise glance to Jade, "my girl."

"Darling," said Beverly, "why don't you go with them? Then when our Jade has to leave Sam, he's not bereft of mechanical assistance. *You* can drive your Hup back."

"And leave you alone in your condition? I should think not. You cannot even get out of your chair without help."

"I'll have Jelani with me." She turned to the young Kikuyu. "You could stay for a few days, couldn't you, Jelani?"

"But the *mundu-mugo*—"

"Will not expect you for a while yet," finished Jade, "not after you were hauled out of the village under arrest." Jelani nodded his assent and started in on the chicken.

"I'll send a wire to the Blue Post Hotel at Thika and ask someone to deliver a message to the Thompsons," said Avery. "Neville ought to be able to spare Maddy to stay with Beverly for a few days, too."

"Maddy'll be wanting to check on any replies to her advertisement anyway," added Jade. "Don't forget you promised to talk to that Berryhill boy for me, Bev." She stood up. "Oh, blast! I never reported the sabotage to the police. Sorry, Sam."

Sam's lips twitched. "It's understandable, considering. And by the time we all handle the plane tomorrow, there probably won't be any usable fingerprints on it anyway."

Jade waved her arms to the door, "Well, we're burning daylight, gentlemen. Let's get a move on."

CHAPTER 17

The most trusted warriors are employed to procure food for the manyatta.
If they need to, they are allowed to take it with force.
Their mission demands it, for the continuing good of the Maasai.
These warriors are called embikas.

—The Traveler

DESPITE EVERYONE'S BEST efforts at throwing together supplies, they didn't exit Parklands until midafternoon. Since
they wanted to avoid driving to Sam's hangar for fuel, most
of the time was spent purchasing overpriced cans of gasoline
at the various supply stores or rounding up empty cans to collect whatever they could salvage from the plane. Sam's tool
kit was back at his hangar, but Avery, deciding he needed one
himself to maintain his new car, purchased a set. Jade took
charge of food, water, cots, and tents. She brought out her
Winchester and ammunition, and Avery added his Enfield
to the stock. No one intended to shoot anything, but then, no
one ever intended to get attacked either.

Avery insisted on being allowed to drive his own car
and opened it up to a blazing 60 miles per hour on the better stretches of road. There weren't many of them, as Sam
noted after bouncing out of the seat over one particularly
bad rut. Still, they made the south end of Lake Naivasha in

decent time and had enough daylight to get to the edge of Hell's Gate before nightfall. The last three miles came at sunset. They might have missed the plane, but for the signal fire maintained by the Maasai on watch.

Jade greeted Tajewo and introduced Sam and Avery. Sam wanted to examine the plane right away by flashlight, but was voted down by a large yawn from Jade. "She'll keep till morning, Sam. You need to sleep right now."

With such a clear night and a palette of stars overhead, Sam suggested they forget the tent and just sleep on the cots. Jade, mindful of Sam's recent bout with malaria, pounded two tent poles in the ground on either side of his cot and draped a mosquito net over him.

"Aren't you kind of closing the barn door after the horse already got out?" Sam asked.

"Always a good idea in case there's another horse still in the barn," Jade replied. "You were lucky last time. You might not be so lucky the next. Use the blasted netting."

"And what about you and Avery?"

"Mosquitoes don't bite me, but I plan to sleep downwind of the campfire smoke," said Jade. "That'll keep the nasty little buggers away."

"And I intend to sleep in the backseat of my car," called Avery from the Hupmobile. He'd tossed the rest of the supplies from the back into the front seat. "I'll drape a net over the open window. Now if you don't mind, good night."

Jade woke just before dawn and, yawning, opened the driver's door to pull out a coffeepot, coffee, and a thick mitt. She filled the pot from their water supply, measured in the coffee grounds, and put the pot on the fire's coals to boil. Then she returned to the car and fetched flour, baking soda, a can of lard, and a pan. Jade cut in enough lard to turn the flour and soda into a mealy mix, then added water slowly until she had a stiff dough. She pulled off sections of dough and spread them around on the pan to make a dozen biscuits. Next, she arranged a bed of rocks on the coals near the coffeepot and set the biscuit pan on top. A lid on the pan and some coals on the lid, and Jade had a working Dutch oven going as the sun rose.

On her final supply run, Jade got her first good look at Sam's plane since her return. For a moment, the sight before her made her stop dead in her tracks, slack-jawed. *Well, it could be worse.* She rummaged in the supplies, brought out a slab of bacon, pulled her knife, and sliced off offerings for a final pan. At the fragrant scent of frying bacon, both Sam and Avery stirred. Jade kept her eyes on the bacon, pretending she hadn't even noticed what had happened to the plane.

"Mmm," said Sam as he stretched on his cot. "Something smells great. Nice to have a trail boss who cooks, too. Will our new friends join us?"

Jade shook her head. "A runner brought in some calabashes of sour milk earlier." She checked the biscuits. "Breakfast is almost ready. Tell Avery to get his sorry backside out of bed." She stirred down the coffee grounds and set the pot aside to brew.

"Will do." Sam pulled aside the mosquito netting and sat up. "And how's my . . . What in Sam Hill happened to my plane?" He quickly scrambled off the cot for a better look.

"Pretty, isn't it?" Jade said as she squatted by the fire, still holding the bacon pan. "I think they meant you an honor, Sam." She looked up to see how he'd take this last offering. Setting the pan aside where it wouldn't burn, she stood and went to his side. "Looks like a good fix, too. I like the red color."

She walked beside Sam as he approached his beloved Jenny and gingerly reached out to touch the colorful wing patch. Scarlet fabric with little white and black circles painted on it had been carefully stitched with a fine sinew into the Irish linen. He touched the seams, which had been sealed with some sort of natural glue.

Tajewo joined them, sporting a wide grin. "We knew the healed skin would please you," he said in a mix of English and Swahili. He pointed to a top wing and the circles within circles painted on it. "We know not what this talisman is, but it protected the top, so we put it here."

"Yes, I see," mumbled Sam, still dazed over the shock of seeing his plane tricked out in such finery.

Jade elbowed him and gave him a significant look. "You were fortunate in your protectors, Sam. The plane wasn't eaten by wildlife."

Sam rallied at her reminder. "Yes," he said with more feeling, "I am very happy. This is a big . . . big and happy surprise." He plastered a large smile on his face. "Thank you."

"I think the ostrich feathers and beads on the spars and handholds are a nice touch, too," added Jade, fingering one of them.

"Ah," said Tajewo, "these are a powerful charm. A black ostrich feather means peace." He pointed to the red beads. "Red is survival. Together, they bring a blessing on the arplane."

"Well, I can't argue with that," said Sam. "I can use all the help I can get right about now." He thanked Tajewo again, shaking his hand.

Avery paused in his return from making a morning necessary visit. "Sweet mother of pearl," he exclaimed, "it looks like a bloody circus came to town!"

THE THREE OF them worked for several hours after breakfast, draining the remaining gasoline, washing off the carburetor screens, and, in general, cleaning out everything on the plane that could possibly be cleaned. After straining the saved gasoline through a layer of mosquito netting, to catch the larger particles, then through cotton sheeting, they poured the fuel back into the tank. Then they repeated the process, again draining the gasoline after it had washed the interior. Each filtering left them with less gasoline.

"It would have been easier if we could have trained an elephant to come over and blow out the blasted tank," said Sam.

"I wonder what our new friends think of all this," Avery said with a nod to the Maasai.

They stood, storklike, and watched with keen interest. Only this time, their attention was fixed on a distant dust trail. Sam swore softly under his breath. The blasted animal crew would be there in a matter of minutes, and when they left, they'd take Jade with them.

It wasn't that he felt any competition from Anderson. But after discovering that Jade had risked her neck flying solo for him, Sam really didn't want her to leave his side. He wiped his hands on a rag. "We've got company."

Standing suddenly after squatting so long made him feel woozy, so he took hold of the propeller for a better balance. Then he helped himself to a long pull on his canteen. *Be danged if I appear weak in front of these men.* After all, he reasoned, he was representing the air corps. Well, he and Avery both.

The two trucks pulled to a stop to the side of the plane. Daley drove one with Cutter riding shotgun. Several hired Africans rode in the back. Anderson drove the second truck, a large wood-and-wire crate in back.

Sam noted with disgust that the only empty seat for Jade was in Anderson's truck. *Blasted son of a one-eyed mule probably planned it that way.* He nodded to the men and forced a smile. "Good morning. Have any trouble finding us?"

Daley leaned out of the window and waved. "Not much. For a while we got mixed up on another set of tracks. Looked like they doubled back to an old shack. Once we got back on yours, we followed them right to you." He nodded to the plane. "Is it fixable?"

"Yes," said Sam. "Just a matter of cleaning out the carburetor." *And the tank,* he added silently, still wondering if one of them was the saboteur.

"Do you need anything?" asked Daley. "Got all your tools?"

"We could probably use another can of petrol," said Avery, "if you have one to spare."

Daley shook his head. "Gasoline's kind of tight right now. No guarantee we could restock in Naivasha."

"We'll be all right," said Sam.

Jade came around from the front of the plane, her trousers grimy and a streak of grease across her face. Sam thought she'd never looked lovelier.

"I hate to head off and leave you shorthanded, Sam," she said. "But we shouldn't be too long. Then I'll help you and Avery finish up and I'll fly back with you."

Sam shook his head. "You're not flying back with me." He'd decided that last night.

Her dark brows furrowed and her eyes snapped green fire. "Why the hell not?"

"Not going to take a chance, Jade. Look, we've just about got this cleaned out, but . . ." He held a finger to her lips to stop her when she opened her mouth to protest. That mouth that he wanted to feel against his right now, grease and all. "There's always a chance that we overlooked something, and I'm not going to risk your pretty neck up there with me."

Jade scowled as though she'd like to see him try to make her go back without him. Sam saw the look and knew he had to get this bird up and off before they returned.

He gave her a gentle push toward the trucks, hoping she'd hop in the back of the first one with the natives. "Get going, now. And thanks for your help. All of it."

"You'd better still be here, Sam Featherstone," she said.

Wisely, he said nothing.

Jade gathered up her bag with her camera and personal effects and climbed into the passenger seat of Anderson's truck. Anderson made sure Sam saw his big smile as they drove off, Tajewo and his companions jogging alongside them, refusing to ride.

Sam and Avery stood for a moment, watching the trucks head on toward the village.

"You asked her yet?" asked Avery.

Sam didn't even pretend to misunderstand his friend. "Working up to it."

Avery shook his head. "Don't wait too long. The bucks are circling."

*   *   *

TAJEWO LED JADE and her companions to an expansive enclosure made of dried mud and dung. Ringing the inner
wall was a series of capacious mud, dung, and wattle huts.
Jade counted forty-nine. She saw older women going about
the business of milking cows and a few goats. The women
were decked out in wide, flat beaded collars, which circled
their slender necks like the rings of Saturn she'd seen in a
photograph. Several girls were busy beading scabbards for
a warrior's knife. The littlest boys played at various games,
pretending to herd cattle or hunt lion. Jade noticed only a
few warriors defending the village. The older men, identifiable by their short or shaven hair, sat talking outside under
a euphorbia tree.

"This is my village," explained Tajewo. "I live here now
but soon I will go with others of my age to the *manyatta*, the
warriors' village, to learn how to become an elder."

"I see five warriors," said Jade. "Are there many living
here?"

Tajewo nodded. "Some are guarding the cattle. Others
are over there." He pointed to a distant hut where two men
lounged, undergoing the time-consuming process of plait-
ing their hair and decorating their bodies. Two others hosted
mock combats with some boys. Jade asked if she could photograph the *kraal*. Tajewo nodded.

"Ask him where our rhino is," said Daley.

She didn't need to. Tajewo understood enough English
to grasp the question. He called to the men in the battle with
the boys. They grinned and ran off to the far side where a few
nanny goats were being milked. Soon they returned leading
one very forlorn-looking little rhino.

"What the . . . ? They painted him," said Cutter.

On his right hind quarters, the rhino bore a bright ocher

circle with a darker red star inside it. Jade recognized the pattern as taken from the Jenny.

"We painted Bwana Mti Mguu's brand," said Tajewo. "He grows well on goat's milk."

Jade photographed the rhino as it stood by one of his guards. "He looks very healthy, Tajewo. Thank you."

One of the girls ran over to the rhino and gazed up shyly at Tajewo. With a giggle, she placed a circlet of green-and-white beads around the rhino's neck. Tajewo pretended to pay her no attention, but Jade detected a slight tilt to his lips. Obviously, this little damsel courted his favor and had found a new way of gaining notice beyond the usual beaded gifts would-be girlfriends made for prospective beaus.

"*Asante sana,*" said Daley, thanking Tajewo in Brooklyn-laced Swahili after the girl had run back to her friends. "Load him up!" he shouted to Cutter and Anderson, who, in turn, directed the two African men in the trucks. But they hadn't counted on the Maasai's fierce reputation getting in the way. None of the assistants, all Kikuyu men, would set foot in the Maasai enclosure.

Tajewo also didn't look pleased that men from a farming tribe might enter. In fact, noting that there was even a remote possibility of their doing so galvanized him into action. He motioned the two warriors guarding the calf to lead the rhino out to the truck.

The Kikuyu ran to the truck and opened the cage door. Hurrying on to Anderson's truck, they retrieved four long boards and placed them side by side to form a long ramp. The confused calf had no intention of walking up them. So, finally, they slid the cage down the ramp and, by coaxing and prodding, induced the rhino to enter. Then they secured the door behind him.

The next step, pushing the cage back up the ramp, was no easy task as the calf weighed close to five hundred pounds. With the Kikuyu pulling the cage from above and Anderson, Cutter, and Daley pushing from below, they managed to get the cage back into the truck, much to the amusement of the watching Maasai. The warriors cheered, brandishing their spears. Two started to jump, stiff-legged, and were soon joined by the other warriors in this show of strength. Jade photographed this send-off, wishing Sam was here to capture it as a motion picture.

As she turned to leave, Jade saw one of the elders walk toward her, a long staff in one hand. He wore yards of red fabric fastened over his right shoulder like a tunic and, over that, a cloak of shimmering brown fur. A container for snuff, fashioned from a very small, painted gourd, hung around his neck. His gray hair was closely cropped, and large loops of beaded wire dangled from his ears, ending in tiny bells and what resembled spear points. In his other hand, he clutched a fly whisk made of wildebeest tail and lion's mane. From the way the other elders moved aside, Jade knew he held rank. Had she broken a taboo by photographing the jumping competition?

Tajewo moved to her side. "It is the *laibon*," he said, "the most powerful elder of all the villages. You may speak if he hands the talking stick to you."

Jade felt her blood run cold and her muscles tense. The *laibon*. She had heard many stories of the supposed power such a man held. To Jelani, a Kikuyu, the *laibon* was the equivalent of a witch. But the witch she'd confronted in Tsavo on her first trip was not a respected village elder, but a man in pursuit of evil and power. She stood her ground and waited.

The elder spoke and Tajewo translated, though Jade was

able to catch some of the words. "Engai, who has wide eyes, watches over you," the *laibon* said, his voice cracking with age. "Sometimes he lets me see through his eyes. I have seen you face raking claws and blood-hot rage with the bravery of a warrior. I see something else: danger before you. It comes with madness in pale yellow eyes. When this killer comes for you again, Simba Jike, you must seek help from your mate." He raised his fly whisk, spat on it, and brushed her face and shoulders.

A cold sweat broke out along Jade's spine, and her vision dimmed. She saw a pair of faceless yellow eyes staring at her. With the image came a distant report, like a rifle's. Jade shook her head to clear it, and the vision passed.

"It is a blessing," whispered Tajewo, nudging her.

Jade extended her hand. The old man put the talking stick into it. "Thank you. I shall heed your warning," said Jade as Tajewo translated. "And may Engai send you many cattle and many children and bring you sweet grass," she concluded in Maa.

The *laibon* nodded, a pleased smile on his wrinkled face. Jade climbed into Anderson's truck. She waved goodbye to Tajewo, and they drove back toward Nairobi with their prize.

Jade looked out the open window as the truck jerked and jolted over the rocky ground on this eastern side of Hell's Gate. A family of rock hyrax, startled from their foraging, raced back into the shelter of the surrounding rocks with several loud squeaks. The last hyrax, a plump adult, turned and exposed its teeth at them before scurrying to safety with the others. Its fierceness and defiance, especially from something so small and edible to so many predators, impressed and amused Jade, until she recognized the creature's fur as the same as in the *laibon*'s cloak. After they disappeared, Jade contented herself by watching the heat ripples that shimmied over the exposed bare ground.

"You're coming in with us, aren't you?" asked Anderson. "I mean, you aren't expected to continue slaving over some dirty airplane engine, are you?"

Jade arched one brow in response. "I'd hardly call it slaving. It's important to keep an engine clean if you expect it to run well. Even more so for an airplane." She nodded toward the truck's hood. "Sounds like this one could use some maintenance. Don't you ever work on it?"

"Well, yeah. We change the oil when it needs it. Cutter handles most of that."

Jade watched Anderson closely, gauging how much he really knew about engines and how much he might pretend not to know. And did he hate Sam enough to frame him or foul his engine? She decided to hit him with a broadside.

"So why did you tell Inspector Finch that Sam hit Stokes?"

Anderson inhaled and swallowed simultaneously, causing him to cough and wheeze on his own saliva. Jade reached over and held on to the steering wheel until he stopped. He wiped his eyes with the back of his hand and shook his head. "What are you . . . ? Where did you get that . . . ? What makes you think *I* tipped off the police?"

His reaction told Jade she'd struck the mark. She simply folded her arms and stared at him. It worked. He shifted in his seat like a guilty child caught in the act.

"You've got a suspicious mind, lady."

"Made even more suspicious by the fact that you're not answering my question."

"Look, no matter who ratted on him, I have it on good authority that he's dangerous."

"On good authority? That means *you* didn't see anything." Jade snorted. "You really hate pilots, don't you?" He didn't reply. Instead, he kept glancing nervously at her right hand. Did he think she was about to belt him or pull her knife on him? *Tempting, but not while he's driving.*

"Who told you Sam hit Stokes?" she asked after she let the silence drag on. He fidgeted in his seat again. "One of our bosses? Or Cutter?" A twitch of his lips told Jade she'd struck pay dirt on that last name. "Cutter said Sam hit Stokes?"

"Look, after they found this Stokes fellow dead, we talked about it by his store with some of the farmers. Cutter said he saw an American man arguing with Stokes. Waving his hand in the air all mad. Took a swing at him. One of those farmers allowed that there'd probably be a reward for that information." He thrust out his chin. "It was my duty to report it."

"But *not* to *embellish* the facts," Jade said softly, in a voice that sounded suspiciously like a low growl. She let the matter drop, satisfied that Finch's so-called eyewitness wouldn't hold up in court. She just wondered who had egged him on with the promise of reward. Something told her that it could have been the real killer looking for a scapegoat.

She ended the conversation with a "Hmph" and turned back to the surroundings. They should be coming up on Sam's plane soon. Jade didn't believe for a moment that Sam would turn her away, especially if it meant she had to ride with Anderson.

She was wrong. Another ten minutes brought them to the spot where the plane had been. Jade called a halt and got out, hoping to find a message left behind by Sam. *Nothing!*

"Looks like he didn't want you after all," said Anderson. "I told you he was no good."

SAM WATCHED THE last of the lake disappear beneath the cockpit. He could still see it if he leaned over and stuck his head out into the slipstream. It felt so good just to be flying again, as far from that hospital bed as he could get. He loved how his Jenny responded to his commands. A nudge on a foot pedal, a slight shift in the stick, and he was banking gently. Why couldn't women be that way? Why did they always have to fight back? It made him wonder why in thunder he or any other man referred to an engine, automobile, boat, or airplane as a "she." *Wishful thinking, probably.*

He'd seen the look on Jade's face when she left this morning. He knew the set of that mouth and the snap of those eyes. She had every intention of flying back with him, as if he still needed mothering. *Probably would have insisted that Avery fly back and she drive me home with a blanket tucked around my lap.*

Well, he'd told her no and he'd meant it. No one was going to risk themselves in his plane until he was absolutely certain they'd gotten her all cleaned out. And they had. She was running like a dream.

She'll be mad at you, you know. That was a perfect example. If he'd told Avery or Neville that he'd be gone when they returned, they'd nod their heads and accept it. And they wouldn't expect him to change his mind and wait for them anyway. After all, saying what you meant and acting on it should be a sign that you could be trusted. Not a woman. A woman would be completely surprised by the fact that you meant what you said.

A little voice in his head nagged at him that Jade wasn't

like other women, which was why he loved her so much. *She'll be madder about having to ride back with that jerk, Anderson.* He had to give her that one. He would be, too. Well, if she was mad, he had a plan in mind for how to soften her up.

JADE CLIMBED BACK into the truck after inspecting the ropes holding the cage in place. All the knots held. "Let's go."

"See, I told you that man's trouble," said Anderson. "Now, *I'd* never go off and leave *you* behind. He deserves to lose you."

"Will you be quiet?" Jade muttered. "Why should Sam and Avery have waited? They had no idea how long we'd be gone." She leaned her elbow on the door top and rested her cheek against her fist. Actually, she had been angry, but listening to Anderson made her ashamed of the way she'd felt initially. Still, she was disappointed.

"What I'm saying," Anderson said, "is that he's taking you for granted. He's assuming that you're stuck on him. That's what *all* those flyboys think. That they're God's gift to women."

Jade groaned and wished she'd ridden in the back, next to the rhino cage.

"Now you take me for instance," continued Anderson.

"No," Jade interrupted. "Wayne, I'm flattered, but please stop."

He looked over to her, his brows arched in confusion. "You getting one of those female headaches?"

Jade stifled a laugh. "Yes, that's it. Some quiet would be good." She leaned out the window and saw the second truck trundling along behind them. They'd taken the lead so that the others could keep an eye on the restraining straps holding their prize rhino in place. The slightest hint that the cage was coming free, and they'd beep the horn for a stop. Not that they intended for anything to progress that far. They'd stop again along the way to check the cage. Jade had even suggested a good spot, the old farmhouse near Mount Longonot. But she had another reason for stopping there. Ever since Daley said he'd accidentally followed tracks to a shack, she feared that someone else had been there. But were they friend or foe to the runaway woman?

A warthog disturbed from his dust bath raced off to the south, his tail sticking straight up. To her right, Mount Longonot rose, its gently sloping blue-gray mass blending into the sky. From Jade's vantage point, it appeared to be supported by all the candelabra-shaped euphorbia growing at its base, like hundreds of slender arms pushing it upward as an offering. Six giraffe browsed among the scattered acacia trees in the foreground. The bulk of the wildlife, Jade knew, resided closer to the lake. She made a note to come back sometime and photograph the animals, especially the hippos and the colobus monkeys, with their stark black-and-white fur, like some bizarre cross between a skunk and a monkey. *A skunkey.* The zebra would photograph well, too.

Thinking of zebra made her reconsider Sam and his movie. What would he do when he completed it? Would he go back to America to try to sell it? Would he tour with it? Would he return to Africa? The thought of him so far away disturbed her. *You know he's in love with you. And yes,* came the returning voice, *you're in love with him.* But Jade wasn't sure which she *needed* more: Sam or her independence. Somehow she didn't think she could have both.

The hot afternoon air and the rocking truck made Jade drowsy. She fought sleep by pulling her notebook out of her pack and writing some impressions of the morning's visit to the Maasai warriors' camp. She would have at least one article for the *Traveler* out of this, perhaps two. She wished she knew more about those enigmatic people.

Jade thought about her promise to Jelani. She knew that her magazine would not be interested in an in-depth look at Kikuyu life and their current problems. She'd already given them a glimpse into village life when she'd written about the *ngoma* during her first trip. *A book? Jelani's story?* Maybe. It would be good if Jelani could sell his own story. Not that she was shirking her duty, but making the boy dependent on any of them would not help his cause.

The boy! She had to quit thinking of him that way. The boy had grown up. Children in difficult situations always grew up fast. How was it that the British system saw Jelani as a man now, but still saw sixteen-year-old Harley as a boy? Sam's plan to take Jelani aloft and let him see Africa from the air was a good one. Leave it to Sam to give the boy wings. It was just the sort of thought that she admired him for. *What are you going to do when he goes back to the States?*

"Is that the farmhouse you said we should stop at?" asked Anderson.

Jade gazed ahead to her right. "Yes."

"Don't look like much of a place to live. Why'd you suggest stopping here anyway?"

"There's a well pump in back in case the radiators need water. We can also refill our drinking-water supply." She jerked her head to the cage behind them. "Junior might be thirsty, too." What she didn't say was that she wanted to check on the woman inside. If she was actually Alice Stokes, as Jade suspected, then she might be in need of help but afraid to ask for it.

Anderson stopped about fifty feet away from the dilapidated house. "I don't think anybody's home," he said when no one appeared at the door. The second truck pulled alongside. Jade got out, leaving her Winchester in the truck, and motioned with her palm out for the others to wait where they were. She didn't relish someone pulling a shotgun on her, so she took a moment to not only show that she had no weapon with her, but to scan the doors, windows, and assorted cracks for anyone pointing one at her. *My knee doesn't ache. I'll be fine.*

"I'll just go ask if we can have some water," Jade announced loud enough for anyone listening in the house to hear. "Anyone home?" she called as she walked to the door. No one answered and she didn't detect any motion at the windows. She rapped loudly on the warped wooden door. "Hello? Can we use your well?"

Jade listened carefully for a cough, a sigh, any little noise that a human might make when trying her best to lie low. Dead silence. Shouldn't that baby she thought she heard on her last visit wake up and whimper? Her stomach knotted. What if something had happened to them? They could both be inside, injured. Or worse!

She tried the door. It was unlatched and opened easily. Jade stepped inside, warily sniffing the air. No stench of death and decay. She heard three truck doors open and shut behind her. Reinforcements coming.

"Jade," called Daley, "what's going on?"

"I'm not sure, Hank," she called back. "It looks like the person here cleared out." It didn't take much looking to see that the two-room house was empty. The boxes of supplies were gone as well. "The pump's around back," she hollered. "I'm going to look around in here a bit more."

She walked into the back room, the one that had been

a bedroom and also a nursery. The only furniture was one worn-out cot with an old mattress stuffed with dried grass, a few empty stacked crates for a dresser, and one empty wooden crate on the floor at the foot of the cot. Inside were a scrap of a blanket and a broken baby's rattle.

Mrs. Stokes and her child had disappeared again.

Had they gone willingly?

CHAPTER 18

Not all warriors are brave, trusted, or follow the Maasai culture.
Some cut their long hair before the appointed time, just before becoming an
elder. Others shirk their duties. The embikas *punish these men.*
It is imperative that this generation of warriors retain its honor.

—The Traveler

AFTER JADE HAD bounced about for more than four hours in a decrepit truck, her headache was no longer a pretense. The grasslands had been rough enough, but once Anderson turned onto the road from Naivasha to Nairobi, he sped up. What he didn't consider was that the dirt of any murram road remembered every rut run into it during a rainy season, and this particular road had a long memory. The colony's public works department didn't do much to erase it either. Since Anderson hit every blasted rut, some deep enough to lose a goat in, Jade's spine soon learned everything the road had to tell.

At least the little rhino fared all right. The cage was just large enough for him to stand with no extra room to be bounced back and forth and slammed around like a tennis ball. Once they arrived at the warehouse, Jade coaxed the little fellow out to drink and have a dinner of goat's milk and a bit of hay.

"That's a fine specimen," declared Perkins. "We'll pack him back up as soon as he's finished eating." He had stayed behind to orchestrate the loading of most of the hoofed animals. "I've got an engine heading south late this afternoon. We'll start boarding those animals, then come back for the rest of them, saving the big cats for last." He reconsidered a moment. "I'll take those kittens down on this first trip, too." He handed two checks to Jade. "One of these is yours. Give the other to that pilot fellow for me."

"What do you want me to do here today, Mr. Perkins?" asked Jade, slipping the checks into her shirt pocket.

He took off his hat and scratched his head. "Well, we won't be needing your roping skills anymore, so once you've got some photos of the animals going onto the train, you should be clear until the others come back. They'll need your help again with that lion Percy. He seems to respond to your voice better than ours."

Jade held out her hand. "I guess this is goodbye then, Mr. Perkins. Thanks for the job."

He shook her hand. "Been a pleasure, Miss del Cameron. Look me up if you ever get back to the States."

"Hey, Bob," yelled Cutter from the truck, "who's overseeing the animal care here and who's going on to the boat?"

Perkins pulled a notebook from his hip pocket and flipped through a few pages. "I've got you staying here, Frank. Wayne will go with me and Hank on the train." He turned another page. "They'll return here for the carnivores and you. I'll stay at the boats." He looked up from his book. "I'll hire workers at Mombassa to help before we ship out."

"So it's just *me* here?" Cutter looked like a kid who'd just learned he had to miss a parade for chores. "Why do I have to stay behind?"

"Because your shoes still stink like polecat, Frank," said Perkins. "Don't want to be in the same train car with you if I can avoid it. Get the damn things cleaned, why don't you?" He waved a hand at the warehouse. "You have men here, Frank. Once everything is locked down for the night, you only need to post the usual watch."

"Yeah, Frank," said Anderson, "you're acting like you're a scaredy-cat."

"I don't see you rushing over to check on those cats, Wayne," retorted Cutter. "That leopard gives me the willies every time he looks at me. Those eyes don't look natural, I tell ya."

"You don't have to feed the leopard yourself," said Perkins. "Just make sure it gets done. You'll be in charge." He clapped his hands twice. "Let's get to work, men."

Jade saw that the rhino had finished his hay, at least as much as he intended to eat. Right at the moment he seemed more intent on pawing through it and bucking in what, she supposed, passed for rhino play. Jade let him have his fun and exercise for another ten minutes, then led him back into a traveling pen before he could curl up and fall asleep on the ground outside. His new pen was large enough for him to move around in, and once inside, he quickly dropped to his knees and closed his eyes.

In the meantime, the others had started pushing and hoisting cages into the waiting freight cars. Jade photographed the loading of the zebra stallion as well as his harem. Next came a young pair of reedbuck, the male's horns barely budding. Following them, the men loaded up two Thomson's gazelles. Their horns had been wrapped in woolen fabric to prevent them from accidentally goring each other during the voyage. It looked as if they sported turbans, and Jade made a point of capturing the image.

As she watched set after set of animals, she had the impression that this was a twisted sort of Noah's ark. Once again, pairs or small herds of animals were being saved, but from a flood of humanity rather than water. The last cage to go up contained one lone female aardvark. She stuck her long, piglike nose between the bars and sniffed. A moment later, her whiplike sticky tongue flicked out and swept the floor, searching for insects.

At least they didn't keep the zorilla.

Jade had finished taking shots of the aardvark when she spied one of the railway workers walking the line, checking to see that all doors were shut and the cars securely coupled. The engineer? No, the engineer was currently backing the locomotive down this side rail. Whatever this man's position, she decided to visit with him. Since Neville's coffee dryer had stood on the siding for several days, this man might have seen or heard something useful.

She stepped forward, her right hand extended. "Hello, I'm Jade del Cameron." The man shook her hand, his brows tipped upward in curiosity. Jade waved her Kodak in her left hand. "I'm documenting this shipment for Mr. Perkins and Mr. Daley. I was wondering if I might ask you to pose by one of the cars for a picture."

"Why, certainly, miss," he said, putting his left hand on the boxcar door handle. "How's this?"

Jade moved to her right to get the approaching locomotive in the background and took two exposures. "Wonderful. Now if I could just get your name and your official title." She slung the camera over one shoulder and pulled out her notebook and pencil.

"David Robertson," he said. "I'm an assistant locomotive superintendent. I oversee special freight cars such as this one. Wouldn't do to have excessive weight behind an engine, you see."

"Ah, an assistant *superintendent*!" exclaimed Jade. "Then I imagine you know everything that goes on around the rail yards, don't you?"

The man dropped his hand from the door and brushed away some dirt from his shirtfront. "Yes. I check all the manifests for weight, oversee loading and unloading, that sort of thing. " He smiled. "Doing a piece for a paper?"

"I write for a magazine," said Jade.

"A magazine," he repeated as he straightened his cap. "Good show. Wonderful what young ladies can do nowadays. If you'd like to photograph my office, I'd be happy to let you. Perhaps a shot of me sitting behind my desk?"

"I think out here in the yards is much more impressive," said Jade. She looked around as though trying to find a proper backdrop. "Considering your importance, you should be in front of some heavy equipment."

"There are crates of tea in the far warehouse," he suggested.

Jade shook her head. "No, I want something that really represents the colony. I know. How about some big farming equipment? Maybe something that has to do with all the coffee they grow around here?"

"You mean such as a pulper?"

"Yes, or a dryer?"

"Sorry, miss. Nothing of that sort here now. And you should be glad you weren't taking these photographs last week. We *had* a dryer on the siding. Sat over there." He pointed to the far side of their animal warehouse. "Man was found dead inside it."

Jade shook her head. "I heard about that. Murdered, they

say. Then you may have seen who did it, too? I imagine the police have asked *you* a lot of questions."

He puffed up, sticking his chest out. "Told them I saw that Mr. Stokes and some other man arguing one day. Yank, by the sound of him. Mad about overpricing him on petrol. Said it looked like the billing had been tampered with. Stokes seemed surprised."

"Did they fight? I mean physically?"

Mr. Robertson shook his head. "Not what *I'd* call fighting. Just loud words. Some fist shaking, posturing, that sort of thing. I think Stokes walked into the Yank's fist once. Made him step back, but that's all. Then that Yank got on a motorcycle and rode off. I think Stokes stayed around, though."

"How shocking," said Jade.

"Unpleasant, I suppose, but not entirely surprising. I've wanted to take a swing at Stokes myself, to speak the truth. He had . . . a way about him. I'm only surprised he didn't have more enemies. Of course," he added hastily, "*I* wouldn't actually go and hit him. Perhaps accidentally trip him in a practice scrimmage, if you catch my drift."

"Did the police interview you?"

"Yes. Inspector Finch, I believe."

Jade wondered if Stokes had been waiting for someone when Sam found him. She also wondered why, if Finch knew all this, he'd ever seriously considered Sam as a suspect. "You're lucky you weren't here longer," she said. "You might have been the target for the killer instead of Mr. Stokes. Pity him standing there all alone."

"Well, he wasn't the only one around at the time. As I recall, there was a farmer hanging about later. And I saw some chap coming out of this animal warehouse. Wiry, blond fellow.

That sounded like Cutter. "What time of day was this? Do you recall?"

"Actually, yes. I was coming off my job, you see, and in a bit of a hurry. The railroad employees' football squad was having a dinner that evening at the gymkhana. I play forward on the team, you know."

"Ah," said Jade, "so it was still early in the day?"

"No. Pushing six thirty, in point of fact. Barely time to go home and change into evening kit." He leaned in as though to offer a confidence. "It's these blasted work hours, you know. Can't even get a game in before dark. Have to play on Sundays. Only reason I could see any of them was because of the light above the warehouse door."

Jade considered what she already knew and matched it against the railroad man's report. Sam had been seen arguing with Stokes. Cutter probably overheard the argument and came out to see what was happening. He saw Sam drive off. He presumably told Anderson, who embellished the story to the police. Added to Sam's print on the harvesting glove, it might have initially been enough to bring Sam in for questioning the night of the dance.

Stokes waited, though. It was already dark, so someone could have killed him and then shoved the body in the nearby dryer without anyone seeing. Then the murderer had staged the suicide. Either he had the glove or he had found it with Stokes' things. Unfortunately, not much blood came out since Stokes was already dead. But there were always natives at the depot selling chickens. It would be easy enough to get one, bring it back, kill it, and pour its blood into the dryer drum. Could it have been Cutter? Jade couldn't figure out his motive, but then, she didn't know him well at all.

The locomotive and its tender edged into the line of

cars. The resulting clang of couplers startled Jade out of her thoughts as the force rippled in waves down the line of cars, making them shudder. The impact, mild as it was, frightened the animals, which responded with a cacophony of bleating, brays, and snorts. Several monkeys screamed.

"Will you be wanting any more photographs, miss?" Mr. Robertson shouted over the din. "Because if not, I believe I need to double-check those couplings so your train can leave."

"Oh, sorry. No. I think this one with the animal train will be good. I can send a print to you if you'd like."

"Would you? That would be splendid. I can send it home. Show my mum that I've an important job and all that." He waved goodbye and strode off down the track, whistling.

Anderson came up beside her. "We're heading out now, Jade," he said. "See you when we return, and mind what I said about that pilot."

"Leave her alone and get on board, Wayne," called Daley from the car's door. He waved and Jade waved back as they and Perkins boarded the lone passenger car attached at the rear. The train chugged out of the rail yards, and Jade pulled her watch from her side trouser pocket. Four forty-five. She'd catch a taxi and head for the Dunburys' to see if Avery and Sam were back. That was when she heard Cutter issuing orders to the native workers regarding the dip tanks.

"Get rid of it." Cutter stood with his hands on his hips and an impatient scowl on his face.

"*Ku-simama!* Wait!" shouted Jade. She was too late. The men, standing on either end of the big metal trough, tipped it over onto the dirt.

"What's the problem?" asked Cutter. "We don't need it anymore. All the animals have been taken care of."

"That's a poison, you idiot!" she exclaimed. "You just had them dump gallons of arsenic. I read in the paper where absorbing enough of it can cook your liver."

"Oh." Cutter watched as the pools of liquid disappeared into the soil and gravel. "Ought to keep the fleas down then," he said, and laughed. "I'm glad you're still here, though. You know some of these natives, right? You speak their lingo? Who's the best one for night watch?"

"Wachiru isn't afraid of the leopard, if that's what you mean. And he understands some English in case your Swahili is bad."

"Which one is he?"

Jade pointed him out as he came out of the warehouse.

"Thanks. I'll let him either pick a pal or keep watch tonight himself." He hurried over to Wachiru. Jade was about to follow when the men by the dip trough called to her.

"Simba Jike, come!" Both men waved to her with one hand and pointed with their others to the ground on the far side of the tank.

Jade walked over. "What is it?"

"We have found something, Simba Jike. It was under the trough."

She stepped around the tank, expecting to see a smelly, bloated rat carcass. Instead, lying on the wet siding was a man's pocketknife.

CHAPTER 19

*A warrior might kill another in mock battle, and then the dead man's family
will seek revenge unless they can be placated in some way.*

—The Traveler

A KNIFE! Jade started to reach for it when she remembered
that it was probably coated with an arsenic-laced solution. Instead, she pulled out her pocket kerchief and used it to pick
up and carry the knife over to a pump, where she rinsed off
the poison.

The knife looked like any ordinary pocketknife, three
inches long with brass edging surrounding a dark wood in-
lay. Jade wanted to examine the blade when she remembered
that there might be fingerprints on it. She had no idea if any
would remain after being ground in dirt and bathed in dip,
but that was a matter for the police to determine. She tipped
her hand enough to flip the knife over on the sopping cloth,
hoping to see a monogram. Nothing.

Because the coffee dryer had sat near here, and there
weren't any other dip tanks nearby, it seemed likely that
Stokes had drowned in this very trough. So, Jade wondered,
had the knife belonged to Stokes? Had it fallen out of his

pocket or his hand when he fell into the tank? Or had it belonged to the killer? Even though it wasn't a murder weapon, maybe it could help Finch connect someone to the scene of the crime. Then again, maybe it simply belonged to someone in this crew. Maybe it was Cutter's. She rolled up the dripping kerchief and shoved it and the knife into her side pocket.

"Hey, Frank," she called, "I've got something under my fingernails. Can I borrow your pocketknife?"

"Sure," he hollered as he pulled his out. "I thought you always toted that big knife in your boot."

"Oh, that's right. I plum forgot it was there. Sorry." She watched him shove his knife back into his pocket, shaking his head at silly females. *Well, it's not his.*

"Frank, I'm heading off now." She retrieved her Winchester from the truck, waved goodbye to him and to Wachiru and the other men, and set off at a brisk walk up Government Road, hoping to get to Stokes and Berryhill before they closed, her camera bag slung over her shoulder.

As she stepped off the distance, she remembered meeting Jelani the first time she'd walked up this road after the war. He'd been working at the Norfolk Hotel and had been sent to haul her and her luggage in a rickshaw. Jade couldn't bring herself to let a young boy act like a beast of burden, so she'd walked beside him, asking him questions and practicing her rudimentary Swahili.

The broad street had changed a lot in the short time since then. There were fewer tossed-together buildings of galvanized tin and more of stone or timber. Rickshaws were still plentiful, but many were powered by motorcycles or bicycles rather than by human legs. In fact, the motorized traffic had increased enormously along with the dust and the noise. She didn't see a single horse cart or oxcart along the street.

Jelani had changed, too. The boy had disappeared. In his place stood an imposing young man, a future leader already harnessing himself in that role. What would have happened to him if she hadn't met him, hadn't interfered in his life? Would he now be working on someone's farm? Would he be happy or at least content with his life, not knowing any other? Somehow she doubted it. His strength, intelligence, and courage had always been there. He still would have chafed and felt the frustration of not being able to do anything about his forced servitude. She hoped he would write; perhaps he could bring the natives' concerns before the governing body. Maybe they'd see the potential for the rest of the Kikuyu in this one young man's abilities.

A car horn beeped, and Jade came out of her daydream and dodged the vehicle as it sped past her. *Better get to the sidewalk.* Ahead one block stood Stokes and Berryhill, *Catering to the Settler* written in wide black letters beneath the name. Jade quickened her pace and went inside.

The store felt cooler, because a few ceiling fans turned lazily overhead. Jade gave the room a quick survey, noting the customers as well as the employees. Mr. Berryhill assisted Charles Harding at a display of pitchforks. The Berryhills' son, Harley, stood with a red face next to an older woman, who was intent on purchasing a lady's cambric camisoles and drawers.

Chalmers was settling a bill with Mrs. Berryhill, a big smile on his gaunt face. He grabbed up a new halter and bridle and shoved a smaller bundle wrapped in brown paper into his jacket's spacious lower pocket. "Good day to all of you," he said as he tipped his hat. "Charles, bring your mare by the next time she's in heat for White Fire to service. I promise I'll only charge half my usual stud fee."

"Won't be necessary, Alwyn," grumbled Harding. He turned his back on his erstwhile friend to one of the forks, a big six-pronger, and hefted it.

Chalmers tossed the tack on top of a large box loaded down with soap, floor brushes, white flannel, and what looked like curtains. Hoisting it, he repeated his goodbyes as he kept on walking and talking, not watching where he went until he bumped into Jade. "Oh, Miss del Cameron," he said. "Please excuse me. I'm terribly sorry." His eyes sparkled in his narrow, weathered face.

"Think nothing of it, Mr. Chalmers. You certainly look happy." She waited, her head tipped expectantly. Chalmers did not disappoint her. He was too pleased to hold back his news.

"My prize polo pony returned. Isn't that amazing? And in time to register for race week and the polo competition."

"That certainly is amazing," Jade replied. "Congratulations. Poor thing must have been starving."

Chalmers shook his head. "The grazing has been fairly good as of yet, I believe. He looked fit and trim. Mane was a bit ragged is all."

"You certainly were searching hard enough for him," Jade added.

"That's the irony, don't you see? I was out again yesterday, and when I came home, he was standing outside his stall, as impatient to go in as if he'd just had a good workout, which, all things considered, I believe he's had. Probably not easy running with the plains animals."

"I'm very happy for you. He must be a very special horse. I've never seen you so . . . ebullient." Once again, she waited, giving him an opportunity to continue.

For a moment, it looked as if he intended to tell her something else. "Actually . . ." He looked over his shoulder at the others, who were now busy buying and selling, and leaned closer.

Just as he took a deep breath, Pauline Berryhill called to Jade, "I shall be with you in a moment, Miss del Cameron. You may set your rifle by the door."

It was enough to break the spell. Chalmers nodded again and said goodbye. Jade stopped him with a hand on his arm. "By the way, I found something today, Mr. Chalmers. I was going to ask if anyone might know who it belonged to. Since you're here, perhaps you can tell me." She took the damp kerchief from her pocket and pulled enough aside to reveal the knife.

Chalmers peered at it a moment and shrugged. "Could be anyone's, miss. I couldn't say for certain. Sorry I can't be of more assistance than that. Now, if you'll excuse me, I have to hurry to get to E. Dobbie's before it closes." He grinned again, which made his red face and long, gourd-shaped head look like a smashed jack-o'-lantern.

Jade watched him leave as she slipped her Winchester off her shoulder. "I'm not certain what I want yet, Mrs. Berryhill," she said. "Please don't rush on my account."

"As you wish," said the sour-faced woman. She shooshed her son into the back room. "Bring out another case of Pearson's carbolic soap," she snapped. "Mr. Chalmers took the last of the ones up front."

"But Mrs. Trumwell . . ." the young man began.

"*I'll* assist Mrs. Trumwell," said his mother.

The lad ran into the back, only too glad, it seemed, to get away from women's underthings, lacey or otherwise, and his mother's temper. Jade wasn't sure, but Mrs. Berryhill seemed to be in a more sour mood than usual.

Jade sauntered past a display of blotters, clocks, and ink stands toward the showcase of knives. "Hello, Mr. Harding," she said. "Thank you again. My friends told me you were the only person they could find to join in the search for me."

Harding seemed embarrassed by the recognition, and merely nodded before deciding on the pitchfork. He set it against the counter next to a bottle of Pinkham's liver pills. "I happened to be in town the evening before."

"That's right," said Jade. "The Volunteer Mounted Rifles dinner, if I'm not mistaken. I think I've seen a photo of you and Mr. Chalmers and you, too, Mr. Berryhill. You were standing next to a zebra." She hoped they would want to boast of their exploits, but Mr. Berryhill merely shot a sideways glance at his wife and started to write up Harding's billing.

"More like stuff and nonsense," scolded Mrs. Berryhill. She'd finished with Mrs. Trumwell and stood, fingertips grazing the countertop. "An excuse to drink and carouse, is all." She glared at her husband. "Bunch of foolish boys playing at dress up." She turned back to Jade. "Have you decided on anything, Miss del Cameron, or are you just . . . visiting?"

"I'm interested in seeing your pocketknives," Jade said. "I found one today at the animal compound. Someone lost it. I thought at first I might keep it if no one claimed it, but I think a lot of arsenide dip has spilled on it." She shrugged, as though to indicate she wasn't sure it would be in very good condition anymore. "But it looked like a nice knife and I was considering getting a new one like it." Jade scanned the display. "There," she said, pointing to the same model. "It looked like that." She pointed to a folding single-blade model.

Mrs. Berryhill unlocked the display case and removed the knife, slapping it on the counter. "A very popular knife. Just sold one to Mr. Chalmers."

"Did Mr. Stokes own one like this?" Jade asked.

Mrs. Berryhill shook her head. "What an odd thing to ask."

"I believe he used the next size smaller," said her husband. "I think it fit in his pocket better."

"Can you tell me who else bought one? Perhaps the person who dropped the one I found replaced it. It might help me find the owner."

"One of those Americans buying up the animals bought one. Mr. Chalmers, as I already said." She pursed her lips. "I cannot recall the others without checking the books."

"Would you mind?" asked Jade.

"I'm really very busy," Mrs. Berryhill snapped.

Jade made a soft clucking sound, shook her head, and led the woman aside, away from the men. "You look very tired, Mrs. Berryhill. May I call you Pauline? I feel I know you well enough. Are you still making many of the deliveries?"

Mrs. Berryhill looked for a moment as if she might burst into tears. Her lips quivered, and she clutched the locket hanging on her bodice. Jade noticed that several blond hairs stuck out of the locket. A quick glance behind the counter verified that both the husband and son had brown hair.

"No," said Mrs. Berryhill, "I'm not making deliveries. It's not . . . necessary anymore." She stifled a sob.

Jade felt a pang of sympathy for this sad woman, who, Jade suspected, carried Alice Stokes' hair in her locket. She reached over and patted the woman's hand.

Mrs. Berryhill straightened with a sniff. "I apologize for my behavior just now," she said. "I'll check those files for the recent billings for you."

While Jade waited, she tried to engage Mr. Harding and Mr. Berryhill in conversation. "That's certainly good news for Mr. Chalmers, isn't it? I must admit, I'd have bet that his pony would only show up in lion droppings." Harding only grunted and Berryhill went to an adding machine to tally up the bill. Jade tried another topic. "Did you sell any more animals to Perkins and Daley?"

Harding pulled his head back in surprise. "Who said I had animals to sell?"

"I was there when you brought in those leopard cubs, remember, Mr. Harding?

"Yes, that's right," he said. "I'd forgotten."

Winston Berryhill returned with the newly tallied bill. Harding paid it and, with a nod to everyone, left the store. Mrs. Berryhill closed the file cabinet and returned to the counter, calling Jade.

"It appears that Mr. Harding purchased a pocketknife a few days ago, as did a railroad man named Robertson. But it looks like we also sold knives to two Americans, Mr. Cutter and Mr. Featherstone."

CHAPTER 20

An innocent man can undergo a trial to prove his innocence.
He will drink blood from an ox and say,
"May God kill me if I did this crime."

—The Traveler

Jade snatched up her rifle and hurried to police headquarters. While she didn't relish seeing Inspector Finch again, she hoped that the knife could be the clue he needed to find the real murderer. Unfortunately, it was not going to help take Sam off the list.

It will if you don't give his name to them.

Could she do that? Could she withhold information? *What's the worst that could happen?*

Jade thought through the most likely scenario. Finch would go to the store to verify her information. Mrs. Berryhill would give Sam's name along with the others. The fact that Jade had withheld it would probably put Sam to the top of Finch's list.

No, it would be better if she gave his name and then stressed how he couldn't be the murderer. While she was there, she'd explain how someone had sabotaged Sam's plane, and how Stokes had been seen standing after Sam left. Mr. Robertson could verify that.

Robertson! He bought one of those knives. It wasn't a far stretch to assume he'd dropped his knife near the dip tank and didn't know where he'd lost it. With all the traffic near there, it would be easy for someone to kick the knife under the tank. So the knife might not have anything to do with the murder. *But it might!* What Jade found most curious was the fact that Mr. Chalmers had just purchased one of those knives and hadn't bothered to mention that to her when she showed him the old one.

Finch can sort it out. As long as he drops Sam from his suspect list. Her decision made, Jade went into the police station, head high. "Inspector Finch, please."

"Sorry, miss," said the constable behind the desk. "Inspector's busy. Absolutely not to be disturbed. Perhaps I can help you." He spied her rifle slung over her shoulder. "You're going to have to check your weapon at the door."

Jade carefully leaned her rifle against the wall, beginning to wish she hadn't taken it with her when they went to fix the plane. In town, it was a nuisance. She dug into her pocket and handed over the knife, explaining where she'd found it and to whom it might have belonged, while the officer wrote down the particulars. "I don't know if you can get any fingerprints off it anymore," Jade said.

The constable picked up the handkerchief with the knife still resting in it and placed it in a small wooden box. He put a note and a label on it and set it aside. "Right. I'll see that he gets it first thing." He turned to his paperwork.

"I'm not finished," said Jade and related the incident with the plane, stressing that Sam couldn't have fouled his own plane as he was sick then. The constable wrote down her information and added that note to the other one.

Jade retrieved her rifle and went out the door, feeling

relieved. She'd finally done something to help clear up this *shauri*. Giving up the knife to the police meant that the situation was literally in their hands now.

She flagged down a motorized rickshaw and headed home to Parklands and her friends as the sun set. Would Avery be back yet? Would Sam be there, too? Would anyone have something to eat? Her stomach rumbled, and she realized she hadn't eaten since the bacon-and-biscuit breakfast she'd made. It was past six now.

Madeline met Jade on the veranda, a smile on her face. "Avery came home a few hours ago," she said. "Sam flew in just fine, but Avery stayed on to help him give the carburetor and tank another thorough cleaning."

Jade wiped her boots on the mat and stepped inside. "Didn't Sam come back with Avery?" She looked around the room, hoping to see his dark eyes flashing at her from some corner.

"Sorry, Jade. No, he didn't. He told Avery he was exhausted, and Avery said he looked it. I don't think either of them wanted to risk a relapse." Madeline laid a motherly hand on Jade's shoulder and leaned closer. "You wouldn't want him back in the hospital, I'm sure."

Jade shook her head, trying to let go of her disappointment. "No, definitely not. You're right. It was . . . a smart plan." She hung her rifle on the gun rack and went over to see Beverly and Jelani, seated at a writing table, heads bent over a paper. Both looked up at her approach and greeted her, Beverly with a bright smile, Jelani with a serious nod.

"Hello, you two," said Jade. "Dare I ask what you're up to?"

"I have started to write, Simba Jike," said Jelani. "I am telling about my village and how the men must leave to work."

"It's very good, too," said Beverly. "Jelani has a powerful voice."

"May I read it?" asked Jade.

Jelani placed his right hand over the paper. "When it is finished, Simba Jike. I do not want anyone to say that you wrote the words."

"I understand," Jade said. It pained her to see the intensity in his eyes. Crusades like his often went the worst for the crusader. Then, just as she was about to turn away and leave him to his work, a spark of the boy returned. His black eyes flashed and his lips twitched as if he was struggling to contain his excitement. "What?" Jade asked him.

"Bwana Dunbury told me that Bwana Featherstone will take me up in the airplane tomorrow morning. We will fly over my village, and I will see *everything*!"

Jade grinned, joining in his enthusiasm. "You'll love it, Jelani. There is nothing like it."

"I thought I would drive him over to the hangar," said Madeline. "I'll go home early tomorrow morning. Then Neville or I will make certain that Jelani gets back to his village without any more incidents."

An idea came to Jade. "Maybe I can go with you? My motorcycle is still at the hangar."

"No, it's not."

Jade turned to see Avery standing in the rear door of the parlor, wiping his hands on a rag. "I brought your motorbike back with me. Tied it on the boot of my car. Just took it off now."

"Come with us anyway," said Madeline. "Ride your cycle. I'm sure Sam will want to see you."

"Thank you. I will." Jade clapped her hands together. "Now, is there anything to eat around here, Beverly? I'm starved."

Beverly glanced at the mantel clock and made several *tsk*ing sounds. "It's only six thirty, Jade. How can you think of sitting down to supper at such an uncivilized hour?" She laughed and shook her head, setting her soft curls jiggling like corn silk and sunlight. Beverly's laugh, so full of mischief and joy, always reminded Jade of a rippling brook. "I suppose this is when the cowboys eat, am I right?"

Jade's stomach growled.

"Ooh, careful, everyone," said Beverly. "The lioness is hungry." She laughed again.

"I haven't eaten since dawn, Bev," said Jade.

Beverly hoisted herself up from the stiff chair she'd been sitting in next to Jelani and waddled over to a softer one near the unlit fireplace. "If you can subdue your appetite for another hour, I can promise you a very fine meal. I have hired a *mpishi*," she said, using the Swahili for "cook," "as well as a maid, a butler of sorts, and several kitchen hands. We are having a very fine roasted chicken."

"I hope he can cook," said Avery as he helped his wife settle into the chair.

"His name is Matthew so, of course, he calls himself Matthew Mpishi. He cooked for Mrs. Bottworthy for three years, but she and her husband are returning to England in another month."

"In a month!" exclaimed Madeline as she picked up a sheaf of typed pages from the sofa and sat down. "Then I wonder how you managed to secure him now."

Beverly grinned. "Offered him double wages if he'd jump ship. Of course, Mrs. Bottworthy is furious with me," she added with a shrug, "but they can eat at her daughter's house for the rest of their stay."

"Do you expect us to dress for dinner?" asked Jade.

Beverly waved the idea away. "As if *you* would, you wild hyena. Besides," she added, "I don't think I have any evening clothes that will fit me at the moment."

Jade found it hard to imagine that Beverly's closet was entirely devoid of something proper to put on, but she knew that Beverly was very attentive to the feelings of others. In this case, she didn't want to embarrass Maddy, who would have only her housedress to wear. Such consideration was one of Bev's more lovable traits and one that endeared her to Jade. She'd seen the extra care Bev had given to the wounded in her ambulance, always speaking to them as though they were her dearest friends.

Another stomach growl broke Jade's reflections. "Better feed her something," said Avery, "or she'll devour the entire chicken." He went off to find something for her to snack on.

"I know what will take your mind off food," said Madeline. "We can tell you all about our interrogation today."

Avery returned with a large slab of bread, slathered in creamy butter. Jade thanked him and bit off a big chunk. "What interrogation?" she asked with her mouth full.

"The *Berryhill* boy," said Beverly.

Jade's eyes widened. She'd forgotten all about him and his statements alluding to blackmail. She looked from one to the other, waiting for someone to continue.

Beverly laughed. "You should see yourself, Jade. Very well, I shall tell you before you explode." She tried to cross her legs to get more comfortable and gave up. Jade pushed an ottoman toward her to rest her feet on instead. "Thank you, love. Now, how to begin."

"Try by telling me what he said," said Jade, growing impatient with Bev's teasing.

"*My* story," said Bev. "I telephoned the store and placed an order for flour and pots and potatoes and—" She cut off her list when she saw Jade's glare. "The point being that it was a large enough order to ensure that the young man would deliver it instead of Mrs. Berryhill, since you told me she does some of that sort of thing now."

"And?" coaxed Jade.

"And he came right away yesterday evening," piped in Madeline, anxious to get to the good stuff. She looked sheepishly at Bev, who simply smiled and motioned with an open hand for her to continue. Before she could, a third voice chimed in.

"He ate an entire tin of biscuits," said Jelani, scorn and indignation in his voice. "He ate like a famished jackal before the lion comes to claim his food."

"Yes," said Madeline, "but, of course, that was the plan. We plied him with food and asked him all sorts of questions while he sat and . . . and inhaled food faster than a Hoover." She grabbed a pencil. "I must use that line in my next book."

Both she and Beverly erupted in girlish giggles. Jelani looked at Jade, rolled his eyes, and grinned. Jade smiled back, letting her friends have their fun. In the meantime, she took another bite of bread, making certain to take smaller ones and chew slowly, lest she supply them with more ammunition against her later.

Beverly wiped a tear from her eyes. "You tell her, Maddy. I can't stop laughing."

"Well, I went back to the pantry to see that everything was stored properly and just eavesdropped, mind you. But Beverly was brilliant. She told the young man that she'd only just come to live here and asked him all sorts of questions about Nairobi and, of course, his father's store. She complimented the young man on his muscular build and asked if he did all the deliveries. Harley said he had started only recently, that Mr. Stokes had handled most of them before. It came out then that Mr. Stokes had been found dead."

"By now I opened up a second tin of biscuits," said Beverly, "but I doled them out to him a few at a time while I pumped more information from the well. It was quite evident that he didn't care for Mr. Stokes."

Jade leaned forward in her seat. "*That* much we knew. Did he say why?"

Maddy finished the tale. "He claimed that Mr. Stokes insisted on doing the deliveries because he saw things other people didn't and shouldn't. Then he used the information against people."

"Right," said Jade. "Harley made the blackmail accusation to Sam. But I was hoping for something more specific."

"Patience, Jade," said Beverly.

"I'm afraid you'll go into labor and have that baby before you get to the end of the story," retorted Jade.

Madeline giggled again, and even Jelani grinned. Avery, wisely, kept his mouth shut.

"Apparently Stokes had seen Harley and one of his school chums engaged in some shenanigans and offered not to tell their fathers if they paid him."

Jade sighed and her shoulders slumped. "That's not much help then, is it? I'd hoped the boy had seen Stokes blackmail his father or someone else on the suspect list."

Avery stepped forward. "You have a suspect list?"

"Yes." She told them about finding the knife as well as the names of anyone who'd recently purchased one just like it. "I'm hoping the killer lost it, couldn't find it in the dark, couldn't come back in the daylight to look without arousing suspicions, and then eventually bought a new one to replace it."

"And you gave the knife and that list of names to Inspector Finch?" asked Avery.

"To one of his constables," said Jade. "Unfortunately, Sam's name was on there, too, so I'm not sure how much attention Finch will pay to the others." She made a fist and pushed it into her other palm. "I hope there are still some fingerprints left on it. He may not know who they belong to, but at least he'll be able to eliminate Sam from the list."

Just then, a slender Somali stood in the doorway. He wore a white turban and an immaculate white knee-length robe over white pants. "Excuse, madam. *Mpishi* says the dinner is ready."

"Thank you, Farhani. You may begin serving then," said Beverly.

Avery helped Beverly to her seat, and held Madeline's chair for her. Jade declined a similar offer with a wave and sat down next to Madeline.

"Jelani," said Beverly, "please sit next to Jade."

Jelani looked uncomfortable joining them at the table, but Beverly and Avery both insisted. They started with oxtail soup, followed by a well-cooked and succulent roast chicken nestled in a bed of vegetables. Fresh bread and creamy butter completed the meal. Avery and Madeline each drank a glass of wine, while Beverly, Jade, and Jelani opted for lemonade.

Jade was too hungry to talk much, and so most of the conversation flitted around local town news supplied by Madeline and Avery, who had both made short trips into Nairobi proper. Madeline had gone to see if there were any replies to her adoption notice. There was one: a lady suggesting that they inquire at Lady Northey's home for children.

"Those children have parents but they're soldier settlers, just now building their homes," said Madeline with a heavy sigh.

Beverly laid a hand on Madeline's arm. "Don't give up hope, Maddy dear. There have been orphans there before. Avery and I will give you and Neville the best character references."

"But how can I pray for a child if it means the poor dear will lose his or her real parents?"

"I don't think you would be hoping for anything of the kind," said Bev.

"Did I mention," said Jade, turning the topic, "that Alwyn Chalmers' polo pony actually returned? He told me when I saw him at Stokes and Berryhill. I've never seen that man so happy before."

"Really," said Avery. "I say, that *is* interesting. What was he purchasing? Do you know?"

Jade thought for a moment. "Bridle, horse equipment. And a lot of soaps and cleaners. Curtains, too, and piles of white flannel. Lord knows he needed all of it. I'd seen cleaner pigsties than his home. He was in a hurry, though. Said he was heading to E. Dobbie's next. Isn't he a watch repairman?"

"Jeweler," said Avery. He put his forefinger to his lips and pondered in silence.

"What, Avery?" asked Beverly. "What are you thinking?"

He shrugged. "It is, of course, pure speculation, but when

a man buys something from a jeweler and intends to clean his house and hang curtains, I'd say that—"

"He's bringing home a bride," broke in Beverly. "Darling, how devilishly clever of you. Just like Sherlock Holmes." She turned to Madeline and Jade for confirmation of her spouse's brilliance. "What is it, Jade?"

"I think he's been looking for Mrs. Stokes. I'd bet my last dollar that she's been hiding *with* her baby at that old farmhouse by Longonot. I saw her when I left the plane for Naivasha on foot, and I heard a child. There were tire tracks leading to the farmhouse and a lot of boxes of canned milk from Stokes and Berryhill.

"Someone was bringing her supplies?" asked Beverly.

"I think it was Pauline Berryhill. She told me she had to make deliveries on a Sunday. I think she hid Alice out there. Remember, it was Chalmers who found me near Naivasha. He said he'd been following tire tracks, which doesn't make sense if he was looking for his missing pony."

"So you think he was looking for Mrs. Stokes?" asked Avery.

Jade nodded. "I think he loves her. He had her photo, the only clean item in his house. Chalmers was very disappointed when he thought he'd been following *my* tracks. But he learned from you and Sam that I'd flown and gotten stranded. So I think he went out there again, found her, and convinced her to go with him. The woman was gone when I stopped back there the next day. Mrs. Berryhill was very distraught this morning and she also said she wasn't making any more deliveries."

"Oh, my," said Maddy. "I'll have to talk to my new friend, Nancy. If anyone would know some gossip, it would be a hello girl."

"But why all this pretense of adopting out the baby?" asked Avery.

"Probably so that Alice could start fresh with a new identity somewhere else," said Jade. "But now that her husband is dead, the pretense is no longer needed. She married the first time because her parents died and she had no one to support her. I don't think she's the type of woman who knows how to take care of herself."

"So she accepted Mrs. Berryhill's help until another man came along," said Beverly. "Very interesting. Perhaps all that white flannel is for nappies, then."

Jade excused herself after dinner to develop her pictures in the separate building that operated as her darkroom. With a red filtered lantern, she took her film through the vats to develop the negatives, then studied them with a lens to look for the best ones to make into prints. To her delight, there were several wonderful photos of the Maasai as well as of the little rhino. She went through them all systematically and finished with a print of the railroad man, Robertson. She could drop it off at the railroad offices tomorrow for him. She was on her way back to the main house when a native came running up, panting hard.

"Simba Jike," he called, "you are needed."

Jade held up the lantern and studied him. She didn't recognize the man, although he looked like a Kikuyu. "Slow down and catch your breath," she admonished.

"No time, Memsabu. You are needed at the animal building, please."

"What happened?"

"I think the big lion is sick. I have been told to bring you. Cannot find Bwana Cutter. Other bwanas gone."

"Very well," she said. "I'll go back on my motorcycle. You can sit on the rack in back if you want."

The man waved her off. "No," he said, breathing harder now. "I cannot ride on such a machine. You go. Hurry, please, Memsabu."

"All right, I will. I'll just tell my friends where I've gone."

"*I* will tell, Memsabu. *You* must hurry before the lion dies."

"Fine. Be sure to tell the bwana at the house where I am." She hurried to her motorcycle, and sped away south to the warehouses, wondering what had happened to old Percy and what in the world she could do about it.

As much as Jade wanted to race through Nairobi, she maintained a slower speed and was careful to wipe free of grime the glass over her cycle's headlamp. The constables had gotten very fussy of late about lights and license tags. They issued fines as readily as most people handed out good morning wishes. *Shame they aren't so particular about finding murderers.*

Still, every time she wondered what was wrong with Percy, she caught herself accelerating. *Who was on watch? Wachiru?* A careful man, attentive to his job. Perhaps Percy wasn't too bad. Maybe Wachiru just felt that someone should look in on him.

I haven't a clue how to treat a sick lion. What if he was dying? What if she had to put him down? That was no good. She hadn't even brought along her rifle.

She wished she'd looked up the name of a veterinary officer in Bev's *Red Book* before she'd left. There wasn't even any phone in the warehouse to use. The railway office wasn't too far from there. Maybe someone would still be there to let her use a phone.

Cutter's probably in some bar somewhere getting tight.

Jade skirted the quiet rail yards, finding her way with a combination of moonlight and the occasional light over a warehouse door. She stopped near their animal compound and shut off the engine. Overhead, a bare bulb glowed weakly under the accumulated soot and grime, providing just enough illumination for her to see that the door was open a crack. Another light shone faintly from inside, flickering as if the old bulb was in its death throes.

"Wachiru?" Jade called as she dismounted. There was no answer except for an explosive bark followed by one shrill screech. *Mama baboon's not happy.* If Wachiru was inside near Percy, he wouldn't be able to hear her over the din. She went inside, leaving the door ajar, and called again more loudly as she walked toward the back wall, where Percy's cage was located.

"Wachiru!"

A cacophony of sounds all but drowned out her call. The hyena's jittery laughter joined with the wild dogs' gruff barks and plaintive whines and the jackals' short yelps. The young lioness snarled and woofed. Jade was about to call again when it occurred to her to listen to the animals.

They're all giving alarm calls.

For the first time, she noted her body's own, unique alarm going off as a deep, pulsing throb in her left knee.

Get the hell out of here!

She turned and sprinted toward the door, but it was too late. The door was shut. She heard the lock click into place outside and knew she'd been set up.

"Open the door now!" she yelled. She didn't expect an answer. The only way she'd have gotten a response was if Cutter or Wachiru had come by, seen the door open, and shut it, not knowing she was within. She grabbed hold of the handle and yanked as hard as she could, but the door didn't budge.

Then she heard a new sound: the asthmatic cough of a leopard. Only this time, it didn't come from the cat pens.

CHAPTER 21

A Maasai proverbs says, "A predator can hide for a time,
but it will finally be killed or captured." Essentially, "Murder will out."

—The Traveler

THE SHIVERING CHILL started in Jade's stomach and spread out along her limbs. Her heart hammered in her chest. She felt the throb in her wrists and throat, heard it roar in her ears. A film of sweat seeped out over her forehead and in the hollow of her neck. The blind woman's warning came to her again, only now it was too late.

Steady now! Slowly and quietly, she wiped her sweaty palm on her trousers. Then she leaned to her right until her hand found the knife hilt. Once she had it safely in her grasp, Jade felt as though she had a slim but fighting chance. She'd have to act fast. *Chui* was a powerful, muscular killer with raking claws that could gut her in an instant.

There had to be another way out of here. *The window!* There were two narrow windows on each long side of the warehouse, eight feet up. She just needed to stack up some of the smaller crates and climb up to one. *But which one? Where's the leopard?*

Leopards, Jade knew, were ambush hunters. Whereas the lion would rush and run down its prey, the leopard would pounce before she even had a chance to make a break for the window. And the cat was an expert climber, too. It would easily follow her up the crates, claw her legs, and pull her down. For all she knew, he was atop one of the cages now, gauging the distance to her with those hypnotic eyes. Her skin prickled at this new fear. There were fewer cages behind her, so chances were he wasn't hiding there.

Are you so sure?

Part of her wanted to run screaming toward the door, the windows, anyplace but here. But reason told her that escape was useless at the locked door or the windows. No. She needed to be smarter than the cat.

Find it and find a hiding place.

A hiding place. There was an idea. Were there any empty pens in the warehouse? *No.* They'd all been removed with the animals. Jade forced herself to focus on a mental layout of the remaining cages.

Anything I can share a cage with? Most of the hoofed animals had been housed near the back door. That area was now nearly empty except for a pair of ostrich. *No help there. I'll be kicked to death.*

The next row of cages housed a honey badger, a catlike genet, and the lone white-tailed mongoose. Those smaller predators, too little to threaten the antelope and zebra, had formed a buffer zone from the larger meat eaters. Unfortunately for Jade, their cages wouldn't fit her. That left the baboons and the larger hunters. Jade didn't relish trying to vacate or share a cage with any of them, not even Percy.

Then it dawned on her. There *was* an empty cage: the

leopard's. But it was on the far end of the row. *You don't have much choice.*

Could she get to it? That depended on where the leopard was right now. The bulb high overhead continued to flicker spastically as Jade searched in vain for the eyes' reflective glow.

Listen to the animals.

Every one of them contributed to the racket, and for a moment, Jade despaired of getting any help from that quarter. She forced herself not to react, and listened again. The baboon had definitely become more agitated. Her barking alarm call had changed to a continual high scream.

The cat was close to the baboon.

The baboon cage is behind me.

Fear, a cold knife, cut into her. Jade felt the hairs on her nape rise. She pivoted and stared straight into the hypnotic glare of *chui*. His eyes, a washed-out citrine yellow, flashed cold hate as he recognized her scent. He screwed up his mouth in a snarl, exposing four daggers. The image, flickering insanely with the sputtering bulb, seared itself like a brand in Jade's brain. Beneath him, the mother baboon shrieked and barked in terror, clutching her baby to her chest.

Jade gripped her knife as tight as the mother baboon did her young and began to make her last apologies to God for every headstrong, bumble-brained thing she'd ever done. One meager chance, that was all she'd get, to drive her knife into the beast's heart. Even if she came out alive, she'd be badly mauled.

The cat screwed up its hindquarters, tensing to leap. His tail lashed from side to side, then twitched, draping over the edge of the cage. That was when Jade found an unwitting ally. Mama baboon seized the tail of her hated foe and pulled. When she had yanked enough into the cage, she sank her own canines into the tail.

The leopard snarled and hissed, slapping at the cage as he tried to twist and pull himself free. Jade didn't wait to see the outcome. Instead, she turned and bolted. She knew once the leopard got free it could easily outrun her. Behind her the cat hissed again and rattled the cage as it thrashed. Anger would increase his speed once he broke loose. Jade didn't have time to make it to the end of the line.

Immediately ahead was Percy's cage. Suddenly, the *laibon*'s words about danger echoed in her mind: *It comes at you with madness in pale yellow eyes, Simba Jike. You must seek help from your mate.* If she was "lioness," then Percy was "lion," her mate. Jade raced for his cage.

Like many of the others, it was held shut with a series of toggle pins. She switched her knife to her left hand, pulled the pins, and yanked open the door, praying that Harry Hascombe's old pet was still friendly.

The leopard thrashed once more, and the noise was followed by a sharp "yak." That sound alone pushed Jade to her limit. It meant the mother baboon's mouth was no longer clamped on the leopard's tail.

"Get out, Percy," she said as she got behind him and pushed him on the rump. Percy took one look at the open door and the young lioness across the way and strutted over to her, his tail curled up like a banner. Jade stayed inside and pulled the cage door shut. She fumbled with one of the pins, trying in vain to find a slot to shove it into. She could barely get her hand through the closely placed slats. The back of her hand scraped against the rough wood, tearing off skin.

"Where's the blasted hole?" she muttered. There! Her

fingertips grazed it and she struggled to get the pin tip aligned with it. A hot breath blew across her fingers, and she instinctively yanked them inside just as the razor-sharp talons raked the wood and her two fingers.

Jade stood pressed against the cage back, her knife blade pointed forward. She waited for the cage door to bounce open as it recoiled from the cat's slap. Her muscles tensed to take the impact and drive the blade into the cat's heart. The charge didn't come. At least not immediately. She'd managed to get the tip of the pin into the slot enough to keep the door closed.

But for how long?

She could see the pin sitting cockeyed in its nook. Outside, the leopard pawed furiously at the slats. One good jolt and the pin would tumble over onto the floor. The leopard supplied it. He gave up on the front and launched himself on top of her cage to reach her from above. As he jumped, a hind paw kicked the toggle and sent it flying. The door creaked open a few inches.

The cat seemed to recognize the sound of an opening cage door and reacted immediately. He leaped back to the floor and swiped at the slats, trying to pry the door open farther. At each attempt, Jade stabbed at his pads and drove him back. The infuriated leopard swatted at the door with greater speed and strength.

His actions attracted Percy's attention. For a while, the old lion had been more interested in making the acquaintance of the lioness across the way and voicing soft *pfff* sounds in greeting. But here was another animal toying with his cage. It was doubtful whether Percy regarded Jade as anything more than a familiar human, one who sometimes talked to him or brought him treats. But he'd marked that cage as his turf, and no other cat, no matter the species, was going to usurp his territory.

With a deafening roar that shook Jade to her marrow, Percy wheeled and lunged for the leopard just as the furious, spotted cat managed to swing the door open. The old lion might never have hunted or made a kill before, but his sheer size made up for his inexperience. One swipe of his huge paw caught the leopard in the shoulder and sent him reeling backward. The smaller cat tumbled twice before righting himself.

Percy didn't know to follow through, however, and the leopard charged, leaping on top of the lion. *Chui* dug in with his hind claws and scratched at Percy's back and head with his forelegs. The actions were useless against the lion's thick mane, but not against his shoulders. Percy snarled, screwing his face into a hideous grimace. He shook himself, trying to dislodge his opponent. When that didn't work, he reached around to bite the leopard.

His reach wasn't long enough to catch hold of the demon on his back, but the action threw Percy into a roll. As he turned over, the leopard pulled away and rolled onto its back, waiting for Percy to show his vulnerable underbelly to the raking hind claws.

Jade watched in horror, knowing that Percy was seconds away from being disemboweled and that her own death would follow soon after. *Not without a fight!* She hurried to the cage door and hurled her knife at the leopard's side, hoping to penetrate a lung at least.

The knife caught the shifting leopard in his shoulder and stuck. The cat screamed in pain and rage, rolling to the side in an effort to rid itself of this newest torment. The movement and the blood scent gave Percy the opportunity and the stimulus he needed. With one bite, he clamped his huge maw around the leopard's throat and held. The smaller cat struggled, his hind feet flailing uselessly, scratching the air. Then he lay limp. Percy held on with his suffocating grip for a moment longer, and Jade used the opportunity to vacate the cage and head for a window.

With apologies to the honey badger and the civet cat, she stacked their cages atop each other to climb up to the narrow opening. That was when she found Wachiru, lying facedown beside the mongoose cage. She felt for a pulse, found one. Fear gave her additional strength as she hoisted him onto her back like a cape. His arms draped over her shoulders, spreading his weight along her spine.

But there was no way she could get him up and out that window. Even if she did, the drop down could break his back. Instead, she half carried, half dragged him to the front door and set him down next to it. Then she rummaged in his pockets for his key so she could unlock the door from the outside.

"I'll be right back," she told him, unsure if he could hear her.

Jade hurried back to the stacked cages and hauled herself through the window, leaving Percy to roar his triumphant call to the night, proclaiming his first kill.

She prayed Wachiru would not be his second.

CHAPTER 22

Maasai do not steal. Well, not from one another.
They once raided other tribes for cattle, but then, since Engai
gave all cattle to them, that's not really considered stealing.

—The Traveler

BY THE TIME Jade had shinnied out the window and dropped
to the ground, she was scratched and bruised, her shirt ripped
open across the midsection. Her legs and arms quivered, the
muscles twitching. Behind her, Percy continued to announce
to his would-be mate that he was lord of the realm. Jade had
heard him roar before, but never with this ferocity. He'd
made his first kill and would leave Africa a wild lion.

But Jade needed to make certain that this was his only
kill. She had to get Wachiru out. The first time she got to
her feet, her knees buckled and she collapsed back onto the
ground. The second time, she used the wall to support her,
willing her legs to move. She staggered around the side to
the door and pushed the key into the padlock, removing the
lock and letting it drop. When she opened the door, Wachiru
tumbled halfway out. Jade grabbed him under his arms and
pulled him clear. Finally she shoved the door closed and
locked it again.

Percy was still loose inside, and eventually they'd have to coax or drive him back into his cage. But not now. Right now Jade needed to ascertain the extent of Wachiru's injuries. She knelt beside him and, starting at his head, examined him for cuts and wounds. All she found was a lump on the back of his head where he'd been hit from behind. The leopard hadn't found him.

Yet!

Jade had no doubts that whoever had set her up had also intended for the leopard to finish off Wachiru, making it look like their combined incompetence had resulted in their deaths. Sam's intended crash was supposed to look that way, too. Apparently, both of them knew something incriminating. She just wished *she* knew what in the Sam Hill it was.

Let Finch sort it out. Right now, she needed to get medical attention for Wachiru. And that meant leaving him long enough to find a telephone. The depot? Probably closed until morning. The railway office. Someone should be on duty.

"Wachiru," she said into his left ear. "Wachiru!" She was rewarded with a moan. "It's Simba Jike. You're hurt. I'm going to find help. Don't move."

"Simba Jike?" He started to lift his head and groaned.

"Don't move! Do you hear? I am going to call for help. I'll be right back." She wondered if he understood. "Wiggle your fingers if you can hear me." He did. "Good. Now, don't move!"

She ran across the rows of tracks to the railroad office housed in yet another tin-roofed, wooden building. One light burned inside, and through the window, Jade could see a man sitting with his feet propped up on the desk, eyes closed and arms folded across his chest, his mouth agape. Jade tried the door, found it locked, and knocked loudly.

"Open up! I need help!"

From inside she heard a startled "Hunh" and the squeak of a chair. "Someone out there?"

"Yes. Let me in! I need help."

The latch clicked and the door swung inward. In front of her was a drowsy-looking man in his midthirties, balding, his tie askew and hair mussed. He blinked several times and yawned. Then his eyes lit on her torn shirt and smudged face. "I say, you look as if you're in a bad way. You'd best come inside and sit down."

Jade stepped into the cluttered office crammed with wooden filing cabinets, boxes, a telegraph set, and a desk. The man straightened his tie and ran his fingers through his hair. "Can I fetch something for you? Tea?" He looked around the room. "I might have a tin of biscuits here."

"I need a telephone," said Jade.

"A telephone? Oh, yes. Quite." He pointed to the one on the wall. "Did you have an accident? Wreck a motorcar?"

"No." Jade picked up the handset, clicked the receiver up, and cranked the handle around several times. "Hello? Operator? Please connect me to the police. Yes, the police. Thank you."

"The police," said the man beside her. "By thunder, did someone rob you?"

Jade shook her head. "No, but—" Her explanation was interrupted by a voice on the line. "Hello. Police? I want to report an attempted murder."

"Murder!" exclaimed the railroad man. "My stars!"

"Yes, murder," continued Jade, trying to hear over the expostulations next to her. "Warehouse number eight. And bring a doctor. There's an injured man."

She hung up the telephone. "Thank you," she said to her

now-agitated companion. For a moment she toyed with ringing up the Dunburys, but it was so late, past two in the morning. They'd be asleep and she didn't want to worry Beverly,
not in her condition.

"Are you certain, miss, that I cannot be of more assistance?" asked the railroad man.

"No, I'll be fine. But thank you, Mr. . . . ?"

"Oswald. Dicky Oswald." He smiled and stood up very
straight, trying to add another inch to his stature.

"Thank you, Mr. Oswald. You've already been a great
help. Now I have to get back. I left an injured man out there."
She stopped at the door and turned partway around. "There
is something else. Do you have a cup or mug that I can use,
please? I need to give someone water."

He filled a drinking tumbler from the crockery water-
cooler. "Perhaps I should accompany you, miss. It seems
you've had quite enough adventure." He looked around the
office. "I should just secure everything here first and . . ."

Jade didn't have time to wait for him to tidy up. She took
the tumbler from him. "If you wish, but *I* must get back now.
Thank you." She hurried back to the warehouse and knelt
beside Wachiru, cradling his head and holding the water
glass to his lips. "Drink, Wachiru," she said. She let some water trickle onto his lips. His eyelids fluttered and his mouth
opened. "Easy, now. Take it slowly."

Jade heard the sound of hasty footsteps from behind her.
"There you are," said Oswald. "I was worried that . . . Oh! I
say. It's a *native*!"

"His name is Wachiru," said Jade as she offered the water
again. "He's been hurt."

"Is *this* the man that set upon you, miss? Be careful! If he
comes to, he may try again."

"You don't understand, Mr. Oswald. Wachiru was hit and left to die by the same man who tried to kill me."

Any further explanation was stopped by an approaching motorcar. Jade recognized Constable Miller as he stepped out along with an African *askari*.

"Miss del Cameron, I believe," he said. "What's all this about an attempted murder?"

Jade explained briefly the evening's events, beginning with the message that Percy was sick and ending with Wachiru's rescue.

"Could this man," Miller asked, "be the one who lured you in? Perhaps he took a fall before he could get out himself?"

Jade shook her head, then stopped when it only increased her growing headache. "No. I know Wachiru. He's a trusted employee."

"Perhaps it was all just an accident, Miss del Cameron," Miller said. "You may be overreacting to think of this as a murder attempt. Not surprising considering the perilous situation you've just emerged from."

Jade scowled and gritted her teeth. Why did all officers think that women got hysterical and overreacted at the slightest provocation?

Before Jade could say anything, Miller continued. "It's very easily explained, you see. Your man there was checking on the animals. He saw the lion seemed ill and sent someone for you. In the meantime, the leopard escaped. Perhaps this man—"

"His name is Wachiru!" growled Jade.

"Yes, of course. Your man Wachiru there might have been feeding it at the time. He fled, hit his head, and there you are. You arrive, the leopard charges, and naturally you know the rest."

"That's a lovely theory, Constable Miller, except that it doesn't explain how the door locked behind me."

"Hmm, yes. Are you certain you didn't shut the door behind you?" asked Miller. "Perhaps you did and the lock caught."

"It's a damn padlock!" shouted Jade. Beside her, Wachiru moaned and either fell asleep or passed into unconsciousness again. "You did call for a doctor, didn't you?" she asked. "Wachiru's hurt."

"Yes, of course. Dr. Garnham should be along in a moment. Rang him up just before I left." Miller seemed to notice Oswald for the first time. "And you are?"

"Richard Oswald, Constable. Most people know me as Dicky, though. I have the night shift this month at the rail offices." He pointed across the tracks to the little wooden building. "The, uh, young lady came to my office for assistance. In need of a telephone."

"Very good," said Miller. "So you've been there all evening?"

"Since seven o'clock, Constable. Same as every night."

"Did you see anyone suspicious loitering about these premises?"

"No, I did not."

"It's a bit difficult to do with your eyes closed, isn't it?" asked Jade. "I believe you were asleep when I knocked on your door."

Oswald's face reddened. "Of course not," he said. "Can't sleep on duty. And speaking of duty, I had best return to mine." He paused and waved his hand in Wachiru's direction. "No need to return the water glass, miss."

Jade watched him hurry back to the office. *Running like a cowardly cur.* "You can't go by his word," said Jade to Miller.

"He *was* asleep when I knocked on his door. He knows that. That's why he skeedaddled just now. It's worth his job."

"I will grant you that much, Miss del Cameron. Many a night watchman has been caught napping while on duty. But the simplest explanation is generally correct. I see no real reason to suppose someone meant murder. At most, someone was negligent and shut the door not knowing you were inside." He turned his head at the approach of another motorcar. "Ah, the good doctor arrives."

Doctor Garnham parked his Overlander next to the constable's Dodge and stepped out, black bag in hand. He was an older man with white sideburns and a generous sprinkling of white hair among the brown. His mustache, too, was white and the full style more old-fashioned than the thin ones now favored by the younger men. "What seems to be the matter?" he asked. "Can't have been a train accident."

"Wachiru's suffered a blow to the back of his head, Doctor," said Jade.

"Have you moved him?"

"Yes, from the warehouse."

"Shouldn't have done that," he said, kneeling down on the other side. He took a small flashlight from his bag, pried open Wachiru's eyelids, one by one, and shone the beam in his eyes.

"It was that or let him be mauled by a big cat, sir," said Jade. "Someone hit him over the head and then locked the both of us inside with a loose leopard."

The doctor's head snapped up. "The devil you say."

"At the moment, that is speculation," said Miller.

"Speculation, my aunt Fanny!" retorted Jade. "This is directly related to Stokes' murder. For some reason, the real killer thinks I know something or have seen something incriminating."

"And have you?" asked Miller.

"I found a pocketknife under the dip tank today. It may have belonged to Mr. Stokes, or it may have been dropped by the murderer and inadvertently kicked under the tank. I turned it in to police headquarters this afternoon for Inspector Finch to examine."

"Anyone might have dropped a pocketknife, Miss del Cameron. This is a busy place. Don't worry. I shall type up all this in my report for the inspector to see first thing tomorrow. In the meantime, you should let the good doctor take a look at you as well."

"Yes, indeed," said the doctor. "Constable, have your man help me get this native into my car. I'll take him to the native hospital."

"We'll take care of it, Doctor," said Miller. He directed the African *askari* to fetch a blanket. "You see to Miss del Cameron."

"You need to keep Wachiru under guard, Constable," said Jade. "Someone made an attempt on his life. He may be able to identify the attacker. That person may try again at the hospital."

"Yes, yes," said Miller. "Don't fret yourself, miss. I'm certain we'll bring whoever did this to book soon enough." Miller and the *askari* rolled Wachiru onto a blanket and lugged him into the constable's vehicle.

"Miss del Cameron," said the doctor, "if you'll please come with me, I do want to see to those cuts of yours." He pointed to Jade's hands. "We'll go to the European hospital."

"I'm fine," she said. "I want to go with Wachiru and see that he's taken care of."

"I insist," he said, laying a fatherly hand on Jade's arm. "If the leopard scratched you, then those cuts could take a very

nasty turn if they are not properly disinfected and bandaged."
He nodded to the rips in her shirt. "You may have suffered
other wounds as well."

"My motorcycle," said Jade, looking for an excuse to stay.
"I don't want to leave it here."

The doctor frowned for a moment. "Let me see your
eyes." He shone his light into each of them in turn, watching
for the pupilary reaction. "You don't seem to have suffered
any head injuries, but I dare not take a chance letting you motor off on your own until I'm certain." He turned to Miller,
who'd just finished placing Wachiru in the backseat. "Take
the young lady's motorcycle to the European hospital. I want
her to ride with me until I know she is all right."

"Certainly. I'll have Andrew here," he said, nodding to
the *askari*, "ride it over before we drop off this native. I'll follow him. If that is all right with Miss del Cameron."

"Take Wachiru to the hospital first," said Jade. "And
remember, I want him to have the best care. I'll pay for it,"
she added, knowing that the native hospital's reputation was
mixed at best with too many men too close together in less
than sanitary conditions. As long as no one made another attempt on his life. "You do know how to operate this?" she
asked the *askari*.

He grinned and replied by adjusting the choke and deftly
kick-starting the engine. Jade sighed and got into the doctor's
car. At least she'd be able to get home without calling for a
rickshaw or, worse, waking Avery. They rode to the European hospital, and she couldn't help but recollect when she'd
visited Sam. The doctor crept along, taking care not to jar
her while going over the ruts. They arrived just as Andrew
zipped by on her motorcycle, followed by Miller.

"Come with me to the examining room, if you would

please, Miss del Cameron," said the doctor. "Have a seat." He pointed to a wooden chair in the middle of the room. "Nurse!" he called out into the corridor.

A middle-aged woman in starched whites and a veiled cap stepped into the room. She waited without a word for the doctor's orders, her gaze never leaving his face.

"This young lady has some wounds to attend to."

The nurse nodded and stepped over to the side table and an enamel basin. She filled it with water, came back with soap, cloths, and towels, and proceeded to wash Jade's hands. The doctor went to a locked cabinet and retrieved several bandages and a bottle labeled MERCUROCHROME.

"This is quite new, but very wonderful," he confided. "Should have liked to have had it during the war." He dabbed the orange mixture onto the newly washed areas. Jade winced. "It does sting just a bit." He capped the bottle. "Let me give you something for the discomfort while Nurse applies your bandages."

"I'm fine really, Doctor," said Jade. "I just want to go home, swallow some aspirin, and crawl into bed.

"Ah, I can help you there," said the doctor with a gentle smile. He stirred a powder into a glass of water and handed it to her. "Drink it all down now. That's a good girl."

Jade swallowed the liquid and started to get out of the chair. "Thank you. I'm . . ." The room started to spin, and the last thing Jade heard was the doctor telling the nurse to prepare a bed for Miss del Cameron.

CHAPTER 23

Now that they are restricted to their reserve, how will the Maasai
hunt buffalo for hides to make their shields? Where will they find
enough lions to outfit their headdresses? And where will they wear
them if they cannot raid or go to war?

—The Traveler

THE SEDATIVE MIGHT have knocked another woman of Jade's
size out for hours, but Jade's strength of will was stronger
than most. Consequently, instead of putting her out into a
mindless, drugged sleep, the medication kept her teetering
on the fringes of consciousness long enough for her to con-
jure up everything that had happened in the past week. Then
fatigue took over and Jade drifted into a dream-filled sleep,
where her mind attempted to sort it all out.

In her dreams the blind Wakamba woman, only a few
vestiges of gray clinging to her nearly bald and liver-spotted
head, stood before her. Her ancient breasts, flattened like two
deflated balloons, hung above her leather apron. She clutched
a ratty monkey skin around her shoulders, staring at Jade with
dead white eyes, which followed every move Jade made. When
Jade, in her dream, stopped and greeted her, the old woman
pointed a bony finger and opened her toothless mouth. "Watch
for the madness in the eyes of a killer," she croaked.

The old woman changed into the *laibon*. He pointed to a set of evil-looking yellow eyes glowing through the darkness. She heard his voice, cracked with age but still commanding. "When this killer comes for you again, Simba Jike, you must seek help from your mate."

Both the woman and the *laibon* vanished into mist, leaving behind two snappish kittens. As Jade picked them up, Harding rode up on a zebra and handed her a skin of milk. He ineffectually stabbed at it with his fingernails, trying to poke a hole. Stokes wandered by, clutching a corn knife, and swiped the end of the bag, spilling the milk, which turned into a poisonous arsenic dip, all over Harding, who sickened, clutching his stomach.

Jade ran into Chalmers' musty and unkempt house, looking for help. All she could find was dusty photographs of him and his friends posing in uniforms next to a zebra. Jade was about to grab the picture when Chalmers leaped out of it and ran outside. He touched Harding's mount, and it sickened and died. Then the two men fought while Stokes looked on, laughing.

Mrs. Berryhill stood in the background, sneering at the foolish men playing at soldiers and dress up. Jade saw Alice Stokes hiding behind Pauline's skirts and called to her. The frightened young woman ran away with a baby, just as Sam flew overhead in his Jenny.

Jade shouted at them to stop, but no one listened. She called to Inspector Finch but he was too busy hauling Jelani and some other Kikuyu away to prison. The natives protested the sentence, one man shouting that he could not work where the animals were bewitched.

Then everyone disappeared, leaving behind one coffee dryer. Jade approached it cautiously, as if she knew what she'd find inside. The door opened on its own at her approach, but when she looked in, the dead man within was Sam.

A wailing moan woke Jade with a start. She sat up quickly, surprised to find herself in a narrow bed. *Where the . . . ?* The moan was repeated, louder this time. It came from a woman at the far end of the ward. *Dang doctor slipped me a sedative.* At least the nurse hadn't bothered to undress her beyond removing her boots, which stood beside the bed.

Judging by the relative quiet and the darkness through the high windows, Jade thought it was still night. The patient at the far end wailed again, a knife-edge to the sound. It was enough to bring the nurse. Jade closed her eyes and feigned sleep as the woman padded past her.

"Now, Mrs. Albright, you're not ready to deliver that baby yet."

They put me in the maternity ward? Jade waited until the nurse's back was turned, picked up her boots, and tiptoed out. The rest of the hospital's halls were vacant, devoid of waiting visitors, and bustling doctors and nurses. A clock showed it was five thirty in the morning. Jade headed for the front door and freedom. Once outside, she picked her way carefully in her stocking feet to the west side, where her motorcycle was parked. She sat on the ground, pulled on her boots, then pushed her cycle to the edge of the hospital grounds. When she was sure that no one would hear her, she adjusted the throttle and choke and kick-started the machine. The reward of hearing the engine finish the stroke went a long way to restoring Jade's peace of mind.

She motored down the long hill just as the sun rose. With it went all hope of getting home before anyone else woke up and discovered she was still gone. Madeline had planned to leave before dawn, and Beverly, always an impeccable hostess, would have already risen to see that she and Jelani had breakfasted before they went.

At the bottom of the hill, Jade paused, idling the motor. Should she try and hurry to catch up to them or head on to Parklands and ease Bev's concerns about her absence? The dream images, especially that hideous conclusion, kept tickling Jade's brain, urging it to make sense of the puzzle. Sam was a key. He was the first intended victim. So what had he seen?

It could be something he saw when he was flying or when he was filming the fair.

She tried to think of everything he'd told her; then she remembered his logbook. Could it contain a clue? *Think! What do you remember reading?* She couldn't recall anything special except . . .

A new idea popped into her head, and she decided she needed to ask Mr. Berryhill a question. His store, which catered to early-rising farmers, opened at six a.m. Jade pulled out her pocket watch. It was already ten minutes after. She set the throttle and headed there, hoping the store would be empty of customers.

It wasn't. Two farmwives examined dry goods, and their husbands debated with themselves over various implements. For a moment, Jade couldn't figure out why the normally efficiently run store seemed to be standing still. One of the women had clearly made her choice and stood at the counter, shifting impatiently from one foot to the other. Then Jade saw that Mr. Berryhill was alone behind the counter. Had his wife gone back to making deliveries? After ten minutes, which Jade spent pacing, Mr. Berryhill finished with the last customer and asked what he could do for her.

"I'm sorry to bother you, Mr. Berryhill," Jade said. "You're alone here this morning." She let the comment hang in the air, hoping for a reply.

Berryhill released a deep sigh. "Yes. Pauline took the truck early this morning. Don't know why. We hired a chap to make deliveries. Unfortunately, she left me with all this paperwork, too." He ran the fingers of both hands through his hair. "I don't do the paperwork. Pauline does. It's left me in a bit of a dither."

"It's a good thing you didn't keep that baby that someone left on your doorstep, or you'd really be busy."

Mr. Berryhill stared at her with owlish eyes, blinking once. "What baby?"

Jade dismissed his confusion with a wave of her hand. "My mistake. Oh, and I've been curious about the Volunteer Mounted Rifles. I've been interested ever since I saw that picture of yours. I think Mr. Chalmers has a copy of it, too."

"Oh, yes. I'm sure he does. Several of us were in the Volunteer Mounted Rifles." He looked around as if he expected to see his shrewish wife make a derogatory remark about them.

"Can you tell me the names of everyone in the photo?"

"To be sure." He brought the picture from his desk to the counter and pointed to the far left. "That's me, of course. Next to me is Clarence Greene. Then there's Charles Harding, and Kip Foster, Martin Stokes, and on the right Alwyn Chalmers."

"Holding the zebra's bridle," said Jade.

"Oh, that's not a zebra. We painted up the ponies to look like that. Shoe blacking, you know. Kept thieving tribes from taking them. A few men just threw a striped cloth over them, but it never looked as effective."

"How interesting," said Jade, thinking back to Sam's side

notation in his log. He'd seen a zebra mating with a horse on one of his flights. She looked up from the photo and noticed a rifle advertisement tacked onto the back wall. It depicted a hunter aiming for a snarling leopard, the cat's terrifying yellow eyes glaring at him. Jade's head spun. Everything else went black around her, leaving only the eyes, like an evil version of the Cheshire cat.

Yellow eyes. Liver pills.

"May I ask you another question?" Without waiting for Berryhill's reply, she pressed on. "I saw Mr. Harding buying liver pills the other day. Does he buy a lot of them?"

"Yes, he does. One might suspect that he drinks too much, but I know for a fact that he drinks very little," Berryhill said. "At least never at our dinners. But he uses so much sheep dip. Too much, I think. I read in the paper that it can cause liver damage. Why do you ask?"

Jade smiled. "Just friendly concern for him, that's all. Thank you very much. Sorry to have bothered you, and good luck with your paperwork."

Berryhill frowned. "You're welcome, and thank you. I shall need the luck. Stokes made quite a mess of the bills. Somehow it even affects some of the new billings. I don't know how Pauline managed to make heads or tails of it all these years. I hope she returns soon to finish these."

Jade thought about calling the Dunburys from the store but decided she didn't need either Berryhill or some hello girl to eavesdrop on the conversation. As much as she didn't want to waste time, she also didn't want to leave Bev and Avery in the dark. She turned to leave, but stopped at the door.

"It turns out I do need something, Mr. Berryhill. Some of your best rope for a lariat."

*   *   *

SAM WAS SORRY to see the flight end. He'd enjoyed watching Jelani's expressions, at least what he could see of them. They ranged from awe as they flew above great herds of kudu grazing on the plains, to amusement as they buzzed by the falls and startled a drinking lion, and finally pride when they passed over Jelani's village. When they landed and Sam helped Jelani out, the lad's eyes were aglow. Sam laughed. He, too, was happy to see Jelani looking more relaxed. It was terrible to think that someone so young should already be burdened with so many concerns. For an hour this morning, Sam hoped he'd lightened those cares and given the boy a vision of his homeland that no other Kikuyu or any other native, for that matter, had ever seen.

Jelani helped Sam pull the plane into the makeshift hangar. *"Asante sana,"* he said, thanking Sam. He held out his right hand.

Sam shook it. "It has been my pleasure. A man who is going to write about his country should see it first."

Jelani smiled and nodded. "I have seen it now."

"Anytime you want to see it again," said Sam, "let me know."

"I will. And now I must go to find Memsabu Thompson. She will take me to my home." Jelani turned and, with head high and back straight, walked toward the distant farmhouse.

Sam was about to get his logbook to jot down some notes when he heard Jelani call to him. He turned toward the lad, who pointed to an old truck bouncing and sputtering up to the hangar. Sam waved back that he saw the truck and Jelani continued his trek to the house. Charles Harding got out and walked over to Sam.

"Mr. Featherstone, I was wondering if I might have your help over at my farm this morning. I'm having a great deal of trouble with my steam engine, and I hear you're a good mechanic and an engineer."

"JADE, WHERE THE deuce have you been?" demanded Avery as he met her at the door. "We rang up the police, who told us nothing. Then we telephoned the railroad office, asking them to find you. Got some chap saying no one could go into the warehouse until they caught a loose lion. What the blazes happened?"

"No one left you a message last evening?" Jade asked. Avery shook his head. Jade wasn't surprised. It was no wonder she hadn't recognized the man who came for her. "Where's Beverly?"

"I made her lie down. She's asleep. Are you going to answer my questions?"

"Yes, but you must promise to remain calm and not wake Bev." Jade dropped her voice to just above a whisper and briefly recounted the previous night's events, noting Avery's stifled swears. She finished with that morning's discovery and her new plan to capture the murderer. "I'm going to the Thompsons' to get Sam first. Call Inspector Finch and tell him where we're going."

"And just where would that be?" called a querulous soprano voice from the back room.

"Bev, I should have known you'd hear. You have the ears of an Airedale." Jade went into the bedroom and found her friend propped up against some pillows.

"I heard everything," said Beverly. "Well, most of it. I definitely didn't catch that last part about where you're going."

"To get Sam," said Jade, omitting the part after that. "Since I was a target, it's only a matter of time before Sam becomes one again."

"Good," Bev said, seemingly mollified by this bit of information. "Bring him back here before anyone takes another stab at him."

Jade squeezed Bev's hand and said she'd do her best. "Get some rest, Bev."

When Jade came back into the front parlor, Avery was just finishing his call to Finch. Jade asked for the phone. "Inspector," she said, "I don't think I need to remind you that we must act quickly before word gets back that I survived the attack. Inspector?"

"Don't worry," peeped a female voice. "I won't tell a soul."

"Who the blazes is this?" asked Jade.

"Nancy, the operator. The inspector's hung up already. But don't worry. My lips are sealed. And I'll ring him back up and tell him myself."

Jade rolled her eyes. "Oh, and Mrs. Thompson thought you might know something about a rumor that Mr. Chalmers is getting married."

"Oh my, yes. I heard someone call Mrs. Berryhill yesterday evening and tell her the good news. The bride is that pretty Alice Stokes. Seems she and her baby have been found quite safe."

Jade thanked the girl and hung up.

"Jade, be careful," whispered Avery as she headed for the door. "I'd tell you to wait for Finch but—"

"But you know it won't do any good," she finished for him as she took down her Winchester. "Don't worry. I'll be fine. I'll have Sam with me."

"That's the only reason I'm not going with you," said Avery.

"That and the fact that your Hup won't keep up with our cycles."

JADE EASED AROUND one of the worst ruts, then coaxed the cycle into second, feeling one gear meshing into another. Then she sped toward Thika and the Thompsons' farm, her excitement rising at the thought of seeing Sam again. Together they'd confront Stokes' real killer and clear Sam's name. The anxiety of that upcoming confrontation tempered her exuberance, creating a worried agitation. But with Finch coming, there shouldn't be too much problem.

Don't be too sure. The man's going to be armed and probably won't go down without a fight. But that was why she wanted to get there with Sam first, to surprise the scoundrel and hold him safely until the police arrived. Otherwise, he might bolt before anyone could catch him.

Goggles on, Jade had eyes only for the potential road hazards as she sped along. But in front of everything, she saw that vision of Sam lying dead. She pushed her Big Twin to its limit, circumventing a little striped skink basking in the dust. Soon she reached the Thompsons' farm and roared up the drive to the house.

Jelani, on the veranda, rose to greet her as Jade parked the cycle and removed her head gear. "I went up in the airplane, Simba Jike," he said. "I have seen my home now as Ngai, the Maker, sees it." He paused and sighed, closing his eyes to recapture the memory. "I could never imagine that my land was so beautiful. I cannot wait for Memsabu Thompson to finish work with the chickens so I may go home and tell my people."

"It *is* beautiful, Jelani. I'm sorry I wasn't here when you landed so you could tell me right away. But I'm glad you haven't left yet. I wanted to ask you an important question."

Jelani's soulful black eyes locked on hers. "On the day that you were arrested," Jade asked, "there was a man who left his bwana's farm because he said the animals there were bewitched. Do you know who he worked for?"

Jelani nodded. "Yes, Bwana Harding."

Jade nodded, her suspicions confirmed. It all fell into place: Chalmers' missing stud pony, the zebra seen by Sam flying overhead as it mated with one of Harding's horses, Harding shooting the female leopard rather than letting her come onto his land, the sudden return of Chalmers' pony with a ratty mane. She also recalled the morning Harding brought in the leopard cubs and the skin of milk. He fumbled in his pocket for a missing knife, the knife she suspected she'd found under the dip trough.

More than that, she remembered his liver condition, probably brought on by his previous contact with the ever present arsenate soda he used on his own sheep. It was the *laibon's* words in her dream that had brought it to mind, his warning to watching for danger in a pair of yellow eyes. He hadn't meant the leopard as much as Harding.

Jade looked around for Sam. "I suppose Bwana Featherstone is still busy with the plane?"

Jelani shook his head. "No. He has gone."

"Gone?" Her skin prickled. Had he been lured away as she had? "Where did he go?"

"Bwana Harding drove up in his truck as I walked back to the house. I think Bwana Featherstone went with him."

The prickling sensation turned to terror for Sam's safety. "Where's Bwana Thompson?"

"He has gone to the far fields today."

Jade started her cycle and prayed she wouldn't be too late.

CHAPTER 24

*To be Maasai is to be a member of a proud race, and the Maasai
respect this and their traditions. As they say in their own proverb,
a person without a culture is like a zebra without stripes.*

—The Traveler

SAM HAD FOLLOWED Harding's truck on his own motorcycle,
his mind playing over all the possible complications that could
break down a big steam engine. It pleased him that Harding
had asked for him. The man had previously seemed gruff. At
least he'd forgiven Sam for flying over his farm. Sam was also
excited about the prospect of working on the engine. As an
engineer, there was little he enjoyed more.

Sam recalled his father needing help fixing a threshing
machine when he and his brothers were still too small to contribute much muscle. It had been damaged in a spring tor-
nado and several neighbors pitched in to set it aright. The
satisfaction he'd found in watching them hammer out bent
parts was one of the reasons Sam had gone on to study engineering.

Harding's farm sat twenty-two miles northwest of the
Thompsons', and they took it as the crow flies, rather than
by the more roundabout roads. Sam knew they'd save many

miles, but he wasn't sure it was worth the wear on Harding's old truck. On the other hand, his own Indian motorcycle, a war veteran like himself, took the hills and skirted the ditches and termite mounds as easily as it had once wound around trenches and debris in Europe. When they came to the fenced lands of the farm, they went around and cut into the lane to one of the barns.

Sam shut off his cycle, parking near a fence post. He slipped off his goggles and leather helmet, draping them over the handlebars. "Now where is that engine of yours, Mr. Harding?" He turned from his bike and found himself staring straight into the barrel of an army revolver.

JELANI HAD TOLD Jade that he had watched Sam and Harding ride off across the fields rather than along the roads. Jade knew she needed to follow their tracks in case Harding tried something along the way. They had a half an hour's lead on her at least, which was about to be lengthened when she noted her low fuel tank. There was no time to try to find Neville, especially if he was on the far side of the huge farm. She pulled up by the hangar and quickly pumped gasoline from Sam's tank into a can and filled up. Then, after a quick check to make sure her Winchester was secure in its saddle case, and the lariat was handy across her shoulders, she picked up their trail and sped off in pursuit.

She moved faster than a truck could, taking less time going over ditches, jumping several rather than bouncing around them. It was a comforting thought. She was shortening their lead. One jump disturbed a sleeping serval cat that responded by arching its back and hissing. Just so long as it wasn't a rhino or a buffalo, she didn't care. The matted grasses displayed the tracks, and Jade picked up the trail after each cutoff. As long as there were two sets of tracks, she knew that Sam had still been following Harding.

Soon, she reached Harding's fields and the native workers laboring in them. Several waved, enjoying the show of another rider speeding by. But Jade didn't ride all the way in. Not when it would alert Harding and give him time to ambush her. When she got close enough, she shut off the engine and pushed the bike around a horse paddock on her way to the barn. Jade stopped behind an outhouse and peered around it. There was Sam, tied with his back to a fence post next to his motorcycle. She leaned her own cycle against the building and slipped the Winchester from its sheath just as Harding went into the barn.

Sam was no more than a hundred yards away. Jade covered the distance in a run, switching her rifle to her left hand and pulling her knife from its boot sheath. With one swipe, she sliced through Sam's bindings.

"Take this," she mouthed and handed the knife to Sam. "I'll slip in the back of the barn and hold Harding until Finch arrives." She ran along the fence toward the barn. She was halfway there when Harding came out and opened fire.

Jade hit the dirt and rolled behind some barrels. She raised her rifle and returned fire, driving Harding back into the safety of the barn. But it didn't stop him from shooting again. Eventually, he'd hit her. For the second time that day, her vision blurred and dimmed, only this time the *laibon* appeared before her. She felt, rather than heard, his advice. A bullet hit the ground in front of her, and the vision vanished like morning fog in the sun.

"Sam!" she shouted. "Get me out of here."

Sam was already on the way. He'd straddled his own cycle and had it running. "Get ready," he shouted. He sped toward her and braked just long enough for her to jump onto the secondary seat over the rear tire. As Jade cradled her rifle across her chest, Harding broke from the barn astride a large sorrel mare. He turned the mare's head away from them and urged her into a gallop with several kicks.

"We can't let him escape," Jade shouted over the engine's roar.

"Hang on," said Sam. He revved the engine and tore off after the fleeing man.

Harding turned in his saddle and fired. Jade needed both hands to hang on as Sam zigzagged. His pattern made him a difficult target, but it kept Jade from returning fire. It wasn't long before Harding ran out of ammunition and concentrated on eluding Sam and Jade instead.

"Can you get in closer, Sam?" Jade hollered in his ear.

He nodded. Jade slipped her Winchester into Sam's own empty rifle bag and pulled the lariat over her head. Sam saw the movement and nodded again, understanding. He kept to Harding's left, giving Jade a free-and-clear throw at the man on her right.

She held most of her rope in her left hand, playing out enough to make a large honda. Then she began to rhyth- mically swing it overhead, gaining momentum. The disad- vantage here was that this time her target was higher than she was. Well, she'd just have to rise a bit and throw a little harder. The horse shied at something and Sam used the op- portunity to pull up closer. Jade gauged the distance, gripped the side of the seat with her legs, and lifted herself up just as she let the rope fly. It hovered for a moment over Harding, then settled near his shoulders.

Jade tugged, not so hard as to choke or snap his neck, but enough to yank him off the rear of the horse. He landed hard and struggled to remove the rope, but by this time Sam had circled him once on the cycle, thereby wrapping the rope around his arms. Sam cut the engine as Jade leaped off, rifle in hand.

"Give it up, Mr. Harding. You're not going anywhere," she called.

His horse, without a rider to urge it on, slowed to a trot and finally stopped. Harding looked up at her from the ground, his jaundiced eyes burning with fear and anger. "That damn Stokes was blackmailing me!" he shouted. "I wasn't going to keep Chalmers' stud for good. It wandered onto my land, and I figured I could at least get a colt from it. Tried to disguise the animal, but that damn Stokes knew the trick. I tried to explain to him, but Stokes wouldn't listen. He was going to ruin my reputation. My good *name*!"

Jade kept the rifle trained on Harding while Sam did the honors of binding his wrists behind him. She didn't trust Harding. A man that desperate might try anything. Besides, she noted, she could see murder in his eyes. Just like in the leopard's.

"Let's go back," she said in a calm voice.

They walked silently back to the barn just as Inspector Finch and two officers pulled into the yard and spilled out of a war-vintage Crossley staff car, painted black. Finch, weaponless and wearing the same tired brown suit, strolled over to them as casually as if he was attending a garden party. Jade recognized Constable Miller and the *askari* named Andrew from the night before. Miller held a revolver in his hand. Andrew, the driver, held a thin club. Something about Andrew nagged at Jade. Where had she seen him before last night?

"Looks as if you did my job for me," said Finch. "We'll take him now." Miller and Andrew put Harding in the backseat, Miller joining him and Andrew standing guard on the other side of the vehicle.

"I got your messages, Miss del Cameron," said Finch. "Very good job. Of course, this last one was probably unnecessary. Once I had his prints from the knife, I was certain we had our man. They matched another set on the coffee drum that we'd just managed to identify early this morning."

"How did you happen to know they were Harding's prints?" asked Sam. "Don't you have to compare them to a known set?"

"Indeed. And I had one. Assuming that our man was local, I had assigned several of my *askari* to act as waiters at the fair's dance. What with their white gloves, they could take a man's glass from him without adding their own prints. They wrapped each glass in paper with the drinker's name on it." He chuckled. "No one noticed them. But who *ever* notices the staff."

"That's why the *askari* looks so familiar," said Jade. "I saw him at the ball."

Finch nodded. "Yes, Andrew was there. I collected quite a lot of drinking and champagne glasses. Been up to my ears in fingerprints to analyze since then. But I wouldn't have had the knife or the motive without all your work, Miss del Cameron. I must say, my confidence in you wasn't misplaced. You lived up to your reputation."

Jade stared at him openmouthed before exploding. "What? You son of a . . . You *deliberately* accused Sam so that *I* would do your dirty work?"

"Well, I knew that if I asked around myself, the killer would lie low. What I needed was someone like you, a reporter, to do the asking. People love to talk to a writer, it seems. And I needed a way to make you want to ask those questions. Accusing your boyfriend here seemed to provide you with good motivation."

"You low-down, sidewinding, stinking son of a butt-faced warthog! You nearly got us both killed!" She clenched her fist and lunged for the inspector, launching a punch right for his jaw. Sam grabbed her from behind just in time and held her back, as she fumed in his grip.

"Easy, Jade. I don't want to see you arrested for striking an officer." She wriggled again and made something akin to a hissing snort. "Settle, settle," cooed Sam. "Temper on safety, as that idiot Harry Hascombe used to say."

Jade relaxed her stance and Sam released his grip, slowly at first, then completely when it seemed she no longer intended to punch Finch. She shook herself free of his embrace and folded her arms across her chest. As soon as she stepped aside, Sam launched his own punch and connected with Finch's left eye.

"Don't *ever* use Jade like that again!"

CHAPTER 25

In the end, only two things are really valued by the Maasai: cattle and chil-
dren. They greet one another by inquiring after both of these prizes and say
goodbye with a hope that Engai will bless the other with more of each.

—The Traveler

THREE DAYS AFTER Harding's arrest, Sam and Jade sat in
wooden chairs on the Dunburys' veranda, a lemonade in
Sam's hand and a coffee in Jade's. Biscuit lounged at her
feet, his tongue lolling. Jade wore her usual duck trousers
and boots and a short-sleeved white cotton shirt, open at the
throat. Sam had dusted off his riding breeches and put on
a clean pin-striped shirt, newly purchased from Whiteaway
and Laidlaw on Sixth Street. The front door creaked open
and they watched as Avery assisted his very pregnant wife to
a new rocking chair, purchased just for her.

"Thank you, love," said Bev as she lowered herself onto
the seat. Farhani followed with a silver tray and two more
lemonades. "And thank you, Farhani," she added. Despite
her bulging abdomen, she still looked beautiful in a buttercup
yellow linen dress with a pleated bodice and white lace at the
edge of the short sleeves.

Jade held her now empty coffee cup in her lap and absentmindedly stroked Biscuit's head. Before her spread the Dunburys' beautiful lawn, Bev's roses once again thriving under her direction. Whinnies from the stables indicated the recent arrival of a stallion and two young mares. "How long do you think it will be before Maddy and Neville get here?" Jade asked.

"I should think within the hour," said Avery. "Signing the papers was merely a formality."

"They may have stopped to do some shopping," suggested Beverly. "Clothes, toys, that sort of thing."

"I haven't known them as long as you have," said Sam, "but I've never seen either of them so happy. For the past twenty-four hours since they got the news, Neville's been wandering around completely distracted. And Maddy's sung every lullaby she's ever heard."

Jade chuckled. "Maybe now she'll be too busy to write any more of those books she claims are about me."

"Don't count on it, lovey," said Beverly. "She's already sold *Ivory Blood* to her publisher, and I've seen part of the manuscript for your Moroccan adventure. She's calling it *The Hand of the Kahina*. It's very good, actually. There's one line in particular I love." She closed her eyes and recited from memory. " 'He'd purchased the lovely hellcat for ten pieces of gold. Now he leaned in close to claim his due.' "

Jade snorted. "It was two pieces of gold, and Mother owns me, not Sam."

Beverly dismissed the contradiction with a wave of her hand. "While we're waiting for the Thompsons, explain to me just what Harding was doing."

"Remember that Alwyn Chalmers sold one of those Somali ponies to Harding with the idea that they were salted," said Jade.

"Right," said Beverly, "only the animal died of some equine disease anyway, correct?"

"That's correct," said Jade. "So Harding felt that Chalmers owed him an animal. As a man with a reputation for being a square dealer, he expected the same from others, especially a friend and former volunteer. Chalmers didn't give him another. He'd lost one himself, so he counted them both as being swindled by the seller."

"Only Harding didn't agree," said Sam. "So when Chalmers' stud broke loose and wandered onto his farm, he kept it to service one of his mares. That way, he'd have his animal. At least by his reasoning."

"Why didn't he just ask Chalmers to lend him the stud?" asked Avery.

"I suppose that Chalmers wouldn't agree without Harding paying the usual stud fee," said Jade. "Or Harding was too proud or too stubborn to ask. Either way, it didn't end up being an overnight sort of affair. His mare must not have been in heat, so he kept the stallion until she was."

"But he had to disguise it," said Avery, "right?"

"Yes," said Jade. "He used the old trick that they'd used in the Volunteer Mounted Rifles of bootblacking stripes on the white horses and clipping the manes to disguise them as zebra from raiding tribes. It worked from a distance, but anyone coming up *close* would see through it, so he had to keep people off his farm. He stopped speaking to Chalmers, feigning a feud, and—"

"And he shot the leopard mother before your crew could come looking for it on his land," finished Avery. "By thunder!"

"And that's why he wanted me out of the picture," said Sam. "I flew over and saw a zebra mating with his mare.

Thought it was odd and even commented on it to him at the fair. If I spread the word around, Chalmers would have figured out that Harding had the pony."

"He told Finch that he never intended to kill you in a plane crash," said Jade. "Apparently he thought the dirt ball would disintegrate sooner and just make the Jenny crack up on takeoff. Then you couldn't fly back over his land in case you wanted to take a closer look at the zebra."

"But Stokes already knew about the zebra?" asked Avery.

Jade nodded. "It appears he really was in the habit of seeing things and blackmailing people to keep quiet about them. Stokes told Harding to meet him after dark at the rail yards. I don't know that Harding ever actually intended to kill him, but when he hit him hard enough to knock him into the animal dip, he didn't bother to pull him out until it was too late."

"And he lost his pocketknife in the brawl?" asked Beverly. "The one you found?"

"Yes. It must have gotten kicked under the trough where he couldn't find it," explained Jade. "I remembered later that he fumbled in his pocket for the knife to poke a hole in the milk bag. He either hadn't discovered it was gone yet, or possibly just reached out of habit. That's why he wanted to kill me. I asked too many questions, including about the knife. In fact, by then, he was getting desperate. He paid a native to lure me to the warehouse."

"But surely he must have known you'd turn the knife in to the police and they'd find him eventually," said Avery.

"Not necessarily," added Sam. "He couldn't know that they had his fingerprints on file. All he counted on was that it was a common knife. He's a sick man, suffering from liver failure induced by poison. He apparently has too free a hand with arsenide dips. I think it's affected his mind."

"So did Harding accuse you, Sam, of hitting Stokes when he needed a scapegoat?" asked Beverly.

"No, that was Anderson," said Sam. "Cutter saw me argue with Stokes about my gasoline bill. He told Anderson, who saw it as a way to discredit me in Jade's eyes."

"Well, what threw everyone off," said Avery, "was the fact that Stokes was—how do they say it?—cooking the books. I rather suspected Mr. Berryhill of doing him in."

"It wasn't Stokes that was skimming money from the store," said Jade.

Beverly choked on a swallow of lemonade. "Will you please stop doing that? You have this terribly dreadful habit of spilling important news just when I'm drinking."

"Sorry, Bev," said Jade. "I didn't do it on purpose. Not this time. You see, when I last visited the store, Mr. Berryhill was alone, trying to cope with the accounts. He said his wife was away and *she* always handled the books. Then he said that Stokes had made such a mess of the bills that problems were still showing up. If the man had any sense of accounting, he'd know that wasn't possible. Someone else must have been doing it."

"Then it was *Mrs.* Berryhill who was stealing?"

Jade nodded. "I think Mrs. Berryhill always planned to leave her husband. She helped Mrs. Stokes run off and develop a new identity for herself, dyeing her hair, adopting her own baby. She was very distraught when she found out that Mrs. Stokes was no longer at that old farmhouse by Longonot, especially when Mr. Chalmers came and bought all those cleaning supplies and curtains and such. And Mr. Berryhill knew nothing about any baby being left with them. Mrs. Berryhill made all that up to help Alice change her identity."

"Mrs. Stokes is with Chalmers now?" asked Sam.

"Yes," said Jade. "Married yesterday. He's apparently always loved her. So, I suspect, did Mrs. Berryhill."

"Mrs. Berryhill always loved Mr. Chalmers?" asked Avery.

Jade shook her head. "She always loved Alice Stokes."

Beverly gasped. "What makes you say that?"

"I saw golden yellow hair sticking out of Mrs. Berryhill's locket. Her husband and son are brunets, so I think it was Mrs. Stokes' hair. Growing up back home in New Mexico, I knew two women from Boston who moved to Taos. They were—how do I say this delicately?—*very* close. People always whispered about them. Anyway, I think Pauline felt that way about Alice and maybe planned to run off with her."

"Only Alice didn't reciprocate," said Sam.

"No," said Jade. "She just needed someone to care for her as she always has. Once her husband was gone for good, she was more than willing to marry Mr. Chalmers. Maybe Mrs. Berryhill will stay with her own husband now."

Avery reached over to an end table and picked up the morning paper. "I think she's already left him. I placed an order for some grain for the horses yesterday, and a new man delivered it this morning in an old, beat-up truck instead of the usual Ford." Avery opened the paper, found an ad, and read aloud: " 'Woman with small capital wishes to meet like-minded woman with intent of starting a farm in the upland territory. Apply box 87, Nakuru.' I would wager that the writer of this ad was none other than our book-cooking friend."

"Oh, dear," said Beverly. "I suppose Finch will have to go after *her* now."

Jade shrugged. "Not unless Mr. Berryhill presses charges, and if he does, Finch had better not drag me into it." Her keen hearing picked up the sound of a puttering motor. "I think Maddy and Neville are coming," she said as she stood for a better view of the road. Sure enough, their old box-bodied car turned past the gate and chugged up the long lane. Jade ran down the steps to greet them. She could see by their broad smiles that they had good news even before she saw the toddler seated between them.

"Maddy, Neville, congratulations!" Jade said as she helped Maddy out of the car and hugged her. Behind her, she heard Sam approach.

"Allow me to join in on that," he said. "Congratulations." He pumped Neville's hand.

Madeline reached into the car and lifted up the child, a towheaded boy who stared at them with huge blue eyes. He stuck a thumb in his mouth and instinctively laid his head on Maddy's shoulder as the strange grown-ups clustered around him.

"Isn't he beautiful?" asked Madeline. She kissed the boy on the forehead. "He's fifteen months old and his name is Cyril Masters, but of course, we're adopting him so it will soon be Cyril Thompson."

"His family left him at Lady Northey's Children's Home last year while they went up north to start their farm," explained Neville. "Soldier settlers, you know. Planned on fetching the little tyke once they had their home built. Seems he drew a bad plot of swampy land, though. Both of them caught yellow fever and passed on two months ago. After applying for relations back in England, the home found that they had no other family."

"So now he's ours," finished Madeline.

Avery had stayed on the veranda to help Beverly to her feet. She stood by the steps, waiting for them. "Maddy, bring the baby here, please. Avery won't let me go down the stairs."

Maddy hurried up with her child. Neville followed and was heartily congratulated by Avery. Jade and Sam stayed below, watching, happy for their friends' joy.

"They'll be wonderful parents," said Sam. "That's one lucky little guy."

Jade nodded. "Just like the Dunburys' baby. Both couldn't ask for better parents or a better place to grow up."

They walked up to join the others. Cyril snuggled into Maddy's lap and dozed.

"Is Inspector Finch going to charge you with assault, Sam?" asked Neville as he stroked his son's head.

"Not unless he wants Jade to call on the governor and tell how he used her to do his investigation." Sam massaged his right hand. "I still owe him for nearly getting my plane wrecked." He leaned against a post and folded his arms across his chest.

"And now all the animals are off to their new homes," said Madeline. "I'm glad Percy is gone. I'd worry about Cyril getting too close, but I must admit, I'm going to miss the old fellow. Still, his saving you, Jade, will make a splendid chapter to my next book."

Jade groaned. "I should think motherhood would take all your attention, Maddy."

"Oh, I'll make the time," Madeline said. "The money will be even more important now."

"You didn't still need Percy for your movie, did you, Sam?" asked Beverly.

He shook his head. "That part is finished, and I just shot some footage of the coffee pulping and drying to round out the feel of farm life." He straightened and relaxed his arms. "You know, if you don't mind, I'd really like to include little Cyril in the movie. Having you bring him home to the farm is a great ending. You know: peace, serenity, life moving on."

Maddy shifted and took her husband's hand as they gazed into each other's eyes, communicating silently as married couples do after years together. After a nearly imperceptible movement of Neville's lips, Maddy agreed. "Certainly, Sam," she said. "And it would help us preserve a very special moment in our lives."

"Is that how your film will close then, Sam?" asked Avery. "With the little tyke toddling among the coffee trees?"

"Not exactly," Sam replied. "I think I'd like to film him on the lawn with the farm in the background. Then I want to pan out, show Africa beyond. After that"—he paused and looked at Jade—"with some help, I want to end with an aerial sweep of the farm and Africa." He cocked his head and studied Jade for a moment. "What do you say, Jade? Late-afternoon light will be best. Long, interesting shadows. Less haze. Shall we try it today?"

She nodded. "Love to. If it's all right with Maddy and Neville."

"We'll meet you in a little while," said Neville.

Jade and Sam waved goodbye and headed for their respective motorcycles. Biscuit got up to follow, but Jade told him to stay. "I'll be back this evening and bring you a nice chicken," she said. When she looked up, she saw Sam and Avery exchange a meaningful glance. Before she could ask Sam what that was about, he'd started his engine.

THEY BUZZED LOW over the Thompsons' farm, Sam at the stick and Jade up front with the camera. She balanced it over the right side and cranked film while Sam executed a gentle spiral, rising higher and higher with each turn. Then he leveled out and headed southwest, allowing Jade to capture the low sun and the distant herds. Jade did her best to film what she hoped was the essence of Sam's vision, then stopped cranking and turned her head to the side to await his next hand signal. He made a short chopping motion, and she set the camera down carefully on her lap. It had been their prearranged signal that filming was complete.

Sam had made a wooden box to house his precious Akeley camera. Jade reached for it from its place on the floorboard. She slid back the catch and opened it, expecting to find it empty. It wasn't. Inside was another small box, nested in a corner. On the top was penned, *Open this!* Jade did.

For a second, everything evaporated around her except the glittering, cerulean blue sapphire ring in front of her. The square-cut stone, a full carat in size, was set in a white-gold ring crafted in the geometric lines of the new art deco style. Two larger claw mounts held the stone at the top and base with smaller ones on each corner. The breeze shifted and brushed Jade's cheeks, bringing her back to reality. She noted the soft whoosh of the wind and the purr of the Jenny's motor. Then she saw the note tucked inside the box lid.

I can't promise you the world, but I can promise you the sky. Marry me.

Jade looked at the stunning sapphire once more and recalled her fears when Sam had been raving sick. Once again, the *laibon*'s words came back to her.

When this killer comes for you again, Simba Jike, you must seek help from your mate.

She had heard these words when Harding opened fire on her, and called to Sam, just as she'd gone to Percy when the leopard attacked. Which yellow-eyed killer had the *laibon* meant? And did it really matter?

The stone matched the sky around her as if a chunk had been crystallized and preserved just for her. She knew that Sam was waiting behind her, silently manning the controls, anxious to know what her answer would be.

She wondered herself.

AUTHOR'S NOTES

THERE'S A TENDENCY to become politically correct in books, but Jade's attitude toward the African natives is in perfect keeping with historic sensibilities. As proof, I refer you to letters from the assorted clergy that appear in the *Leader of British East Africa* and the *East African Standard* during those years. People in London even formed antislavery societies, protesting the forced labor of the native tribes. There is also an excellent book, *Kenya*, written by Norman Leys, MB, DPH, a health officer in Mombassa. Published in 1925, it exposes the travesty that enforced labor laws wreaked on Kikuyu life and culture.

For a beautiful look at the Maasai tribe, see *Maasai* (1980) by Tepilit Ole Saitoti, photographs by Carol Beckwith. The author is a Maasai, so the text is written with excellent insight into the culture. Maasai proverbs and beliefs are explored in *The Masai, Their Language and Folklore* (1905) by Alfred C. Hollis.

One of the most famous men to capture wild animals, Frank Buck, has written several books describing his experiences, including *Bring 'Em Back Alive!* Chapter four of Harold J. Shepstone's 1931 book, *Wild Beasts To-Day*, gives an excellent description of the capture and shipping of wild animals.

Mapping 1920 Nairobi required its own detective work. No one seemed to include any maps in the handbooks and guides. The closest I came was a proposed redevelopment of the downtown area in the September 4, 1920, issue of the *Leader of British East Africa*. As Mr. Jim McGivney of Kenya Books, Brighton, UK, surmised, "The only important road would be the one that led from the station to the Norfolk Hotel bar!" But *The Traveller's Guide to Kenya and Uganda, 1936* (published by the Kenya and Uganda Railways and Harbours) does include a Nairobi map. Combining this with local newspaper ads from 1919 to 1920, I was able to piece together an idea of the town in 1920.

Old Nairobi and the New Stanley Hotel (1974) by Jan Hemsing has many interesting photographs and notes on early Nairobi, but the best view of all came from Nairobi's own newspapers: the *Leader of British East Africa* and the *East African Standard*. These are available on microfilm, and through their personal columns, ads, and letters to the editor, I gained a window into life in 1920 Nairobi. The plot of this book was inspired by an actual missing-person notice and a pitiful plea for someone to adopt an orphaned baby boy. These microfilms are an excellent example of why newspapers must be archived in their *entirety*, instead of saving an electronic cache of the headline stories. Otherwise, how will future generations be able to see into *our* thoughts and daily lives?

Readers interested in more tidbits about life in Jade's time can visit my weekly blog, "Through Jade's Eyes," at www.suzannearruda.blogspot.com or by clicking on "Suzanne's Blog" on the Web site at www.suzannearruda.com.